MAR 0 8 2023

D0712275

MURDER AT HAVEN'S ROCK

Also by Kelley Armstrong

Rip Through Time
A Rip Through Time

Rockton
The Deepest of Secrets   *Watcher in the Woods*
A Stranger in Town   *This Fallen Prey*
Alone in the Wild   *A Darkness Absolute*
City of the Lost

Nadia Stafford
Wild Justice
Made to be Broken
Exit Strategy

Cainsville
Rituals   *Deceptions*
Betrayals   *Visions*
Omens

Age of Legends
Forest of Ruin
Empire of Night
Sea of Shadows

The Blackwell Pages (co-written with Melissa Marr)
Thor's Serpents
Odin's Ravens
Loki's Wolves

Otherworld
Thirteen   *Living with the Dead*   *Industrial Magic*
Spell Bound   *Personal Demon*   *Dime Store Magic*
Waking the Witch   *No Humans Involved*   *Stolen*
Frostbitten   *Broken*   *Bitten*
Haunted

Darkest Powers & Darkness Rising
The Rising   *The Reckoning*
The Calling   *The Awakening*
The Gathering   *The Summoning*

Standalone novels
Wherever She Goes   *The Masked Truth*
Aftermath   *Missing*
The Life She Had   *Every Step She Takes*

MURDER AT HAVEN'S ROCK

KELLEY ARMSTRONG

MINOTAUR BOOKS
NEW YORK

First published in the United States by Minotaur Books,
an imprint of St. Martin's Publishing Group

MURDER AT HAVEN'S ROCK. Copyright © 2023 by KLA Fricke Inc.
All rights reserved. Printed in the United States of America. For information,
address St. Martin's Publishing Group, 120 Broadway, New York, NY 10271.

www.minotaurbooks.com

Library of Congress Cataloging-in-Publication Data

Names: Armstrong, Kelley, author.
Title: Murder at Haven's rock / Kelley Armstrong.
Description: First Edition. | New York: Minotaur Books, 2023.
Identifiers: LCCN 2022046167 | ISBN 9781250865410 (hardcover) |
    ISBN 9781250891655 (Canadian) | ISBN 9781250865427 (ebook)
Subjects: LCGFT: Novels.
Classification: LCC PR9199.4.A8777 M87 2023 | DDC 813/.6—dc23/
    eng/20220923
LC record available at https://lccn.loc.gov/2022046167

Our books may be purchased in bulk for promotional, educational,
or business use. Please contact your local bookseller or the Macmillan Corporate
and Premium Sales Department at 1-800-221-7945, extension 5442,
or by email at MacmillanSpecialMarkets@macmillan.com.

First Edition: 2023

10 9 8 7 6 5 4 3 2 1

For Jeff

MURDER AT HAVEN'S ROCK

PROLOGUE

The longer Penny works on building this strange little town, the more obvious it becomes that the company is lying. Lying about everything. They say this tiny community deep in the Alaskan forest is owned by a private firm conducting climate and environmental research that's both valuable and potentially controversial, given the political divide over climate change.

The owners want to conduct this potentially very lucrative research unhindered, and they were willing to pay a small fortune for the construction crew's discretion. Every member of the crew had been hand-selected from across North America. They'd signed ironclad NDAs and been provided a "working on an oil rig" cover story for family and friends. All electronic devices had been confiscated at the airport. They'd been flown out in a private plane with darkened windows.

The others didn't care what the reason was. Research, climatology, environmental engineering, it was all so deathly dull. As far as they were concerned, any company willing to pay a year's wages for a quarter's work could insist the crew work wearing clown noses.

While Penny had accepted the story herself, there was a reason she'd grown up in a bedroom filled with cats. It was her mother's joke—and a not-so-subtle reminder. *Curiosity kills the cat, Penny. Be a little less curious, and you'll live a lot longer.*

That was like telling Penny to breathe less air. She thrived on mysteries and puzzles, especially when it came to houses. Yes, most people don't think of "houses" as puzzles, but that's because they aren't architects. A new client comes to you, eyes glittering with the dream of their perfect home, and you need to make it a reality, even when everyone has told them that their vision won't work. Penny's specialty is making it work.

That's why she's here—to take this company's dream and make it a reality. They wanted to minimize their town's footprint while maximizing both function and comfort. The last part sold her. This wasn't a firm trying to stuff worker bees into the smallest hive possible. While they did need to be small—to keep others from investigating—they didn't want to sacrifice livability. That made them good people, right? At least decent as far as corporations went.

The budget ignited the first whisper of doubt. Not that they were asking her to cut corners. She expected that, and she expected to discover that their insistence on "maximum livability" was mostly advertising for the scientists and technicians who'd live here. No, the problem was that they *didn't* amend her plans, even when she warned it'd take the project over budget.

She'd run a test asking for something ridiculous. If they'd agreed, that would mean they were fleecing investors with a fake project, which would be disappointing but none of her business. Instead, they balked at the overage and asked her to scale it back.

Something was going on, and after nearly twenty years in the business, she thought she knew all the scams and tricks, and she couldn't figure this one out, which had her cat whiskers tingling.

She'd started sneaking into places she shouldn't be. Listening to conversations she wasn't supposed to hear. And all she caught were tidbits that made her more suspicious without answering any of her questions. For a curious kitty, that was catnip.

Penny had just finished eavesdropping on a conversation when the participants stormed off. That happened a lot between these two: Bruno, the engineer, and Yolanda, the contractor. Yolanda was trying to keep things on schedule, while Bruno kept finding issues that needed to be addressed. Tonight's argument had been different.

When it broke up with both participants storming off, Penny was left musing in her hiding spot, idly watching Yolanda stalk across the jobsite. Now Yolanda stops, peers into the gathering dark, and then slips into the forest.

That gets Penny's attention. They aren't allowed into the forest. That's been made *very* clear. It's dangerous and untamed Alaskan wilderness, filled with grizzlies and wolves and killers. Okay, no one said "killers" but they all know Alaska is where serial killers run when they need to escape the police.

The person who enforces the "no forest" rule, with strict penalties? The same person who is going in there now.

Penny jogs to a building on the edge of town, ducks into the shadow of it, and peers around the corner. When Yolanda turns again to peer back, Penny's heart stops, but after a slow and careful look around, Yolanda disappears into the forest.

Penny counts to five and then takes off in pursuit. She tracks the whisper of branches brushing Yolanda's nylon jacket, the crack of a twig under her work boots, the sudden explosion of a startled bird taking flight. Penny has never been what anyone would call outdoorsy—she once rolled in poison ivy to get sent home from summer camp—but she's pleased with herself here, picking up those sounds and tracking Yolanda without getting close enough to be caught.

Admittedly, Yolanda is on a path—one hacked out for the approved "group walks"—so it's easy enough to follow her. And it's also easy for Penny to keep on that path and let her mind wander and fail to realize that the sounds up ahead stopped a while ago.

When Penny finally does notice it, she stops to listen . . . and realizes just how silent it is out here. Not just silent either. It's dark.

She peers around the gloom and shadows. It'd been dusk when she set out. Yes, noticing that, she'd realized she should have grabbed a flashlight, but her eyes had adjusted easily enough, and it wasn't as if it was fully dark.

Now it is fully dark.

How is that possible? She left the town just a few moments ago, right? Well, no, it's been more than a few moments. Once she'd realized Yolanda was following a path, she'd focused on piecing together the bits and pieces she'd accumulated in her quest to solve the town's mystery.

So how long has she been gone?

And when did she stop hearing Yolanda?

It is at that moment that Penny realizes her mother was right. Curiosity is dangerous, and not just when it leads her to listen in on a private conversation. It's even more dangerous when it leads her into the goddamn Alaskan wilderness, at night, with no flashlight and no weapon sharper than the mechanical pencil in her back pocket.

She takes a deep breath. There's moonlight, and she can see the path well enough. She just needs to follow it back to town.

She gets about five paces before the moon disappears behind

cloud cover. Penny blinks to clear her vision and continues walking, feeling her way, trees close enough to touch on either side, pressing on—

Her foot sinks in snow, and she pulls back. There were no snowy patches along the path. She'd have noticed that. There *is* still snow here and there, in dark crevices, but she definitely hadn't stepped in any. Therefore, she is no longer on the path.

She bends and squints at the ground, only to see a half dozen large canine prints in the patch of snow.

Wolves.

She backs up fast and tries to retreat to the path, but she gets turned around and ends up back at the snowy patch. Or is this *another* snowy patch? With *more* wolf prints?

Deep breaths as she calms her racing heart. She's fine. She can't be more than a half mile from town. She just needs to find—

There! She spots a clear path through the undergrowth and sets out on it, walking resolutely back to town. She's fine, just fine. A bit of an adventure, that's all.

When her watch says thirty minutes have passed, she starts peering ahead for signs of the town. Then she remembers she's not going to see any at this hour. There are strict light rules past sundown. You can use a penlight to get from building to building, but indoor lights are only allowed if the blackout blinds are drawn.

She keeps going. Ten minutes pass. Then twenty.

Did she miss the town? No, the path goes straight to it.

Is this definitely the path?

It has to be, doesn't it?

She looks around. The path does seem narrower than she remembered, with branches poking her as she walks. But it has to be the one. She just isn't there yet.

Penny takes ten more steps. Then something crackles behind her. She wheels to see a figure stepping onto the path, a dark shadow against the night.

"Thank God," she says with a small laugh. "I thought I heard something in here, and I was only going to take a peek, and I wandered off the path."

The figure doesn't move.

"I went farther than I thought," she says. "Can I head back with you?"

The figure snorts, and it's an odd noise, one that has her squinting. The shadow moves, and she catches sight of flicking animal ears . . . two feet above her own head.

Penny falls back with a yelp. Her foot catches on a root and twists, and then she's falling for real, the ground flying up as she crashes onto her back.

I am dead.

That's all she can think. A grizzly found her, and now she's dead.

The creature snorts again, and she looks up as the moon peeks out just enough for her to see the animal. It's not on two legs. It's on four. Four impossibly long legs, like a giraffe's. The head looks like a horse's. Then she catches sight of massive thick antlers.

Moose.

A memory flashes. A magazine photo of a majestic moose grazing in a twilit bog. That's the one animal she wanted to see up here. A moose. Now she is seeing one, and holy shit, she had no idea how big it would be.

If she'd spotted it through a car window, she'd have gazed in wonder and awe. Seeing it standing a few feet from her—while she's flat on her back—is nothing short of terrifying. It might not be a grizzly, but one wrong move, one moment of fear and panic, and those massive hooves will trample her to a pulp.

Penny slides backward as she rises. The moose only watches. She keeps backing up. When it snorts and shakes its antlers, she turns and runs. Runs blindly, even as an inner voice screams that she's overreacting, it's a moose for god's sake. A giant *deer.*

She doesn't care. She runs until she is certain it's not charging after her. Then she stops to catch her breath, looks around, and realizes she's left the path far behind.

Penny squares her shoulders and heads back the way she came. Back toward the path. But after a few strides, she hits a solid wall of trees. This isn't the way she came.

She's lost. She's completely—

Calm down. Look around. Get your bearings.

The moon has slid free of its cloud cover. Use that as her guide. Where was the moon before? Uh, overhead?

Wait, there's moss on the trees. That only grows on the south side, right? Or is it the north? Is that even true? She vaguely recalls some online trivia saying it wasn't.

Breathe deeply. Gather her thoughts. There has to be something she remembers seeing. Mountains. Of course. There are mountains to the west of the town, which makes the sun set earlier than it usually does, but leaves spectacular sunsets that had her itching for her camera.

She looks up . . . and sees trees. Pines rocket into the night sky and block any mountains she might see behind them.

All right, but she can see the mountains from the jobsite, which means she needs to get to a clearing. Pick a direction and start walking.

She does that, and twenty minutes later, she's blind again, the moon disappearing. She's walking with her hands in front of her face while she tells herself everything's fine. It's getting too dark for predators, right? And while it's hardly the warm spring evening she'd be enjoying at home, Alaska in May isn't nearly as cold as she expected. She's warm enough in her jacket and boots and gloves. Worst case, she'll need to hunker down until morning and then find her way back.

When she hears a noise to her left, she veers right and starts to jog, hands out in front of her face. Then she stops. It sounds like water. The burble of a stream.

Where there's a stream, there could be a clearing, right? Also, where there's a stream, there is eventually a lake, and there's one right beside the town, which means she could follow the stream back.

She picks her way in that direction. It's slow going as the trees get thicker. Then she stops as she catches an odd metallic sound. A faint tinkling, as if the water is running over something metal. That's a definite sign of civilization.

She moves faster as the clouds thin, allowing a filtering of moonlight. Too fast, too confident, and when her foot hits a taut wire, she pitches onto her hands and knees. A trap. She's been snared in a trap.

She flips over fast, and there's a crack and a snap, and a billowing sheet drops onto her. Penny flails, struggling to get out from under the sheet that dropped over her. Her hands touch clammy fabric. She yanks it off and finds herself looking down at a canvas tent. She tripped over a guyline and brought the whole tent down.

She goes still, listening. If there is a tent here, there is a person here. Every story about serial killers in the Alaskan wilderness slams back. She carefully extricates her feet from the guyline. Then she rises, peering around. The clouds have passed enough for her to see that she's in the middle of a campsite.

A hidden campsite.

As soon as she thinks that, she wants to dismiss it as fear and paranoia. But as she looks around, she realizes it's more than that. She just left a town that's being specially constructed to disappear into the landscape. Someone has also tried to hide this camp. That's why she didn't see it until she literally tripped over it.

The tent is dull brown with splotches of green for camouflage. There's a box that must hold supplies, and it's painted the same colors.

She peers around again and then makes her way to the box. It's locked, but someone has forgotten to fasten the lock. She bends and twists it open, and the squeak of the metal almost—but not quite—drowns out the crackle of dead leaves behind her.

Penny spins, arms going up to protect herself. When she sees who it is, she lowers her hands.

"You," she says. "What the hell are you—?"

A burst of pain, exploding through her skull. And then . . . nothing.

CHAPTER ONE

I'm pressed against the glass of an airplane window, looking for a dream come true, and I'm absolutely terrified. I don't have dreams. Ambitions, yes. Plans, certainly. Get a degree. Go to police college. Become a detective. Get on the homicide squad. Very practical aspirations, devoid of people or places. Get a dog? Have a circle of good friends? Fall in love? Move into the countryside? Nope. I excised all that from my life plans at eighteen, when I took a gun to confront a guy who put me in the hospital, and I pulled the trigger, and I spent the rest of my life waiting to be caught for it. I didn't dare live a life where others might get hurt. Where *I* might get hurt, when the inevitable end came. I couldn't afford dreams.

Now I have one. I have so damn *much* these days that it scares the shit out of me. Good friends. A husband. A life focus. Even a dog. All of that swirls together around the nexus of a place that has been born from my idea, shaped by our shared dream, now taking form in the Yukon wilderness. Taking form somewhere below me.

Haven's Rock.

I shouldn't be able to see it from here. If I can, then it's not hidden, and we've paid a lot of money for nothing. That doesn't keep me from peering into the endless forest, straining for a glimpse of a roof, a glitter of metal, something that doesn't quite fit in this vast forest.

"See it yet?" drawls a voice through my headset.

I glance over at Dalton sitting beside me. One leg bounces, his fingers tapping against it, and I have to smile at that. My husband is used to being in the pilot's seat, and that leg has been bouncing since we boarded the plane in Dawson City.

"Just give me the damn coordinates," he'd said when Yolanda said someone would fly us out. She'd refused, and I saw the power play there. The latest in a series of them. This will be our town when it's finished. Until then, it's hers, and we'd better damn well get used to that.

"One more month," I say over our private channel. "Then construction will be done, and we can say thank you very much and put her on a plane." I catch his expression. "All right. *I'll* say thank you very much, and *you* can put her on a plane."

That makes him snort. Our dog, Storm, lifts her huge, black Newfoundland head, and Dalton gives her a pat as he leans over to look out my window, hand going to my knee.

His gray eyes squint. Then he says, "Right there," and points.

I peer out the window and see nothing but trees and lakes and mountains—in other words, I see the Yukon. He directs my attention, but I shake my head. There's nothing there. Just one of hundreds of small lakes and the endless green of the boreal forest.

When the plane veers in the direction he's pointing, I say, "No way. I don't see . . ."

And then I do. We've flown low enough that I can make out the buildings. Or what I know are buildings, though the structural camouflage makes it look like a rocky clearing. A little lower, and my breath catches.

Dalton's hand tightens on my leg. "Just like you imagined it?"

I bite back the urge to say "like *we* imagined it." It's my nature to deflect when attention turns my way. I'm not shy—it's just how I was raised. Share credit; accept blame. But when Dalton tenses, waiting for me to correct him, I smile and say, "It's perfect, isn't it?"

He brushes a kiss over my cheek. Haven's Rock was my idea first, but it was *our* dream, and now I see it unfolding below, and my chest clenches so hard I have to fight to draw breath.

I throw my arms around Dalton's neck. There's a moment of surprise. Again, this is one hundred percent *not* Casey Butler behavior. But after that spark of shock, he hugs me back and whispers in my ear, "We did it."

I hug him tighter. "We did."

Haven's Rock. The town may be new, but its roots go down into the permafrost. Even the name is significant. Rock for Rockton, the town where I went to work as a detective four years ago and met a hard-assed sheriff and fell in love—with him and the town and the Yukon itself. Rock for stability, too, a bedrock foundation, the thing we lacked in Rockton.

And Haven? Well, that's the most important part. Haven's Rock is a sanctuary for those in need. It's a place to hide when the law isn't enough to protect you from persecution for your beliefs or lifestyle, or from a stalker or abusive partner. Rockton was supposed to be that, and it was for some, but for the owners, it was a purely financial investment. This will be different. This time, we're in charge.

The plane lands, and Dalton's still opening the door when a woman strides into the hangar. Yolanda. We've never met, but I know her cousin, Petra, and her grandmother, Émilie, and there is enough of them in her that I know her on sight. She's taller than her cousin and grandmother, with dark curls and skin a couple of shades darker than mine, but her expression is one I know well—it's Émilie or Petra on a mission and ready to do battle.

Great. We aren't even out of the plane yet, and we're already the enemy, even after dropping everything and flying a thousand kilometers to help her.

Dalton climbs out as I snap a leash on Storm. The dog sighs at that, jowls quivering, and thumps her bulk back onto the floor of the plane.

I laugh under my breath. "Yes, it's a leash. Don't worry, we're not in a city."

When we take her to Dawson City or Whitehorse, she only needs her leash in a few places. To her, a leash means a big city, like Vancouver, which she likes as little as Dalton does.

"Sheriff Eric Dalton," Yolanda says outside.

I turn to peer through the open door. She's striding toward him, her expression a little smug, as if she's pleased that Dalton is nothing more than the cowboy she imagined. A modern-day Wild West sheriff, complete with boots and faded jeans and flannel shirt and even a Western-style brimmed hat. He has the rangy build, the steel-gray eyes, and the gun at his side. Tanned white skin and close-cropped dark blond hair complete the look. If there's anything she might not expect, it's his age, and he's actually younger than she probably thinks—three days of beard scruff masks smooth skin, and he has crow's feet on his eyes, from squinting into the sun. He's thirty-four, a year younger than me and about ten years younger than Yolanda.

They shake hands as I bring Storm out the door. Yolanda's gaze goes straight to the dog, with a frown of puzzlement. When it rises to me, that expression doesn't change.

Dalton might have been what she expected. Evidently, I am not. It could be that my name led her to expect someone whiter. It could be that my job title led her to expect someone more physically intimidating. I'm neither. I'm a slightly built, five-foot-two woman who takes after her Asian mother more than her Scottish father.

"Casey Butler," I say as I walk over with my hand out.

"What's with the dog?" she says.

My brows rise. *Good to meet you, too.*

I don't say that. I'm the good cop in this relationship—the reasonable one that everyone prefers to talk to. Everyone who doesn't know us well, that is. Dalton and I have learned the benefits of this particular game, and so I bite back anything even mildly sarcastic and only smile.

"This is Storm," I say.

"Uh-huh."

"She's our dog."

"I see that."

Dalton's jaw flexes. "She's our dog," he says, in a tone that tells her nothing else should need to be said.

Our dog. Our town. Yes, her grandmother invested in Haven's Rock, but the majority of the money came from my inheritance and my sister's, and even that is none of her business. Yolanda was hired to oversee construction of our town. We can bring in an elephant if we want.

So far, I've been calm, even conciliatory, in recognition of the fact that Yolanda is a damn fine builder, even if, like so many experts, she's a pain in the ass. I guess, if you're at the top of your game, you have that luxury and the confidence to use it, and I completely respect that . . . it just doesn't make her any *less* of a pain in the ass.

We'd expected to be up here, helping build our town and

getting a sense of this corner of the wilderness as we did. Yolanda vetoed that. If we wanted her, we had to stay away. She wouldn't work with the "homeowners" peering over her shoulder.

"I have two missing crew members," she says. "I called you in to find them. This isn't a site visit."

Dalton points at Storm's nose. When Yolanda narrows her eyes, he says, "The dog is here for that thing on the end of her snout."

"Her nose?"

"Yep."

"She's a tracking dog," I say.

Yolanda's look says this is a very fine excuse. We don't argue, because she's fifty percent right. Newfoundlands are water-rescue dogs. Dalton used the tracking-dog justification as an excuse for buying me my dream breed and pretending it was a practical choice.

"May we go into town and talk?" I ask.

"No."

My head jerks up. "Excuse me?"

"I said 'no,' because once you're in town, you're going to want to look around, and I need my people back."

Dalton's jaw tenses, and his gaze shifts my way, lobbing this grenade in my direction.

"While we are certainly interested in seeing the town you built for us," I say, trying hard not to emphasize those last four words, "the missing people are our priority, and we're quite capable of focusing on that."

"Not being easily distracted children," Dalton mutters.

Yolanda turns to him. "You built a town in the middle of the Yukon wilderness for people in need of sanctuary, and you're convinced it'll work out, despite it failing spectacularly the last time."

"Rockton didn't fail," I say, as evenly as I can manage. "It saved hundreds, thousands even. Which you well know, being the descendant of some of the people it saved. Your grandparents believed in it enough to devote themselves to keeping it alive for as long as possible."

"And all it got them was heartache and disappointment. No, you aren't children. You're something worse. You're idealists." She waves away any protest. "Which is none of my business. It's your money and Gran's. My concern is my missing people, and I need you out there now, looking for them."

I glance at Dalton. His expression is dark, but he says nothing. My call.

"I'll need scent markers," I say. "Recently worn clothing for both your architect and your engineer."

"I'll bring it."

"Once we find your missing people, we will do a site visit. Then we're staying."

"We're not—"

"Ready for that? We accept that our home may not be ready, and we've brought supplies to avoid using yours. We need to stay and get things ready, since we apparently have residents moving in next month, a year ahead of schedule."

Yolanda grumbles under her breath. For once, those grumbles aren't directed at us. They're for her grandmother, the one pushing the timeline forward. She's found people in urgent need and convinced us to open our doors right away, rather than living in the town for a year on our own, as planned.

"We're staying," I say. "After we find your missing crew members."

Dalton mutters, "Who failed to obey the first fucking rule of this town."

"Rules one through three, I think," I say to Dalton. "Stay

out of the forest. Stay out of the damn forest. Goddamn it, what part of 'stay out of the forest' did you not understand?"

Yolanda stares as if we're speaking a foreign language. We are, in a way, though it's one anyone who spent a week in Rockton would have understood.

Finally, she says, "I did not fail to impart that rule. Imparted it, reinforced it, and *enforced* it. But short of an electric fence, you can't keep people from sneaking out."

"Electric fences don't work either," Dalton drawls. "We tried that. Course, they probably work better if you have electricity."

I snort a laugh. Yolanda doesn't crack a smile.

"We know exactly how hard it is to keep people in," I say. "Especially if they're the outdoorsy type, surrounded by the fabled wilderness of the north. So tell us a bit more about who we're looking for. Your engineer and architect. A man and a woman who went missing at night. The obvious answer is that they were hooking up. Any sense of that?"

"I would have no idea," she says. "My crew's social lives are their own."

"All right," I say. "Then I'm going to need to talk to someone who actually knew them. There are a dozen possible scenarios here and knowing which is most likely will help us find them."

"How? You're tracking them. You don't need to know *why* they're out there."

"It helps if we do," I say calmly. "Tracking isn't a perfect science. Storm will do her job, and Eric will do his, but there will be times when they lose the trail, and we need to make a guess. Being able to make an *educated* guess will help."

I brace for an argument, but she nods. "Understood. All right then. We have two missing people. One is Penny, the architect. Early forties. Single. Sexual orientation unknown, as you were asking about a possible entanglement. She's never shown any interest in the forest or in Bruno, who is my engineer and the other missing person. Late forties. Married to a woman."

"Has anyone mentioned seeing them together in a social setting?"

She pauses long enough that I add, "I know people are here to work, and they're being paid extra to work long hours, but I'm presuming there's still some social scene, even if it's only hanging out around a campfire with beers and marshmallows."

"I wouldn't know."

I glance at Dalton and then say, "I'm not asking whether you've noticed who participates in social gatherings. I'm just wondering whether there's someone I can speak to about them."

"I presume there are social gatherings, but when my workday finishes, I'm in my office, working some more."

In other words, she'd hesitated because she's honestly not sure how her crew socializes, much less who hangs out with whom.

"Did Penny and Bruno seem to get along in a professional sense?" I ask.

"As well as can be expected for an architect and engineer."

Dalton rocks, a subtle show of frustration, and she says, "The architect has the vision and the engineer has to make it work. There is always conflict, but it was minimal, as far as I know."

"Have either of them been known to go into the forest for any reason?" I ask.

"Bruno joined the guided walks that you two suggested. I allowed them, recognizing that while they're an inconvenience, they might cut down on people wandering off on their own."

"And Penny?"

"She never joined them. Before you arrived, I asked the young woman in charge of the walks. I also reviewed our initial interviews." She's relaxing now, on familiar ground. "Bruno mentioned he'd love to work in Alaska again—we've told them it's Alaska, not the Yukon. He'd worked in the north before and enjoyed it. Penny said nothing about the environment. The setting seemed inconsequential to her."

"Two last questions before we take off. Was there any evidence they took anything with them? Clothing or other equipment?"

"I had people check their lockers as soon as they were reported missing. All clothing is accounted for except for what they would have been wearing. Each crew member was issued a high-powered penlight and a utility tool with a knife. Penny's are in her bunk. Bruno's are not. However, I have seen Bruno carrying his on the job."

"Meaning if they're missing, that doesn't necessarily mean he prepped for a trip into the forest. Penny definitely didn't, which brings me to the final question. Is there any evidence that either of them was taken by force?"

Yolanda shakes her head. "No. Both their beds show no signs of being slept in. Several people saw Penny earlier in the evening. The last person to see Bruno seems to have been me. We were discussing the schedule, and we parted at around nine. No one reports seeing him after that."

I'd rather ask around myself. I'd also rather get a look at their sleeping quarters myself. But we have a trail that's growing cold, and if I'm being truly honest, even my focus might waver once I see our new town.

"All right," I say. "If you can bring those scent markers, we'll set out."

CHAPTER TWO

As we're heading out of town, I spot a small house nestled in the forest, and my breath catches.

"Is that our—?" I cut myself off and wrench my gaze away, as if I've caught a glimpse of my presents before Christmas morning.

Dalton leans to my ear without breaking his stride. "I think it is. Do you want to take a peek?"

I glare up at him, and he laughs, easing back into himself now that Yolanda is gone and he can drop the steel-eyed sheriff act. He throws his arm around my shoulders.

"I could take a peek and report back," he says. "Since you're the detective assigned to the case."

"We're tracking . . . and you're the tracker."

"You have Storm. Don't worry. I'll catch up in a few hours. Just give me time to check our new home, sneak into town and explore, maybe—"

I poke him in the ribs, hard enough to make him yelp.

"You deserved that," I say.

"Just trying to be helpful."

"You know what would be really helpful? Picking up the damn trail and finding these two before they become bear chow."

"Nah, wrong time of year for that. Grizzlies have been out of hibernation long enough not to be starving, and it's too far from autumn for the old ones to get desperate. While we could be getting some sows with cubs, the biggest danger these two are going to face is their own foolishness."

"By which you mean 'lack of wilderness survival skills.'"

I get a hard look for that, which I accept. Dalton might have little patience for fools, but he understands the difference between being careless and being clueless, and he excuses the latter as a lack of opportunity. He really does mean foolishness—the issues that come when people *think* they know what to do in the forest, because they read survival tips in an online article once.

"Okay," I say. "Let's hope they didn't do anything *too* foolish."

"They went into the Yukon wilderness at night. That suggests we're starting at foolish, and just hoping we don't work our way down."

I shake my head and lift two bags, each containing a sample of clothing. "Let's give Storm a sniff of these and then we'll circle the perimeter and try to figure out where they went into the forest."

Dalton points down. I frown at him.

He gestures at the faint trail we've been following. "They went this way. At least one of them did."

"Someone went this way," I say. "Multiple someones, it seems. They've been using this when they need to go into the forest."

"Yep. And someone used it last night."

I look along the path. Like a game trail, it's lightly trodden, with the undergrowth parted, leading the way deeper into the forest.

I glance down at the ground. Shoe prints and boot marks, mostly scuffs, from multiple treads.

"Nope," he says. "The ground's been dry for days, so those don't mean anything except that it's been used."

I peer at broken twigs.

"Nope," he says. "Those are old breaks, at least a week ago."

"So how can you tell the trail was used last night? By one of our targets?"

"Lucky guess?"

I shake my head and open the bag with one of Penny's shirts. Storm takes a good sniff, and then lowers her head to the ground and looks back up at me.

"Seems I'm a good guesser," Dalton says.

When I narrow my eyes, he says, "You want a clue?"

"What's it going to cost me?"

"The temporary irritation of realizing, as the detective in this duo, you should have figured it out yourself."

I ignore him and take out the second piece of clothing—the shirt belonging to Bruno. Storm sniffs it, and this time, she gives the trail a harder sniff, walking along it and then back to me before lying down, which means she doesn't smell Bruno on this particular trail.

"Huh," Dalton says. "That's not what I expected."

I understand then that he was making an educated guess when he said they took this trail . . . because there aren't going to be many trails from Haven's Rock into the forest. This isn't Rockton, where we organized hunting and fishing and logging trips as well as recreational hikes. These people are here to work and work fast. Everything they need has been flown in. Except for those hikes, they have no reason to enter the forest. They'll have carved out this one trail, and anyone who ventures in will use it, knowing that otherwise they take the very real risk of getting lost.

I peer around. It's thick woods and brush here. That's part of the reason we chose the building site—it's in part of the forest that won't attract visitors. The Yukon might be a popular tourist spot, but it's hardly the Appalachian Trail. In over fifty years, no more than a dozen people—hunters and miners mostly—stumbled onto Rockton.

If Bruno went off-path, he had to either follow a creek or chop his way through.

"Your call," Dalton says.

Do we follow Penny's trail or go back and find Bruno's? I weigh the options. Two people went missing on the same night. It's unlikely these two trips *aren't* connected.

The obvious answer is a romantic liaison. The uglier answer is a stalking situation—or a luring one. Another possibility is that they were meeting for a non-romantic purpose, maybe a job-related discussion they didn't want others overhearing.

All that boils down to one thing: it is almost certain that they went into the forest for a shared purpose. Even if Bruno's trail isn't here, he would have met up with Penny.

"We'll track Penny," I say.

Before I came to the Yukon, I presumed one section of forest was the same as another. Oh, I knew there were different types of forest—though in my vocabulary, that'd have been "evergreen, hardwood, and jungle." But if you were in the same geographic zone, unless you had specific landmarks—like lakes or mountains—it'd all look alike. Even with those landmarks, well, a lake is a lake, and a mountain is a mountain.

I came to understand that areas of forest are like urban neighborhoods. If you aren't from the city, they all look like endless rows of houses. Even if you are, one neighborhood built in the same era looks like the next. But *your* neighborhood is always different. Your neighborhood is unique. There's the fire hydrant you tripped over as a kid and needed three stitches. There's that house with the garden gnomes that always gives out full-size chocolate bars at Halloween. There's the perfect climbing tree in the Millers' backyard—just don't get caught on their property. Dozens of markers and memories that make that neighborhood yours, and when you move, you need to start the process over as you're plunked down in a neighborhood that looks like all those other soulless replicas.

The forest is the same. I knew Rockton's forest, in a way that I don't think I realized until I left it. I knew the trails Storm liked best. The trails where my horse—Cricket—could break into a gallop. The trails with just the right hills for my dirt bike to launch airborne. I knew the best spots to hunt or fish or gather, and I could find them without trails. The tree where Dalton first kissed me. The cave systems I'd crawl through with our deputy, Will Anders. The places where people I cared about laughed and lived. The places where people I cared about had died. And the places where they'd betrayed us.

I miss Rockton, but I think I miss *our* forest more. And if I ache for it, I cannot imagine how Dalton grieves. Compared to him, I was a newcomer to the neighborhood. He was born there, grew up there, lived there his entire life.

Now we are in new forest. We've been here many times as we scoped out the area, but it isn't ours yet. We haven't mem-

orized landmarks, and certainly haven't made memo
Storm follows the trail, Dalton and I are both quiet,
around, taking it in, excited by the promise of this ne
but, deep down, feeling like children who've been
scuffing around the new neighborhood, grumbling th
the same, not the same at all.

We will make this forest ours. It's not the same as be
into a new neighborhood. We chose this one. Pai
chose it to have everything we loved about Rock
ronment and everything Dalton would have done
We border a lake now—one with fresh water and fi
ground springs provide fresh water. We're perfectly
to have access to mountains for hunting, while b
sun's southern path all day for better solar power.

We will love this place as much, if not more, tha
It's just going to take some time.

The official town path ended after a kilometer
had rolled his eyes at it. Yolanda's idea of a trail w
a straight line into the woods and then you tur
march back to town. The path didn't wend arou
pass by a beaver dam or head up an incline for a
could get the same experience walking into a
inside a city.

When the trail ended, Penny kept going, th
of sparse trees and brush. Had she not realized
There's safety tape marking a tree, but she'd b
and might not have seen it.

According to Storm, Bruno didn't join Per
on the official path, which seems to make it ur
meeting up. A thousand meters isn't far in tl
thirty-minute hike through dense forest. If it
they'd have united by then.

So what was Penny doing in here at night without her penlight? If she left at dusk, she might not have thought she needed one. Maybe ventured in the forest, not for the forest itself, but for the privacy it afforded. Working through a problem and needing some peace and quiet. She's walking and thinking, and doesn't realize she went beyond the path until it's dark and she tries to get back to . . . and the path is gone.

Where is Bruno in that scenario? I have no idea, and I can't worry about it. We have Penny's trail. Once we find her, we can focus on Bruno.

We've gone about a half kilometer past the end of the trail when Penny seems to realize she's no longer on the path. She hit a patch of snow. It's May, and there are shaded hollows where the snow hasn't yet melted. She stepped into one of these, her boot prints clear. Another thing is clear too: wolf tracks.

There's a wolf pack in the area, which doesn't worry us. Oh, we'll need to be careful, but there's plenty of game, and if we stay out of each other's way, all will be fine.

Penny wouldn't know that. She'd crouched here, seen big canine prints, and decided she was getting her ass back to town, fast. Except it was night, and probably dark, and she'd been trailblazing without realizing it. There was no path to get back on, and she seems to have wandered a bit before resolutely striking out . . . in the wrong direction.

What Penny followed is a game trail. To a newcomer, the forest seems blazed by endless trails from all the people who came before, and surely those trails all lead somewhere interesting, right? Well, that depends on whether you consider "a stream" or "a safe clearing for resting" or "a nice patch of vegetation for grazing" to be someplace interesting. These aren't human trails. They're made by animals, often moose and caribou here, carving paths between all the spots they

consider interesting—or at least useful. The roadways of the forest.

Penny got on one of these and decided she was obviously back on the trail to town, only she was heading in the same general direction she'd been going before. In other words, she was getting deeper and deeper into the woods.

Since she's following game trails, Storm is able to follow *her* easily. We continue on for a kilometer and then a second kilometer. Here she seems to start to realize she should have reached the town by now, as she meanders a bit, as if looking for it.

When Dalton stops, Storm's hackles rise in a low growl, as if she noticed something a split second after he did.

"And we have a moose," Dalton says, walking forward and dropping to a crouch. He pulls back undergrowth to reveal one massive hoofprint in soft ground.

"Woman versus moose, to be exact," he says as he points out a boot print just behind us.

Two boot prints, I see now. As if Penny had stopped short, seeing the moose.

Dalton pokes about, examining the ground.

"She went that way," he says, pointing slightly off the game trail we've been following. "Moose came out behind her. She spun around, saw it, and decided to get the hell out of its way . . . by continuing in the direction she'd been already going."

"Farther from town."

"Yep. Only she panicked and ran off the game trails. There are running footprints through a softer area just to the left, along with a sign that she fell at some point—there's a hand-print in the dirt."

He pauses and mutters a curse. "And now that I say that, I see she fell here, too." He points out the marks. The ground here is harder than where the moose stood, but there's a scuff mark right behind those two clear footprints. She saw the moose, and it must have done something to make her stumble back. She fell, got up, and then ran.

Ran headlong into the darkening forest.

"What were the conditions last night?" I ask.

"Partly overcast," he says.

"Which is worse than overcast," I say. "If there's no moon, you know it's dark. She heads into the forest without a light, the sun sets, but there's enough moon to see by . . . until there's not. She bumps into a moose, panics, and runs back the way she was going, thinking she's heading toward town."

"Yeah, looks like she veered—"

Dalton goes still. One hand reaches for Storm. The other drops toward his holster, and as I see that, my own hand does the same.

I touch the butt of my gun as I scan the forest. When Dalton pulls his weapon, I do, too. His gaze sweeps the woods. Then it stops. He sees something. I follow his line of sight, and I tell myself I'm just not aligned right to see whatever he does, but the truth is that whatever he's spotted is probably right there, too camouflaged for me to make out.

Dalton raises his gun to his side. It's a revolver. Yes, a modern one—a .357 Smith & Wesson—but still a throwback to another era. I've always suspected the gun is more for show than protection. He's an excellent hunter, but handguns are not his thing, and if he takes it out, that's more than nerves. It also means that whatever he sees is human.

An animal would have Dalton reaching for his bear spray. Oh, he'd shoot a bear—or wolf or wolverine—if he needed to, but if a predator is charging, the bear spray is more effective. Guns are for threats that will see them and stay back. Guns are for people.

"I can see you," he says after a moment. "You're twenty feet in front of me, behind two pines. If you can see me, you know there's a gun pointed at you. What you probably don't see is the second gun, to my left. Now, I'm a fair shot. She's a better one. Still, neither of us has any interest in pulling a trigger today. We're looking for two people who went missing—"

The crash of undergrowth. My arm swings up, finger off the trigger, but even before it's raised, I know whoever is in that forest isn't running at us—they're running away.

Dalton lets out a string of curses and starts after the fleeing figure. He makes it two steps before glancing back at me.

"Go," I say. An old injury to my leg means I'll never run as fast as I used to. "I have a gun and a dog. I'll stay right here."

He lifts a hand in thanks, and then he's gone. I keep my gun raised, my body tensed, waiting for any sign that the person is leading him into a trap. The crashing of undergrowth says otherwise. It's a panicked run.

Penny? Bruno? Or an innocent hiker who bumped into two people armed with handguns? In their place, I'd run, too.

I'm really hoping it isn't a hiker. Oh, I'd feel bad for scaring them, of course, but I'd be a lot more concerned about us encountering tourists on our first post-build foray.

That really is our biggest fear. We surveyed the area as well as we could, making sure there were no active mining operations or hunting cabins or any sign that people—even a lone seasonal trapper—used the area. That doesn't mean we couldn't find ourselves in the middle of a route that suddenly became internet famous among dedicated hikers.

Even then, the land still isn't free for the taking. It's Crown land and Indigenous land, and we're squatting on it, only hoping that our altruistic intent at least mitigates the trespass.

I survey my surroundings. It's boggy to the east, where the

moose had been grazing. To the north, low mountains are barely visible through the tall pines.

Dark shadows on the mountains promise cave entrances. I consider climbing a tree for a better look, but pines really aren't as climbing-friendly as the maples and oaks of my youth. Still, I eye a possible contender, also as a way to get a better look at the landscape while I'm waiting for Dalton.

I said I wouldn't leave this spot, and yes, I'm an adult, capable of walking twenty feet and returning to this location, but I won't give him the heart failure of returning to find my spot empty.

I'm still eyeing the tree—thinking that when he comes back, he can boost me to the lower branches—when I realize I'm alone. Oh, obviously Dalton took off, but a moment ago there'd been a Newfoundland beside me, and now there is not.

"Storm?" I say, swinging around in alarm as I scan the trees.

She whines, and that has my heart tripping faster until I finally spot her half hidden behind brush. She lowers her head and whines again.

I exhale and stride toward her, presuming she walked away to do her business, that whine telling me she knows she shouldn't wander, but she had a reason.

She's not crouched to relieve herself, though. She's snuffling the ground.

"Tell me you don't smell blood."

She cannot, of course, tell me anything of the sort. I'm concerned because her whine tells me she hasn't just picked up Penny's scent, which is all around.

I take out the scent markers. I open Bruno's bag to ask if that's what she smells—our other missing person—but she doesn't lift her head even when I call her. She just whines another apology for disobeying.

I glance in the direction Dalton went and then over at Storm. She's about fifteen feet away, and if I can see her from here, then he'll be able to see me if I go to her.

I walk over and bend beside her. She lifts her nose and paws at the ground. A tree fell here, and the earth is covered with dead branches and moldering leaves. I dig with one hand, but only find dirt.

I straighten and look around. Then I take a step back for a better angle, trying to see what might be bothering her, and my foot slips.

I presume I've slid on those rotting leaves, so I'm only paying half attention as I adjust my balance, but my boot keeps sliding backward, and the next thing I know, I'm falling, arms windmilling as I topple.

I don't hit the ground. I keep going, Storm giving a bark of alarm as I plummet, the earth disappearing above me.

CHAPTER THREE

I hit the ground hard, and as I scramble up, my ankle and wrist scream in protest, but I keep going until I'm upright . . . and looking at Storm eight feet overhead, woofing in alarm.

"I'm fine," I say, and my voice comes out as a winded croak.

I peer around. It's some kind of pit. It's been dug into the permafrost, meaning it was dug out in summer, years ago by the looks of it. I'm standing at the bottom, looking up at the top covered with the branches of that dead tree. Intentionally covered? I try not to be paranoid about that. If there are people living out here—and there certainly will be, somewhere—they hunt for their dinner, and that's what I've fallen into: a pit trap. Not exactly a common method of hunting in North America, but in the Yukon, we get all kinds.

I'm brushing myself off when Storm gives another deep woof. Then her head disappears.

"Don't go far," I say. "I—"

Paws thunder over the ground, brush crackling.

"Storm?" I say.

I try to shout it loud enough to bring her back, but I'm still winded. I'm also a little dazed, and it takes a moment to realize my query wasn't a command.

"Storm!" I call. "Come!"

She's too far away now to hear my hoarse shout. I don't have Dalton's piercing whistle, and I'd spent part of last year training her with a dog whistle. That would be so much more useful if it weren't in my backpack . . . which is up top, after I removed it to get the scent markers.

I keep shouting, and my voice is clearer, but she's long gone. Off to fetch Dalton to rescue me, which is very sweet, but I'd rather she let me try doing it for myself.

"What's that, Lassie?" I mutter. "Timmy fell in the well. Again?"

I shake my head. At least I haven't gotten myself in this *exact* predicament before. Sure, I've stumbled off a cliff and been left hanging on a ledge, but this is far less dire. I'm on the bottom, and the top is only a few feet overhead. There are plenty of roots, too, which means I should be able to get out.

I grab one thick root up over the permafrost level, dig the toe of my boot into the frozen ground of the side, swing up . . . and the root flies free.

Step one: make sure the damn root is actually attached to something.

I find another root and test it. Seems secure. Grab it. Dig in my toe. Heave myself up—

A branch cracks overhead. I freeze, suspended on the pit side like a rock climber.

I slide back down as I listen. Dead leaves whisper, as if under a bear's paw. I take out my gun and peer up.

I can't see beyond the spot where I fell through. The rest is covered by that dead tree and the leaf debris that's fallen on top of it.

Fallen? No, the leaf debris that was placed on top of it to hide the pit.

I ease back into the darkness under that overhang. More crunching overhead. Then a grunt, and I tense and curse myself for leaving my backpack—with bear spray—up top. I should have had it on a utility belt. Too excited about being in our new forest home, I made the tourist mistake of stuffing it into a backpack pocket.

A shadow falls over the sunlight shining through that opening. I brace myself for the inevitable bear muzzle to poke into the hole. It's just curious. Like Dalton said, this is the wrong time of the year for desperately hungry bears, and I can't be threatening a cub down in this hole. Bears are curious. Just let it be a black bear rather than a brown, please.

No muzzle appears. Instead, I see a rounded head against that patch of sun. A smooth head with something on it that is *not* a furry pair of ears. It's a hat. I catch the distinct shape of a brim. A ball cap or a safari-style hat. Or a Western-style, like Dalton's? It's not him. He'd have said something by now.

Still, it's definitely a human up there. Male? Female? I only see the shadow of a head. Then there's another grunt, and I realize it's the soft exhale of someone rising—the first grunt being when they crouched.

Someone is out there. That is the reality I'm trying to hide under the cover of figuring out *who* it might be. If someone is out there, I need to make a choice.

Should I say anything?

I don't think they've noticed me. They must have seen my backpack, though. It's right there. So they spotted a random backpack beside a hole and crouched to look in.

Crouched, but didn't say anything. Didn't ask if someone

was in there. Didn't bend inside to be sure no one was lying on the ground, injured.

Is that because they *did* see me? They know I'm here . . . and they aren't offering to help. They aren't asking whether I'm okay.

Footsteps sound again. A slow crunching that I track all the way around the pit. They stop at the spot where I fell in.

Another soft grunt, as if crouching. Outside, the forest has gone completely silent, and when I focus, I can hear breathing.

Another sound comes. A whisper, like fabric dragged along the ground. Then a clink that I do recognize—my carabiner hitting my bear spray can. The person has picked up my backpack.

I tense, imagining they're pawing through it. Instead, footsteps retreat, and soon, all is silent again.

Did they just *steal* my backpack?

Did they find a backpack, in the middle of the Yukon wilderness, beside a hole where someone has fallen into a pit . . . and they took it? Took what could be someone's only hope of survival?

I holster my gun, march to the edge of the pit and grab the root that had supported me earlier. I heave myself up, and in my mind, I'm already out and going after whoever the hell just stole my damn backpack. I'm focused on that, and this time, I don't notice when the root gives way. I'm dangling, feet on the side, weight held up by that root, and it jerks from the earth, and I fall flat on my back, wind knocked out of me again.

I lie there for a moment, reining in my temper. Yes, I'm reasonably sure someone just took off with my backpack. I'm even reasonably sure that they knew I was down here. But I can't go running into the forest after them. I promised Dalton I'd stay here, and now Storm has gone to find him, which is going to bring him running in a panic. I must be here when he gets back.

When my breathing slows, I declare myself calm enough to stand. I reach down on either side, bracing myself to rise. One hand sinks into the dirt. The other sinks . . . and hits something. Something that is not rock or root. Something soft and pliant and cold.

I don't jump up. I stay where I am, letting my fingers touch what I know is flesh. Cold flesh.

I ease to the side, away from what I am touching. Not escaping it, but minimizing the damage I might have already done.

Am I really that calm while touching what I think is a buried body? No, but this is how I deal with it. Switch into detective mode while telling myself it's probably a dead animal. After all, this *is* a hunting pit.

I ease to the side, and then I scramble up until I'm crouched. I'm blocking the light, so I inch upward until the sunshine hits the dirt here, and I see a pale patch of skin that I know is not any animal out here.

I carefully brush away the dirt. The patch of skin becomes the back of a hand. Then fingers, long and slender. Two delicate rings, one woven gold and one with emeralds.

I keep clearing. A watch. A gold watch. I keep clearing. A shirt sleeve. Then a jacket sleeve pushed up a few inches. The sleeve becomes a jacket, zipped tight against the chill spring evening. I keep going, up the neck. That's where I stop. It's bent at an odd angle. Snapped.

I process that, and I keep going, gently clearing until I see the pale face of a white woman with light brown hair. A woman in her early forties. With a gold watch and rings and trimmed, clean nails. Not a hiker. Not a miner. Not a hunter. A professional working in this forest.

I've found Penny.

CHAPTER FOUR

I'm still clearing the dirt from Penny when running footsteps pound overhead.

"Casey?" Dalton shouts. "Casey!"

"Down here," I call back, and then quickly add, "I'm fine. I fell in a pit trap, but I'm fine."

More pounding of footsteps. The first head that appears in the hole is big and shaggy.

"Hey, Storm," I say. "You brought help, huh?"

She gives a low woof, and then backs out, tugged aside by Dalton, who crouches.

"Who the hell builds a pit trap out here?" he says. "You could have been—Shit."

"I found Penny."

He curses, and then shines in his flashlight and says, "I was about to say someone could break a leg falling in. Penny must have run from the moose and fell into this trap." He shifts the light beam up her body, stops at her obvious broken neck and curses. "She was buried?"

"Yep. Also, that hole you're looking through is from me. It

was covered when I got here. That's how I fell in. Storm was sniffing, distressed about the body, I'm presuming. I made a wrong step and . . ." I motion around.

"So either she fell in and broke her neck and someone covered it up . . . or someone killed and hid her here. Any signs of other injuries?"

"I hadn't gotten that far. I want to examine her before we move her, but I need a light."

"Right." He hunkers onto his heels, partly disappearing. "Your backpack is up here?"

"It was. I took it off to get out the scent markers for Storm. Before I found Penny, someone found me. Found my backpack at least."

"Someone *stole* your backpack?"

"That depends. Is it sitting two feet to your right?"

He looks and lets out a string of curses.

"Did they know you were in—?" He waves off his own question. "Let me get down there, and we'll talk while you work."

"As much as I'd appreciate the help, I think someone better stay up there with Storm . . . or she might get snatched next."

He snorts. "Like to see them try. But yeah, better not have us both in that hole if your thief does come back."

He stretches out on his stomach and reaches the flashlight low enough that I can stand on my tiptoes and grab it.

"What else do you need?" he asks. "You got your phone for photos?"

I pause and then curse.

"It was in your backpack?" Dalton says.

My grumble is answer enough. I'm not used to having a cell phone anymore. They were prohibited in Rockton, where the owners had argued they'd be nothing but paperweights.

That was true once upon a time, but these days, even without service, a cell phone is a Swiss Army knife of utility and recreation. The council just didn't want residents using the limited electricity, which makes sense. We have more solar, though, so we'll be allowing cell phones when we get enough sun, which means I'd brought mine with me. And it's now in the hands of whoever stole my backpack.

Along with . . .

"Shit," Dalton says. "The sat phone."

That's also new. We'd had emergency radios in Rockton, which didn't work worth a damn. Here we'll have satellite phones. We'd brought one . . . and I'd been carrying it in my backpack.

"Note to self," I mutter. "Don't be cheap. Invest in extra sat phones."

Dalton only shrugs. With an undertaking like this, we do need to keep overages to a minimum. We have two sat phones—one in town and one for an "away team."

That means, however, that we're going to need to get Penny back to Haven's Rock by ourselves.

"I could use any bags you have for evidence," I say.

Dalton takes rope and a knife from his backpack and then passes it down to me.

"Take what you need and conduct your examination," he says. "I'll rig up a sled for Storm."

As I conduct my examination of the body, I can hear my physician sister's voice, huffing about how I'm not a medical doctor and certainly not a medical examiner. I've had April's voice in my head for my entire life, and it has always been a voice of criticism, not unlike my father's and sometimes my mother's.

The steady barrage of "not good enough." Not smart enough, not driven enough, not *singular* enough. The last was most important. Oh, I was smart and I was driven, but compared to them, I was a very ordinary sort of above average.

Now, hearing April's voice, I don't hear criticism. I hear . . . well, I just hear April. My sister has come to realize she's on the autism spectrum, a late-in-life discovery that she has embraced because it helps so much of her experience make sense. It also helps me to understand her. April's words would be partly rebuke, but also an excuse to let her leap into the investigation.

"Wish you were here, April," I murmur as I check Penny's pockets.

She will be, eventually, but for now we are back to where we often are in our investigations, with me performing the role of coroner, pulling on what I learned growing up in a household of medical professionals.

Her pockets contain one used tissue and one empty condom wrapper, which really makes me hope the tissue was used for nose-blowing. I bag both.

I place the items into baggies. Then I look at her hands again. I've already examined the nails and noted that they seem clean. There's a cut on one hand that could mean she at least raised it to defend herself, but the lack of broken nails or tissue in her nail beds suggests she didn't have a chance to do more.

I hunker back on my haunches and consider. Except she did fall. We know that from the handprint on the ground near the moose encounter.

Could she have been wearing gloves? It's cool enough at night for light ones. If she'd worn gloves, whoever buried her might have removed them, correctly interpreting they could carry trace materials.

I record a note into Dalton's phone. Then I remove Penny's jacket. As soon as I do, I know she wasn't the one who zipped it up, despite the chill. The front of her T-shirt has been sliced, the weapon cutting into her abdomen. Blood soaks the bottom half of her shirt.

I check her jacket more carefully. There's some blood on the inside, but not a lot, and no obvious traces on the outside. I fold the jacket and put it carefully into a second bag. Then I pull up the bottom of Penny's shirt.

I try to estimate the wound length. I remember I have Dalton's cell phone, which means I have an actual ruler—we'd downloaded an app and calibrated it. The wound is five and a half centimeters long. I take a photo. Then I use a wooden matchstick to prod open the slice. Maybe a centimeter deep, going just beyond a light layer of fat into the muscle.

I roll up Penny's shirt. I don't remove it—we won't want to drag her naked body through the brush. I'm looking for more torso injuries. None on the front. I'll need Dalton's help to check her back.

Next I peel down her jeans. I have them to her thighs when I stop. There's a deep slash across her left thigh. The depth and the position make me wonder whether it severed the artery. If so, there's no blood, not until I look closer and see smears, as if someone cleaned it away.

I check her jeans. No, I hadn't missed a slice in the fabric. They're whole.

"Makeshift stretcher ready," Dalton calls down. "How're you doing?"

"I found two cuts from a sharp instrument. One's across her abdomen, and the other—deeper—on her thigh. The one on her torso went through her T-shirt, and then someone zipped up her jacket to cover it. The one on her leg didn't go through her jeans, meaning she wasn't wearing them. I also found an empty condom wrapper."

"Huh."

"That suggests she was in her T-shirt when she was attacked. She may or may not have been wearing panties, but she was definitely half naked."

"Huh."

"The leg wound may have pierced the femoral artery. It's in the right general area. No blood, though. Not under her body or on her jeans. There's a smear, as if she was washed up."

"And the torso?"

"That bled through her shirt, but the jacket was put on after it was done bleeding. That's definitely not the cause of death, though."

"So she bled out?"

"Mmm, possibly? That'd be an April question. Or a question for Yolanda's on-site medic, if he has that kind of training."

I turn back to Penny and continue examining her. "I never asked about the person you were chasing."

"Not much to tell. I didn't get close enough for a good look. They went to ground maybe a half mile from here. I was trying to figure out where they were hiding when Storm came."

"I presume 'they' means you didn't get close enough to guess at their sex."

"I caught a glimpse. I'd lean toward male, but it could have been a stocky woman. All I saw was a dark jacket and jeans."

"Any kind of hat?"

"Yeah. Looked like a ball cap."

"Whoever came around after I fell was wearing a hat. I could see a brim."

"Does the timing work?"

"I realized Storm wandered off after I couldn't hear you any-more. I came over here, fell in, and she took off. Maybe five minutes passed before I heard someone out there. Probably less."

"Could have been the same person. I was trying to figure out where they holed up, but instead they'd circled back here."

"Possibly."

"Am I right in remembering that Bruno was last seen in a dark jacket, jeans, and ball cap?"

"You are."

"Huh."

"Agreed. Now do you mind checking for evidence out there while I finish up in here?"

"On it."

I tell Dalton what to look for, and he heads off to do that. He's not a trained detective. Not a trained police officer, either, in the proper sense of the word. Hell, he didn't even attend elementary school. His education was all informal, and he's uncomfortable about that, but it's enviable to me—a life spent pursuing what-ever interested him, with no need to learn anything that didn't affect him. For detective training, he chose to learn what he needed to assist my investigations.

When I first met Dalton, I couldn't have imagined him tak-ing training—or instruction—from anyone. He was the sheriff. He was in charge. Again, that's a useful fiction. He was only in his mid-twenties when his adoptive parents retired south, leaving him as sheriff.

Fake it 'til you make it, and baffle them with bullshit. Those are Dalton's keys to successfully convincing a town that he's in charge. The reality is a whole lot different.

I continue examining Penny. I don't find much else of interest. I don't conduct an internal exam for recent sexual activity. The empty condom wrapper suggests the answer to that is yes, and either way, that evidence won't change when she's moved. I need to check everything that might be affected by that move.

I do discover one more thing. The soles of her feet are dirty. That leads me to realize, a little belatedly, that her boots are on the wrong feet. No new information there—it just supports my conclusion that she'd been attacked while wearing little more than a shirt. She is also, I note, braless. That could mean she wasn't wearing one. It could also mean that her killer didn't put it back on when he redressed her. She'd put her shirt back on for a bit of warmth after sex, and then she'd been attacked.

Attacked by her partner, who I suspect was Bruno? Or attacked *with* Bruno? Is he out there, dead or injured?

Yes, the person we saw roughly matches his description, but I'm not making any presumptions. All I know for now is that we have Penny, dead and buried in a pit, with stab wounds inflicted while she'd been in a semi-naked state, on a night cool enough that you wouldn't have undressed unless you were doing something that required it, like having sex with your secret lover.

CHAPTER FIVE

It's another hour before we leave. Dalton has combed the area up top, but after he helps me climb out of the pit, he wants me to double-check his work, and I appreciate that—it'd be awkward if I had to suggest it myself.

That's the downside of any work-plus-personal relationship, one made even more awkward when one party is technically the other's boss. Here is one of many reasons I'm grateful for Dalton's unusual upbringing: he doesn't carry the typical cultural baggage. I am the detective. He is not. Therefore, I should check his work, for the sake of the victim.

He didn't find any footprints up top, and I don't either. Whoever buried Penny in the pit didn't leave any obvious evidence. I didn't see any prints below either.

"What would someone be catching in that pit?" I ask as Dalton straps Penny's body to the stretcher. We've used lightweight rain jackets from his backpack to wrap her, as best we can. I move to the edge of the pit. "Have you ever seen something like this? For trapping?"

"Too much work. Also, do you want to come check it and find you caught a pissed-off grizzly?"

"Fair point."

"It'd work for moose or caribou. They'd break a leg falling in. Helluva thing to do." He moves to the edge. "Could be for wolves, too, if they were a problem."

"Really hoping they're not."

Dalton shrugs. "For most people, just having wolves around is a problem. We know better. Could also be wolverines. Hell, I'd set out a trap myself for them. The pit seems to be years old. It definitely wasn't just dug—thawing the permafrost takes time. More likely it's long abandoned."

"And whoever killed Penny knew about it and used it to hide her body."

"Yeah."

I look over at Penny, her covered body roped to the make-shift stretcher.

"Let's get her back to town."

The stretcher is tied to a harness on Storm. She tolerates that. She'd much rather play bloodhound than sled dog, but she knows this is a rare request. As we walk, we don't say much. I'm deep in thought, working through the lists of questions I'll have for the crew's medic and the people I'll need to interview. I use Dalton's phone to record some of my questions—the ones I fear forgetting—and he suggests a few more. Otherwise, it's a silent walk.

We've made it about halfway when I notice he's lagging. I'm in front, with Storm following behind and Dalton bringing up the rear. I glance back once to see him peering into the forest, having dropped a few feet behind the stretcher. When I look back again, he's even farther back, frowning into the trees.

He asks Storm to stop and slips around the stretcher to come up beside me.

"I think we're being watched," he whispers.

I look in the same direction he was.

"Can't say for sure," he says. "It's a feeling and a few noises. There's a rise maybe fifty feet that way. If we *are* being watched, they're up on that. I can't see anything, though, so maybe I'm just antsy. Unfamiliar forest."

"You want to check it out?"

He shakes his head. "Not after the last time. All I accomplished was letting them lure me away so they could circle back to you."

"They wouldn't have had any way of knowing I'd stay behind."

"Yeah, but you did, and they took advantage."

"Unless my backpack thief wasn't the person you chased. But, yes, I take your point. Also, even if they did realize I was down in that pit, they didn't try to hurt me. Sure, stealing my backpack might have condemned me to death, but I don't think we're dealing with an immediate threat." I peer into the woods. "Though I *would* like my cell phone back."

Dalton turns toward the forest and fingers his backpack strap, as if considering handing it off to give chase again.

"I was kidding," I say. "I can afford a new cell phone, and unless they're a hacking genius, mine's nothing but a brick until they wipe it."

"Notice I'm pretending to know what you're talking about."

I smile. "Sorry. The passcode and facial recognition mean

a thief isn't getting my data. They'll need to reboot it from scratch, giving them a lovely new phone, but I'm more worried about my personal information, which they will not have."

"Good."

"To be really safe, I can remote-wipe my phone, which I'd like to do, but that will require being in Dawson City. So for now, fingers crossed that we haven't stumbled over a world-class hacker in the middle of the Yukon wilderness."

I shield my eyes and squint, just making out the ridge he'd referred to. "I'll add my vote for leaving them alone, at least for now."

We're close enough to Haven's Rock to hear an undercurrent of noise. That's always a concern, and it's one reason why we're not running generators—along with the obvious issue of bring-ing in fuel. The crew is minimizing the sound of construction by minimizing the use of power tools, but even the slap of one plank hitting another rings through the forest. One reason we'd chosen this location is that there's a waterfall nearby, and we plan to construct dams between the fast-flowing streams and the lake, both for power and for added noise. All that means is that we don't hear the town until we're about a hundred feet away.

That's where we realize we have a problem. We don't dare walk into town with a body in tow. Everyone will stop what they're doing and demand explanations and assurances of their own safety.

While we won't be able to keep this from the crew—not when we're investigating a murder—there's a wrong and a not-quite-as-wrong way to do it.

"We need to get Yolanda," I say. "Tell her we'll put Penny . . . well, I guess we'll put her in our cabin for now. Not exactly the housewarming omen I'd like, but necessity wins out."

"We'll move her to the medical clinic as soon as we can. Go on and get Yolanda. I'll wait here."

I hesitate. In order to bring out Yolanda, one of us has to go into town first. One of us gets to see it first. It's an inconsequential thing compared to a murder, but it's still significant to us.

"You go first," I say. "I'll wait."

He pauses, eyeing me. Then he waves for me to follow him, saying, "We should get closer. Just in case we were followed."

We continue on, and then he motions for me to wait. I ease back and start unfastening the ties binding Storm to the stretcher. We can pull it the rest of the way ourselves. When I glance up, I see that Dalton is only standing about twenty feet away, scanning the forest.

"You!" he says, making me jump. "Get over here."

Whoever he's talking to clearly doesn't do what he's asking, not surprisingly. A stranger is hailing them from the wilderness. Dalton's lucky they don't break into a run, shouting a warning to the others.

He takes two more steps. "You! In the red jacket. I need Yolanda."

It takes another moment, but then a guy in his forties tentatively steps in our direction. I raise a hand in greeting, and as his gaze goes from me to Storm, he relaxes. The scary guy barking at him from the forest is with a woman and a dog. That's okay then.

I jog toward him. "Bring Yolanda, please. Tell her Casey and Eric need to speak to her in private."

"Oh, you're the folks who came in on the plane. Sure, let me grab her."

We wait no more than a few minutes before Yolanda comes, alone, at a run.

"You found them?" she says. Before we can answer, she sees the body wrapped on the stretcher, and she falters. "Oh." A sharp intake of breath, and then another "Oh."

"It's Penny," I say, lowering my voice. "We didn't find Bruno. We spotted someone vaguely matching his description and gave chase, but then we found Penny."

"Oh." She blinks and gives a sharp shake of her head. "I keep saying that, don't I? This is . . . It's not . . . I didn't . . ."

"I'm sorry," I say. "Hopefully, Bruno is still out there and fine, but for now, we really need to quietly get Penny's body someplace. I was thinking we could put her in our house until we can inform people that there was an accident, and then we'll transport her to the medical clinic for examination."

"Yes, that's . . ." She trails off, as if losing her train of thought. Then she snaps back to herself. "We can take her directly to the medical clinic. There's no one working in that quadrant, and there is a rear door, with access to the forest. I'll go ahead to clear the way. The door should be unlocked."

"Great. Can you bring the medic? I'm going to need a postmortem examination."

Her brows knit at that. Penny just suffered an accident, didn't she? I don't clarify. Not yet.

After a moment, Yolanda nods and says, "I'll bring him along."

We're in the medical clinic, which will also double as April's new house. I'd made the mistake of questioning whether my sister actually wanted to live where residents can come banging on her door at 2 A.M. for headache meds. That earned me a spread-sheet, where she had calculated projected personal time lost by living above the clinic versus projected personal time gained by not needing to travel back and forth—including weather-related clothing changes—particularly when she has a patient requiring regular check-ins. So April will be living above the clinic and honestly, knowing my sister, I feel kind of sorry for the first person who decides their headache is worth waking her.

We get Penny's wrapped body onto the table. Then Dalton hands me his phone.

"Take pictures for April."

"We can't transmit them to her."

"I mean pictures of her new clinic."

"So she can stop asking whether we are absolutely certain we communicated her full list of requirements?"

"Yep. Also to make her happy, which means taking lots and lots of pictures of all the perfectly organized storage areas."

I laugh under my breath. "That *will* make her happy. But I'll do that later. I don't want Yolanda and the medic walking in to find me snapping new-homeowner pictures while their architect's body is on the exam table."

Yolanda and the medic haven't arrived, so I undress Penny and place each piece of clothing on a shelf, awaiting proper bags. I'm setting aside her boots—after photographing them being on the wrong feet—when footsteps sound on the front porch.

Hearing the others approach, Dalton shakes out a bedsheet. I take the other end and help him lay it over the corpse. I don't know how close either Yolanda or the medic was to Penny, but they shouldn't walk in to see her naked body on an exam table.

Yolanda enters, followed by a burly guy in his late thirties. He's white, with balding brown hair and a beard, and he's dressed in short sleeves and wearing a tool belt.

"This is Pierre," Yolanda says. "He's a carpenter, but also our medic. He served as an EMT before switching careers."

I hesitate. Yes, we couldn't afford a full-time doctor for the crew, but we'd been clear that we wanted someone with as much medical training as possible, even if that meant they'd spend most of their time doing nonskilled labor for physician wages.

"How long were you an EMT?" I ask, as casually as I can.

"About a year," he says with a light Quebecois accent.

I glance at Yolanda, whose lips tighten. She knows this isn't what we agreed to, and I don't think she was cheating us—she just wasn't about to give up a precious crew spot to a doctor who couldn't do more than hold boards while someone hammered them in.

"Okay," I say. "I don't suppose you have any experience working with medical examiners?"

He stares blankly at us.

"We weren't expecting to be conducting autopsies," Yolanda says. "Pierre can set bones and he can stitch cuts. That's what we've needed, and it's what we got."

Pierre's gaze goes to the exam table, as if he's seeing the covered body for the first time. He quicksteps back. "Uh-uh. I don't know anything about performing an autopsy."

"We don't need a full autopsy. I'm mostly looking for your medical opinion on what killed her. I have a doctor I can link in. We'll need your help assisting—"

"No," he says, taking another step back. "Sorry, but no."

"You were an EMT," Yolanda snaps. "Don't tell me you never had to handle a corpse."

"Yes, I did. Once. An old guy who'd been dead in his apartment for a month, and no one noticed until he missed his rental payment. That's when I remembered how much I enjoyed carpentry in high school."

"That's fine," I cut in, trying to sound as if I mean it. "Our victim isn't decomposing yet, but if you really don't feel you can help . . ."

"I can't. Sorry. I was hired to tend to the living. No one said anything about working on the dead."

He's gone before anyone can respond.

"I'll help," Yolanda says. "I may lack medical training, but I'm not squeamish."

"Thank you," I say. "I know first aid, but that's about it."

"Casey's being modest," Dalton says. "But yeah, none of us are medical professionals. We'll need to use the sat phone to call Casey's sister to guide us through this."

"She's not going to like doing it long-distance. Be prepared for complaints."

"Understandable," Yolanda says. "Do you have your sat phone handy?"

"We don't have it at all," I say. "Someone stole my backpack while I was in a pit finding Penny." When Yolanda's brow furrows, I say, "Long story. Short version is that the thief may have been Bruno, who may . . ."

I remember that Yolanda is missing a key detail, one she's going to need to know fast.

I continue, "Earlier, I said we'd need to let people know that Penny suffered an accident. It wasn't an accident. She was murdered."

Yolanda's face gives nothing away. She just stands there, seconds ticking by before she says, "You're certain of that?"

"I'm certain she was stabbed twice," I say.

Another pause. I wait it out.

"I'll get the other sat phone," she says finally.

"Thank you."

I fold down the sheet as Yolanda leaves. She's halfway out the door when she stops.

"Do you need anything else?" she asks as she turns back. "The clinic is stocked but—" She stops, her gaze on Penny as she blinks.

"Would you prefer I kept her face covered?" I ask.

"No," she says slowly. She walks back and stares down at the body. Then she looks at me.

"That's not Penny."

CHAPTER SIX

The dead woman lying on our examination table is not Penny. She resembles the architect, only in the most superficial way. She seems roughly the same age, she's white, and she has light brown hair. In any other missing-person case, we'd have gotten more details, starting with a photograph. No one saw a reason for that. Exactly how many missing women did we expect to find wandering around the forest? The answer, apparently, is: at least two.

"Is this a member of your crew?" I ask.

When Yolanda hesitates, Dalton's brow creases. While Yolanda has already indicated that she doesn't sit around drinking after-work beers with her crew, there are only a couple dozen people here.

"No one else has been reported missing," she says.

"Okay."

"Yes, you think I should be able to answer that definitively," she says, her voice cooling. "And if I can't, then I'm a cast-iron bitch-boss who doesn't even recognize members of her own crew. We have thirty people on the crew. Twenty-two are women. And I have difficulty retaining faces."

"Ah," I say. "You're face-blind."

Her cheek twitches. "I have mild prosopagnosia, which causes some difficulty with facial recognition. And before you ask, yes, I am absolutely certain this isn't Penny. We worked together closely enough for me to recognize her. The problem would come with those crew members with whom I have less interaction."

"Can we get someone in here who can tell us whether she's a crew member?"

Yolanda hesitates. Then she says, "Of course," and turns on her heel. A moment later, she's gone.

"I handled that badly, didn't I?" I say to Dalton.

"I'd have handled it worse." He leans against the counter. "My guess is that she's uncomfortable admitting she has . . . What did she call it?"

"Prosopagnosia. It's an inability to recognize faces. More commonly known as face blindness, but I think she prefers not to use that term."

"And she'd prefer not to admit she has it. Having not admitted it to her crew means she now has to figure out how to explain why she needs someone else to ID our victim."

"Shit. Okay, I see the issue. Personally, given the choice between people thinking I have a neurological disorder and thinking I just don't care enough to remember who the hell they are, I'd go with option one, but that's me."

"Yep."

"See, *you* would have handled it better."

He snorts. "You know how I would have handled it."

"Told her your opinion of the situation and how she should fix it, which no one wants to hear from a near stranger?"

"Yep. There is a time for blunt honesty, and a time when it's really better for all if I throw you to the lions."

"Thanks."

The door opens, and Yolanda strides in, followed by a woman. The newcomer looks Indigenous, with dark eyes, brown skin, spiked blue hair, and a nose ring. She can't be more than twenty-five.

"This is Kendra," Yolanda says. "She's our plumber, and she is pursuing her master's degree in social work, which satisfied your requirement for someone with mental-health training."

Yolanda's tone is brisk and emotionless, but I remember the battle we'd had over this particular stipulation. Yolanda hadn't seen the need for a mental-health expert, even after our *own* mental-health experts explained the issue—thirty people, who've never met, thrown into extreme isolation together for three months.

She'd only agreed when we threatened to send our former psychiatrist, Mathias. Five minutes on a call with him, and she changed her mind. Mathias has that effect on people.

Yolanda didn't see the need for a mental-health professional . . . and Yolanda doesn't see the need to admit to her own neurological condition. Knowing the first part, I shouldn't be surprised about the second. Or vice versa, I suppose.

"Also," Yolanda continues, "as per your instructions, all crew had to disclose any psychological conditions to Kendra, and mine was included in that."

Interesting use of the passive voice there. "Mine was included," not "I included mine." Was that Émilie's doing? Or Petra's? At least it meant someone here knew about Yolanda's condition.

"I'm not sure how much Yolanda explained—" I begin.

Yolanda cuts in. "Kendra is aware that Penny is missing. Again, as per your instructions, I had already consulted with her to determine whether either Penny or Bruno had any issues that might have led to their disappearance. She is now aware that a body has been found, which is not Penny's, and that we require her to identify it, if possible."

"I'm up to speed," Kendra says with a quarter smile. That smile is strained as she glances toward the covered body and squares her shoulders. "Onward, then?"

"Have you ever seen a dead body?" I try not to sound *too* gentle, which could imply she needs coddling.

That smile twists. "I grew up in a village five hundred kilometers north of here. One of my earliest memories was finding my cousin after he committed suicide. So, yep, I've seen a few. Got into social work in hopes of seeing a few less."

The automatic impulse is to say that I'm sorry. I don't. She didn't share this for sympathy. Just stark facts.

I fold back the sheet from the woman's face. Kendra doesn't even hesitate before saying, "Nope. She isn't one of us."

I'm now supposed to ask whether she's sure, but that seems silly, given the small number of people on-site.

Without me asking, she moves forward and studies the face further. "I've met everyone who's worked here. There were a few supply drops, though, and I didn't see the pilots."

"One pilot," Yolanda says. "I know him."

Kendra glances at the dead woman again. Her gaze drops to the left hand, peeking out after I adjusted the sheet. She walks down to peer at it and then looks at the clothing folded on shelves.

"Is that hers?" she asks.

I nod and take the clothing down, silently unfolding it.

"If you don't recognize her face," Yolanda says, "you're not going to recognize her clothing."

Kendra takes no offense at the snap in Yolanda's voice. Instead, the corners of her mouth twitch, her dark eyes dancing. "Are you sure? What if it was Penny's clothing? Or *your* clothing? Now *that* would be a mystery."

Yolanda only sighs, as if this is to be expected from Kendra.

"The clothing doesn't look as if it belongs to someone living rough in the forest," I say. "Nor someone who came here to enjoy the wilderness. Same as her hands. Not your typical hunter or miner or hiker. Which doesn't mean she isn't one of the above—just not what you'd expect."

"Damn," Kendra says. "And here I was hoping to be the first one to make that observation."

I extend a hand. "Proper introductions. I'm Casey, former homicide detective."

"A cop?" Her brows shoot up. "You don't look like one." She nods toward Dalton. "He does. You don't."

"And you don't look like a social worker," Yolanda says.

"Pfft. Then you haven't met many social workers. I totally look like one. Now, a plumber? Maybe not. But with this hair, I'm definitely a social worker." She turns back to me. "Yes, this woman's clothing and her hands suggest she's not—as you say—a typical hunter, miner, or hiker. Still could be a tourist."

Dalton nods. "If she convinced someone to fly her into the bush dressed in blue jeans. Pay enough, and they'll take anyone."

She peers at him. "Now *you're* from around here."

His brows rise.

"You've got the look," she says. "Your dead woman does not. Death by misadventure, I'm guessing."

"We're still determining that," I say.

"Murder?"

"I didn't say—"

"You didn't say yes to misadventure, because you don't want

to outright lie, which means you suspect—or know—it's murder." She looks at Yolanda. "Is there a security risk?"

"That remains to be assessed," Yolanda says. "In the meantime, I will proceed as if there is, with a curfew from dusk until dawn and a buddy system. I would have done that anyway, with Bruno and Penny."

"Who are still missing," Kendra says.

"I'd like to talk later, get your insights into both of them," I say.

"And that is my cue to leave," she says. "You'll find me working at the commissary."

"You found a *dead woman* in the woods?" April's voice crackles over the line, and I could blame a bad connection, but it's probably just April. "Less than twelve hours in town, and you're already out in the forest looking for cases to solve? And you call me a workaholic."

When I pause, she says, "That was a joke. Mostly. Perhaps sixty percent. The other forty percent of me fears that, if I believed in omens, this would be a very bad one."

"But we don't believe in omens, so we're good."

"I am also not certain whether to be glad it isn't the missing architect . . . or to be more concerned that you're finding unrelated bodies." A beat. "Or *is* it unrelated? Could our missing duo have happened upon this woman and murdered her, lest she report them for some nefarious deed? Or, perhaps, she is the third member of a polyamorous relationship, whom they were meeting for a tryst when things went horribly wrong."

Part of my sister learning to relax and not work every waking hour means reading, and she has discovered a passion for mysteries.

"Ready to start?" I say.

"That would depend on you, Casey, as I cannot see the body, much less wield the scalpel, and therefore I am unable to influence the timeline. I should be there."

I lower my voice. I'm alone with Dalton in the exam room, but I don't know how far Yolanda went.

"I agree," I say. "I have suggested that, but at this point, it's hard to argue for bringing you out to perform a postmortem examination on a woman who isn't even one of ours."

"Does that make her less deserving of proper treatment?"

"No, but it does mean she isn't entitled to that treatment from *us*. We're in the middle of building a town. I only brought her back because I thought she was our missing architect. Now I'm stuck. We considered returning her to where we found her, but we risk leaving trace evidence."

"You are conducting an examination on a woman despite having just said you can't investigate her death."

I put the probe down, clacking it against the stainless-steel tray. "Do you have a better idea, April? If you do, I would love to hear it, particularly if you know a way for me to turn this poor woman's body over to the Mounties and focus on our own missing people."

Silence. Dalton is busy prepping and wisely staying out of this.

"Eric and I ran through the options before we called you. Return her to where we found her? That risks having left evidence if she's discovered. Find another spot where she will be found, so her family can claim her? Again, the risk of leaving evidence. Any way that gets her to the proper authorities puts us—and Haven's Rock—at risk. The only alternative is to bury her and move on, and that might be the smart solution, but we can't do it. Especially if there's a chance that her murder is connected to our missing people or our build."

More silence. Then, her voice gentle, "I wasn't questioning whether you'd thought this through, Casey, though I can see how it might have sounded that way."

"If you have an ethical objection to assisting in the examination of a woman who might, eventually, need to be quietly buried and never found, then say that, April. I'll understand."

"I do not." Another pause. "I was questioning your assertion that she is not entitled to your investigative efforts, because I would prefer to be there, conducting the procedure. I apologize."

"I'm being testy. I didn't expect to be called in to hunt for missing construction crew members, and I certainly didn't expect to be dealing with a murder victim. The council in Rockton may have made things so much more difficult there, but there are a few things they made easier. Now we need to make the hard choices."

"Pretty sure we always did," Dalton says. "If this happened there, they'd have told us to bury her and move on. And we wouldn't have been able to do it. So we'd be right here, conducting an examination we have no real right to conduct."

"True enough," I say. "Let's get on with it then. We'll be recording this session, April." I clear my throat and motion for Dalton to hit the record button. "We have a Caucasian female, approximately forty years of age . . ."

We don't need to conduct an autopsy, thankfully. I would have been truly uncomfortable cutting into this poor woman, a procedure that would have made it impossible to ever return her to her loved ones.

April thinks our victim bled out from the leg wound. Without an actual autopsy, she won't definitively give that as a cause of death, but the evidence strongly supports that conclusion. The body has lost a great deal of blood, with minimal lividity. I know enough anatomy to confirm that the wound on her thigh did sever her femoral artery, which would have led to death if untreated. There is no indication that anyone tried to treat it by stanching blood flow, even with a tourniquet.

Our mystery woman bled out in the forest, where she'd been attacked. Then someone did a quick cleanup job, dressed her, and transported her to that pit.

There's no easy way of telling which wound was inflicted first, but the one to her abdomen wouldn't have been fatal. Her killer had paid less attention to it, as well, not bothering to clean it, just zipping up her jacket over it.

Someone stabbed her, twice. Someone cleaned her wound. Someone hid her. Presumably the same person did all three, though I'd never ignore other possibilities—for example that someone found her dead, cleaned her up, and "buried" her in that pit. To reject that possibility would be to reject the reality that not everyone in this forest is mentally sound.

I'd estimate her weight at about one-forty. How far could someone carry her to that pit? We saw no signs that she'd been dragged or hauled, but we'd need to rule out that possibility before concluding she was carried, which means we'd likely be looking at a male killer and a nearby crime scene.

Does that mean I plan to find her killer?

Not unless I stumble across more clues. For now, we can only put her body in a hole in the permafrost, our version of a morgue freezer.

I am, however, committed to finding Penny and Bruno, and if their disappearance is connected to this death, then yes, I will need to solve her murder. Yet if they had nothing to do with this, then she was murdered by someone possibly residing in this area, and *that* is our problem. We will not bring innocent refuge seekers into a dangerous situation. We've done enough of that.

CHAPTER SEVEN

With the examination completed, April gone off to write up her own notes, we have finally reached the point we've been waiting for. The point in this visit that, with everything that has happened, we've actually forgotten. Deep in the mystery of who killed this stranger, I've forgotten where we are, what lies beyond these walls.

Haven's Rock.

Our new town.

When Dalton says "You ready?" it takes a moment to make the connection. He's at the door, hand on it, looking at me expectantly. I've covered our mystery woman and cleaned the area, and now it's time to step through that door.

I give a little "Oh!" and his mouth twists in a half smile.

"Not exactly the way you dreamed of it?" he says.

I *have* dreamed of this moment. I've dreamed of stepping off a plane and walking into town, and seeing it laid out before me. Dalton and I would come alone, after the construction crew had left, and a few weeks before *our* crew would arrive. Our honeymoon, the others joked, but really, that's what it would be. We'd been married in a small service, and we hadn't wanted to spare any time for a honeymoon. We'd have this instead— two or three weeks alone in our new home, the two of us exploring and settling in and making plans.

When the schedule shifted, our first residents due to arrive sooner, our "few weeks" became one week—maybe five or six days alone before the others arrived.

We can still carve out that time, if this wrench doesn't throw construction too far off schedule. Yet it will be different, because we will already have been here. I could mourn the loss of that fantasy, but I accept it as more of a passing fancy. The important part is that we are about to see Haven's Rock.

Dalton stands ready to head out front. I shake my head and motion to the back door instead, the one we came in through. Dalton frowns slightly, but only follows me down a small hall and out the rear door.

There's a deck here, behind the clinic. That wasn't part of April's plan, but I added it. A small deck, with the forest beyond, where she can sit with a book and a glass of wine. My sister won't care much about the forest view. She hasn't taken to the wilderness the way I have. To her, it's simply another environment. What I think she will appreciate is the privacy of being out here. I added a balcony, too, off her bedroom, and I see it above us, acting as a roof for the deck.

"She's going to love it," Dalton says as he catches me looking up at the balcony. "She won't say that. She'll fuss about the added expense. But she's going to love it."

"I hope so."

I lead him around the side of the building. The neighboring one is Kenny's workshop, with his own residence overtop. Kenny is *our* carpenter, and head of our militia. April doesn't know his house is beside hers, but this, too, will please her.

They're friends, and I keep hoping that'll turn into more-than-friends, but they're in no rush to get there.

We walk between their two buildings and out the front. All the services form an outer ring, with the common residences in the middle. It's the opposite of Rockton's setup, but it'll be safer this way, with only our core group having homes at the forest's edge.

We head left. There's no one in sight, though we hear the sounds of construction inside the buildings. From the exterior, the town is complete, and it is exactly the vision we gave to Yolanda and Penny, of a modern wilderness town with a touch of the Old West—or, in this case, the Klondike gold rush—in the wooden buildings and rustic porches and dirt "roads" that are really only walking paths in a town with no vehicular traffic.

The buildings might look old-fashioned but they are as modern as possible, at least in terms of eco-consciousness. For a self-sustained town, that's more about common sense than environmental awareness, but it's also Yolanda's specialty—she recycles old building materials to produce high-efficiency homes. These are built to the highest standards for northern living, from thick insulated walls to the quadruple-paned windows that cost us a small fortune but will ensure maximum light for minimum heat loss.

Earlier, we'd left Storm behind the clinic, and now she's with us again, and when someone notices strangers, it's the dog they see first, as a woman steps out and quickly retreats on spotting a huge shaggy black beast. I call a greeting and assure her we're invited guests—and Storm is not a black bear—and she waves tentatively before returning to her work.

We pass buildings, ticking them off in quiet voices. The general store. The toolshed. The community center and library.

When we reach the next one, we stop. It will be our bar and coffee café, fashioned just like the last bar, reminiscent of an old saloon. That's no accident, not in design and not in materials. When we broke down Rockton, board by board, Yolanda rescued as much as possible to recycle, and our new "the Roc" is constructed with the DNA of the last one.

I walk onto the oversized front porch and lay a hand against the weathered wood.

"Think Isabel's going to like it?" I say.

"I think she's going to find everything that the builders did even slightly wrong, but allow that it will do the job."

"But, since it is not *exactly* as requested, she'll feel free to renegotiate the percentage of credits she's allowed to retain."

He snorts. "She can try."

I push open the wooden doors and step inside, and I'll blame swirling dust for making my eyes tear, but it is the smell of the place. The sawdust is from the construction, but the Roc always smelled of that, sawdust used to line the floors, an easy way to clean up spills and keep the less savory scents at bay.

It's more than that, though, and when I turn, I even see "our" table, the one in the corner that every resident knew to steer clear of, even if the sheriff wasn't in the building. I picture our friends, an ever-changing cast revolving around a few core faces. I see people long gone, and people recently gone, having decided not to join our new venture. I see those who will return immediately, and those who will return after we are settled, and those who may join us only temporarily to get us through the opening.

I mourn for the friends and allies we've lost, and I mourn for those who are going to step away, while completely understanding their reasons for doing so. I look forward, too, to the day when I'll sit at our old table with those who remain and with those yet to come.

It's a fresh start that pulls in just enough of the past for comfort and stability. I take Dalton's hand and squeeze it, and we gaze at that table, dust motes swirling around it in the sunshine, and we anticipate the future. Then we turn our backs on the past and focus on the present.

Time to get to work. We haven't seen everything yet, but we've seen all save the most important: our new home. That will be our treat at the end of what I expect will be a very long day.

As we cross through town, I get a look at the residences. In Rockton, there'd been a variety of them, and what you got depended on how essential—and difficult—a job you performed. In a town like this, everyone has a job, and there is nothing more valuable than quality of life. It also, however, led to endless envy and resentment, with residents—quite rightly sometimes—questioning housing decisions that could seem arbitrary or, worse, fueled by factors such as the resident's friendship with core staff.

In Haven's Rock, there are only two types of housing: that given to permanent staff and that given to everyone else. April, Kenny, and Isabel all get quarters over their place of business. Anders will have an apartment over the police station. Everyone else is in dormitory-style living, with tiny private bedrooms and communal kitchens, living rooms and bathrooms.

Are the new residents going to love that? Nope. But when they decide to come here, they'll know what to expect. It's this or nothing.

We continue past the block of residences to the police station. Yolanda has set up shop in it, and I rap, and then step in to find it empty.

"Quick look?" I say to Dalton.

He nods, and we bring Storm inside. This is one building that isn't significantly different from the Rockton version, in the spirit of "if it ain't broke, don't fix it." The second-floor apartment for Anders is new. He'd had a whole chalet before, but as he says, less living space is less space to keep clean. He pretty much just needs a bedroom anyway, not being the sort to cook his own meals or spend his free time alone in his quarters.

Our one stipulation was soundproofing between the station and his quarters. He usually takes the evening shift, and he's not going to get much sleep if we're dealing with a situation below.

Do we expect to have situations? I would dearly love to say no. In fact, I'd love to say that we don't need a police department, much less a three-person one. We are hoping that our roles shift to be more managerial—looking after the daily running of the town—but there will always be a need for some law enforcement, even if it's just to handle inter-resident disputes. To that end, though, what we call the "police station" will officially be known as the town hall. Are we going to keep referring to ourselves as sheriff, detective, and deputy? That part is still under review.

We poke about in the town hall for a few minutes. Then we head past the commissary, which is going to require a more appealing name. What was once two separate structures—one for dine-in and one for take-out—is now one big kitchen and food-storage area, set up for both dining in and taking out.

We head into the commissary, where we find Kendra hard at work on the septic system.

"That looks complicated," I say as we walk over to her.

"You guys gave me a challenge," she says, pulling her head from under a sink. "And I appreciate that. This is the real reason Yolanda hired me, despite the fact that she thinks I'm a pain in the ass. I cut my teeth on northern plumbing. Well, not literally." She pauses. "Or possibly literally, since Mom says I lost two baby teeth trying to work a pump handle."

Plumbing is another area where we're very excited about innovations. When Rockton was first built, they used outhouses and hauled water. Seventy years later, we'd barely progressed from that, relying on chemical toilets and reservoir-and-pump systems. We can do better now. The nearby lake gives us freshwater access, and between Kendra and our solar expert, we're going to have a decent supply of running water. We're also going to have a septic system, with Kendra's use of cutting-edge technology insulating the system and eliminating the need for heating it. Lots of science involved, most of which I don't pretend to understand. I only know that while we won't have truly hot showers or a maintenance-free septic system, what we have will be a damn sight better and healthier than before.

"Can we talk about Penny and Bruno?" I ask Kendra.

"Sure can. Just give me a minute to tighten these screws. Grab a hot drink if you like. The kitchen's open."

CHAPTER EIGHT

Dalton takes Storm for a walk while I talk to Kendra. That's partly exercising the dog, but mostly that he wants another look at the perimeter, to see whether he can figure out where Bruno exited last night.

I make myself a hot chocolate and eye a package of store-bought cookies before opting for a piece of sponge cake instead. One bite of the cake tells me I made a mistake. I'm terribly spoiled, having spent two years in a town with a world-class baker.

I take my snack into the empty room that we're calling the private dining room. The commissary has two main dining areas. One is cafeteria style, with long communal tables. Take-out food can be eaten in there. The other area is a more intimate dining room, with private tables and a server, where it'll cost extra for the more "restaurant" experience.

When Kendra joins me, I'm dunking my sponge cake into my hot chocolate. That makes her laugh.

"Tastes like shit, doesn't it?" she says as she sits. "I'm pretty sure it's just our extra Styrofoam, painted to look like cake."

"The hot chocolate's not bad, though." I take out Dalton's phone to jot notes. "Do you want to grab something to eat before we start?"

"I'm good. So you want to know about Penny and Bruno. First, whether there's any indication they may have run off together or left temporarily together for any reason. Second, in light of what you discovered, you're going to want my opinion on whether they could have had anything to do with that."

"Yes, but unless you have specific concerns regarding the second part, I don't expect you to make a guess. That isn't fair."

She exhales dramatically. "Thank you. Okay, now, every crew member is required to have at least a brief session with me weekly. Like I told Yolanda, nothing that either Bruno or Penny said to me in that setting would lead me to conclude that they would leave town together for any purpose other than a professional one. That said, professionally, they *did* work closely, being the construction engineer and the architect."

"Worked closely together well? Or not well?"

"That is the big question, isn't it? And the answer doesn't come from our sessions but from working with them, which isn't privileged information. They butted heads. A lot. From my experience, though, that's not unexpected. This was a complicated job, and I get the feeling Bruno was in over his head while Penny was in her element. Her brain was zipping at a hundred miles an hour, and Bruno was always reining her in."

"They clashed."

"Yep, but so did Bruno and Yolanda, and Penny and Yolanda, and pretty much everyone here above the general-crew level. Yolanda hired a freaking dream team of experts, and that means a lot of conflict. Even I've had a shouting match or two, and that is absolutely not my style."

"If there was a dispute, though, it would be possible for either Penny or Bruno to see the other one heading into the forest and follow to confront them out of earshot of others. Or for one to go into the forest to escape the other . . . and be followed." I wave my hand. "That's not a question. Just speculating."

"Well, if it was a question, Penny wouldn't have gone in on her own. Either she'd follow Bruno or she'd have accidentally stomped in there to avoid him."

"She didn't like the forest."

"She had a complete disinterest in it, coupled with a healthy respect for it. I handle the hikes, which aren't hikes so much as straight walks into the forest and back."

I smile. "I noticed."

"Not my idea. That is pure Yolanda. Even our hikes are efficient. But I can say that Penny never joined them or expressed any interest in them."

I jot notes. "How connected are you with the crew on a social level? If I were looking for someone to talk to—or to tell me who best to talk to?"

"Because that person is definitely not Yolanda?" She laughs. "Yeah, I'm connected enough. I can tell you who Penny and Bruno hung out with. For Penny, the answer would be anybody and nobody—she was friendly with everyone but too busy to do more than have a drink now and then, and she'd just join whatever group was gathered. As for Bruno, well, he mostly stuck with the Y Gang."

"The Why Gang?"

"Y chromosome. The guys."

"The men stick together?"

She leans back. "Some of them. It's sociologically interesting, really. I've worked a lot of jobs where I'm the only woman,

but on some big ones, there will be several of us. It's not uncommon for women in a male-dominated workplace to stick
together. Is it the same principle here? Maybe, but I get the
sense that for some, it's the discomfort of being outnumbered
in a setting where you usually dominate. There are eight guys
on a crew of thirty. Three of them are cool with it, hanging out
with anyone. The other five tend to stick together, especially
for socializing, some of them to the complete exclusion of socializing with the women."

"Interesting."

"Right? An intriguing social phenomenon. Of course, we
also speculate that in some cases, with the married straight
guys, there might be more to it. I get the sense Bruno is one
of those."

"Avoiding temptation? Or avoiding a misinterpretation of
interest?"

"Can't say. But if you want to know more about Bruno, definitely ask the Y Gang. The women haven't had more than passing contact with him."

"Got it."

"I'll give you names. That takes us to the bigger question of
our . . . unexpected guest."

"It does."

"I can't help you there. I'm not sure anyone here could.
We've been completely isolated for two months. Like I say,
I've led the hikes, and I haven't seen evidence of anyone else
out there."

"Do you get the sense anyone is venturing out alone?"

"Besides me?" When I give her a look, she shrugs. "I grew
up in this forest. I figured the rules didn't apply to me, but I
wasn't going to argue my case with Yolanda. I slip out now and

then. Walk around the lake at dawn. Hike toward the mountain on my lunch break. I haven't seen or heard anyone."

"Any warning signs with either Penny or Bruno?"

"That they could secretly be serial killers, driven into the forest in search of victims when trapped too long in an enclosed environment where they don't dare exercise their compulsions?"

"Possibly."

"I was kidding."

"I'm not."

She sinks into her chair with a dramatic sigh. "And this is why I'm in social work instead of psychiatry. I prefer a life where that *was* a joke."

"I doubt they're serial killers, obviously. But is there anything at all, from your sessions, that might make you think either one could be responsible for this?"

"'This' being murder. I'd say either one could kill in self-defense. Otherwise?" She shrugs. "We don't get that deeply into sessions. For one thing, I'm not trained for it. For another thing, we all passed the entrance psych exam. My job was to ensure no one was too badly affected by the isolation."

"Were either of them?"

"Less than average for Penny. For her, it was three months to immerse herself in one project, with spare time to catch up on her technical reading, and even do some fiction reading."

"Like a sabbatical."

"A very well-paying sabbatical. We shared that in common—with no kids or partners waiting for us at home, this was a chance to unplug and focus."

"And Bruno?"

"It was tougher for him. Not the isolation but being away from his family." She pauses. "My sessions aren't covered by patient privacy—and that was made clear in the waivers—but I don't want to seem as if I'm blabbing away about people who confided in me professionally." She shifts position. "I know I can seem like the type who'd do that."

"As the person relying on your insights to find two missing people, I appreciate anything you can tell me."

"Bruno is separated from his wife, with the separation beginning with this project and—he hopes—ending with it."

"Ah. Things were rough at home, and he thinks if he gives her three months of uninterrupted personal time, she'll welcome him back."

"Yep. Also, for the sake of full disclosure, the issue was an affair. He had a fling. She wanted him gone. He left . . . hoping to return."

"Which may explain his reluctance to socialize with the women here. Either avoiding temptation or avoiding any sense of impropriety. The fact he had an affair might make him more likely to have one with Penny. Or it might make him *less* likely, if he really did regret it."

"Yep."

"As for Penny, did you get any sense that she'd be interested?" I ask. "In an affair or a one-nighter? Yolanda couldn't confirm her sexual preference, which is obviously Penny's own business, but it is a factor here."

"No sense pursuing the fling theory if she wasn't into guys. On a professional level, it never came up. On a personal level? I may have tested the waters in that direction myself. I like Penny. We have a lot in common, and I couldn't get a read on how she gravitates, but my overtures went undetected. She wasn't ignoring my pitch—she never saw the ball."

"Suggesting she's straight."

"In my experience, yes."

I ask Kendra a few more questions, before Yolanda strides in looking for a postmortem-exam update. I thank Kendra, who promises to get me those names she mentioned.

I give Yolanda her update, which only takes a few minutes— yes, it was murder and yes, the knife wound was the cause of death. She wants to know what I got from Kendra. I'm vague there. In the waivers, it stated that the results of the therapy sessions would not be private, but the waivers were ten pages long, and we know from our Rockton experience that no one reads them thoroughly, which is often to our advantage. I'm still not telling Yolanda anything she doesn't need to know.

Once that's done, I interview the people Kendra suggested, but get nothing new, so Dalton and I head into the forest looking for Bruno and Penny. Dalton found what he believes is Bruno's entry point. We expected that to be mostly just a box ticked off the list, something that would have bugged Dalton until he found it.

It turns out to be more. Possibly a lot more.

What we discover is a trail that someone—that someone seeming to be Bruno—has been using routinely, enough that it's a clear path into the woods. From his residence, he'd been cutting between two buildings on the perimeter and going into the forest. How do we know it's him? Well, Storm says yes, based on his scent marker, but there are also the boot marks.

This being a jobsite, steel-toed boots are mandatory. Yolanda had chosen the ones we issued. They're high-end, designed for cooler weather and comfort, and the crew had been pleased. All except Bruno, who needed special boots with arch support, so he'd been allowed to bring his own. That means that everyone's boot treads are the same except Bruno's. And the treads we find on that path are not the standard issue. Multiple iterations of that tread, sometimes atop one another, mean he's used this path many times.

We continue along the path. After maybe two hundred feet, it joins up with the main one.

"Well, that's less helpful than I hoped," Dalton says. "Gotta give him a little credit for the ingenuity, though."

What he means is that the two paths don't *exactly* join up. Bruno's path ends on a rocky patch, which he then used to cross onto the main one without leaving any sign of a branch.

I show Storm the end of the trail. She follows Bruno's scent over the rock to the main trail. Then she whines, ears plastered to her head.

"Something wrong?" I ask. "Or are you apologizing for not picking it out earlier?"

She can't answer that, but her look says guilt rather than concern. I pat her head. She's not a professional tracker, and there are enough scents on the main trail that I don't blame her for not realizing her second target had joined it. She'd been focused on Penny.

We follow the main trail to the point where it ends and Penny kept going. I ask Storm to check for Bruno's scent on the path Penny cut. Her reaction says it's not there.

"So Bruno came out through his secret spot, and joined this trail, but doesn't seem to have taken the same off-ramp as Penny. I can see their initial paths being separate if they were secretly meeting. Not sure why they'd separate here."

I take Storm a ways down the path and then back, but she doesn't figure out where Bruno left it. By then, the sun is dropping.

"Call it a night?" Dalton says, peering up.

"I think so."

"Really call it a night? As in, we aren't going to go back and do more investigating because we're exhausted from spending the last eighteen hours getting here, searching for missing people, finding a dead person, autopsying that dead person, searching again for missing people . . ."

"Feels more like eighteen days. So the answer is yes. I can officially declare the case—or cases—set aside for the remainder of the night."

"Good. Then let's get back and see our new house."

CHAPTER NINE

The outside of our new house is exactly what we dreamed it would be. Exactly what we envisioned, after nights poring through designs and hammering out floor plans and making our endless list of requirements.

I remember how nervous I'd been, sending that list to Yolanda. I'm not a person who asks for things, at least not for myself. I'm certainly not a person who demands extras that'll make her life easier while making someone else's—in this case, the architect's—difficult. I take what I'm given and make the best of it. Or that's the old Casey. The new one is a little more confident in asserting her own needs, yet I still wanted to give a dozen qualifiers when I sent in the plans.

This is just an idea.

We aren't professionals, of course.

If it can't work quite like this, we understand.

I said none of that, having realized by that point that if it couldn't be done, Yolanda wouldn't hesitate to tell me. But I'd never heard a peep back. Now I realize, a little belatedly, who made our demands a reality without a word of complaint. Penny.

The house is separated from the town by twenty feet of trees, giving us both privacy and the sense of being tucked in the forest, which Dalton needs. It's a small, two-story cabin, with a wraparound deck, huge windows—I shudder remembering *that* expense—and second-floor balconies front and back. Inside we had enough demands for a two-thousand-square-foot home squeezed into a thousand square feet. People need to pay to come to Haven's Rock, and we can't have them looking at our house and thinking *that's* where their money went, even if it came from my inheritance.

We needed a living space big enough to entertain, with doors that open onto the back deck to expand the entertainment space. A decent-size kitchen—Dalton prefers to make our meals. A bathroom with a tub. Yes, a tub, which is a ridiculous luxury in a town that rations water, but Dalton insisted on it for me. We need a fireplace in the living room and we wanted one in our bedroom, mostly so we can leave the windows open even when it's well past that time of year. We wanted an office upstairs. We're both prone to working late hours, and we both want to be able to spend those late nights at home. Then there's storage. Maximum storage for two people who want to make this their forever home. And that doesn't even include all the little extras, like window seats for the deep walls.

Was it even possible to put all that into a small house?

We stand at the back door, both our hands on the knob, mine over Dalton's.

"Ready?"

He turns the knob, and we throw open the door to see . . .

Darkness.

"You bring a flashlight?" he says.

"Uh . . ."

He laughs under his breath and takes out his phone. He shines the light around, and we spot a lantern beside the door. A moment later, it's lit, wavering light shining over . . .

"Oh!" I say. "It's . . ."

I don't finish. I grab the lantern, leaving him laughing, and I run into the middle of the living room. A huge stone fireplace dominates the space. The walls are wood, like the floor, and there are as many chairs as could be crammed into the space, along with an oversized sofa. Bearskin rugs—Dalton's—cover the floor, and the chairs are piled with blankets and pillows. Beside the fireplace is a raised cushion. I run over and pat it.

"Up, girl," I say to Storm.

She comes over and climbs on.

"Your own couch," I say. "Right beside the fire."

"Which I am going to get going," Dalton says.

"Excellent idea," I say.

I throw my arms around his neck and kiss him. It's meant to be a quick, spontaneous kiss, but something ignites. Joy, I realize, as it takes a moment to identify the emotion. It's one that had been missing from my life for so long, and now, there are times when I feel like a glutton, gorging on it.

The past eighteen months have been studded with spots of joy, but so much work, too, and frustration and trepidation and fear—the utter terror that we are in over our heads, children indulging a pipe dream. Now, we are here, seeing that dream realized in our new home, which is as wonderful as our old one and yet even better because it is truly ours.

I kiss Dalton, and he kisses me back in the same way, deep and hungry with exhilaration and relief.

"You want to see the rest of the house first?" he asks as I push his T-shirt up his torso.

"Do you?"

"Hell, no," he says, and lowers me onto the bearskin rugs.

We go to sleep on the balcony off our bedroom. We'd insisted it be built big enough to accommodate that, another oddity that Penny hadn't questioned. When I first came to Rockton, I didn't consider myself particularly outdoorsy, but something about my bedroom balcony called to me, and I found myself dragging my bedding out there. When Dalton caught me sleeping there, I'd been embarrassed. It was an odd thing to do, and I grew up learning that "odd" was concerning. Odd behavior meant there was something not quite right about you.

What did Dalton do, when he realized his new detective was sleeping on her balcony? He got me a folding mattress so I could do that more comfortably. That's the moment when I realized our sheriff might not be the guy I thought he was. And finding I was sleeping out there was the moment when he realized I might not be the person he thought I was either.

We sleep on our balcony, atop a folding mattress, blankets piled over us. I start off sleeping soundly, but then I keep waking, hearing a distant wolf or a nearby owl. I startle awake, remember where I am, cuddle back against Dalton, and sleep again.

When another sound wakes me, I'm not sure what it is at first. I lift my head and strain for wolves or owls or any other night music. What I hear is musical, but a very different sort.

Bells.

I'm hearing the soft tinkle of bells, like a wind chime. I lift onto my elbows and peer into the darkness. The sound continues, and I slide from bed, taking one of the top blankets to wrap around me as I move to the railing. Storm rises from her own pile of blankets and pads over.

The night is still, and I'm not sure why my subconscious notices that until I realize that "still" means there's no wind. I look up over the treetops into a sky lit to indigo blue by a blanket of stars and a bright moon. My groggy brain starts mentally reciting the constellations—taught to me by Dalton—until the bells sound again, and I remember why I'm awake.

I inhale, drinking in sharp, fresh air with the faintest hint of woodsmoke. I glance toward town, but see nothing. Good. We'd been particularly careful about the light pollution that could signal a settlement, every building having the best blackout blinds and shutters for the winter months when lights go on by late afternoon.

Another tinkle of bells tugs my brain back on track.

Is that coming from town? While I'd hate to be the killjoy who complains about such a simple pleasure as wind chimes, we really can't have them. At night, it is so quiet that we'd catch a whisper from someone on their porch.

I'm making a mental note that we'll need to ask about the chimes when the sound comes again, and it seems even closer . . . and from the direction *opposite* town. I move to that side of the balcony and squint out into the night.

Darkness. That's all I see. Unrelenting black.

When another sound comes, it takes me a moment to realize it's Storm growling. She's pressed up against me, the barest growl rippling her flanks.

"Eric?" I whisper. I crouch by his head and squeeze his shoulder. "Eric?"

He wakes with a start, blinking around in confusion. I'm about to remind him where we are, but he gives a grunt of recognition. Then the chimes sound, and he cocks his head, frowning.

"It's not from town," I whisper. "It's out in the forest."

That gets him up. He doesn't bother with a blanket to wrap himself in. It's probably ten degrees Celsius, but he's grown up in a cooler climate and to him, this is warm enough.

When the jingling comes again, his eyes narrow as he peers into the dark.

"I thought it was a wind chime," I say.

He shakes his head. "Bear bells."

I know what bear bells are, of course. Most negative bear encounters come from people accidentally startling a bear that didn't hear them coming. A bell prevents that. I've used them when I walk in the forest alone with Storm, but I don't do that often. Being part of a group—preferably a chatty group—is safer.

Knowing what the sound is makes me relax for a split second. Then I remember where we are and where it's coming from.

"Someone's out there," I say.

Dalton grunts again, turns from the railing, and reaches for his jeans.

"Any chance Penny or Bruno took a bell?" I ask as I retrieve my own clothing from the floor.

"Let's hope so."

CHAPTER TEN

As we head out, Dalton tells me that he had bear bells on the stock list and told Yolanda to have everyone use them whenever they go in the forest, even as part of a group. Bells aren't really his thing, but they're one more safety measure for the inexperienced. At the very least, the bells remind people that they are in a forest with bears.

There's no path leading from our house into the forest. We'll need to figure out what to do about that. Obviously we want one, but we don't really want residents seeing our house as a potential landmark to visit on their hikes. All the paths will need to be planned, staked, and watched for a year to be sure they don't flood or cross sensitive areas. That was why we hoped to have a year up here before taking residents. We'll work it out. For now, Dalton finds the best route into the forest, heading in the direction of the bells.

We've only gone a few steps when he pauses.

"Is the sound receding?" I whisper.

"Think so."

Earlier, I'd only heard the occasional jingle, as if someone had been moving erratically, stopping and starting. Now it's steady, as they walk away from town.

I'm not sure whether that's good or bad. Bad if it's Penny or Bruno, and they got this close, only to wander away. And if it's a stranger? Then it's good if the person had accidentally been close to Haven's Rock, and they've moved on. Bad if they'd been there intentionally, and are now moving on before we can get a look at them.

Either way, we break into a faster walk. We've gone maybe twenty paces when Storm freezes. Her nose lifts to catch the breeze, and every hair on her body seems to rise as her head lowers, a growl vibrating through her.

We turn in the direction she's looking. It's ahead to the right. In the direction of the retreating figure? It's hard to tell from here.

Dalton peers into the forest. Then he takes out his gun, and I do the same. Dalton motions for Storm to lead the way. She does, and I fall in behind her, Dalton behind me. We brought a flashlight, but the night is bright enough and our route is clear enough that we don't need to risk alerting whoever's out here to our presence.

Storm walks maybe twenty feet. Then she stops, planting her bulk in my path as she growls.

Something growls back.

Dalton slides up beside me. When his hand lifts, I go to raise my gun. Then I realize he's lifting the flashlight. He hits the button. One second before that light turns on, I see what's ahead. A ghostly gray four-legged beast, ten feet away.

"Wolf," I whisper.

The light comes on, and there it is. A gray wolf.

The wild canine is as tall as Storm, but it's all long legs and lean muscle to her mastiff bulk. I grew up seeing animals like this in zoos, and that was nothing like seeing them in their natural environment. What has always struck me most is how *healthy* these wolves look. Of course, I've seen sick and elderly animals in the wild, but one like this, in its prime, looks like it's ready for a dog show, all gleaming coat and rippling muscles and sharp eyes. While there's a scar under one eye and one ear tip is ragged, it is still a magnificent beast.

Magnificent and dangerous, because it's a lone wolf who isn't backing down from a bigger canine and two humans. Most wolf encounters I've had up here have been fleeting glimpses. The only exception was when Storm was in heat, but that's not the issue now. The issue now is that we've come upon it while it's eating. It's standing in front of its prey and—

My gaze drops, and I suck in a breath. I'd briefly noted a shape on the ground. Large and light brown in color, like a caribou. Now I see the head. A head with black hair—human hair.

The wolf is standing over a person wearing deerskin clothing.

No, I realize with a blink. The person isn't wearing clothing. They're wrapped in skins. It's a grown man wrapped like a swaddled baby, only his head protruding. The man has been laid on his back, his face up, and when Dalton's light moves, I can make out his face. It's a man with light brown skin and a beard.

"Bruno," I whisper.

At the sound, the wolf looks up at me. It's a mild look, only vague curiosity. Then it turns its attention back to Storm and laser-focuses on her.

"I think that's Bruno," I say.

"Matches the description, anyway."

"Is he wrapped up? Like in a cocoon? Or am I seeing things?"

"You're not seeing things."

"I can't tell if he's alive."

"Presuming not," Dalton says. "That's what drew the wolf in."

"Damn."

"Yep." Dalton takes a slow breath, audible in the silence. "I'm going to try to scare it off. You got it in your sights?"

I lift my gun. "I do."

He doesn't tell me not to fire unless I need to. He knows I won't. He also knows that I won't hold back longer than I should in hopes I won't have to pull the trigger.

Out here, there is room for common civility toward other predators, giving them a chance to retreat. There is not, however, room for sentiment. The beauty of this creature might take my breath away, and I will regret it if I need to pull this trigger, but if that's what it comes to, I'll do it. Those bearskin rugs in our living room aren't trophies—they're honoring encounters gone wrong by making use of the beast Dalton had to shoot.

"Ready?" Dalton says.

I lay a hand on Storm's back. I don't grab her collar. That's respect, too—I acknowledge that she's intelligent enough and mature enough to make her own choices. I'm asking her to stand down, and she tenses as Dalton moves forward, but she stands her ground as she holds the wolf's gaze.

"Hie!" Dalton says, waving his arms. "Hie! Hie!"

The wolf's gaze flicks Dalton's way, but with only the mildest of interest, and that sends a chill down my back. There are three things it should do at this point. Be startled and run. Be annoyed but back away. Or, if we're unlucky, attack.

Fight or flight. That is nature. But the wolf only glances at Dalton and then looks back at Storm.

"Eric?" I say.

"Yeah, I know. Something's not right."

I don't ask if it could be rabies. There hasn't been a reported case in the Yukon in nearly fifty years. That doesn't mean it isn't possible. Same as distemper. Uncommon in wolves, and uncommon here. We still get Storm vaccinated against both, though.

This doesn't seem to be either of those obvious answers. The wolf gives no sign of being confused or even unnaturally curious. It just isn't bothered by us.

"All right," Dalton says, his voice louder than usual as it rings through the forest. "We seem to have ourselves a situation here, sir. You want that poor man. You might also want our dog, but that's a little less clear. Either way, we're going to need to refuse, and you're going to need to move along."

This time, the wolf's ears flick Dalton's way. They stay in that direction as he talks, and while its gaze remains on Storm, I'm reminded of when I talk to Storm and she listens for words she recognizes.

"Get ready," Dalton says. "I'm going to need to lunge at it."

I adjust my grip on the gun.

Dalton lunges, stopping a few feet short of the wolf. The canine's eyes roll that way and then back.

"I . . . think the wolf just gave you side-eye," I say.

"Huh." Dalton crosses his arms and stands tall, only to get another sidelong look from the wolf, one that makes me choke back a laugh.

"Someone has not developed a proper appreciation for our position at the top of the food chain," I say.

"Because someone knows that's bullshit."

Dalton takes another step, and that's when the wolf reacts. It drops its head in a warning growl. Storm feints, snapping and snarling her own warning. The wolf glowers at her and then growls at Dalton again.

"All right," Dalton says. "He's chill until we get near his dinner. This is going to require a little extra incentive—"

A sharp whistle sounds. I don't jump—I can't, not while I have my gun trained on the wolf—but I do give a start. The wolf's head jerks up. Another two piercing whistles in succession, and the wolf lunges, and here is where I am glad I have learned my lesson about having my finger near a trigger. If I did, I'd have fired before my brain registered that the wolf wasn't lunging at Dalton or Storm. It's leaping into the forest.

One huge bound, and then it's running, and all we see is its pale form darting through the trees until it's gone. We still stand there, poised and listening. A moment later, the bells tinkle again, and I realize they'd stopped. Now they're on the move again, heading away.

Bells in the same direction that the wolf ran. The same direction that the whistle came from.

"Did someone just call their pet wolf?" I say.

"Seems like it."

"That *was* a wolf, right? Not a husky? Not a sled dog?"

"That was pure gray wolf."

I ease back onto my heels as I holster my gun. "I thought this place was going to be less weird than Rockton."

"It's the Yukon. It's always going to be weird."

"All right. Well—" I stop short, seeing the wrapped body and then wheeling in the direction the wolf ran. "Shit! We heard those bells over here earlier. That cannot be a coincidence."

"Whoever left the wolf also left the body."

I stare into the forest. The bells have faded into silence.

"We should go after whoever that was then," Dalton says. "While the trail's fresh."

I glance down at the body. "I hate to leave him here but—"

I blink. Then I scramble over to crouch beside the body. I stare at him a moment, unsure of what I saw. When I see it again, I lay my fingers on the side of his neck.

"He's breathing," I say. I look up at Dalton. "He's still alive."

CHAPTER ELEVEN

We aren't about to chase a person through the forest when our "dead body" is alive—barely alive. His breathing is shallow, and when I try to unwrap the tightly wound deerskin, I see blood. I quickly refasten it. As I do, Dalton crouches and fingers braided strips of leather wrapped around the person that we presume is Bruno. Then he walks a few steps into the forest, bends, and examines the ground.

"Whoever left him here dragged him," he says. "That's what the straps are for."

"So the question is whether we drag him into town or examine him on-site," I say. "At least Pierre was an EMT. He should be able to tell us whether we can move him or not."

"Any preliminary assessment?" Dalton says.

"Besides the fact that I'm trying to stay calm while inwardly freaking out that if we wait for Pierre, Bruno might not live that long?" I glance up at Dalton. "I need you to leave me here, with Storm, while you run to town."

Dalton's gaze travels over the dark woods, and I'm about to say something, but then he nods.

"I don't like it, but I'll be quick," he says. "Just . . ."

"Be careful because it could be someone trying to separate us again?"

He nods and then bends to lay the flashlight at my side and kiss the top of my head. Two seconds later, he's loping through the shadows.

I turn to Storm. "Watch," I say, motioning around us. She walks over to me, turns, and—with her back to me—keeps an eye on the forest.

I check Bruno's breathing. Still shallow, but steady. I press my fingers to his neck. Heat throbs from him. The heat of feverish skin against my night-cold fingers. My touch doesn't make him flinch, though. I lay a cold hand on his forehead. He still doesn't move.

Definitely fevered. His skin is clammy, his hair plastered down by dried sweat.

"Bruno?" I say. Then I try a little louder, but if he didn't react to my cold touch, he's too deeply unconscious to react to a voice.

I sit back on my haunches to look at him. My fingers itch to undo those bindings, but I can't until Dalton and Pierre arrive.

When Storm growls, I glance over sharply, but she's only standing there, and while her body is held alert, it's not in danger pose, as it had been with the wolf. She growls and snaps, and brush crackles as some smaller predator slips away into the night.

I stare out into the forest. It's pitch-black now under a tree canopy thick enough to block out the moonlight. Another sound, a scampering rustle. Storm tracks it, but doesn't growl. I keep looking and listening. Minutes pass in silence. Then comes a sound I'm waiting for—a sharp birdcall from my left. Dalton telling me he's on his way and not to be alarmed by the sound of their approach.

I move back to Bruno. After one last, uneasy look around, I trust Storm to detect trouble long before I do, and I start unfastening the hides. As I do, I make a mental note of the quality. That's not a distraction—it will be important in figuring out where they might have come from. The work is professional-quality tanning. Dalton is good; this is better. There are no embellishments. No embroidery or beads or anything remotely fancy. Just solid workmanship. And yet the owner had no concern about getting these bloodied and abandoning them.

Bruno still wears his jacket, over two layers of shirts. Blood soaks the front of it, but when I open it, there's little staining below. I pull up both his jersey and undershirt and wince. Unlike with the mystery woman, there are no stab wounds, but the damage might be worse. A deep purple contusion mars his ribs, and something pokes against the skin of his torso. April can warn me against practicing medicine, but I'm going to say that "something" is a broken rib, and if it is, we might have internal bleeding.

I touch the bruise. It's big and it's ugly. A blunt strike? Could be a blow or a fall. I check his hands. One moves in a way that tells me his wrist is broken. When I shine the light on his palms, there's embedded dirt and several puncture wounds. I move up to his head. His face is fine, but I finger the back of his skull and my hand comes away bloody.

I'm touching the wound, feeling the size of it, when my flashlight beam catches something around his neck. I pause and reach to find a thin cord, light brown, blending with his skin color in the darkness. It's looped off to the other side of his neck.

A necklace? The cord is rawhide, and together with the skins, it gives me pause. I pull up the other side of it and lift what looks like a piece of bark that had fallen to the side, maybe when I unwrapped him.

I tug the bark. The cord runs through it. I finger the piece. It's maybe the size of my fist.

Why would someone tie—?

It hits then, and I turn the bark over to see someone has burned letters into the underside of the bark.

I shine the light down and read the single word.

LEAVE

A crackle of brush sounds, Dalton breaking through with, "It's me."

I glance up to see Pierre struggling along behind. I set down the bark message and focus on the man lying in front of me.

"Please tell me this is actually Bruno," I say.

"It is," Pierre says.

"Contusion on the right lower rib cage," I say. "Possible rib fracture. Another contusion on the back of his skull, with what could be a serious loss of blood. One broken wrist. Damage to his palms suggesting a fall." I quickly amend, "Which could be an accidental fall or falling to the ground after being struck."

"Got it," Pierre says.

The man might have been hesitant with our mystery woman, but here he dives in, all business, checking vitals and assessing damage. It's only when he goes to examine the lower extremities that he pauses.

"Did you wrap him like that?" he says.

"No," I say. "He was found wrapped to his neck. There's board bracing behind his head and under his back. Someone brought him here."

Pierre only nods and keeps working. When he notices that rawhide necklace, he hesitates. I tug it off and show the message.

"From whoever dropped him off, I presume," I say.

Again, there's no hesitation. We have a seriously injured patient. There isn't time for curiosity about anything that doesn't directly affect Bruno's chance of survival.

"Rib fracture," Pierre says. "Two, possibly three ribs affected. One is badly fractured. There's the possibility of internal bleeding, but I hope not because . . ."

"Because you aren't trained to deal with that."

"Not to deal with it, and not even to diagnose it without proper equipment. I know there're some in the clinic, but it's been arriving in boxes that I don't open, because I wouldn't know how to operate it anyway."

He keeps unwrapping Bruno's legs as he talks. That's when he does stop for a moment, his gaze going to the pant leg, soaked in blood. There's a tourniquet below his knee and then bindings below, but even without removing the binding, we can tell by the protrusion what lies below. A compound fracture, the bone breaking through the skin.

"We need to get him back to town now," Pierre says.

Dalton and Pierre carry Bruno back while I jog ahead with Storm. I reach the edge of Haven's Rock and stop short as my gaze swings around the town. It's pitch-black, as it should be, especially at this hour, but as I look, I realize I have no idea where to find Yolanda.

I'd expected she might be staying in our house before we arrived, and that would have been fine, but it'd been obvious no one has occupied it. There are apartments over most of the service buildings, and those will be the next best homes. I survey my options and then run to the most obvious choice. The town hall/

police station, with Anders's new apartment over it. I run inside and up the stairs, only to find a place as unused as our house.

I run back down and straight to the nearest residence building, where I bang on the door. It takes a minute. Then the door opens, and the guy who stands there is maybe in his late twenties, wearing a pair of very small briefs.

His gaze travels down me. "Well, hello there. You must be new."

Someone shoves him aside. A man moves into the opening. He's red-haired, maybe forty, and dressed in pajama bottoms.

"Excuse this idiot. He's been in the woods a bit too long." He looks at the other man. "This is one of the people who came to search for Penny and Bruno." He turns back to me. "You're staying in the executive retreat, right?"

"The . . . ?"

He makes a face. "Sorry, I mean the place outside town. Is everything okay?"

"I need to speak to Yolanda. Where does she sleep?"

"Women's residence." He grabs a jacket from the darkness. "I'll run you over."

I don't get the guy's name. He can tell it's urgent, and he doesn't stop for introductions. A minute later, we're in the women's residence, where Yolanda is sleeping in a regular room, like everyone else. My escort disappears with a murmur, and I wait in the hall until Yolanda appears in sweats and a head wrap.

I wave her outside before I say, "We found Bruno. He's alive but injured. They're bringing him back—Eric and Pierre. I'm going to need your sat phone again so I can call my sister."

She nods and leads me to the town hall, where her sat phone is locked in the small safe under the desk. As she opens it, she rattles off the combination and says, "You're welcome to use the phone, obviously. There's also a gun in there. That's mine, and I would prefer you didn't use that."

"There's a gun locker," I say. "It should have a rifle and a shotgun for animal control problems. I believe you have a few hunters on staff to deal with that."

"Yes, Kendra and a couple of others."

As she opens the locker door, I catch a glimpse of her gun. It's a Glock. I say, carefully, "I understand you might feel safer in the forest with that. I carry one myself. But it's not going to stop a grizzly, not unless you hit it just right."

"I know."

She takes out the phone and hands it to me. "How bad are Bruno's injuries?"

"Bad enough that I'm bringing April in. I'll need to consult with Émilie to get her on a flight."

I brace for the argument that's sure to come.

"Understood," she says. "No need to bother my grandmother. I will make the arrangements."

"Thank you," I say, but there must be a note of trepidation in my voice, because Yolanda glances up.

"There won't be a sudden emergency requiring the plane and preventing her from arriving," she says. "*This* is the emergency. One of my crew is seriously injured, and another is out there and could be seriously injured when she's found. Whatever my feelings on the bullshit you're pulling with this town, I'm bringing your sister because it's the right thing to do for my crew."

"Bullshit?"

She rises. "Let's get this out of the way. You're preying on my grandmother. I can't say that to her because she'd tell me she's not some little old lady falling into dementia, giving money to a nice woman on the phone. Absolutely true. But Gran has one weakness, and it was Rockton, and now it's this town that's supposed to replace it."

"We're not conning your grandmother. I sunk my inheritance into this place, as did my sister."

"And, as someone who also comes from money—so much fucking money—I know that's not the same as sinking in your own life savings. Two possibilities here. Either you've invested your inheritance in a long con, or you're idiots, thinking you can succeed where others—my brilliant grandparents included—failed."

"We aren't conning anyone."

"Then you're idealistic idiots?"

"Never claimed otherwise."

She shakes her head. "You know that's worse, right?"

"Maybe so, but I'm not the one who set aside three months of her life to build a town for people she thinks are cheating her grandmother."

"Oh, I'm not building it for you. I'm building it for her, because she's a scary bitch, and I am too chickenshit to tell her no. Also, because she's eighty-five years old, and I love her to death, and I am not stomping on this dream. It's for her. It's all for her. And if you do anything—*anything*—to fuck it up, intentionally or not, I will come for you."

"Noted. For now"—I hand her back the phone—"my sister needs someone coming for *her*. Can you please arrange pickup, and then I'll make the call."

"How long will she need?"

"It's April. She'll already have a bag packed."

CHAPTER TWELVE

The clinic has its first critical-care patient, and my sister is furious about that. Furious, I think, that she needs to travel for hours to get to him—precious hours that could mean the difference between life and death. She doesn't say that. She upbraids me for getting our new town off to such an ominous start. Missing people, dead strangers, and critically injured residents. Did I not learn my lesson the last time?

I used to think my sister was cold, even unfeeling. Now I've begun to realize the opposite is true. She feels things—feels them deeply—and doesn't quite have the tools to handle those emotions, and so she says things that she doesn't realize will hurt others, especially me. I'm already smarting from Yolanda's outburst. I don't need April's, which feels uncomfortably close to the same thing. Uncomfortably close to a truth I fear? That we are indeed idealistic idiots of the most dangerous kind—those who don't realize they're chasing an impossible dream and drag others into it, and end up doing more harm than good.

I don't believe that. I can't. We aren't leading a bunch of gullible dreamers into a promised land. Everyone on our team is smart and savvy and, for some, as far from idealists as you can get.

So yes, I'm still smarting from Yolanda's words and, worse, I don't blame her one bit. If it were my loved one investing their hopes in this project, I wouldn't trust us either.

I put that all aside. We have that critically injured patient to worry about. Again, Pierre is in his element, and I leave him in charge as I fall into a support role, doing whatever he needs to be sure Bruno is stable. In the end, "stable" is the best we can hope for until April arrives.

Pierre does what he can, and then tells me he can take things from there. In other words, I can leave.

Here's where the suspicious bitch in me must take over, the homicide detective who has seen too much to trust anyone she doesn't know well . . . and sometimes those she does. Bruno was badly injured in the forest. I have no idea what happened yet—accident or attack—but there are a limited number of suspects, and most of them are right here in this town. That means I am not leaving anyone alone with Bruno.

I finesse it as best I can. Pierre was dragged out of bed in the wee hours of the morning, and Bruno is stable, and April may need Pierre's help. So he should return to bed while he can, and Dalton and I will watch Bruno. Pierre doesn't argue. He asks us to bring him as soon as April arrives, and then he leaves.

We secure the back door, and then we go into what will be April's office. Right now, it's a small room—walk-in-closet-sized—with a bookcase and a filing cabinet, because those were her priorities, far more than a desk and chair.

Dalton wheels in chairs from the waiting room, and we sit in there, with the door open so we can keep an eye on Bruno.

I tell Dalton what Yolanda said about us. His response is seven words, all of them profanity.

"Is she wrong?" I say. "At least, wrong to be concerned for Émilie?"

"No, that's the cause of my uncharacteristic use of foul language."

That makes me laugh. Dalton is known for his colorful language. Or he was, and I know I'm always going to get outbursts like that, but post-Rockton, without the need to present a certain persona, it's not quite as much a part of his everyday vocabulary.

"I prefer our enemies to be evil," he says. "That makes it easier to ignore them."

I snort another laugh. "Yolanda isn't our enemy."

"An antagonistic force of opposition, then. Or, in colloquial terms, a royal pain in our asses."

"Well, she has a reason to be, and I wanted you to know that. We're not con artists, and we're not hippies in rose-tinted glasses, but we need to accept her point of view as valid and move on without trying to win her over."

His brows shoot up. "Me try to win someone over?"

"Fine, you don't try. You just do."

"Right back at you."

"Mmm, I think I do try, at least a little. But yes, neither of us is exactly the people-pleasing type, and in this case, it helps to know where the resistance is coming from, and acknowledge that it's a valid place."

"While counting down the days until she gets on a plane, and we can go about our business without the stern looks of disapproval?"

I smile. "Twenty-three, by my count." I pull my legs onto the chair, crossing them as I get comfortable. "All right, so let's talk about what the hell just happened out there."

"Bruno? The tame wolf? Or the person who apparently

tamed the wolf and left it to guard Bruno's badly injured body, which they'd transported close enough for us to find, while leaving a clear 'get the hell out of Dodge' message around his neck?"

"Yes. All of it. The obvious big question is whether Bruno's injuries are also a message."

"Did the person who left him also injure him? Seems likely. Beat the shit out of him but don't kill him. Drag him close and then hope we stumble over his body before the critters eat him alive."

"Presumably the wolf was there to prevent that but, yes, it would have made more sense to bring him closer. They either didn't care or they didn't dare. Dead or alive, he's still a message."

Dalton sighs. "I hoped we were done with this shit. Get away from Rockton. Get away from all the history there, all the *people* around there, and find ourselves an empty space. How hard can that be?"

Theoretically, it *shouldn't* be hard at all. The Yukon is as big as Texas, with forty thousand people, most of them in Whitehorse.

"The problem," I say, "is that if we think this particular piece of land is perfect, someone else will, too. We might not have found anyone on our forays, but we both knew that didn't mean no one was out there."

He grumbles under his breath. It isn't as if we're a couple who bought a piece of property and now we're complaining that someone else is moving in next door. We *need* that isolation. It's what allows us to offer sanctuary.

Someone else is out there, and we need to deal with that. Dealing with it will—I hope—mean convincing them that we come in peace. Or that will be the plan if our "neighbors" turn out to be miners or trappers or off-grid settlers. We promise that we'll keep to ourselves and that we have no interest in minerals or furs or whatever limited resources they might be here for. We just want the privacy, and we will be ideal neighbors—so quiet and tidy that you'll barely know we're here.

It's a whole lot different if the person we're dealing with has beaten our resident into a coma.

"You think it's the same person who killed our mystery woman?" Dalton asks.

"If it's not, then that means more than one person out there to deal with. Imagine someone attacks our mystery woman. Kills her, realizes what they did and quickly hides the body. But then there's Bruno. Maybe he was with her, or maybe he saw her body. The killer attacks him with plans to use him to send a message to the place he comes from."

"Which is not the place *she* comes from."

I sigh. "And that's where it gets complicated, because our dead woman isn't Penny, and we have no idea who she is. Also, she was attacked while undressed."

"She doesn't look like she lives out here. Maybe someone Bruno knows? I have no idea how she'd track him here—or how he'd *invite* her here."

I sigh and rub my temples. "I'm getting ahead of myself. With any luck, Bruno will wake up and fill in the blanks. In the meantime, as much as I want to be here for April, we need to get back out there searching for Penny."

"Why don't *I* get out there searching. I can take the girl with the blue hair."

"She has a name."

"Kendra. I know. I'm just slipping back into Sheriff Dalton mode, where I don't give a shit about anyone's name, because I'm an uncaring asshole."

I roll my eyes. "Fine, Kendra knows what she's doing out there, so if she's free, take her. I'll stay here in hopes that Bruno wakes up and can tell us more."

"Also maybe get some sleep?"

"After I jot down my notes."

He sighs and shakes his head. "Let me go rustle up some breakfast then."

I'm alone in the clinic jotting down notes in a book I stole from my sister. I know I'm going to catch shit for that. I always did. She'd have a shelf of untouched notebooks and journals, and I'd take one, and she'd give me hell because she'd been saving that particular one for a particular purpose, even if it was the same size as ten others on that shelf. I know better than to argue now. I just take a picture of the notebook and resolve to replace it with this exact one.

During my time in Rockton, I always had a notepad at hand. I had to. There was nothing else to use for writing and organizing my thoughts. At first, I'd found it frustrating when I couldn't cut and paste or reorganize a page of clues and theories. Before that, paper had always been nothing more than a temporary storage device between my brain and my laptop.

Now I have Dalton's phone, and I will have a laptop . . . and I find myself swiping one of April's journals instead because jotting on Dalton's phone is driving me to distraction. I can't see nearly enough of the page, and I can't make margin notes or add arrows linking thoughts. My brain has changed, and this is what works, scribbling clues and theories and ideas and questions.

When the door opens, I'm so wrapped up in my note-taking

that I think it's Dalton bringing breakfast . . . which he brought two hours ago, and we ate together, and my now-cold cup of coffee still sits at my elbow on April's filing cabinet.

"Hey," an unfamiliar male voice says.

I look up to see the guy who answered the residence door in his briefs. He's wearing a bit more now, but it's still not what I would consider seasonally appropriate, given that it's ten degrees Celsius and he's in a ripped tank top. When he notices me looking, he gives a little flex that has me struggling not to roll my eyes.

"So you're some kind of detective, huh?" he says as he slides into the room.

"Some kind," I murmur, and I put the pen down on the pad with a decisive thwack, drawing attention to the fact he's interrupted my work. "May I help you?"

"The question is whether I can help you." He waggles his eyebrows suggestively.

"You have a tip about the disappearances?"

His lips twitch in disapproval. I'm not playing his game, and that is no fun at all.

"What would you give me if I do?" he asks.

"The satisfaction of knowing you've helped your fellow crew members."

"Mmm, I was thinking of something else."

I keep my expression neutral. "Such as?"

"A smile." He rocks back on his heels. "I don't think I've seen you smile, Ms. Detective. And, yes, I know you're here with your husband. I have been warned by several parties. I'm not asking for anything like that. Just a smile from a pretty girl."

"How old are you?"

His grin sparks. "Old enough."

"Not old enough to be calling a woman five years your senior a 'girl.' Too old, however, to be pulling this bullshit. If you have a tip, then you have two options. You can give it to me freely, and I'll thank you, and you can leave, happy in the knowledge you did a good deed. Or you can be an asshole, demand a smile, and deliver your tip from the floor, with my boot on your throat."

One brow rises. "You're serious?"

"Do you see me smiling yet?"

He shakes his head. "You're a hundred pounds soaking wet. You aren't ever going—"

A grunt of surprise. Then a thud, as he hits the floor, flat on his back.

When he tries to scramble up, I press my boot into his throat. "I'm a hundred and twenty pounds dry, thank you very much. Now, as you seem to have selected option B, I'm really hoping you'll tell me what you know, and I'll still thank you, and we'll part on a better understanding of the world—that understanding being that no one likes to be asked to smile."

I'm ready for him to get pissy. To scowl and swear and then stomp out. Instead, when I take my foot off his throat, he puts out a hand for me to help him up.

I take his hand, braced for him to try throwing me. He only uses it to help himself rise, and then makes an exaggerated show of dusting himself off.

"Yolanda's a bitch," he says.

"Excuse me."

"She's a bitch," he says. "I'd say she's got some angry Black woman thing going on, but then you'd accuse me of being a racist, so I'm not saying it."

"You just did."

"She's a bitch, but I don't blame her. In this business, she's going to have a rough ride. The point is that, while acknowledging she's a bitch, I actually respect her for it, just like I respect you for telling me to stuff my bullshit."

"Uh-huh."

"I'm serious. Well, half serious. I'm never fully serious about anything, which is why Yolanda's tough-as-nails routine just rolls off me. It's also why I'm not sulking over some woman half my size throwing me on the floor. That was a dope move."

"Thanks," I say dryly.

"All this is to say that I don't have a grudge against Yolanda. I like her. Hell, I was kinda hoping she'd be impressed enough with my work to take me onto her crew when she leaves. I like her work ethic. I like her style. I like that she hires so many women, and that's only partly because they make a much more scenic work environment than a bunch of sweaty guys."

"The point, it is coming . . ."

He chuckles. "It is. The point being that there are people here who'd love to knock Yolanda down a peg, but I am not one of them. Which makes this tip really awkward."

"It's about Yolanda."

"It is." He rocks on his heels, hands in his back pockets. "The other night, Penny went into the woods, and everyone thinks she was following Bruno, because we all know Penny wouldn't go in there on her own. Yolanda and Bruno had just come out of a meeting where they had a bit of a dustup. Bruno must have stalked off into the forest, and Penny must have followed."

"So Bruno *didn't* go into the forest?"

"Oh, he did. Eventually. See, I've got this place I like to hang out, up in the rafters of one of the storage buildings. It's great for chilling with a beer and taking in the sights, like a nosy old woman peeking out her window. Also, well, there are some women who know if they're feeling lonely, I'm up there, ready and willing to make their night better. So it's a good place for me to hang out."

"And that night you saw things."

"I did. I saw Yolanda and Bruno come storming out, after I heard raised voices from the town hall. Then, a while later, I saw Bruno slip off down his secret path into the forest. Have you found that?"

"Over by the storage sheds? Yes."

"He sneaks off a lot. One night, I was up in my perch until two and never saw him come back. Course, I was occupied for an hour or so, and he might have come back then. But he's fairly regular in his trips. I think he might have been meeting someone, though I never did figure out who. Not Penny, that's for sure."

I make a mental note that if I want gossip, here's where to come.

He continues, "That night, though, it was about a half hour before he left. By then Penny was long gone."

"Because it wasn't him she followed into the forest, was it?"

"Nope. It was Yolanda."

CHAPTER THIRTEEN

I don't need to track down Yolanda. Just as I'm trying to decide who can take over my Bruno-watch, she walks in.

"Any change?" she says.

I shake my head. "He's stable. That's all we can hope for. April should be here at any moment. I'll need to head to the hangar as soon as I hear the plane, so I can talk on the way back here—she won't want to waste any time on an update. That means we need two people to watch over Bruno briefly."

"Two?"

"He's been badly injured. We have no idea who did it, but there are a limited number of suspects."

"You think someone *here* did that to him?"

"Are we going to presume not and take the risk of leaving him alone with someone who might not want him waking up?"

"Fine. Two people. Briefly. But it was someone in the forest who did this. Gran and Petra have told me what kind of people live up here. You know it firsthand, which is yet another reason why I can't believe you're trying this bullshit again."

"Penny didn't follow Bruno into the woods. She followed you."

Yolanda physically pulls back, her brow furrowing at the sudden change of subject.

I continue, "Penny was spotted following *you* in the forest that night."

"Let me guess. Gunnar?"

"I didn't get his name."

"Oh, you can't miss him. Serious clothing allergy, but with abs, pecs, and bis that mean no one complains. I know he likes to watch from his perch. I know he likes to do a lot in his perch. Not from personal experience, mind you. He's a very pretty boy with a very generous soul. A damn fine worker who offers a bonus that some of my crew have very much appreciated."

"Okay . . ."

"So Gunnar saw me go into the forest."

"It's not personal," I say. "He wanted to be clear on that. He finally decided he had to step forward, even if it might cost him a spot on your permanent crew, which he was hoping for."

She rolls her eyes. "Ah, Gunnar. I'm actually surprised he came forward at all, when he had a personal stake in keeping silent. He gets a point from me for that. As for why I didn't mention going into the forest that night, it was irrelevant, and I didn't want to muddy the waters."

"You thought it was irrelevant that Penny followed you and then vanished?"

Yolanda leans back against the filing cabinet. "I had no idea she followed me. If I had, I would have mentioned it."

"So why were you in the forest?"

"That'd be my business."

"Not during an investigation into one missing crew member, one badly injured crew member, and one dead stranger."

"I had nothing to do with any of that."

"Am I supposed to just take you at your word?"

"I don't know what choice you have," she says. "You aren't actually law enforcement here. This isn't actually a public investigation. It's a private one, and as a private citizen who is not in any way under your control—having signed nothing to that effect—I don't have to answer your questions. I will, if I choose, but otherwise . . ."

She shrugs before continuing, "If you want to make an issue of it, then you only have one card to play. Threaten to throw me off your property. Which, technically, is not *your* property, but we won't get into that. You can threaten to expel me, before the job is done, and maybe I'll cave and maybe I won't. If I don't, that means I walk away, taking my crew with me."

"That's how you're going to play this?"

"It is."

"Then you become my primary suspect. You're lying about not seeing Penny follow you. You know what happened to her. You might even be responsible for it."

"No to all of the above. But feel free to make me your primary suspect out of spite."

"It's not spite. It's logic. You wouldn't block me if you had an innocent explanation. Ergo you must be responsible for what happened to one of those three people."

"Or maybe I have an explanation, and I'm just letting you know where you stand, in case you start thinking you have any authority over me."

I'm about to answer when a plane buzzes in the distance.

"I need two people watching Bruno," I say. "And if you tell me to find them myself, then yes, I will call your bluff, because right now, I'm thinking I'd be a lot happier if you and your crew walked off this job and took the problem of Bruno and Penny with you."

I walk out before she has a chance to reply.

By the time I get outside, the plane is already visible. I set off at a jog for the hangar, and I reach it just as the little bush plane is touching down on the lake. It taxis in and stops outside the hangar. As when we arrived, the pilot stays on board. A side door opens, and April appears. She's a few inches taller than me, with the same heart-shaped face and dark straight hair. Her skin is lighter than mine, and she inherited Dad's blue eyes rather than Mom's brown ones.

I grab for her bag, expecting her to shoo me off, but she lets me have it . . . mostly because she has two more inside. I get the small piece of personal luggage. She hefts a box that looks as if it contains fifty pounds of medical equipment. Then she turns and hands it to someone else inside the dark plane. I can't see the third party, and before I can wonder who it is, April is walking out with yet another box.

"Packed light, I see," I say.

"Oh, she actually did," says a voice behind her. "She tried to bring two more boxes, and when we told her no, she tried bargaining to take one and leave her personal luggage instead."

The other passenger descends the stairs with two of April's boxes.

"Good to see you," I say as I embrace him. "Nice job, stowaway."

"The pilot never even noticed me."

I have to laugh at that. It is impossible not to notice Will

Anders. Our deputy is a six-foot-two Black man with a build to rival Gunnar's. He's also gorgeous, with a military-short buzz cut and a black-inked US Army tattoo on one bulging biceps. He sets the boxes down to envelop me in a bear hug, lifting me off my feet.

"Been a while," I say. He hadn't been around when we left, having been spending time with his sister and her family. "You're back early."

"Got antsy. The kids are great. My sister and her husband are great. I just started going stir-crazy back in the burbs. Since this isn't Rockton, I'm allowed to actually leave and see them every now and then, so we agreed I should get my ass back here and help prepare."

The pilot calls something about wanting to leave, which Anders takes as the cue to grab his backpack. Then we all clear out of the way.

"There's a cart in the hangar," I say. "Those boxes look heavy, even for you."

"They are," he says. "April? Pass over that box and you can take my backpack . . ."

"This box contains sensitive and delicate equipment."

"Which is why I don't want you stumbling and dropping it."

She narrows her eyes, and then hands it over. "Fine. Be careful."

"Always."

He takes off to get the cart, as April and I continue on.

"I'm sorry this isn't quite the arrival you expected," I say.

"That's not your fault." She adjusts Anders's backpack. "Before I left, Kenny pointed out that you are probably already upset over what seems an inauspicious beginning, and that I will not help by calling attention to that. He also said I may even be making you feel as if you are somehow to blame. I think it is obvious that I could hardly hold you responsible for crimes that occurred before you arrived, but in the event he is correct, I will clarify that the person I actually blame is Yolanda for not allowing you on-site during construction. She has a poor grasp of the forest's dangers."

I clear my throat as a figure appears at the end of the path. "Yolanda," I call, alerting my sister to her presence. "This is my sister, April."

Yolanda strides down the path, and the two women size each other up in a glance.

"You're the neurosurgeon," Yolanda says.

"And you're the woman who allowed—"

I cough, cutting April off, but Yolanda doesn't seem to have heard. Her gaze has gone behind us. There's one split second where she stares—just stares—but that's gone in a blink as her eyes narrow.

"You're not my pilot," she says.

"No, I am not," Anders calls as he pulls the cart to us. He catches up and extends a hand to Yolanda. "Will Anders."

"The *deputy*? What the hell are you doing here?"

Anders only arches a brow, in the mildest look of reproach. Then he answers, his voice calm, even light. "With everything going on, it seems like you could more law enforcement, at least temporarily. More importantly, I am here to assist April."

"Are you a doctor, too?"

"No," he says. "But I played one in the army."

Her eyes narrow more, as if he's mocking her.

"Let's do the background check," he says. "Premed in college. Decided to join the army instead. Trained as a medic there. Did some medic work before being moved to policing. And before you presume that means I flunked out as a medic, no, I did not. The army recognized that I had more valuable skills as an MP. My specialty is conflict resolution, which is gold when dealing with frustrated soldiers. I get the feeling that might also be my most valuable skill here right now." His gaze flits to me. "Just a hunch."

I roll my eyes where only he can see it.

"Also," he says, "because Casey is shit at defending herself—or avoiding blame of any kind—let me clarify that she had no idea I was coming."

"That is true," April says. "I asked him to join me for his medical skills."

"If I'd known Will was back," I say, "I'd have asked him to come along myself. Now, can we get to the patient, please?"

When Yolanda hesitates, Anders turns to her. "I'm sure this has been a pain in the ass. You're on a tight schedule, and this has taken your attention away from that. But I can assure you that between the four of us, we have everything covered. If you have time later today, I can update you on the patient's condition and the investigation. Maybe over lunch? If that works?"

"I don't stop for lunch."

"I won't need you to. I can talk while you're working. Or we can choose a better time."

"Noon," she says as she walks away. "I'll be supervising work on the commissary."

I update Anders and April on Bruno's condition, and then we're in the clinic, where they can see him firsthand. I work on unpacking what April has brought while Anders prepares Bruno for a more thorough assessment and April looks through the boxed equipment. A couple of things she brought are already here—she wasn't taking that chance—and I help her set up. Then my services are no longer required.

I'm at loose ends then. While there are a few things I could do, my focus has shifted to Penny. There's no sense further investigating Bruno's situation or the dead woman before April has had a chance to look at both. Penny is still missing.

I find a crew member and ask her to show me where Penny sleeps. I should probably go to Yolanda, but that's guaranteed to derail me. The crew member shows me Penny's bunk and locker, which is unlocked, and then she heads back to work while I search.

Penny has mostly standard-issue gear. There are a couple of T-shirts, and both make me smile. They're ironic goth—an adorable reaper and a kitty vampire.

I also find an ebook reader with a battery pack. I remember Kendra saying that Penny seemed to spend her spare time reading, and this is how she managed it without a massive stack of books. This is how we'll manage it, too, in Haven's Rock. Oh, we'll have physical books, but we'll also have e-readers stocked with titles that residents can borrow. They don't take much power to charge or need charging all that often. That's what Penny's done, with Yolanda obviously giving her permission to charge that backup battery now and then.

I open the e-reader and skim the contents. There are years' worth of architectural journals, and that makes me smile again. I know what that's like—when you see enforced offline time as an opportunity to catch up on your professional reading. There are architectural books there, too, along with a bunch of popular-fiction titles—mostly science fiction and fantasy.

The only other personal items are photographs that look as if they were hastily printed and put into a cheap photo album— probably when Penny realized she wouldn't have access to her phone and pictures on the jobsite. Photos of family, photos of friends, photos of someone that I realize by the reaper shirt must be Penny. I take that photo out and lift it into the light.

Penny looks nothing like our dead woman, except in superficial ways. About forty, white, full-figured with blue eyes and ash-blond hair to her shoulders. What catches my attention most in the photo are those eyes. They sparkle with something that makes my heart clench, thinking of what has probably befallen her in these woods. This is the woman who gave us our dream home. Our dream town. Who saw it as a challenge and dove in without a word of complaint, however ridiculous our demands.

I slip the photograph into my book to show Dalton. It will help to have a mental image of who we're searching for.

I'm leaving the residence when I hear a deep woof. I shield my eyes against the sun and see Storm running for me, leash dangling, Dalton sauntering along behind.

A few people working stop to watch the dog. One woman puts out her hand, as if to call her over, but Storm is on a mission, and that mission is me. After all, we've been separated for nearly five hours. That's five weeks in dog time.

I hug and pet her while Dalton makes his way to us. I don't ask whether he found anything. He'll tell me, and when he only lets me cuddle Storm, I know the answer is no.

"Heard the plane," he says. "Figured I'd head back, grab you and lunch, and set out again."

"Anything out there?"

He shakes his head. "I had a couple of hunches. Thinking of what happened to Bruno, I wanted to check out places where Penny might have gotten herself into trouble, near where her trail ended. Storm couldn't pick it up past that point. Neither could I. We checked a few places. Nothing. I figured you'd want to go back, though. Get a look at the crime scene."

"I do. Thanks."

"Let's see what they're serving in the commissary, and whether we're authorized to eat any of it."

We eat lunch with Anders. April is too busy to join us. Afterward, we head out and soon we're back at the spot where we found the dead woman. I've searched up above again, as has Dalton, but we don't seem to have missed anything. Then it's down into the pit. With a flashlight, I make a more thorough examination of the floor, looking for prints. I detect a few impressions, but nothing that would serve as an identifier.

What I mostly find is hair. Dalton identifies several that seem like they belong to animals—black and gray strands that he'll tentatively say are black bear and wolf. Was that the purpose of the pit then? Trapping predators? There are much easier ways of doing it. Unless you want them alive and relatively unharmed.

I think of the wolf we saw. The tame wolf.

"Nah," Dalton says when I offer up a theory. "I mean, yeah, some moron would certainly try that. Oooh, a pet wolf. How cool." He snorts. "Not cool at all. Not for the human or the wolf. That one was tame enough that I'm going to hazard a guess and say it was reared from pup-hood. Still not a domestic dog, but with the proper handling, it'd be tame enough."

"Like Raoul." That's Mathias's wolf-dog. We'd found it as the sole survivor of an attack, and he'd taken it in and reared it. "Though in that case, being part dog helps."

"Yep." Dalton looks around the pit. "If someone was trapping live predators, it wasn't for that."

I have the exemplar hairs on a piece of paper, the ones he identified as animal set aside. There are several more. One I suspect is mine—black and straight and over six inches long. Two others might be the dead woman's. The last one is shorter. Either black or dark brown. I take them all, but that's the one I'll concentrate on.

After that, I focus on the part where the woman was buried. I've brought a sieve from the kitchen, and we take turns working through the excavated dirt. It's backaching work. I turn up several more hairs that seem to be from our dead woman. When we finally do find something, though, it's big enough that we didn't need the sieve. A small piece of white paper gleams from a spot where I'd removed the dirt hiding it.

I pick up the paper, and it feels oddly soft and malleable. Not notepaper but some kind of thick tissue. A disposable napkin, I realize as I unfold it. The napkin is emblazoned with a logo for Air North. That's the Yukon's airline, flying mostly from the Yukon to BC, Alberta, and the Northwest Territories. On the napkin, someone has scribbled three sets of coordinates. Two are crossed off. One is not.

I pass the napkin to Dalton.

He reads it and then says, "They're all around here. Three sites, maybe ten miles apart. This last one?" He taps the one that hasn't been crossed off. "It's near us." He takes out the sat phone and hits a few buttons. It takes a moment, but then it zeroes in on our location. He enters the numbers. Then he points.

"A half kilometer that way."

CHAPTER FOURTEEN

We are standing on the spot that the GPS insists is the correct coordinates. There's nothing here, and no sign that anything has been here.

Dalton peers around. "It won't be perfectly accurate. We're going to need to take a look around."

We mark the spot. Then we circle out from it. Ever-growing circles until we reach a creek. We look up and down it, still seeing nothing.

"Cross?" I say.

Dalton shakes his head and motions for us to follow the creek. When we catch a tinkling sound, I go still, turning that way.

"Bear bells?" I whisper.

Dalton shakes his head. He's right. The sound is pitched different and more erratic. We continue walking as the sound grows louder. It's a plinking, like rain but not quite. Then I see what's making the noise. It's some kind of metal contraption for sieving something from the water. Dalton reaches into the screen and picks up a flake half the size of my pinkie nail. He holds it out to me, and as the sun catches the flake, sparkling, I suck in a breath.

"Is that . . . gold?"

"Seems like it."

He surveys the shore. Then, with a grunt, he strides to something.

At first, I have no idea what caught his attention. Then I see the tent. It's mottled tan camouflage, with evergreen boughs leaning against it to disguise it better. Dalton pulls his gun and clears his throat.

"I'm standing outside your tent," he says. "I don't want to startle you. I'm looking for a friend who went missing out here on a hike. Can we talk to you?"

Silence.

"Actually," Dalton drawls, "I'm stretching the truth there. I think I'm the missing one. I wandered away from my buddy to take a leak, and I don't know what the hell happened, but we got separated, and I could really use your help."

Still nothing.

I motion to Dalton. Then I creep to the tent flap, approaching from the side. He positions himself out of the line of sight—or gunfire—and I yank open the tent flap. When the shadows inside stay still and steady, Dalton shines in his flashlight.

"Clear," he says.

I cautiously move to look inside. It is indeed clear, with nothing but a rolled-up sleeping bag and a small trunk. I crawl to the trunk and open it. Inside there's clothing and military-style rations and nothing else.

I back out and tell Dalton what I found. He's located another trunk. That one's locked.

"Placer mining," he says. "Looks like someone found themselves a bit of gold."

"Please do not tell me we're building a town five kilometers from the site of the next Klondike gold rush."

Dalton snorts a laugh. "That'd be *just* our luck. Nah, a flake doesn't mean a find. And whoever has this spot is keeping it well hidden. People around here have learned their lesson about that. The problem is that, well, miners can be a paranoid bunch, even the most stable among them."

"Great. . . ." I look around. "And I think we can safely say that *this* is where those coordinates lead?"

"Yep."

"Which means that gold plus one dead body plus one injured lost person and one still-lost person are likely not unconnected events."

"Yep."

"Shit. . . ."

Our dead woman had a list with three sets of coordinates, two of them crossed off. That's not an invited guest. She was looking for this spot. Looking for this camp. Did she find it and was killed to keep it a secret? If so, the miner was hardly going to leave those coordinates with her.

We still search for signs that the crime scene might be here—the place where our mystery woman bled out. If so, then the blood would attract critters, and we see no evidence of anything digging at the dirt, looking for what was presumably buried there. There are no boot prints or any other obvious signs of trace. It's a micro mining operation minus a miner. That's all we can tell, and if either victim—Bruno or the mystery woman—is connected to this camp, then we aren't eager to stick around until that miner returns.

"Okay," I say, my voice low. "The trunk is how I found it, and I don't see any signs of our footprints. Anything I'm missing?"

"The traps we sprung?"

My brows shoot up. "Traps . . . ?"

"If the miner hid their tent like that, they're worried about someone stumbling over the claim, so they're going to set up alerts to let them know if someone did." Dalton starts pacing around the site. Then he drops to a half crouch and lifts what looks like very fine thread, invisible against the dark ground. "One."

He moves to the tent and shines his light on the flap. Another hairlike thread dangles from the zipper. "Two."

He walks across the site and shines a light at the hidden trunk. "There's one on the lock, to show if someone jangled it. I didn't, so I only have two to repair. Well, two that I found."

"I'll keep looking."

We don't find more alerts. If there are others, Dalton says the miner will likely expect wildlife to trip some of them, so we've probably covered our tracks. If not? We'll deal with "if not" later. For now, we know that we need to ramp up security at the jobsite. There's definitely someone out here, and they are paranoid with good reason.

Strike that, there are definitely *two* people here. We saw no sign of a canine in residence, and Storm would have let us know if she did. That means the miner is not the person with the tame wolf.

As we said, we knew better than to hope no one lived around here, even part-time. Still, we'd really hoped our empty land would be a little more empty.

Back in Haven's Rock, we go straight to the clinic, where April is on the back porch, drinking coffee while standing at the railing.

"There *is* a chair," I say, pointing at it. "Two, in fact."

"The patient has internal bleeding," she says. "I have operated and addressed the worst of it, but he is going to require a specialist, as I fear he has further injuries I am not qualified to assess."

"Got it. I'll tell Yolanda—"

"We have already contacted Émilie, who is sending a plane first thing in the morning to take him to a private hospital in Alberta."

"Good."

She doesn't reply. She only turns her gaze to the forest again. I climb onto the back deck.

"I'm sorry, April," I say. "I know this is . . . not ideal."

"It is not." She backs away from the railing. "However, it is significantly better than it was in Rockton. With Émilie's assistance and her hospital, we no longer need to fight to have a resident flown to proper care. It will be no different than a remote facility."

"Better," I say. "Neither of us is a fan of private health, but in this case, it means top-notch care with no questions asked."

"I don't approve of private care, nor of the way Émilie's family made their money"—they're Big Pharma, with everything that implies for those who grew up around doctors—"but I approve of the way she is using her funds in this particular instance."

I nod and say nothing. I know better than to push.

"This is my first patient in our new town," she says finally; then she lets that hang there, as I wait for more. When no more comes, I realize that's the entirety of it. That's what's bothering her.

"And you already need to turn his care over to someone else."

"Yes."

"I'm sorry."

I could say it's not her fault she isn't qualified to heal the first patient. It's an extreme case, and there will be twenty more after Bruno that she won't even need to consider sending elsewhere.

I could tell her that I feel the same way—my first "case" and I have one guy in critical condition, one woman missing, and a total stranger dead. I don't say any of it because it will not help. Nothing will help except moving forward to more typical medical cases that restore her feeling of competence. We have that in common, and it has nothing to do with her autism and everything to do with our upbringing. We thrive on feeling competent . . . and we stumble—hard—when we don't.

I give her a moment, to be sure there isn't more she wants to say. When she doesn't speak, I say, "I know you've had a long day already, and I can come back later, but I would like to discuss what you found regarding his injuries. For the investigation."

She snaps back to herself, brisk and efficient and—I suspect—grateful for the distraction. "Of course. We should discuss that immediately, as it will impact your case. His injuries are consistent with a fall, as you suspected. However, that includes the blow to the back of his head. He was not struck and then injured himself falling to the ground. It would be impossible to do that degree of damage to his torso from a fall of a few feet, Casey."

"That's why you're the doctor, and I'm the detective."

"Well, you detected correctly in presuming a fall, though it would have been a substantial one. As for the fact he has injuries to both the front and back of his body, I believe that suggests he struck both in his fall."

"He rolled on the descent. Fell from a height, struck his head and then struck his torso. Or vice versa."

"No, it is most likely in that order, given the wrist injuries, though I doubt it matters for your purposes. The head and leg wounds are consistent with a sharp strike on something like rock. Dirt embedded in the wound supports that. When he landed, it was on his stomach, with injuries to his wrists and hands suggesting he was still conscious at that time. He hit something hard. Likely more rock."

"So injuries consistent with taking a tumble in the dark. He fell off a height, hit his head and leg on the way down and then landed and hit his chest."

"Yes, though I would not waste too much time investigating the sequence of events. I relieved the swelling on his brain, and I expect him to wake soon. He can give you his story then."

CHAPTER FIFTEEN

Dalton brings dinner, and I don't even get a chance to eat it before Bruno is awake. I give my hot food to my sister, and Dalton urges her to eat it, which might actually work. The first time my sister met Dalton, she'd described him—to his face—as just another of my short-term lovers, using a term that was breathtakingly rude for my very proper sister. Within a month, she'd done a complete about-face, questioning whether *I* was good enough for *him*. Dalton might say he doesn't try to win anyone over, but he does it anyway, at least for those who value competence as much as my sister does.

Once Dalton has asked her to eat my dinner—promising he'll get more for me later—we head inside, leaving her on the porch with Anders while I conduct the interview.

Bruno lies in the bed, staring blankly, his light brown skin almost ashen. If he hears us enter, he gives no sign of it.

"Hey, Bruno," I say.

He glances my way then, but his dark eyes remain empty, devoid of even a spark of curiosity.

"I'm Detective Butler," I say. "I'd like to talk about what happened to you. Do you think you feel up to that?"

He seems to weigh his answer.

"I know you probably don't feel like talking, but we're still looking for Penny, and I could really use your help."

His brow furrows. "Penny?"

"She went missing the night you did."

"Penny?" He seems to take a moment to rouse himself. "I don't understand."

"Neither do we," I say with a self-deprecating smile. "Which is where you come in."

"I . . . Penny?" He gives his head a shake and then looks like he's going to vomit from the sudden movement. He swallows. "You're saying Penny—the architect—went into the forest when I did, and now she's missing?"

"Yes."

"I . . . I know I hit my head, so maybe I've forgotten something, but I didn't go into the forest with Penny or see her in there. If we both disappeared that night, I . . . I don't know what to tell you."

"Let's start by talking about you then. Can you tell me what happened to you?"

He relaxes into the bed with a twist of his lips. "I did something really stupid. I went walking in the forest at night. I had a flashlight, but I was shining it ahead of me. The last thing I remember, I took a step, and there was nothing under my feet. I fell over a cliff or something. Hit my head, blacked out for a second and woke up when I hit the bottom."

"And then?"

"I lay there for . . . I have no idea how long. I tried to crawl, but my wrist and leg hurt too much, and I kept losing consciousness. Finally, I lost it altogether and passed out."

"Did you wake up after that?"

"I'm . . . not sure." He lifts his hand, as if to make a gesture, but pain crosses his face, and he lowers it again. "I had what I think were just some really weird dreams. Maybe I was delirious?"

"Can you tell me what you thought was happening?"

"I dreamed that a wolf found me. And then the wolf was a person, and I started thinking it was some kind of werewolf, you know? A wolf one minute, a woman the next. It kept going back and forth. I'd see a wolf. Then I'd see a woman. Someone was cleaning my wounds, and I thought it was the wolf, but its tongue was cold. Then I was being wrapped up and dragged."

"You say it was a woman?"

"I *imagined* it was a woman. It had to be a dream, right?"

"Someone *did* find you and bring you here."

His brows knit.

"Can you describe the woman?" I ask.

"It was dark, and she was wearing a hood trimmed with fur. I couldn't see her face. I just thought it was a woman. Maybe it wasn't?" He chuckles, the movement making him wince. "I could describe the wolf better."

"Did the woman speak? Maybe the voice is what suggested she was female?"

He shakes his head. "I remember trying to talk to her, but she ignored me. Or I think she did. I kept losing consciousness. Next thing I knew, I woke up here."

"Let's go backward. Can you tell me why you were out there?"

He looks sheepish. "We're not supposed to leave the town, but . . . I needed to clear my head. I was upset over the schedule. We get a bonus if we finish on time, but between Yolanda and Pe—"

When he stops himself, I say, "Penny."

"Look, I respect Penny. She's a pro, and she's freaking brilliant. So is Yolanda, and sometimes, that's a problem. They're idea people. They live in their heads, and I'm the one that needs to take that and make it real, and sometimes I can't. We're on schedule to get that bonus, if we make a few changes. The people who're building this town, they have all these big dreams, and that's great, but I don't really see the point. I'm an engineer. I've worked on northern projects. The clients don't expect all these fancy extras. They're just here to make a few bucks and get home."

"So you wanted to simplify things to get the bonus."

"Sure. Tell the clients to scale back their expectations, give them something decent, and get out of here. I have a wife waiting for me. I just want to get home, and if I can get a bonus for being done on time, that's gravy."

"Yolanda and Penny were digging in their heels, wanting it done according to plan."

"Yeah, which I get, like I said. That night, I'd just had enough, so I went into the forest to cool off."

"Which you'd never done before?"

He lets out a long, slow breath. "No, I've done it before. Like I said, I've worked in the north. I'm not like most of these guys, who really shouldn't be in the forest. I mean, other than Kendra, *none* of them should, and maybe I shouldn't be either, but I felt confident enough to go in. I had a pocketknife and a flashlight, and I always followed the same route. Or I usually did. The other night, though, I needed more, so I went off-path, and that's where I got myself into trouble. I turned around to go back and started passing landmarks I didn't recognize and then realized the mountains had moved." A wry smile. "Which meant I was heading in the wrong direction. I panicked a bit, and that's how I stumbled off a cliff."

"Did you see or hear anyone else out there?"

He pauses. There's a flicker on his face, as if he's just remembered something. Then he struggles to douse it and mumbles, "No, nothing."

"You're sure of that?"

He curses under his breath in Spanish. "Fine, I saw Yolanda. That's actually how I got off track, now that I remember it. I always go into the forest on my own trail, but I join up with the main one. That night, I was on the main one when I spotted her, and I stepped off the trail before she saw me. I still needed time alone, so I went my own way."

"And that's when you got lost."

"Yeah."

"Yolanda was heading out?"

He nods. "In a hurry. Seems I wasn't the only one in a temper after our meeting. She was a woman on a mission. I decided to stay the hell out of her way."

It's night. Dalton convinced me to eat dinner, and then we spent another two hours looking for Penny.

I don't know how much longer we can keep up the search. I hate feeling as if I'm ignoring the fact that we still have a crew member in the forest, but we've exhausted every lead. Her trail is cold. We can only keep heading out in that general direction in hopes of finding her. We've mapped out the area in a grid, and we'll search new sections when we're able.

It's dark now, and we're in the town hall. Anders settled in upstairs and then came back down to join us for a fire. While normally that'd be a bonfire outside, we can't discuss this within anyone's hearing, so we're sitting around the town hall fireplace, drinking beer and bringing Anders up to speed on the investigation.

"So Bruno is an accident," Anders says. "He wandered and fell. No one pushed him off that cliff. The mystery then is who found him and used him to deliver the 'Go Away' message."

"Unless the person who delivered him also pushed him and *that's* the real message."

"Go away or else."

"We also have an unidentified murder victim, with no way of identifying her, let alone figuring out who killed her, which is really not our jurisdiction anyway, except it is, because we accidentally took possession of the body, thinking she was ours."

"Yep."

"Then there's Penny, who disappeared in the forest, with the only lead being that she followed Yolanda, who refuses to say why she was in there. What are we doing about that?"

I glance at Dalton. "This is going to have to be your call. Sorry to dump it on you but . . ."

"That's the perk of being the boss," Anders says.

"Yeah, I know," Dalton says. "I'll make the call, but I need input on the options."

I nod and take out my notebook, flipping to the right page. "Option one, we drop it for now. Option two, we call her bluff. If we go with option two, we take the chance that she walks away from the job, unfinished, and takes her crew with her. Would she do that to Émilie? I don't think so, but we can't pull that trigger unless we're ready to accept the consequences."

"Which are that she leaves," Anders says. "And we need to muddle through the rest of the construction. Could we do it?"

"'Muddle' would be the key word," I say. "But the bigger issue is that if we call her bluff and she leaves, we not only have an unfinished construction job—we could be letting her walk away from a crime."

"How likely do you think that is?"

I glance at Dalton. "What's your read on it?"

He shifts in his chair and takes a swig of beer before saying, "Fuck if I know. She's a pain in the ass, and this is complete bullshit she's pulling. I'm damn tempted to call her bluff just to show she can't do that. Which is the completely wrong response. As for whether she could have done something? Hurt Penny? Killed this woman? Again, fuck if I know."

"I don't think she did," I say slowly. "I'm being careful with that, because I've made the wrong judgment call before."

"We all have," Anders says. "Part of the job."

"I know. But looking at this from a purely logical perspective, taking Yolanda herself out of the equation, I can't imagine anyone would murder Penny and then urgently call us in to investigate her disappearance. She'd have sat on it for a while, and then said she figured they took off together and would make their way back."

"Did she seem to recognize the dead woman?" Anders asks.

"That's complicated. She has mild prosopagnosia. She wasn't sure whether it could be one of her crew—one of the members she doesn't know well enough to identify her without other cues. That'd be a weird thing to lie about. *Oh, sorry, I don't recognize her because of my face blindness.*"

"Yeah, that *didn't* seem fake," Dalton says.

"She also would have needed to preemptively lie to Kendra, who knew about it. Pushing past that, though, it comes down to a simple question of what she hopes to gain by blocking us.

If she hurt Penny or killed this woman, why not just say she went for a walk, like Bruno did? Fought with Bruno, needed a moment alone, and didn't see Penny."

"It's a power play," Dalton says. "She's letting us know where we stand."

"In a place where we can't touch her," I say. "She's in charge, and just in case we start to think otherwise, she's reminding us that until she's done the job, this is her town."

"She's being an ass," Dalton grumbles.

"Agreed, and you and I both want to show her that we can be bigger assholes, which is why it's a good thing we now have . . ." I glance over at Anders.

"Yep," Anders says. "In a pissing contest, I prefer to stay on the sidelines. Also, to mix my metaphors, I don't yet have a dog in this fight, having not been in town long enough to form an opinion of Yolanda. She's tough as hell, and prickly as hell, but I'll give her the benefit of the doubt and say she probably has a reason."

I nod. "Gunnar summoned the angry-Black-woman stereotype. Someone like Yolanda is going to get that thrown at her every time she asserts herself strongly, which is unfair."

"Yeah, and she's dealing with more than that. She comes from serious money. Billionaire money. And that's the white side of her family, which adds complications on complications. Now, what she's doing—blocking your investigation for what seems like a power play—is still shitty, and I'm not excusing that. But maybe don't turn this into a pissing contest."

"Step down."

He shrugs. "Refuse to play. That's easier than giving ground. Just move on, as if her blocking you is of no consequence. Now, if something comes up that suggests she's a suspect, obviously that changes. Otherwise . . ."

"Let her focus on her work, while we focus on ours."

"She'll be done and gone soon enough."

"And then the town is all ours."

Anders smiles. "It is."

I rise, beer bottle in hand. "Have you had the proper tour yet?"

"I have not."

"Come on then. Let me show you around your new home."

CHAPTER SIXTEEN

Another long day. Another restless night. We're sleeping on the balcony again, and this time I keep thinking I hear bear bells and wolf howls, and at one point I wake thinking I hear Penny in the forest, shouting for help. I dream of everything that has happened, all mixed up, as if my brain is trying to store the memories in its filing cabinet and keeps opening the wrong drawer.

I dream of being in the forest, with that wolf, only it's Storm standing over the body and when I look down, it's Dalton's still form she's protecting. Then I'm back in the pit, and when I dig, instead of finding a napkin, I find Penny, buried under where the mystery woman had been laid. Then I'm in the clinic, interviewing Bruno, except it's not Bruno in the bed, it's Gunnar.

"Yolanda was heading out?" I say in the dream.

Gunnar's brow furrows. "No, she was coming back."

I tap my notepad. "That's not what Bruno said. He spotted her on the path, heading out right after they fought."

"He couldn't have. I told you he didn't head out directly, right? I saw Yolanda leave. It was about a half hour before Bruno left."

I startle awake. Then I sit up and replay it. Dream-Gunnar was right. He'd told me there'd been a decent gap between Yolanda leaving and Bruno leaving. But Bruno made it seem as if they'd both taken off at the same time. He said he saw her heading out, and she was presumably angry about their disagreement, just as he was.

But if he was angry about their disagreement, why did he take half an hour before heading into the forest?

Oh, there are explanations here. Bruno could have mistaken the direction Yolanda was going, and she was heading back to town, not away from it. He'd tried to cool down, realized he was really pissed off, and *then* went into the forest.

But if Yolanda *was* heading back, then she hadn't been in the forest long, certainly not long enough to do anything to anyone. And where the hell was Penny, if Penny followed Yolanda out?

"You've had a thought," Dalton drawls behind me.

I lean down to press my lips to his. "No major revelation. Just something I missed."

"Share?"

I tell him, and as I do, his head tilts.

"I don't like it," he says.

"Which part?"

"All of it." He pushes up to sit. "Three people go into the forest. Two seem to be cooling off from a fight, and they pick the same way to deal with it? Then a third person follows one of them. Why? To catch her boss going into the woods when she's not supposed to?"

I shake my head. "That doesn't sound like the Penny anyone has described."

"So why did she follow Yolanda? Did she think Yolanda was up to something? Three people go into the forest. One comes out fine. One's found after a fall. One's still missing. And a fourth party is dead. Yet none of these have anything to do with the other."

"They must, obviously." I glance through the railing, my fingers tapping the floor. Then I pull my hand back. "I'll talk to Bruno in the morning."

"It is morning."

I give Dalton a look. "My sister would kill me for waking up a seriously ill patient to question him at four in the morning."

"His plane will be here at six."

I swear under my breath.

"Yep," Dalton says. "His plane arrives at six, and April's going to need to get him up soon to prepare him for the flight. She won't appreciate a four A.M. wake-up, but she also won't appreciate you peppering her patient with questions as she's getting him ready to leave."

He pauses. Then he hits me with "Also, if Bruno really is holding back, he knows the timeline. He can use it to his advantage."

He's right. If I wait until five, then all Bruno has to do is stall—feign mental confusion or sudden pain—and I'll lose my narrow window. No one, including me, is going to force him to stay longer just so I can get answers.

Dalton rises and gives Storm a shake. "Come on, girl. We're getting another early start to our day."

Dalton offers to wake April, but I'm not throwing him in front of that particular bus. I believe this is the right thing to do, and I'll take the hit myself.

The door to Bruno's clinic room is closed, and I won't even peek in to see whether he's awake. No end runs around my sister, however tempting that might be.

I leave Dalton and Storm outside and take the stairs to my sister's apartment, while making a mental note to ask her to keep the outside door locked, please. We can install a bell for anyone who needs emergency assistance.

The clinic is bigger than our house, which leaves plenty of room upstairs for a decent apartment. The stairs open into a combination living room and kitchen. That leaves three doors—a closet, a bathroom, and a bedroom. The bathroom one is open. Of the other two, I make my guess—based on the layout of the building—and rap on the door.

"April?" I call. "It's Casey."

When she doesn't answer, I try again, louder now. Still nothing.

Do I have the wrong door? I open it carefully. Moonlight shines through the window onto the foot of April's bed. My heart leaps into my throat as I remember that unlocked door below and dash into the room to see—

April lies in bed, curled up on her side, and I tumble back to a childhood memory. Me, at five or six, in a chair in April's room, watching her sleep as I shivered from a nightmare. A friend had told me that she actually liked having nightmares, because it meant she had an excuse to go sleep with her big sister.

I'd sat in that chair, watching April and dreaming of crawling in and having her arms go around me, hearing her tell me it was all right and I could stay if I wanted.

I never tried that. I knew better. But I'd dreamed. Oh, how I'd dreamed, imagining the day when I'd finally do something that would make her love me.

I could grieve for what we missed, but I only whisper a silent apology for not understanding why she couldn't give me that. A silent curse, too, at my father for insisting his oldest daughter was fine, just fine. We were all fine, thank you very much. Except we weren't, and I might have suffered for it, but April suffered so much more.

Yes, I missed out on having a big sister that I could curl up with after a nightmare. Yes, I blamed myself—my inadequacies—for her seeming lack of love. But I will be honest here and admit that I was not a child who suffered in silence. April didn't want to be a "proper" big sister? Fine, then I wouldn't be a proper *little* sister. I'd be a brat, a troublemaker, a thorn in her side, and I would let her know that I didn't need her. Didn't need her one bit.

"I'm sorry, April," I whisper. Someday, maybe I'll be able to say that when she's actually awake and listening. Someday, when I figure out a way to say it that won't seem as if I'm trying to unburden my own guilt or, worse, expecting her to apologize back.

I don't need to worry that she'll hear me now. There's a reason she didn't wake up. April always had trouble sleeping, and she often uses earplugs and an eye mask. That does, however, pose the problem of how to wake her without scaring the shit out of her.

Shaking her shoulder is out of the question. Any kind of waking touch is. Instead, I move up beside her and say her name louder, then louder still, until she scrambles up, ripping off the mask.

I flip on the bedside lantern. She blinks at me, taking a moment to remember where she is. Then she frantically waves from the lit lantern to the open window blind. I close it as she removes her earplugs.

I explain the situation as succinctly as I can. By the end, she doesn't seem to be listening anymore. She's frowning at a box over her nightstand. It's a small speaker. She flicks the volume dial, and then turns to me.

"Did you turn this off?" she says.

"I don't know what that is."

"The monitor. It's hooked up to the patient monitor and will sound an alarm if there's a problem. Even with my earplugs, I can hear the beep of the monitor."

I stare at the silent box. "I didn't shut—Shit!"

I'm at the stairs in a few running strides and then scrambling down them, calling "Eric!" He's inside before I reach that closed door. I throw it open and run in. There's the monitor, dark and silent. And there are the electrodes . . . dangling from an empty table.

CHAPTER SEVENTEEN

April stands at the clinic bed, holding those electrodes.

"Shouldn't an alarm have sounded when they were disconnected?" I ask.

"It is programmed to sound an alarm if they are accidentally removed," she says. "Someone turned off the machine." Her head whips up, gaze on the door. "How did you get in here?"

"Through the back door."

"It wasn't locked?"

"Nope," Dalton says as he comes into the room.

"I locked both doors and double-checked them. Who else has a key? Yolanda, I presume."

"Probably?" I say as I look around the room. "But there's the problem of getting Bruno out of here. No one person could have picked him up and carried him. I know you set that fracture in his leg, but he still couldn't walk on it."

"He *shouldn't*."

"But could he?" Dalton asks.

The answer should be no. Yet that bed is clearly empty.

I open a cupboard. "His clothing was in here. Did you move it?"

"Certainly not."

"It's gone. Everything except his ball cap." I stride to the door.

"You think someone forced him to dress and leave? I would have heard . . ."

She trails off, realizing she'd be wearing earplugs.

"You'd have heard sounds of a struggle," I say. "Or raised voices."

I circle the room, taking in the scene. I pause and shine my light on the floor. Muddy boot prints lead from near the cupboard to the back door. Bruno's boots had been dirty when I put them away, and I'd left them like that, in case he hadn't said his fall was accidental.

"The door opens from the inside, right?" I say, as I walk over and answer my own question. "It does. It's a one-sided key lock."

"You didn't answer my question," Dalton says. "Could he walk out of here? If he was determined enough?"

I remember something I noticed in the other room and stride back in there. A cupboard door is ajar, and my sister leaves nothing ajar. I open it and see a small assortment of assistive walking devices.

"Anything missing?" I ask April as I wave at it.

She only needs to glance inside. "One pair of crutches. There should be two. But I cannot imagine he'd leave of his own volition."

"It'd be painful," Dalton says. "Not just the leg, but the broken wrist."

"He was on enough medication to make him comfortable, but I was very clear that he shouldn't even be getting up to use the toilet. I provided a buzzer. He knows he has injuries that require serious medical attention and any weight bearing could further injure his leg or ribs."

"He was motivated then. Damn motivated."

"Fleeing a murder charge by fleeing into the forest?" April says. "He wouldn't survive long, and he realizes that."

"Then he's not going far," I say. "There's something he needs to do before he's shipped out."

"Someone he needs to talk to?" Dalton says.

"Or something he needs to hide."

We have the advantage of Bruno not realizing we have a tracking dog. So while he's careful to stick to hard ground and not leave any footprints or crutch marks, he makes a beeline for his target. Which is good, because he does not go where I expect.

When his trail leads into the forest, I figure he's circling around to his target. Instead, it keeps going into the woods. When I see that, I quickly escort April back and ask her to stay locked in the clinic. Then I hurry back to Dalton, who's still on the trail with Storm. He hasn't gone much past where I left him, and before I can catch up, he motions for me to stop.

I halt, and after a moment, I catch it: the low murmur of voices.

I creep up to Dalton and Storm. Dalton leans down to my ear and whispers, "He came to meet someone. He must have been waiting. I heard him say 'finally.' Then they lowered their voices."

I nod and turn to listen. I can still only make out the murmur of voices. Two people? Three? I can't tell. I gesture that I'm going to get closer. Dalton nods and tells Storm to stay with him. Then he takes out his gun. I do the same and then start walking.

I get maybe ten feet before Bruno says, "I don't care. You—"

A twig cracks to my left. A blur of red-brown at ground level. A young fox. It must have caught a whiff of Storm. It's running, and the crackle of undergrowth has a flashlight beam slashing across me.

Bruno lets out a curse in Spanish. A pause. Then a cry of pain, and the thump of someone hitting the ground.

"Stay where you are!" I call. "I have a gun, and I am not alone."

"Detective Butler?" Bruno calls. "Is that you? Help me, please."

A crashing through the forest. Someone running away.

"Please!" Bruno says. "I'm hurt!"

I approach with caution, as Dalton circles up beside me.

Bruno kneels, clutching the wounded spot on his torso. "Please. I think I . . ." He collapses face-first to the ground. It's a fake collapse. I can tell by the way he throws himself down, but when he lands, he lets out a genuine shriek of pain.

"Goddamn it," Dalton snaps, and we run to Bruno.

Bruno faked his stagger and his collapse to distract us from seeing whoever he'd been meeting with. Except now he's in genuine distress, meaning we can't say "screw this" and chase down whoever is fleeing.

"You go," I say as I drop beside Bruno. "I've got this."

"Yeah, and meanwhile, they can circle back and club you over the head," he mutters. He glares down at Bruno. "Thought you were being smart, huh? Joke's on you, asshole. You think you're leaving in an hour. Oh, hell, no. You're . . ." He trails off. "Oh, *fuck*."

Bruno isn't hearing Dalton. He's curled on his side, his eyes wide with shock. The front of his shirt is wet with blood, as if his bindings soaked through, but that stain is spreading fast . . . because in his fake fall, he landed on the broken trunk of a sapling, the sharp end of it sticking up six inches from the ground and glistening with blood.

Dalton doesn't want to leave me with Bruno, but that's exactly what he needs to do. I stay on alert, gun ready, Storm at my side as I strain for sounds from the forest. When those sounds finally come, they're the crashing of Dalton bringing April from town.

Dalton leaves my sister with me, and then he has to run back to town for the stretcher and for help carrying it. I stand on guard as April stabilizes Bruno. Dalton returns in less than ten minutes with a stretcher and Anders. We load Bruno onto it and the guys carry him back to town while I jog ahead to get the clinic open and ready.

Once we're back, I help April and Anders get Bruno situated, but after that, I'd just be hovering, waiting for answers and stressing out my sister. Also, there is something else I need to be doing.

I head out back. Dalton's there with Storm, waiting for me.

"Done," I say. "Let's go."

We return to the spot where we found Bruno in his meeting. I don't have an exemplar scent for Storm, but fortunately, she knows everyone else who was at that spot, so when I ask her to pick up the scent of a stranger, she finds it.

Storm only finds the one trail, which means either one person or more than one person taking that same route in their escape. Dalton's search finds multiple signs of passage, but that's because multiple people showed up at this site—Bruno, me, Dalton, Anders, April, and whoever met Bruno.

The trail goes in as close to a straight line as possible, skirting fallen branches and wending past trees. Where does it go?

Straight back to Haven's Rock.

That's where Storm loses it. Once the trail is in town, where thirty people have been working, she can no longer parse it out from the endless network of scents.

In a movie, the next step would be to line everyone up and have Storm go from person to person, bursting into barks of alarm when she finds the right one. Is that possible? Maybe with a true scent hound. Storm is a part-time tracker and full-time companion dog, and I wouldn't have it any other way.

Storm has told us that whoever met with Bruno came back here. To Haven's Rock. It's up to me to find them.

The first thing I do is return to the clinic to check on Bruno's condition. My sister drives me out. As I'm retreating, Anders catches my eye and shakes his head.

The prognosis is not good. Not good at all.

"Have someone wait outside," Anders says. "We'll send them to find you if we need you back here in a hurry."

If it looks as if Bruno's not going to make it.

"Where is that plane?" April snaps. "That's something you can do, Casey. Get that damn plane here. It's after six."

She's right, I realize as I check my watch while leaving. It's almost six thirty, and there's no sign of the plane.

While Dalton takes Storm on another round of the perimeter, I track down Yolanda. She's still in her residence, and I meet her as she's stepping out.

"The plane hasn't left the airfield," she says by way of greeting. "I got a call at six, and I've been on the phone arguing ever since. We had permission for a predawn departure, and that was rescinded. Now they're being held back by fog. A warm morning after a cold night. They should be here before nine."

"That's not—"

"There's nothing else I can do. We flew your sister in to deal with this, and apparently she can't, so let's hope she can keep him stable for a few more hours." She stops and yanks up the zipper on her jacket. "That was unfair, and I apologize. But last night, she assured me Bruno was stable, and so, while this isn't ideal, it'll have to do."

"That isn't the problem."

I lead her across the road, lower my voice, and tell her what happened.

"He left the clinic?" she says. "On his own?"

"As far as we can tell. The clinic door was opened from the inside and he seemed to have been waiting in the forest for whoever he was meeting. I suppose it's possible someone helped him leave. Is there another key to the clinic?"

She swears under her breath. "There's one hanging in the community center. We had a situation where someone had been injured and it took a while to find Pierre and get the first-aid kit. Turns out he was just in the bathroom . . . for a long time. We put a key in the community center and locked the medicine cabinet in the clinic."

She follows me as I head for the community center. The key is right there, which doesn't mean it's been there all night. I remove it—I don't want April sleeping in a place anyone can access.

"How bad is Bruno?" she asks.

"Bad," I say. "April's not giving me details. She's too busy trying to stabilize him, and it's not going well. She's going to freak out about the plane, but I'm not sure it'd make much difference. She can't put him on it if he isn't stable. She's just going to take it hard. I'll be the one to tell her."

"I'm not afraid of your sister yelling at me, Casey."

"April doesn't yell. She can just be . . . She can say things that seem rude and hurtful."

"I have been warned that your sister is on the autism spectrum, and one can hardly work with brilliant professionals without encountering some of that. I've had people suggest I be tested myself. I don't have autism. I'm just an unfeeling bitch."

"Well, having autism doesn't mean April is unfeeling. She just doesn't display emotion in the same way."

Yolanda's voice drops, softening just a little. "I get that. It's fine, Casey. I promise not to let her reaction bother me or to take it wrong and get her riled up." She jams her hands in her pockets. "What a fucking idiot. I thought Bruno was better than that. Smarter than that."

"Having no idea why he went into the forest, I can't judge his choice there. I can judge his decision to fake a fall. But in the heat of the moment, he didn't think it through."

"And in the darkness, he didn't see he was about to fall on something sharp." She shakes her head. "Of all the shitty luck."

"Yes, and now we cross our fingers that April can stabilize him, preferably enough that I can get him to tell me who he was meeting."

"Because whoever it is, it's one of my crew." She raises her hands. "Yes, I know that includes me as a suspect, but I'm probably one of the few people who has an alibi. I was up at five thirty to meet the pilot, in case he arrived early. I saw Kendra on my way out. She was coming back from the toilet."

"Coming back from it? Or *seeming* to be coming back from it?"

"Well, unless she met Bruno in the woods while wearing killer-bunny slippers, I think she was really in the bathroom."

"I'll need to confiscate the slippers to test for trace."

Yolanda stares at me.

"I'm kidding," I say. "I'm just going to confiscate them because I want a pair of killer-bunny slippers."

Yolanda shakes her head.

"So Kendra and you are covered," I say. "Did you happen to see anyone else?"

"No. I only stepped outside to listen for the plane. When I didn't hear it, I came back in where it was warmer."

"I'm going to need to get everyone's whereabouts," I say. "I can track them down, one by one, but I'd rather call a meeting, under the guise of updating everyone on Penny and Bruno, and then hold them up for interviews afterward. I know that'll make everyone late for work, and you're under a time crunch. Obviously, Émilie will extend the bonus deadline, all things considered."

"She already has. We can announce that as well. Just understand that while the bonus is a big deal for some of them, most of them just want to go home. Sticking to the schedule for the sake of the bonus was an excuse."

"What about Bruno?" I say, remembering our interview. "He said that's what you argued about the other evening. He wanted to cut corners to make the deadline. He figured the new owners wouldn't notice anyway."

Her lips quirk in a humorless smile. "Failed to mention that you *are* the new owners?"

"It didn't come up."

"Yes, well, in Bruno's case, I think it was half about the bonus and half about getting back to his wife. Just be prepared for complaints about the delay. People want to get out of here, and at some point, promising them extra money isn't going to matter."

"Then they'll have every incentive to talk to me and get this over with."

CHAPTER EIGHTEEN

I hold the meeting in the town square, and it feels like old times. We've even had a wooden podium stage made for exactly this purpose, along with the bell from Rockton. By seven thirty, everyone is gathered. Dalton, Storm, and I get a few curious glances. We've been here for two days, but we haven't exactly been hanging out in the common areas, and while I recognize most faces, there are some that I haven't seen before.

Yolanda provides the introduction. We're security for the mining operation that's going in here, and we've been brought in to find Penny and Bruno. That situation has become more complicated, and so the mining operation owners have agreed to extend the bonus deadline by two weeks.

"What?" a woman in the back says. "You mean we're not going home next month?"

"We were already running behind," Yolanda says. "Everyone was aware of that."

"No, everyone was aware that the assholes who own this place set unreasonable expectations, dangling the carrot of a bonus we weren't ever going to collect."

"I set the schedule," Yolanda says. "Not the owners. And now you will meet that date, and you will get your bonus. They are being exceedingly fair."

The woman snorts. "Fair would have been giving us the extra staff we needed to get this shit done."

"We are being delayed because two of our people went missing," Kendra says. "If it was you, you'd expect the same."

"I wouldn't *go* missing, because I'm not foolish enough to go into the forest."

"On that note . . ." I say, raising my voice as I step forward. "Let me update you on the situation. Penny is still missing, so we continue to search for her, which will not impact your work. Bruno, as most of you are probably aware, was found yesterday. He'd suffered a fall, and we rushed in emergency medical help, who were able to stabilize his condition."

"Great." It's the same woman, petite and white haired. "Now that we've all been called away from work to get an unnecessary update on his condition, can we go? Some of us have families to get home to."

"Seriously, Mary?" Kendra turns on her. "Either shut up and listen, or you're going to lose extra time attending mandatory therapy for that concerning lack of empathy."

"If my lack of empathy becomes more concerning, can I get sent home?"

"Mary?" Yolanda cuts in. "Go to your quarters. Pack your things. After Detective Butler interviews you, you'll be taking the flight out with Bruno."

"What?"

"You heard me. You're off this job. You'll be paid up until today, with no bonus—"

"I was kidding, okay? It was a joke." Mary waves at me. "Go on, Detective Whatever. Finish your story."

"My *story* is that, at some point last night, Bruno left the clinic. We do not know whether it was of his own volition or not, but given his condition, we suspect it was not." Yes, that's a lie, but it serves my purpose. "This person took him into the forest, where he was more severely injured and is now in critical condition."

"What?" someone says, echoing a half dozen others.

"You're saying someone forced Bruno from the med clinic and attacked him?"

I peer at the speaker and recognize him instantly. Gunnar.

"I don't have the clinic key," Pierre cuts in quickly. "It's in the community center."

"No one's blaming you, Doc," Gunnar says. "I'm asking if I'm understanding this right. Someone from the forest—from out there—tried to kill Bruno."

"Not someone from out there," I say. "Our dog followed the trail back to town."

Now the chaos starts, everyone babbling, shock and anger and fear mingling. I glance over at Yolanda. I've been waiting for her to say we don't actually think someone from town kidnapped Bruno, and even this second injury is accidental. But she only cuts her gaze my way, with a look that says I'd better know what the hell I'm doing, misleading her crew.

I clear my throat. When no one seems to hear me, Dalton shouts "Hey!" and everyone stops, looking at him like he materialized from thin air.

"Thank you," I say. "To answer Gunnar's question, we don't know what happened. The solution might be more innocent than that. Which is why I'm standing up here asking for answers. If you were the person in the forest with Bruno tonight, and you *didn't* force him out there, and you *didn't* hurt him, then I need to speak to you. I'm hoping we can resolve this quickly and efficiently, especially if it's all a misunderstanding. We'll get everything back on track—and be able to search for Penny again—once we can put this aside. Otherwise, I have an attempted-murder investigation to conduct."

I glance over at Dalton, and he steps forward.

"Okay, you heard Detective Butler. We need to interview everyone, and we want to do it fast. We're dividing people in groups. When your group is up, you need to come to the town hall and wait outside until you're called in. First group is sur-names starting A to F. Go wait at the town hall. If you're G to K, head to work and come by at nine. L to P will . . ."

I really *am* hoping for a quick resolution to this. I want someone to have an innocent reason for meeting with Bruno. "Inno-cent" in the sense that—compared to being investigated for at-tempted murder—they'll decide to confess. That's the scenario I've set up. Scare them with the idea that we think someone kidnapped Bruno and tried to kill him, so the guilty party will come forward and say, "No, no, we were having a fling, and I just wanted to say goodbye before he left."

Okay, I'd like to think Bruno wouldn't be foolish enough to go into the forest with serious injuries to say goodbye to a lover, but I'm hoping it's something on that scale. A secret, but not one they'll keep when faced with a murder charge.

That doesn't happen. I interview the first six people, with Dalton sitting there, silently judging as only Dalton can si-lently judge. That part works. He gets a lot of nervous sidelong glances, and I get a few confessions, but they're not the sort I'm looking for. Someone admits they weren't in their bed last night—they were in someone else's. Someone else admits they got into a disagreement with Bruno the day he disappeared—about him always going overtime in his shower slot.

Round two is much the same. Anyone who might have any reason to be nervous—they were out of bed last night or they had a recent dispute with Bruno—confesses it, just so we don't think they're holding anything back. One woman says she's seen Bruno going into the forest a few times, but we already knew that. One guy says Bruno had a fight with Yolanda that night, but we knew that, too.

I also use the opportunity to get more on Penny, or Penny and Bruno, or just Bruno. Anything suspicious? Anything that might help me understand why Penny went into the forest? Or who Bruno might have been meeting?

The story on Penny never wavers from the one I got. She kept to herself, but she was open and friendly, just really hardworking. She didn't argue with anyone about anything other than work. No romantic entanglements that they know of. Nothing between her and Bruno except work, and the usual architect-versus-engineer disagreements there.

As for Bruno, he'd been more sociable but only with the guys, as Kendra said. Polite to the women while avoiding them in social situations and being clear he was married, just in case anyone had any ideas. Some of the women had been amused. Some had been offended. Most just rolled their eyes and moved on. You always get guys like that on a jobsite, they said, the sort who seemed to think that ten seconds of social conversation was the first step to a torrid extramarital affair.

From what I'd heard of Bruno's marital problems, he seemed to be simply going out of his way to avoid temptation. Dalton had plenty to say about that between interviews—mostly that if you're that easily tempted, you've got bigger problems to worry about—but for my investigation, it only suggests that Bruno didn't sneak out this morning to meet a lover.

We're starting on the third group when a woman raps on the door. She's about fifty, with dark skin and short gray hair.

"Sorry to interrupt," she says. "Dr. Will asked me to come and get you."

It takes me a moment to realize that "Dr. Will" is Anders. He'd probably just introduced himself as Will and she presumed, since he was working in the clinic, that he's a doctor.

"Got it," I say. "Thank you."

"Do you want me to stay and give my statement to your partner? I know you're getting everyone's."

"Come along, and you can give me yours on the way. Eric?"

"I'll tell the next group to come back in thirty minutes."

"Thanks."

The woman who came to get me is Nanette. She's one of the general crew. As for her statement, it's the same as nearly everyone else's—she'd been asleep and hadn't heard anything. I ask her to please stick around the clinic, in case I need to get a message to anyone. Then I go inside.

Anders joins me in the waiting room. Our eyes meet, and he shakes his head. Then he pulls the door shut behind him and strides over.

"He's not going to make it," Anders says. "We've been working on him for hours, but between the puncture and the older injuries and the stress of going out last night . . ."

"Is he awake?"

Anders nods. "We sedated him for emergency surgery, but

once we'd done as much as we could, April had to call it. She brought him out of it. He's groggy. We pumped him full of pain meds. But we wanted him to have the chance to say any final words."

"Has he?"

"He dictated a message for his wife. Now he wants to talk to you."

I exhale. "Good."

"He doesn't have much time."

"Got it."

Anders leads me into Bruno's room. The blinds are half pulled, and there's a hush that makes me hesitate as I enter. This isn't the first "final words" I've taken from someone about to die, but with the other two I'd arrived as they lay dying from their wounds. This feels different. This feels like my sister's province. Not a person lying on the ground with a gunshot wound, but a patient in a hospital bed.

At a crime scene, there is a frantic air of chaos, everyone gathering evidence while the victim is drawing their last breaths, still certain it's all a mistake and they'll pull through. Here, Bruno has been told the end is coming, and that feels so much worse. I catch a glimpse of my sister's face, the anguish and the anger in her eyes despite her stony expression.

"Would you like me to leave?" she asks.

I open my mouth to ask what she wants, but that will only waste precious moments as she sticks to insisting on doing what I want.

"Stay," I say. "In case we need anything."

She nods abruptly and stays where she is. I walk over to Bruno.

"I fucked up, didn't I?" he says, his voice hoarse.

"You made a mistake," I say. "I'm sorry this happened. I'm sorry all of it happened."

I pull over a chair and sit down, as if we have all the time in the world.

"Did someone force you to leave last night?" I ask.

"I did it for Maria," he says. "All for Maria."

"That's his wife," April says.

"I owed her," he says. "I broke her heart, and I owed her."

"Let's talk about what happened last night."

His head jerks back, and he gasps, pain searing across his face. April comes forward and presses a button, giving him more morphine.

"He won't be awake much longer," April murmurs to me. "I'm sorry, but I can't . . ."

"I know."

She can't force him to face the end in agony just so I can get my answers. I open my mouth to ask Bruno what happened, but another wave of pain hits, and I have to wait until it passes. By then, his eyelids are fluttering, my window closing fast.

"Who did you meet last night?" I say, cutting to the chase.

"It's for Maria. Need to protect Maria."

"You can't tell me because you're afraid they'll go after your wife? Even if you *don't* tell me, Bruno, they won't know that. They could still think you did. It's safer for Maria if you tell me. We can protect her."

"I owe her. Broke her heart." His words start to slur now. "Lied to you. Protecting her. Thought if I kept quiet, it'd be fine. Better be fine. I did my part. Kept my mouth shut."

"I'm sorry, but whoever you were with last night knows I'm in here talking to you. They're going to presume you told me everything."

"Make sure she gets the money. Maria. Make sure she gets it all."

"Your pay and bonus? Of course."

"No, all of it." He's slurring so badly I can barely make out his words. "I kept quiet. I didn't tell. Did this to me, and I didn't tell."

"Who did what to you?"

"Said I fell," he says, his voice barely audible. "Said I fell. Didn't fall. I was pushed."

"Last night? In the forest?"

"No, before that. The cliff. Pushed me off the cliff."

CHAPTER NINETEEN

Bruno loses consciousness after that. Oh, I damned well try to find out who pushed him. I keep trying until April orders me out of the room. I'm in the doorway, watching, when Bruno codes, his heart stopping. Anders rushes in then, and they try to bring Bruno back, but I can see by their faces that they don't expect it to work. They knew this was coming, and they only try as a last-ditch effort, in case there is some hope.

There is no hope.

Twenty minutes after those last words, Bruno is dead.

Dalton and I are in the town hall. We've interviewed everyone. As much as I wanted to put that on hold, I knew better. This is now a murder investigation, and I can't give the killer time to come up with a story.

No one has anything else for me. Nearly everyone was asleep when Bruno left the clinic, and the few who weren't had been indoors, either unable to sleep or using the restroom or just up early, waiting for the rest of the crew to wake before venturing out of the residences. Because even if you're awake at five, unless someone's brewing coffee, you're not going outside when it's barely dawn and barely above zero.

Because all the bedrooms are private, it's easy to just stay in your room reading until a reasonable hour. It would also be easy to sneak out and meet Bruno in the forest without anyone noticing because *they're* all in *their* rooms. Even Gunnar reports it'd been a quiet night from his perch. He'd had no "visitors," and he'd gone to bed just after midnight, having seen no one out past eleven.

Once the interviews are done, I'm alone in the town hall with Dalton and can finally tell him what happened in the clinic. The man has the patience of a saint. Well, no, it's more that he knows me well enough to realize that once I started talking about it, I'd never get on with those interviews. So he kept his curiosity in check.

"Huh," he says when I finish.

"'Huh'? I don't even get a mild profanity?"

"I'm trying to cut back."

I snort a laugh. "I don't get a profanity because you aren't all that surprised. Did you suspect he'd been pushed?"

"Nah. I just suspected—as you did—that there was more to his story than that bullshit about going out to walk it off and stumbling over a cliff. This makes sense."

"So Bruno went to meet someone that night. He's been going to meet them regularly. I won't presume it's the same person he met last night, but it seems that way, which means they are also from town. He was going out to meet them to discuss some kind of scheme. Something to do with money, which he planned to take back to his wife as an extravagant apology.

That night, though, his partner in presumed crime pushes him off a cliff. He keeps his mouth shut and meets them in the forest last night."

"Giving them a second chance. He promised to keep his mouth shut on the condition he still got his share. Generous of him. Not sure I'd trust someone who pushed me off a fucking cliff, though."

"Or maybe he was using it as blackmail."

"Give me more than my share, or I tell the nice detective what you did."

I sip my coffee as I think it through. "Blackmail or simple desperation, willing to let a murder attempt slide if he got his money. Because if he tattled, he'd get the satisfaction of ruining his former partner, but he'd also lose the money, and I get the feeling the money was all that mattered. Also, depending on what he was up to, he might not have dared tell me what happened to him."

"Because then he'd need to admit what they were doing." Dalton leans back in his chair, hand dangling to pet Storm. "Any theories on that?"

"It must have had something to do with the build, if he was working with another crew member. He knows there's a lot of money going into this town. He also admitted he was urging Yolanda to cut corners."

"Is there anything here he could sell? Anything he could sabotage?"

"I have no idea. I don't see any obvious source of cash, not on the scale where he'd be willing to cover for someone who tried to kill him. But I must be missing something. I'll speak to Yolanda."

At his expression, I add, "Speak to Yolanda, while recognizing that it's possible that I could be talking to the very person who tried to kill Bruno."

"Yep."

I end up *not* asking for Yolanda's input. She already knows about Bruno's death—I wasn't going to keep that from her while I finished interviews—and now she's at the clinic waiting to speak to April personally. I resist the urge to mediate and protect my sister from any questions that might have her feeling worse than she already does. Anders is there. He will make sure that Yolanda doesn't misinterpret my sister's lack of reaction as a sign that she doesn't care.

Nanette is still outside, waiting to run any messages, and I give her two: to tell April that we're off pursuing a lead and to tell Yolanda that I finished the interviews and I'll talk to her this evening.

As for the lead we're pursuing, that's a half-truth. Maybe a quarter-truth. The half-truth is that I want to get back into the woods looking for Penny. My gut says that I have a reasonable idea what happened to her, and it means I'm unlikely to find her alive.

The night Bruno disappeared, he went into the forest to meet someone. Penny also went in.

Is it possible she was the person Bruno was meeting, not for romance but for whatever scheme he was working on? Yes, but it seems Penny was following Yolanda, presumably suspecting she was up to something. Is Yolanda the person Bruno met? That's the obvious answer, but even if it's not the right one, then I think Penny still stumbled on Bruno and his meeting. She overheard the discussion. She saw the other person push Bruno off the cliff. The would-be murderer realized Penny had seen, and killed her for it.

To find Penny—presumably her body—I need to find where Bruno went over the cliff. There is someone who knows the answer to that question: whoever brought him back to Haven's Rock. The person with the tame wolf.

I also need to get away. My brain is whirring with too many complications and not enough data. One dead engineer. One missing architect. Someone in town pushed the engineer off the cliff, and both were involved in a moneymaking scheme that our architect may have overheard them discussing. Then there's the dead woman. She must be connected. I just don't know how.

I only have one suspect for Bruno's partner: Yolanda. Yet I lack a shred of evidence connecting her to this, beyond the fact that she had also been in the forest that night, which is purely circumstantial.

As we walk, I talk to Dalton, which is mostly just rehashing what I know, in hopes that he'll see a connection I've missed or that, in vocalizing it, I'll make one. Neither happens. I need more, and right now the only way to get it is to pursue this lead while hoping for an "aha!" moment.

We find the spot where Bruno was left and set Storm on the trail of the wolf. Dalton remembers the direction the beast left, and after walking around there, Storm gets the idea that we want to track the wolf. It's an easy trail. The wolf was just getting from point A to point B, with point B being the person waiting in the forest. From there, the trail is equally easy to follow. At least, it is for Storm.

"Good thing we've got her," he says. "I'm no help at all."

"The person covered their tracks?"

"No, they picked a path where they don't need to cover it." He motions around us. "Open land." A wave down. "Rocky ground. I'm sure it's possible to find signs of passage, but they were making sure that wouldn't be easy."

The open and rocky ground, however, does make it easy for Storm. But it's not a straightforward path—the person had to actively select the right landscape for avoiding tracking, which meant a wending path rather than a straightaway—and when I finally see where we're going, a pang of disappointment shoots through me. It's the opposite direction from the mining camp. That means it's also in the opposite direction from where Penny's trail led and where we found the dead woman. We walk for about ninety minutes, taking us at least five kilometers from Haven's Rock.

"Did they drag Bruno all this way?" I say. "That's some serious effort."

Dalton shakes his head. "I haven't seen signs of dragging in a while. I suspect they came from someplace closer and then headed back home this way."

"Which means we should have found the entry trail instead."

"That's the backup. You're going to want to talk to this person, and the wolf's scent will fade faster than the signs of dragging."

"Good point."

"I've got your back."

I smile. "I know."

He shields his eyes against the sun. "Looks like we're coming into dense forest."

I see what he means. We're on a rocky expanse now, but Storm is heading straight for the forest. Once the trail enters that, Dalton's able to pick up signs that prove we're going the right way. Most of them come from the wolf—a paw print in soft ground, a few hairs caught on a bush. The human part of the duo is being extremely careful, even back here, so deep in the forest.

Someone doesn't want to be followed.

Someone doesn't want to be found.

We're approaching the foothills of a mountain, making our way through that thick forest, when Dalton's hand flies up. I stop. He lifts his head and inhales, just as Storm does the same. Then even I catch the scent, thick and musky, coming from upwind, toward the mountain.

"Bear," I say.

"Hmm."

If even I can smell it, that suggests a den, probably in the mountainside and not far away.

"Well," I murmur. "Now we know why our target carries bear bells."

"I'd say we should make noise, but I also have a feeling we're reaching the end of our journey."

"And don't want whoever's out there to hear us coming."

Dalton lowers a hand to Storm's head. "Careful."

That's the command for her to be on guard against potential threats. We trust she'll let us know if we aren't alone out here.

We keep going, slower now, and Dalton frees Storm from tracking so she can focus on the environment. He follows the trail, which even I can make out, as a path cut through the dense forest. We've gone maybe fifty paces when he stops. He pivots, so slowly that I raise my bear spray as I check the wind direction. He catches my movement and shakes his head. Not the bear. Something else.

Dalton stands there, head tilting. I peer into the woods, but I don't see what he does. He backs up to me and lowers his lips to my ear and then points as he whispers, "Look carefully."

I look. I blink. I look some more. Nothing.

When I arch my brow at him, he grins. Then he prods me two steps in that direction.

"Now?" he whispers.

I can only shake my head. I presume it's an animal, but it's too well camouflaged for my amateur forest-vision. Dalton takes me another step. And then I see it. Or I think I do.

It's not an animal. I'm . . . not sure what it is. It's like looking at an optical illusion. Or one of those hidden picture puzzles, where you finally detect something that doesn't quite match the background.

Dalton takes my hand in his, his fingers warm. He gives Storm the command to wait. Then he leads me off to the side and ducks under thick vines draped between trees. We continue for five more steps as we approach . . .

A cabin.

Or that's what my brain concludes as the only possible answer for what I'm seeing, though part of it still insists I'm mistaken. Yes, it's a structure, but it seems almost otherworldly. Like something out of a fairy tale. A couple and their dog go into the forest one day, following a trail, and it leads them to a magical little house, inhabited by fairies or a forest witch.

The structure is no more than ten feet away, and yet I think I could walk right past and not see it. Yesterday, we'd found that camouflaged mining tent. Compared to this, that was a novice effort. This is a master class. Not simply a well-camouflaged house but *art*.

I have no idea what the base material is. Wood, I presume. I can't see that. Instead, I see what looks like a combination of actual greenery—branches and boughs and vines—with painted greenery underneath. The painting—if I'm interpreting correctly—uses stretched hides as a canvas.

I can't tell the shape of the building because of how well it blends, but there seem to be soft angles and curves, making it even more natural. There are windows, too, or vaguely rectangular shapes that I presume are windows, with closed shutters, also painted.

That's when I see an Arctic hare, peeking from under a bough. It isn't a real hare—it's painted on, almost invisible among the rest, a hidden picture within a hidden picture. Once I've seen that, I see others, forest creatures both painted on and woven from twigs.

"I want a house like this," I whisper to Dalton. "Can you make me one? Please?"

"Can't paint for shit. You okay with stick figures?"

I punch his arm. "Did you forget I've seen your drawings?"

He makes a face. As a child, he'd captured the world around him in sketchbooks. When we'd been on our hiatus, between towns, I'd hoped he might take that up again, but we'd been too busy for hobbies.

"I want woodland critters on our house," I say. "And you know how much you love to give me what I want."

He rolls his eyes. "I thought I was supposed to be getting over that."

"When it comes to showering me in gifts, yes. Painting our house is an entirely different thing." I look back at the cabin. "Do you see signs of habitation?"

He points out signs that someone is living there, but it's hard to tell whether they are currently at home.

"Approach with caution?" I say.

"Yep."

CHAPTER TWENTY

Dalton pulls on a light jacket to hide his gun while keeping it within reach. I adjust my own jacket. Then we step into the clearing. Dalton nods for me to take the lead. Even at its gruffest, my voice sparks fear in no one.

"Hello?" I say. "My name is Casey Butler. You brought an injured colleague of ours home. I wanted to thank you for that and ask a few questions about his accident."

Silence.

Dalton whispers something in my ear, and I nod.

"I apologize for coming on you like this," I say. "I know it's not what you wanted, but we weren't sure how else to reach out. We'll leave as soon as we've thanked you."

More silence. All the windows stay shut, no movement to suggest someone has cracked one open to peer out.

Dalton taps my arm and nods. We circle the house and find the "front door" around the back, up so tight against two trees that it would be impossible to completely open it.

"Nicely done," I murmur. "For the record, I'd like a hidden

door, too, so no one can come banging on it when we're trying to take a few minutes to ourselves."

"Nah, I'm going to put a note on ours asking people not to knock unless it's an emergency. People are understanding about things like that."

I snort a laugh. I have seen Dalton's Do Not Disturb signs. They don't "ask" anything. They inform you—with all possible profanity—that if you bother him for a non-emergency, you will pay the price. He never specifies the price. No one tries to find out.

I knock on the door. Then we wait. And wait.

"Shit," Dalton mutters.

I glance over at him.

"No wolf," he says.

I frown. Then I wince as I realize what he means. "Duh, right. If anyone was here, the wolf would be here, and the wolf isn't going to let us get this close without making some kind of noise."

I glance at the door.

Dalton touches my elbow. "I'd rather not."

I turn my gaze on him.

He looks uncomfortable as he shrugs. "If we have to go inside, okay, but we brought stuff to leave a note, and I'd rather do that. Yeah, we went into the miner's tent. This is different."

That was a workplace. This is a home. More than that, anyone who lives out here does so with an expectation of privacy they don't get down south, and their neighbors should respect that.

Dalton himself had grown up like this. His parents had met in Rockton and fled into the forest rather than be sent home. They'd had two sons out there, and this is where Dalton lived until he was nine. He understands what kind of people live out here. Some of them have mental issues. Others—like his parents—are modern-day pioneers, only seeking a different way of life. No matter what their reason, though, one thing is guaranteed—if they're living in a hidden cabin, they do not want visitors.

As Dalton says, we brought paper and a pen for a message. I also brought a bottle of over-the-counter pain relievers as a peace offering. Yes, as "gifts" go, that's a little weird, but I've come to understand what sort of things people out here prize most. While coffee and tea top the list, those could be adulterated. Ammunition also ranks high, but I don't know what sort—if any—this person might want. Booze is always popular, but that implies the person drinks, and if they turn out to be Indigenous, that's insulting. An unopened container of painkillers seems both safe and universally useful.

I write the message, telling who I am and why I'm here. I add instructions for leaving a return message or arranging a meeting. I keep my language simple. Again, I don't want to make assumptions, but that also means not overestimating their ability to read, especially when their message to us had been a single word.

I'm finishing the letter when Dalton's head jerks up. He swivels, following a noise I didn't hear.

"Bear?" I whisper.

No answer, which means he doesn't know. He motions for me to finish quickly. I set the message and offering on the doorstep, and then we hurry back to Storm. Dalton leads us both into a pocket of forest.

It only takes a moment before I notice movement on the path. A figure appears. Small, with a hood drawn up. The clothing is handmade from skins. The boots, though, are . . . well, they're not only modern but they're expensive.

Down south, I was hopeless when it came to footwear. One pair for each function, only to be replaced when they were no longer wearable. Up here, I have become a shoe fashionista. Or, more accurately, a boot one. In this terrain, decent footwear makes a bigger difference than any other article of clothing, and I have a shelf of boots, none of them cheap. That's what I'm seeing on the person approaching. High-end waterproof hiking boots. *Women's* hiking boots.

Bruno had said his rescuer was a woman. Judging by those boots and the size of the figure, he was right.

The woman keeps walking along the path. The wolf follows at her heels, and both seem calm and relaxed.

They reach the spot where they'd need to cut over to the house. There they both stop, in a small clearing, and the wolf moves up beside the woman.

"Hello?" she says.

I glance at Dalton.

Before we can decide whether to answer, a sigh ripples through the silence.

"I know you are there. You can hardly expect to follow my path without Nero alerting me to a stranger. If you do not step out, I will presume your intentions are hostile, and I will respond accordingly." She pauses. "Or Nero will. He is somewhat more formidable than I."

I glance at Dalton, and then I step out and lift my hands. "I come in peace."

I can't see her reaction. I can't see her face at all, hidden in the shadow of that hood. She turns her gaze to the spot beside me.

"I see you are unarmed," she says. "At least, not readily armed. I cannot say the same for the person with you."

When I lift my brows, she sighs again. "I know you are with your dog. Nero caught her scent first. As I do not see her, that means either someone is holding her back or she is a very poor companion indeed, hiding in the shadows while you encounter a stranger."

Dalton steps out. He has his gun in hand but raised over his head, letting her see that he *is* armed. Storm brushes my side and growls.

"Is that a Newfoundland dog?" the woman says. "What a pretty girl she is."

"Storm. I'm Casey. This is Eric."

"Storm? Please tell me that is for the white streak on her ear. I will be terribly disappointed if it is not."

I smile. "Yes, she's named after the X-Men character."

The woman raises a hand and pushes back her hood. As it falls, I blink. Well, that isn't what I expected. When I saw the cabin and then realized it belonged to a woman, I'm afraid my brain jumped straight to fairy-tale land. The forest witch or the ancient healer, at one with the wilderness around her.

This woman isn't much older than me. Mid-thirties. Maybe late thirties. White skin. Dark hair swept back in combs. A stylish pair of glasses. Bright blue eyes.

She looks . . . Well, if it weren't for the home-tanned clothing, she'd look like any well-groomed professional woman I might meet on a Vancouver street.

"Lilith," she says. "That isn't my real name, but up here, we get to reinvent ourselves, and I've always like that one." She nods at the wolf. "This is Nero, as you may have guessed. Yes, he's a wolf. No, I didn't work fairy magic and entrap him. Found him as a pup, raised him and he decided to stay." She looks at us. "There, that's me. Your turn. Oh, wait. No. I think I know everything I need to know about you already. You're the ones building that . . . whatever it is."

"A mining outfit."

Her brows shoot up. "Oddest-looking mining town I've ever seen. I don't suppose you'll take the advice I left for you."

"No, sorry."

"It was worth a shot. Mysterious messages from wolf-taming forest denizens. If you were the superstitious sort, you'd already be gone. Since you are not, that leaves us with a quandary." She meets my gaze. "I don't want you here."

"I know. I apologize. We scouted the region as best we could, and it seemed uninhabited."

"Really? That's odd. Not that you scouted—I believe that—but if you're a mining operation, do you not simply build wherever the gold is? Or the copper or silver? If that is the story you plan to tell, you're going to need to do better."

"Whatever we are doing," I say, "I can promise that it is no threat to anyone out here."

"Or to the environment," Dalton says. "We'll hunt and gather in our area, and if you have a specific region you'd like us to avoid, it will be avoided."

She peers at him, shifting to the side as if to get better lighting.

"Do I know you?" she asks.

"Don't think so."

"No, I've seen you before. Or I think I have."

It's possible she's seen Dalton's brother, Jacob, who tipped us off to this place as a good potential area. Dalton only shrugs.

"Born and raised out here," he says. "So maybe."

"Born and raised?"

"Never lived outside this forest."

She eyes him closer. "Huh. That is not the usual story. Not unless you grew up about ten miles from here."

Where there were several settlements . . . including Rockton.

"Could be," he says. "But if you have seen me, then I am certain you have not seen me doing anything that raised alarm bells."

"No, that I'd remember. So you're a proper sourdough." She turns to me. "And you? What's your connection to this fellow?"

"I'm his wife. I'm from Ontario originally."

"Thought so. I recognize the accent."

"What accent?"

That makes her smile. "Exactly. I recognize the lack of one, to my ears, which means you and I are both eastern transplants. So you're both part of this new settlement?"

"It's ours."

Her brows rise. "Yours?"

"We run it," I say.

"Oh-ho-ho." She leans back. "Now I know what's going on out there. A fellow who grew up nearby, building a secret town that won't bother me at all." She shakes her head. "All right then. Let's leave it at that. I still don't want you here, but I can see that I'm not going to have a choice, so later we will negotiate our terms of cohabitation in these woods. For now, I'm going to rub my magic ball and predict that you are here to ask about the fellow in the gorge. I hope he's recovering?"

"He died this morning."

She blinks, her expression sobering. "I'm sorry to hear that. I couldn't judge the extent of his injuries. I'm no doctor."

"Well, we have one, and there was internal damage."

"Which is why I do not want you in my forest. Your town isn't even finished, and people are already poking about and getting themselves killed."

"It didn't happen in town," I say. "It was a member of the construction crew. Can you tell us how you found him?"

"Nero did. The man had fallen into a gorge. We managed to get him out. I knew he had to be one of yours, so I patched him up for the journey and took him closer. I heard you in the forest and left him there for you to find."

"Can you tell us where you found him?"

"I can, and I will."

"Did you see anyone else? A woman perhaps?"

"Please don't tell me you're missing more than one."

"Yes."

"I have not seen any women in this forest. Not in a very long time."

"There seems to be a miner's camp about three miles from here," Dalton says. "Have you seen it?"

"I have, despite the valiant attempt at camouflage." Her lips twitch. "That is a man. One man. I decided to skip introductions. A woman living alone can't be too careful out here."

"Can't be too careful anywhere," I murmur.

"True enough. At least in the city, I would be slightly less afraid that he'd kidnap me for his wilderness bride. *Slightly.*"

"Did he seem unstable?"

"I didn't get close enough for a prolonged observation. I noticed someone was there. I realized it was a man on his own, mining. He seemed to be minding his business, and so I noted the location and have been avoiding it."

"How long has he been there?"

"I found his tent two weeks ago. The last time I was in the area was about a month previous, and I didn't see it."

"Anything else you can tell us?"

"No, Officer." Her lips twitch again. "Please tell me I am right in that guess. This feels very much like an interrogation, however polite."

"I have experience in law enforcement," I say.

"I am pleased to see that you continue to protect your people, but whatever you think happened out there, I only found a man who appeared to have taken a tumble into a gorge. Nothing suspicious about it."

"Let's hope so. Can you point us in the right direction?"

CHAPTER TWENTY-ONE

We are in the spot where Bruno fell. It's at the top of a gorge carved out through rock with a stream thirty feet below. Lilith had found Bruno by walking from the other direction, where the gorge opens up into flatter landscape.

While the other route would be easier, we needed to see where he fell from. She told us exactly what landmarks to look for and then she left.

We're in the spot, and it's nasty. Not a straight drop, but a jagged one, with plenty of jutting rocks to hit on the way down. Yet if you stepped off it accidentally, the slope is gradual enough that you'd probably land on your ass and slide down.

"Definitely pushed," I say. "No one's going to step over this even in the dark."

It's open land up here. Rock covered in moss and lichen, and while someone could slip on that, it'd have the same effect. You'd hurt yourself, but it'd be a slide down rather than a drop.

"He must have been here, on the edge, looking down. His companion snuck up and gave him a shove."

Dalton's pacing along that edge. Every few moments, he stops and peers down.

"He went over here."

Dalton points, and I come closer. He motions for me to bend, and when I'm low enough, I can make out the crushed moss. I scan the area, now that I know what I'm looking for. There's that spot near the edge, where the moss has been trampled and dislodged from the rock. There is another spot, about two feet over, where it's been crushed underfoot. From the person who shoved him? Digging into the ground to brace for that push?

I point it out to Dalton and tell him what I think, and then add, "I'm not seeing anything useful, though. No prints unless I'm missing them."

He surveys the area beyond, and we fan out to check the spots where dirt has accumulated enough to collect impressions.

"Got a boot print here," I say. "It's Bruno's, though."

"Another partial over here, but it's smudged."

I walk over and crouch. It's definitely a print, and it looks thinner than Bruno's, but there's no visible tread. I still take photos. We keep looking, and then I set Storm on the trail. She finds where they walked in from the bush, but the ground there is hard, no prints to be seen. We follow until she loses it on more rock.

"Time to go down," I say.

Dalton looks off to the east, where there's easy access to the spot.

I shake my head. "I want to take Bruno's route. Preferably without the pushing-and-falling part."

"That shows a lack of proper job dedication, Butler. I'm disappointed."

"Add it to my next job evaluation."

"You want me to actually start doing job evaluations?"

I shake my head and walk to the spot with the trampled moss. "I'd like to climb down this way, in case there are any clues."

"You think he scratched his attacker's name on the rock as he was falling?"

"Ha-ha. Humor me, okay? You can take the easy route with Storm."

"Will you wait until we're down there first, please?"

"I'm not going to fall."

"Humor *me*."

Dalton is in place below. What do I actually expect to find as I climb down? I don't know. I just want to figure out what happened. Put the picture into my brain.

As I descend, I do find something. A spot of blood with hairs embedded into it. This is where Bruno must have hit his skull, and when I see it, I have to wince.

He wasn't standing at the edge when someone snuck up behind and gave him a shove. He had his back to the edge. He saw his attacker. He was facing them, and they pushed him backward.

He fell back onto a ledge that might have saved him if he'd tumbled forward. Instead, he smacked down and his head hit a protruding rock hard enough to leave blood and hair. That's the source of the head injury. He kept falling, cracked his leg hard enough for the bone to break the skin before he landed on more rock at the bottom. There are twin blood pools from his head and leg after he struck down. I can also see the rocks he landed on, rough chunks that look innocent enough, but if you fell on them? Broken ribs and internal injuries.

Bruno was lucky to have survived. And he wasn't supposed

to. That much is obvious. He'd been near the edge. Maybe his partner asked him to look at something. He turns around to talk, putting his back to the edge, and he's shoved, hard.

He said he'd been conscious briefly after he landed. Did his would-be killer stand on the edge, looking down, seeing blood blooming from his skull, his body motionless, and presume he was dead? They must have.

I'm peering up, imagining it when I notice something white on the cliffside. It's about seven feet overhead and tucked back, hidden from my sight as I'd climbed down. When I start climbing to get it, Dalton walks over and reaches up, hand hovering beside it.

"You want this?" he says.

I glare at him.

"You could have just asked," he says. "I'm always happy to help the vertically challenged."

I flash him the finger . . . after he passes over the object. It's a tissue wrapped around something small, with a bit of heft. A rock? I peel back the tissue, and sun gleams off the bright yellow nugget.

"Gold," I whisper.

CHAPTER TWENTY-TWO

Is it possible that someone randomly tucked a nugget of gold into a tissue and stuck it in the cliffside for safekeeping? It would be if we were in the city, finding a gold ring hidden near where a victim had been pushed from the roof. Out here that'd be coincidental on a mind-boggling scale.

This tumbled out of Bruno's pocket as he fell. It landed on that small ledge, where it would have stayed if we hadn't come to check the scene.

I finish my search, finding nothing else of note. Then we head back to Haven's Rock. Dalton hails the first person we see with "You!" and she turns, brows rising.

"We need to speak to Yolanda," he says.

"I think she's in the town hall."

"Thanks," I say, Dalton already striding in that direction.

I ask Storm to wait on the town hall porch. Dalton may have gotten there ahead of me, as if he were going to stride in and demand answers to our questions, but now that he's arrived, he's waiting. He opens the door and lets me go in first.

Yolanda is sitting at the desk, tapping onto a tablet. When we enter, she looks up quickly, but after a glance at our faces, she sinks back into her chair.

"Nothing," she says.

"No sign of Penny," I say. "I'm sorry."

"It's been forty-eight hours," she says. "Isn't there a rule of thumb about that? If a missing person isn't found within the first forty-eight hours, the chances they'll be found alive . . . ?"

She doesn't finish that sentence. We both know what comes next. The chance of being found alive plummets.

"It doesn't apply out here," I say. "At least not in decent weather, with plenty of fresh water."

"But if she hasn't been found, something is keeping her from getting back here."

"Yeah," Dalton says. "The lack of a GPS. Or even a damn compass."

"She could be lost," I say, "and heading in the wrong direction. We're not giving up hope."

"Percentage-wise, how much hope do you actually have, Detective?"

"I always have some. I'd just prefer not to stick a number on it."

Her lips twitch in a humorless smile. "Understood. We'll just keep saying there's still hope, and telling ourselves we believe it."

"We did find something else," I say. "Possibly about Bruno's death. Do you have his work history on file? He said he'd worked in the north before. I'd like more on that."

She taps the tablet. "It's right here. He worked in the Yukon maybe five years ago. It wasn't construction, but he had done that before, and I thought the northern work experience would help."

"You said it wasn't construction. What kind of operation was it?"

Another tap. "He has—" She clears her throat. "He *had* two engineering degrees. Two specialties. Civic and geological. Up here, he was doing the second."

"Geological."

"Right." She passes me the tablet. "Working on a mining operation. Gold mining."

I spend the next two hours with Yolanda's tablet. She's given me free access to the crew's files. I haven't told her that Bruno said he'd been pushed, only that we found some evidence to suggest the possibility. I also don't tell her about the gold nugget. She's still one of my two prime suspects, and I can't afford to panic her. Yet I don't mind worrying her just a little. Suggest he *might* have been pushed off that cliff. Ask to see his records but don't explain why. If she is the confederate who betrayed Bruno, then having her on edge could be to our advantage. Let her frantically try to cover her tracks rather than call in a plane and flee the scene.

I now have a theory about what Bruno was up to. He's a mining engineer, and he realized he was in the Yukon, not Alaska. He'd been sneaking into the forest. Did he have a better idea of where we were and know there was the possibility of gold? That seems like a long shot—if a mining engineer knew there was gold up here, the place would be crawling with speculators. Instead, there's one very small placer mining camp . . . where someone *has* found gold.

I think Bruno stumbled over that camp. He knows this wilderness. He felt comfortable out there. He may even have been playing around with a bit of panning to ease the boredom. He finds the camp, and he knows he's struck literal gold. The fact that it's someone else's gold? Well, that depends on whether this miner is following the rules, and given the camouflaged tent, he might not be.

Placer mining is legal in the Yukon . . . with a registered claim. To stake a claim, you must stake out the area. That means you have to be on-site and place actual stakes in the ground. Then, having done that, you must file an application, which is usually done in person as it needs to be notarized. Once you have your claim, you're allowed to mine.

The problem is that miners are a secretive bunch, even paranoid. Let's say our miner is poking around, looking for a place to stake his claim. He finds gold. Serious gold, judging by the size of the nugget that seemed to fall out of Bruno's pocket. Is he going to want to leave the site to file an application? What if someone sees his application—or his stakes—and suddenly he has one section along a river filled with miners.

It's very possible he's doing more here than just staking a claim. He's mining, illegally. While his application is being processed? Or before making one?

If so, what happens if someone stumbles over his camp? Someone who recognizes what he's found, because that's their own specialty? Someone who may have the contacts needed to steal a one-person mining operation and sell the claim?

Bruno was shoved off a cliff less than a half kilometer from the camp. That's not insignificant. Not when he had a gold nugget in his pocket.

Bruno finds the camp and pulls someone else in. Someone with connections. Or he didn't pull them in at all, but they followed him and demanded their share.

Selling the claim, in conjunction with another person, fits the conversation we overheard in the forest that night. It also fits what Bruno said before he died. Something he did for his wife, something to make money. He wanted to be sure she still got her share.

Is it possible that Yolanda is that second party? That he pulled her in because she has connections, access to a plane, and access to a satellite phone, all ways to start that claim application while they're out in the forest. Maybe that's what they were arguing about that night. Not the job but the claim.

Yolanda demands something. Bruno is furious—it's *his* find. He storms off. She goes into the forest, heading for the claim site. Penny follows. Bruno figures out where Yolanda's gone and goes after her. Penny sees them argue. They kill her, fight over it, and Yolanda gets rid of the sole witness by shoving him off the cliff. Or Yolanda shoves him off the cliff and then kills Penny as the sole witness.

Do I believe that's what happened?

In my gut, no. I'm still pissed off at Yolanda blocking me about why she'd been in the forest that night. I know she was up to something. It could be something criminal. But meeting Bruno, knocking him into a gorge, and killing Penny and another woman who'd witnessed something or been a part of it? On the surface, that's the obvious answer. Yolanda had means and opportunity. Motive, though? There's where it gets trickier.

Yolanda is the granddaughter of a billionaire. Émilie obviously adores her, so there's no chance of being cut out of the will. From what Yolanda said about inheritances, though, she's a lot like me when it comes to family money. Oh, it's a whole other level for her. My parents were just well-off professionals, leaving enough to vault their daughters into the world of investment bankers and stock portfolios.

Still, the principle, I suspect, is the same. I shoved my money into that portfolio and never thought of it again until we considered a new Rockton. Then it became a tool. Same for April.

We didn't put everything we have into Haven's Rock, but only because the others wouldn't allow it. Neither of us cared. It wasn't actually our money, any more than a lottery win.

Yolanda grew up in a family with boggling amounts of capital. She stands to inherit far more than I did, and with Émilie being in her eighties, she's not going to have to wait long. Yet she still went out and built her own company. She's a successful professional heir to a billionaire . . . who seems completely focused on her career, living in residence with her crew, expecting no special treatment.

Is this woman going to kill two people to steal a gold claim? No, but the woman I see might not be the real Yolanda. Could she have gotten into recent financial trouble? Facing a lawsuit we know nothing about? Desperate for a sudden infusion of cash?

Then there's Penny as Bruno's potential partner. Did she really follow Yolanda into the forest? Could she have thought she was following Bruno, wondering why he was going out to "their" claim at night? Could she have been the one going to it, and we only presume she was following Yolanda? Could Bruno have realized Penny was gone and suspected she was up to something?

I like Penny. Or I like the version of her I've gleaned from others. That has nothing to do with how thoroughly I'll investigate her as a suspect, any more than I'd target Yolanda because I don't like her. That's a lie anyway. I'm pissed off at Yolanda, but I respect her and I think it might even be possible to like her if I didn't get the impression she'd really rather I didn't.

I once killed someone in cold blood. You can throw around excuses for that, but I don't, and I also know that I don't present as the kind of person who'd do that. Few people do. Penny could have pushed Bruno off the cliff. Yolanda could have pushed him and killed Penny and our mystery woman.

It could also be someone else in town, and that's the possibility I spend the evening pursuing, reading through employee records and trying to find connections. Any overlap with Bruno? Past jobs that could have brought them into contact? Yolanda has put together a crack team, and some of them have worked together before. I find none of that for Bruno. Nothing obvious, at least. That doesn't mean no one here has crossed paths with him before. He's an engineer. He'd have contact with a lot of people on a lot of jobs.

I'll need to dig into this more tomorrow. For now, we need to get to bed at a decent time. We'll have an early start in the morning, heading out to talk to one person who might have answers. The person unwittingly at the center of what has unfolded here. The miner at that claim site.

CHAPTER TWENTY-THREE

We're up at five thirty, with plans to leave at six. Dalton has commandeered breakfast ingredients from the kitchen, and he cooks while I make coffee and feed Storm. We're eating when someone bangs on the door.

"Fuck, no," Dalton mutters. "Can we go one night without an emergency?"

"Technically, it's morning."

He grumbles and waves me down as I go to stand. Then he ambles to the door, taking his time.

"It's not even six," he says as he pulls open the door.

"Tell me about it," Yolanda grumbles back.

I walk into the living room to see her on the front porch, shoving the sat phone at Dalton.

"It's for you," she says. As she walks away, she calls back, "We need to talk. I'll be in the commissary."

Dalton shuts the door and lifts the phone to his ear. "Hello?"

I hear a woman's voice answer. Dalton grunts, lowers the phone, and switches to speaker.

"It's Isabel," he says. "And Phil."

"Please tell me you're just calling to check in," I say. "Tell me you're in Toronto and forgot about the time difference, and that this isn't an urgent call and the next words out of your mouth will not be 'we have a problem.'"

"We have a situation," she says.

I sigh and slump into one of the living-room chairs.

"My apologies," she says. "That was rude. How is the town? How is your house? How are you? Now, about this problem . . ."

I smile as I shake my head. Sometimes I think that the surest way to know whether I'll get along with a woman is to see how fast she skims through the pleasantries and gets to business. I seem to surround myself with women who have spent their careers being told to be nicer, be less direct . . . and stuffed that advice in the bin where it belongs. There are exceptions, of course, but Isabel isn't one of them.

"What's up?" I say.

"The schedule has accelerated."

I glance at Dalton and ask, cautiously, "By how much?"

"We'll have ten new residents arriving in two weeks."

"What? No. Absolutely not. I need to speak to Émilie."

"We already did, and we argued. She isn't jumping the gun. It's an urgent situation."

"*How* urgent?"

"We let her find us residents, Casey. We admitted that we have no idea how to go about that, and she does, so we turned it over to her. She's done what we asked. Found people in serious need of refuge. Serious enough that they can't wait a moment longer than necessary."

I mutter under my breath.

"I can read you all the cases," she says. "If that's what you want."

"Are they the same ones or new?"

"Some of both. There are three new extremely urgent ones. A couple and their teenage daughter. They need sanctuary now. Émilie is providing that while we scramble for the exit plans. She can manage two weeks tops. Of the rest, two are from the previous group, their situations more urgent. The remainder don't need to be in there quite so quickly, but as long as we're taking some . . ."

"Might as well take them all."

"Would you like the case details?"

I glance at Dalton. Then I sigh. "No. I trust Émilie. I just don't know how the hell we're going to open in two weeks."

A throat clearing. Then Phil comes on. "I have that covered."

I manage a wry smile. "I'm sure you do."

"The build cannot be completed sooner. However, it is possible to reprioritize tasks and keep on a very small crew of workers after the residents arrive."

"A crew who think they're building a town for research? And obvious civilians show up, including a family?"

"Yolanda will handle that. She will prioritize critical occupation needs but also tasks that require certain professionals, who can be sent home once those tasks are complete. In addition to the current crew, we will come up—those of us who planned to be there from the start."

"Isabel and Kenny."

"And myself. It is an urgent situation, and so I will assist."

I glance at Dalton again. He rolls his eyes. Dalton thinks Phil is going to come to Haven's Rock, and he's just dragging his heels, telling himself he's not joining us, when the truth is that there's no way in hell he's breaking up with Isabel.

Phil used to be our council liaison. A faceless voice on a

radio that relayed their orders and suffered through our complaints. I always pictured a middle-aged guy, passed over for promotions, stuck in a dead-end corporate job and acting as officious as only such a middle-management drone can. Then he was exiled to Rockton to "help" us, and he turned out to be a couple of years younger than me, a brilliant strategist and consummate project manager, without whom I'm not sure there'd be a Haven's Rock. He also ended up with Isabel, our fortysomething former-psychologist bar owner who controlled enough of Rockton's money and secrets to make her the most powerful person in town.

They're a formidable couple. They are also two of the most commitment-phobic people I've ever met. I don't think managing Haven's Rock is Phil's idea of a permanent career move, but Isabel is making Haven's Rock her home. They'll work it out or they won't, and I just hope neither gets hurt along the way—or gives up more than they're willing to.

If Phil is coming, though, even just for now, that's good. The only good thing I've heard in this conversation.

"So you'll all come out and pitch in?" I say. "Iz? You're going to wield a chain saw, right?"

"I'll have you know that I have done several renovations in my time," she says. "Yes, Kenny will be more help in that area, but I know the difference between a Phillips screwdriver and a Robertson. Now Phil might be another matter."

"Which is why Phil will devote himself to administrative tasks," Phil says.

"In other words, you'll tell us all what to do," Isabel says.

"I embrace my strengths."

"I still don't think we can be open in two weeks," I say. "Eric and I are eyeball-deep in this investigation, with Will assisting.

April might be able to help with something while she's here, but she's got as much experience wielding a hammer as Phil does."

"April can focus on preparing the clinic," Phil says. "But the other three of you need to start assisting Yolanda. Effective immediately."

"Excuse me?" I say.

"Let me translate," Isabel says. "We need you three pitching in as soon as humanly possible, which means you may need to rethink this investigation. You have a dead stranger and a missing woman who has been missing for days. I'm not saying you need to stop looking for her but . . ."

"You need to accept that it is unlikely she'll be found," Phil says.

"And the dead engineer who was trying to steal a mining claim?"

Silence.

"I thought you'd found the engineer alive," Phil says. "That's why April was sent in."

I bring them up to speed on yesterday's events.

"So while we don't know who the mystery woman is, we do know what happened to the architect," Isabel says. "She was in cahoots with the engineer and pushed him off a cliff and then went into hiding."

"Maybe. Maybe not."

"That's the most likely scenario, Casey. At the risk of sounding heartless, I'm not sure solving this man's death matters. He died because he went to meet someone who tried to kill him. Someone who is almost certainly our missing woman."

"But the killer came back to town, and Penny isn't here."

"Diversionary tactics. Even if it's not her, though, is solving this man's murder a priority over getting the town ready to receive victims in critical need of refuge?"

"It is if the killer is someone who doesn't leave town with the others. Penny is a prime suspect. So is Yolanda."

Isabel swears softly.

Phil cuts in. "I would never tell you how to do your job, Casey, but you need to consider reprioritizing. Yes, look for this architect. Yes, try to find out who the engineer was working with. Even try to identify the dead woman. But if you are hitting dead ends . . ."

"You may need to drop it," Isabel says. "Let this one go and get the town ready."

CHAPTER TWENTY-FOUR

We've barely hung up when someone raps on the door.

"Go away!" Dalton shouts.

The door opens, and Yolanda walks in.

"That is *not* going away," Dalton says.

"It's my personal translation," Yolanda says. "When one door closes . . . you kick it back open. So you got the message from on high, then. Abandon the investigation and help me get this town open."

"We got the advice from on high," I say carefully. "But this is why we're the bosses now. So we don't have to obey orders from anyone, even our primary stakeholder."

"Good." She plunks onto the sofa. "Because if you abandon this investigation, I'm abandoning this job."

I arch my brows at her.

"One of my crew is missing," she says. "One is dead. You think someone on my crew is responsible for one or both. Yes, Bruno dropped onto that branch himself, but he wouldn't have been in that situation if someone hadn't tried to kill him. That's what you've been suggesting, right? That someone from town pushed him over that cliff? That's why you wanted their records."

"That's the working theory." I take a deep breath. Then I say, "Bruno said he was pushed."

"What?" She stares at me. "You didn't tell me—"

"My investigation. My choices. If you'd care to discuss why you were in the forest that night, maybe I'd be a little more forthcoming."

"And if I was the actual killer, I'd lie, wouldn't I? Make up some bullshit story like Bruno did, about needing to walk it off?"

"As you are not my superior officer, you are not entitled to details of my investigation, except when they may endanger your crew."

I expect her to pursue it. Instead, she waves a hand. "Fine, whatever. But I'm serious. If you abandon my people, I abandon yours."

"We aren't abandoning your people," I say. "However . . ." I glance at Dalton.

"We can't abandon ours either," he says. "Ours being the new residents. If your grandmother says it's urgent, then we trust it's urgent. You agree?"

"Yes, but—"

"But nothing. We're here for these people, so we have to match her damn timeline. Phil has a plan."

"I heard it," she says. "Reprioritize. Reschedule. Repopulate . . . with your unskilled labor replacing my skilled labor. I have a feeling I'm not going to like this Phil guy much."

"Oh, he's fine," I say. "It's Isabel you need to worry about. The alpha-female energy in this town is about to spike, and it was high enough already."

A quirked smile. "Fine by me. I've spent my career on jobs with too many big dogs, all of them with something to prove. Dealing with big bitches will be a refreshing change of pace."

"Everyone's going to need to get their egos in check and work together on this."

Dalton's brows rise. "Why are you looking at me?"

"Because you didn't remind us that we still have at least one big dog to deal with."

"That goes without saying."

Yolanda snorts a laugh. "You've been more subdued than I was led to expect, Sheriff Dalton."

"Conserving my energy. Now that you need someone cracking the whip, though?" He shrugs. "Time for me to get back in shape. Does Phil's plan work?"

"With tweaks."

"Then you tweak it. I'll reassign Will to construction duty and talk to April. Casey and I will head out this morning, but when we return, there will be another town meeting, and I'll tell them what's what and handle any fallout while Casey continues investigating, which she will continue to do only—"

"As long as there are leads," I say.

"Yep. And I'm sorry as hell about that, but this is where I'm going to need to step in and, if needed, be the asshole who says we need to stop looking." He turns to Yolanda. "At that point, if you think I'm wrong, then you will be free to carry out your threat and leave. Your priority is your crew. Casey's is the investigation. Mine is the new residents."

"Yours trumps ours," I say. "I get that."

He's right. Émilie's right. Isabel's right. Either I find something or I have to drop this. Leave Penny lost in the woods.

Leave Bruno's killer free. And never identify our dead woman, let alone discover what happened to her.

Time to get moving. Get moving and find something. Fast.

We're still hitting the trail by seven, thankfully. As we walk, we talk about what just happened. Part of that is mutual reassurance—Dalton being sure I'm not pissed off at him for setting parameters and me being sure he isn't pissed off at me for wanting to pursue the investigation.

Yolanda and I may have joked about alphas, but there's no room for that in a personal relationship. Dalton is accustomed to being in charge. I am accustomed to having someone in charge . . . while ignoring them when it comes to what I think is best for an investigation. Although we try to separate the personal from professional, we've come to realize that those are largely artificial boundaries. We both need to compromise more than either of us is accustomed to, and there is plenty of headbutting, but we work it out. For now, we have worked this out. The problem will only come if we reach a point where Dalton decides the leads have dried up and I disagree.

We talk it out, and then we rehash the investigation, bouncing ideas off each other. We're talking about Yolanda when Dalton stops walking. His gaze swings left, hand going to his gun.

We're on the game trail we've been using, which is widening into more of an actual trail, with all our tromping up and down it. This part is open land with low brush and rocks that rise to the foothills of the mountain closest to town.

"Someone's on the ridge," Dalton says.

I peer at where he's looking, one of many ridges along the foothills.

"Thought it might be a bear, up on two legs watching us, but then it moved."

It walked on two legs, that's what he means.

"Disappeared as soon as I looked over," he says.

"Lilith?" I ask.

He shakes his head. "Don't doubt she's keeping an eye on us, but that wasn't her. Not unless she's changed into a modern jacket."

"What kind of jacket?"

"Dark. Black or navy. Lightweight."

"Penny left wearing a navy fleece jacket."

"Yep."

"And if she ducked out of sight, then she's not lost." I pause. "Unless she isn't sure whether we're friend or foe."

"Yep."

"I'd like to check it out."

"I know."

I give him a look. "You know and agree? Or you know and disagree?"

"I agree that if we don't, you'll be up all night worrying that we found poor lost Penny and abandoned her to her fate . . . even if I'm damn sure that any reasonable person, lost in the woods for three days, is going to take that chance. And Penny seems like the definition of a reasonable person."

I sigh. "She does."

"But you still want to be sure."

"Please."

Storm makes our life better in so many ways. Makes our job easier, too. This, however, is one of those times when having a hundred-and-twenty-pound Newfoundland does not help. We need to sneak through the forest. We don't dare split up. And we sure as hell aren't leaving the dog behind. To minimize the noise, Dalton walks thirty feet ahead, motioning back to me when he can hear the dog tromping through the undergrowth, and I shift her to a barer or greener walking path.

Finally, we're close enough to the ridge that we slow to a creep as we listen for signs of whoever is out there. Someone is. Even I catch a twig crackle and then the scuffle of a misplaced boot quickly corrected. That tells us where to go.

I'm guiding Storm over a particularly noisy part when I catch Dalton's frantic wave. I think he's motioning for us to stay where we are, but when I grab Storm's collar, he shakes his head and points. There, up on the ridge, maybe twenty feet away from Dalton, someone stands against a tree. They have their back to it, and that seems intentional. They've seen or heard us, and they're trying to hide.

Dalton beckons for me to catch up. I do, and then he bends to my ear.

"I'm circling around. Cover me."

I nod and take out my gun. He heads off through the thick trees. The person stays where they are. I'm closer now, but they're actually harder to distinguish from this angle, being too far above me. I back up a few steps, and that gives me what I presume was Dalton's line of sight. I can only make out the figure and the dark jacket, with a hood pulled up.

I bend beside Storm, petting her as I try that vantage point. It's better, and I can see blue jeans. It's still too hard to determine a physical size or shape, with that tree marring the person's outline.

I'm trying to work out a better angle when the person raises their arms. Arms that seem ridiculously long and—

A rifle. The person is raising a rifle, pointed in Dalton's direction.

I whistle. It's the only thing I can think to do short of shouting. Even as I hear the sound, I realize how foreign it sounds in these woods, how obviously human. That gun swings in my direction and fires.

I dive over Storm. I knock her to the ground and cover her, my gun raised as I look up the ridge. A crashing to my left. Far too loud a crashing to be Dalton, I think at first. Then, as the rifle barrel swings that way, I know that's exactly who it is. Dalton making as much noise as he can, diverting fire away from us.

The person fires again, and I stifle a cry. If I make any noise, I'll drown out the sounds I do not want to hear—the thud of Dalton falling to the ground, the scream or gasp of pain.

None of those come.

As the woods stay silent, I wrap my hand around Storm's collar and very slowly lead her to the left. When the shooter swings the gun our way, I freeze, but the shot hits back where we'd been, exploding a tree branch.

I turn to keep leading Storm. Then I see Dalton making his way in our direction. When he arrives, he motions me down, and we crouch behind a pair of trees.

The figure on the ridge moves the gun in a slow arc. Another shot, well to the right of us.

"Suppose you *still* want a closer look," Dalton whispers in my ear.

I nod.

He shakes his head but only mutters, "Fine."

CHAPTER TWENTY-FIVE

Being the one who wants a closer look, I should be the one to take the risk and sneak up. Dalton tries to veto that by pulling rank, until I counter that the person staying here is actually in greater danger, being the person hiding with the giant dog.

"How's your aim?" I ask.

"Not as good as yours."

"I don't mean with your gun."

I hand him a stone. His eyes narrow. He knows what I'm saying. If that rifle swings in my direction, he can pitch a rock to divert it the other way, and while I might be the better shot, my throwing arm isn't as good as his.

Dalton hesitates, and I can tell he wants to keep arguing. Then he points back the way he came.

"Circle wider. I saw a better spot to get up there if you stay on the west side of the fallen pine."

I kiss his cheek. "Thank you."

I take the route he suggested, and I send up a mental thanks because it's damn near perfect, which is probably why he didn't insist on going in my place. The path is heavily wooded and leads up the ridge and then down the other side, allowing me to approach behind the shooter while staying in the forest until I am less than ten feet away, looking up at their back.

The shooter still has their rifle raised. They continue scanning the forest. When that barrel lifts, just a little, I know they're about to fire, and I tense, my gut screaming at me to run up there and stop them. My brain intervenes, pointing out that the barrel isn't directed at Dalton. It's aimed off to the left and high, and when it fires, the bullet sings through the trees, well above head level.

A warning shot. The forest below has gone silent, but they know someone is still down there. Someone who did not flee in terror, crashing through the bush.

They don't know what they're doing. That thought hits as I watch the shooter scan the forest. Do they not realize how exposed they are, poised on that ridge? They don't—to them, they occupy the high ground. The safe ground. They can see anyone coming at them . . . unless that person has circled around to the rear.

I creep up the ridge, placing each foot with extreme care. The shooter might not have considered how open they've left their back, but the crunch of a single stone will have them spinning and firing.

Place a foot. Rock forward to test my grip. Lift the back foot. Repeat.

From this angle—the other side of the tree they're "hiding" against—I can see the person's arm and the rifle barrel. That's it. When that arm stiffens, I freeze. Below, dead foliage crunches underfoot. The rifle fires, and it's definitely aimed well overhead.

The shot hits a tree below and something crashes through the forest, running for its furry life. It's very obviously an animal, but the person fires again, and I take advantage of that to cover the last few quick steps. Then I am poised on the other side of that tree.

I pause there to catch my breath in slow, silent inhales. I see now why they feel safe. It's the tree at their back. Clearly no one can get the jump on them. Which is laughable, but I understand the impulse. The tree is tall and solid. It is protection.

It is also protection for me, and as the person with a short-barreled gun, I have the advantage, standing a mere foot away from my target.

I slow my breathing. Then I look around my feet. There are no convenient loose stones here, so I reach into my pocket and take out half of an energy bar. I draw back my arm and pitch it to my right. It's a half-assed underhand toss, but it does what I need it to do, landing with a crackle of the wrapper that has my target spinning that way . . . and I swing around the other side of the tree and put my gun to their back.

The shooter goes still. From this vantage point, I can only make out the dark jacket, hood pulled up, the person four or five inches taller than me and wider. Definitely not Lilith. Possibly Penny.

The figure starts to pivot, rifle rising.

"Uh-uh," I say. "That's a gun you feel. Not a rifle either."

Their shoulders twitch at the sound of my female voice. It's not what they expected. Another advantage to having me here instead of Dalton.

"This isn't the way I like to say hello," I say. "But you started it, shooting at my dog."

"Dog?"

Now I'm the one tensing at the voice. It's male. Damn it. As much as I didn't want it to be Penny shooting at us, at least it would have meant we'd found her . . . and solved our case.

"You shot at my dog," I say. "I kind of take that personally, so you're going to lower your rifle to the ground and then we're going to have a more civil conversation."

"I wasn't trying to shoot anyone. I was aiming well over your heads."

"Gun on the ground."

As he bends, I'm tensed for a sudden move.

He sets the gun down and then straightens, hands lifted. I whistle, two short bursts to tell Dalton I'm fine, though I'm sure he can see that.

"They were warning shots," he says. "I didn't see a dog. Just two people."

"And you randomly fire warning shots at people walking through the forest?"

"May I turn around?"

"If you keep your hands lifted."

He starts to turn. Then brush crackles below, and he stops.

"That's my husband," I say. "He'll be joining us in a minute, with the dog."

The man nods and continues turning. When he's facing me, I tell him to push off the hood. That's when I get a proper look at him. He's about forty, with a trim beard. White skin. Sandy hair. Brown eyes. A very average-looking guy, with an average build, a little shorter than average at maybe five foot six.

"Care to explain why you shot at us?" I say.

"I saw you walking, and I was watching where you were headed, and then you spotted me and veered my way. I was trying to dissuade you from that."

His voice is calm and reasonable, with just the faintest waver of concern. That suggests he's not your typical paranoid forest dweller. My gaze trips over his outfit. Light jacket, jeans and boots.

Dalton appears on the ridge, and I glance over, while tensing again, in case the man mistakenly thinks I'm distracted. He only shifts his own gaze.

I lower my gun. Dalton does the same, and the man turns to look at him. A momentary pause, as he assesses Dalton and straightens. When his gaze drops to the dog, he smiles, just a little.

"Don't know how I missed that beast. He's a big one."

"You always fire warning shots at strangers in the woods?" Dalton says.

"I do if I think they're a threat." The man looks pointedly from Dalton's gun to mine. "Seems my instinct was correct."

"No," Dalton says. "Your misguided instinct is what brought these out. We're looking for someone, and we thought you might be her. We were just coming in for a closer look. We're a half mile from your mining operation. No need to get trigger happy."

Mining operation? My gaze flicks over the man again, and I note that the boots are waterproof with thick soles. Gloves hang from his pockets, and there's mud on his knees.

Damn it. Well, that was some shitty detective work. Worse, the reason I didn't consider him for the role of our miner is that he didn't look like what I expected, any more than Lilith looks like a wolf-taming forest witch. And to add an extra layer of "worse," I *know* that placer miners can certainly look like this. Some are characters straight out of the Klondike gold rush, with long beards and wild eyes, but I have met others in Dawson City who look as much the urban professionals as Lilith.

"Mining operation?" the man says.

"You want to play it that way?" Dalton says. "Sure. Let's pretend you're just some guy out here enjoying our fine wilderness. I don't actually give a shit . . . unless you're going to keep shooting at us while we're out here hunting for our missing woman."

The man eyes us.

"Do we look like miners?" Dalton says.

"You look like cops."

"Good call. We're private detectives, called in to look for this woman. Even if we were the Mounties, though, we're not the ministry of natural resources or the mining commission or whoever the hell handles that. We don't give a shit what you're doing out here . . . unless you want to shoot at us and make us take an interest."

The man eases back. "Okay. I've seen your missing woman, but I don't get the feeling she wants to be found. Lots of people up here like that. I pretend I don't see them."

"Which is fine," I say. "We just need to be sure she's okay."

"Oh, she is. I've spotted her once or twice, maybe two miles from here. Seems to be some kind of photographer. Looks pro, though with folks up here . . . ?" He shrugs. "For all I know, there's no film in that camera and she just thinks she's taking pictures."

"A photographer . . ." I say slowly.

"Yep. Dresses like she tans her own hides. Has a pet husky, too."

Lilith. I try to hide my disappointment. "We've met her, and she's a local. The woman we're looking for went missing three nights ago."

He looks startled. "A tourist? Damn. No, I definitely haven't seen her."

"Are you sure?"

"I think I'd remember, but that's not what you're asking. You mean did I see her and fire warning shots, one of which actually hit her and I'm covering it up."

"Something like that."

He shoves his hands into his pockets. As he considers his next words, we wait. Finally, he says, "Yes, it's my camp. My claim. I did not see your missing woman. However, someone was in my tent a few days back. I have triggers to show me whether anyone has been on the site. One was tripped."

"Two days ago?" Dalton says. "That was us. We stumbled over your camp looking for our missing woman. I reset the triggers, but I must have missed one."

The man shakes his head. "This was the day before that. The night, that is. I was out hunting at twilight. Got tired of canned stew. I screwed up—misjudged the light and went farther away than I should have, so I had to come back in the dark. When I arrived, I found the trigger tripped."

We take a moment to confirm dates. That can be tricky out here, where it's easy to confuse Wednesday for Thursday or three days ago for two. The man is adamant about the timing, and the trigger he found tripped had definitely been reset by Dalton.

The night he found it was also the night Bruno and Penny disappeared.

"We need to talk to you about your claim." I lift my hands. "Nothing about whether you have or haven't found any silver or whatever." *I'm not even mentioning the possibility of gold.* "Nothing about whether it's legal or not. We don't care. But we have reason to believe someone else knew about it. There was . . ." I search for an easy way to say this. There isn't one. "We found a dead body with the coordinates to your camp in their pocket."

He stares and then gives his head a shake. "Come again?"

"Someone had the coordinates to your camp in their pocket. They were found dead nearby."

"I . . ." He keeps shaking his head. "You're serious, right?"

Before I can answer, he says, "Obviously you are, and maybe I shouldn't be so shocked. I've heard . . . Well, you hear stories. I've been mining in the summers since college. Seen some weird stuff, but never had anyone try to steal a claim site."

A sharper headshake. "Now I'm babbling. You're telling me that someone knew about my claim and came here to check it out and suffered some kind of accident."

"Did anyone know where you were? A partner who might have come to join you?"

"No. It's a one-man operation. I learned from the old-timers. Don't tell anyone until you have something, and then *definitely* don't tell anyone. At least not until you've locked up the claim." He pauses. "Not that I've found anything yet."

Dalton says, "So our dead woman is definitely not your partner, right?"

"W-woman?" He stares at us. "You found a dead *woman* with my camp coordinates in her pocket?"

"Yes," I say.

Something passes over his face. Something that looks a lot like panic. "Take me to her."

"She's in her early forties—"

He cuts me off with a frantic wave. "Don't. Please. Just take me to her. Now."

CHAPTER TWENTY-SIX

We don't get any more out of Mark—that's his name, or the one he gives us. He's in an absolute panic, and I think I know why, but I don't even suggest it.

We can't take him back to town, obviously. But we do have two sat phones, now that Anders and April brought a replacement for the one I lost. So we place a call and set a spot to meet.

Mark knows about Haven's Rock, at least in the sense that he realizes there is something being built five kilometers from his claim. He doesn't know what it's for and doesn't care. Whatever he's doing to legalize his claim, he obviously plans to have it finalized before he'd need to worry about people from Haven's Rock.

We don't tell him about Bruno. Unless we think he had something to do with it, there's no point. And I don't see how he can have anything to do with it. Is it possible Bruno found the site and Mark murdered him to keep it a secret? Yes, but the altercation would have happened at the camp, not a half kilometer away. Also, Bruno would have happily told us who pushed him, to exact revenge by uncovering Mark's claim. No,

Bruno was pushed by his business partner, with whom he was conspiring to steal Mark's claim.

There is zero advantage to letting Mark know one of our people plans to yank his claim out from under him. I will tell him eventually. He doesn't deserve to be screwed over. I just need to do it in a way that suggests the would-be thief has nothing to do with Haven's Rock, and that'll be a complicated bit of tap dancing.

Right now, I don't think he'd hear me even if I told him of the danger. He is moving as fast as he can, and when we spot people through the trees, he breaks into a run. He pulls up short seeing Anders, but it's only a moment of surprise before his gaze goes to the wrapped body on the ground. Anders has wrapped her and brought her—with Gunnar's help—on a stretcher.

When I look at Gunnar, my brows raised, Anders murmurs, "He already knew about her."

"I know everything," Gunnar says. "See everything, know everything." He turns to Mark. "Hey, man. So you think you can ID our—"

I shake my head to cut Gunnar off. He raises a quizzical brow and then looks at Mark, standing there, staring down, his entire body quivering.

"Fuck," Gunnar whispers.

Anders discreetly shoulders Gunnar back and steers him out of the clearing. We all stay on the edges while Mark bends beside the body and, with shaking fingers, pulls back the sheet over her face. Then he lets out a horrible gasping groan.

I step away and Dalton follows, Storm staying close. Anders and Gunnar join us.

"He knows her," Gunnar whispers.

"Yep," I say.

"There's a serial killer out there, isn't there?"

Anders motions for him to lower his voice.

Gunnar continues in a whisper. "It's one of those guys who runs up here to escape the law, only now we've brought victims to his doorstep. Us and this guy." He pauses. "Who is this guy?"

"A hunter," I say.

"And if you say one word to him about serial killers . . ." Anders whispers.

"You'll kick my ass into the Pacific?"

"No, Casey will. I'll just watch."

Dalton murmurs something, and when I look over, he nods toward the clearing. Telling me it's time to step in.

I do that, while the guys stay where they are. Mark sits on the ground beside the dead woman, brushing hair back from her face.

"I'm sorry," I say. "She was . . ."

"My—" He chokes and takes a moment before he says, "My wife. Denise."

"I'm *so* sorry."

"What happened to her?"

"We're trying to figure that out." I lower myself to the ground beside him. "Eric and I were called in to find a woman who disappeared from the construction crew, and when we found your wife, we presumed it was our missing person and brought her back."

"Thank you. For . . . for finding her."

Earlier, we'd presumed the dead woman couldn't have been joining the miner. That napkin had three sets of coordinates, with the first two crossed off. That meant she was searching for the camp and had a few leads.

Unless the napkin wasn't hers.

What if whoever had the napkin had been searching for the camp and found it while Mark was hunting? The napkin could have belonged to Bruno or his partner. They could have been at the camp when Denise showed up and overheard something or demanded to know what they were doing, and they killed her. That would connect our dead woman to our crime.

But it also leaves a huge question. If Mark was expecting his wife, why didn't he wonder what happened to her?

There's a simple explanation—when she failed to show up, he presumed she'd been delayed. I just need that answer from him.

"She was coming to meet you?" I say.

"Apparently."

"You . . . weren't expecting her?"

He leans back, presses his palms to his eyes, and exhales. "No, I . . . I hadn't told her where I was."

I don't comment. I just wait for more. It takes him a moment to give it.

"When I'm checking out a potential claim, I can't let anyone know where I am."

"Even your wife." I say it as a statement. A question will sound accusatory, even if my mind boggles at the thought of Dalton disappearing into the forest, alone, for weeks, and not even telling me where he is.

"I know how it sounds, and I wish I could say it was for her own safety or that she didn't want to know, but . . ." He swallows. "She was definitely not happy about it."

I nod, again letting him proceed at his own pace.

"We've only been married a few years. Three." A pained smile. "Three years, two months, five days. Second marriage for both of us. She knew I do this. I'm a professor, and I come up here for most of my summer term. My first wife would join me. Denise . . . It wasn't her thing. I thought Denise was fine with the arrangement, but I realized it's one of those things where you're in love and you tell yourself something isn't a problem when it really is."

He smooths another lock of his wife's hair back. "She told herself it didn't matter and I told myself she didn't mind, and we were both lying. This year, I think she started to realize that I wasn't telling her where I went because I didn't trust her."

"Started to *realize* it. Meaning you *didn't* trust her."

"It wasn't her fault," he says quickly. "She just didn't understand the need for secrecy, and we have friends who mine, and I just . . . I decided it was better if she didn't know. After all, what did it matter? It's not like she can hop on a train and come visit."

"So you were out of contact while you were here?"

"I fly down every third weekend."

"No satellite phone?"

He shrugs. "It's expensive, and it's a security risk. I did promise to look into one of those satellite text things for next year, but it's still a GPS signal, right? That's not safe. I know it sounds paranoid, but I've heard stories—so many stories."

"When you fly down, someone picks you up? Someone you trust with the location?"

"It's a friend, but he picks me up a day's walk from here. Like I said, I'm paranoid."

"Yet Denise managed to find you. She had three sets of possible coordinates, and one led here. If there is a chance someone else was involved in your wife's death, then I need to know how she got here. Who could have brought her. Who could have told her where to find you."

"No one except me has that information."

"*Some*one did."

He shakes his head. "She got it from me. From my research notes. That's the only possibility."

"Your research notes."

He sits back, his gaze still on his wife. "Every year, I work in a new area. When I'm out here, I'm mining but also scouting for those potential new sites. I usually have two or three in mind, within a general area. I start at one, and if I don't get anything, I move to the next."

The list of three sets of coordinates. "This was one of your potential sites."

He nods. "Last year, I scouted over here. I have a scientific model based on a number of factors that predicts a potential site. It's my area of academic expertise. I use that to find a general area and then I study it in person. This year, I had a list of three potential sites."

"She found that list."

He throws up his hands. "Somehow. It's not as if I left it lying around. It's all on my computer. A dedicated laptop that is never connected to the internet. The laptop has a password, of course, but there's additional security on the files, though it's not exactly state-secret level."

"Just enough to keep someone from casual snooping."

"Or serious snooping. But it's my laptop, kept at home, off the internet. I shouldn't have needed more."

"If Denise hired someone to hack it . . ."

"It would take more than some kid who's good at computers, but she works in IT. She has connections. I just never expected—" He swallows the rest with a hard shake of his head. "She'd had enough. I knew that, and I was telling myself we'd work it out when I got back. Last time we talked, she wanted to come out and stay for a week, prove she could do it. I said we'd try that next year."

Because this year, he'd found gold, and he might have loved his wife, but he didn't trust her to understand the importance of keeping that a secret. So she hacked his laptop, found his three potential locations, and came out to show him she could survive a week in the woods.

Only she never got that chance.

CHAPTER TWENTY-SEVEN

We have identified our mystery woman. We have notified her next of kin. So, what happens next? That's where it gets tricky. If we turn Denise's body over to Mark, he's going to realize those knife wounds are not from a wilderness accident. We could forewarn him, but then he might bring in the Mounties, and our town would be in jeopardy. We are prepared for that. We must be, as Rockton was. If we are exposed, Émilie says she'll handle it. Apparently, Rockton did not survive for seventy years without a single government official ever realizing there is an entire town illegally built in the Yukon wilderness. It was handled. It can be handled again. Yet we certainly don't want to deal with that before we've even opened our doors.

Here, though, we can use Mark's own paranoia about his claim. He sure as hell doesn't want to call in the RCMP when he's illegally mining. With us, he has an alternative. We will investigate. We will figure out what happened to Denise, and he can take it from there. There is no other next-of-kin. Her mother is dead, and Denise had no children and little contact with her father. With Émilie's help, this can be handled in a way that allows Mark to lay his wife to rest without the authorities getting involved. That is what he wants, and we will give it to him, because it is to our advantage to do so.

I question Mark further while sidestepping any mention of his mine or its legality. That keeps him on safe ground, and he tells us what he can. Once I'm done, he heads back to his camp, leaving his wife's body with us, where we will continue storing it in the permafrost level to ward off decomposition.

We're back in town now. I've been making notes while Dalton holds the town meeting to present the new timetable. I've resisted the urge to join them. He's got this, and I need to focus on my investigation.

When Dalton is done there, he joins Anders in helping out with the construction for a couple of hours. Then both join me for dinner in the town hall.

"I think Bruno or his partner—or both—were at Mark's camp that night," I say. "They knew he was gone, and they were checking it out."

"And triggered one of the traps?" Anders asks.

"Possibly? But that can't have been the first time they were there. They should have known about the triggers, and the one set off was on the tent, which they'd have no reason to enter. That leads into the question of why Denise was half naked when she was killed."

"Surprising Mark," Dalton says. "She gets there while he's out. Figures he'll be back soon because it's getting dark. Goes into the tent, setting off that trigger. Gets partly undressed for a sexy welcome."

I nod. "He's going to be angry with her for hacking his files."

"But a lot less angry after hot reunion sex."

"Distraction and mollification," I say. "But instead, Bruno or his partner show up. Denise goes out. There's an altercation that turns violent. Mark asked what personal belongings I found with the body. I had to get creative with that, to explain *why* she didn't have anything with her if I think it was likely an accident. But it did give me an opportunity to ask whether she would be armed—does she carry a gun or whatnot. He says she has a pocketknife. It was a gift from her first husband before he died of cancer. An in-joke about needing to take care of herself after he was gone. She carries it everywhere."

"Could that be the murder weapon? She confronts whoever is in her husband's camp and they turn it on her?"

"I'm going to have April examine the body and see if we can come up with a blade size. I also want her to reexamine Bruno for defensive wounds."

"Yeah," Anders says. "We did fingernail scrapings for you, but that's it."

"I have a theory, then, one that ties Denise to the rest of it. Now I need evidence."

After dinner, the guys continue to help with the build while I take over as April's medical assistant for examining Denise and Bruno. The knife wounds on Denise are consistent with a pocketknife blade. It could be any pocketknife, but also, tearing around the edges suggests the blade was not exactly razor sharp. These were thrusting wounds rather than slicing ones. That would match a pocketknife someone might carry for self-defense in situations where they are almost certainly never going to need to do more than wave it around. It's not as if Denise would have been sharpening it before heading into the urban jungle to buy groceries.

I'd examined her earlier for defensive wounds and found a cut on her hand that suggested she fought. But it does not provide any link to her assailant. No tissue under her nails. No foreign hairs on her clothing. If she did manage to stab her killer, any blood on their skin was either washed off or smeared together with her own blood, and while I can test for blood type, it all comes back to O positive, which is also hers.

On to Bruno then. We know he wasn't stabbed, but now we're looking for even a jab or prick, something that suggests Denise got in a blow with her pocketknife. There's none of that on his body. No defensive wounds either.

"I want to check his clothing," I say as April begins to cover Bruno's body.

"It's where you left it."

"No, I want to check it against his body."

She frowns at me.

"Just don't cover him up yet," I say. "Can you help me put a sheet on the floor and move him onto it?"

She doesn't ask. She finds a sterile sheet and spreads it as I get out Bruno's clothing. The two of us lower him onto the sheet. He's off to one side, with a few feet of the sheet empty to his right. That's where I lay his clothing, as if setting it out for a paper doll, each piece placed beside the appropriate part of his body.

"I'm lining up his injuries," I say. "There's a lot of blood on his clothing. I'm looking for any place he might have blood that doesn't seem to have come from his own wounds. Some of it may be transfer, from when Lilith found and moved him, but if I have a limited number of areas to work with, I can test for blood type."

"Because Denise, Penny, and Bruno all have different ones."

I nod. We knew Bruno's and Penny's from their intake forms, but we'd retested Bruno's to confirm. We'd also tested Denise's. While we may not be able to match DNA easily here, you can test blood type with a kit bought at Walmart. The trickier part comes with taking a sample from clothing to test. I have what I need for that, though. I just can't go running an entire bloodied shirt through it. I need small samples for discrete testing.

We work together and start at his head. Lots of scalp bleeding means that the massive bloodstains on the top of his shirt are his. Are they *all* his? Again, while it's possible to test that, it's not easily done under these conditions, so I set that aside. I can come back to it if I need to.

Some of the blood on his torso could also be from his head wound, splattered as he fell. We know from the blood and hair on the rock that his head was bleeding at that point. April and I have a bit of, well, I hesitate to call it fun, but there is a bit of mental puzzle work there that we both enjoy, setting up make- shift models and figuring out the pattern of his fall based on his injuries, which then gives us an idea which blood droplets come from that.

He also has cuts and scrapes from the fall, but none of those tore his clothing, so all that blood is inside his clothing. Then there's his left leg, where the compound fracture soaked the pant leg with blood.

Once we have removed all that, we are left with three po- tential spots that might not be his blood. One is a spray of small droplets across his shoulder. The other is a single drop on his hip. The third, which we'd initially mistaken for dirt, is a smear of blood on the right knee of his jeans.

I start with the droplets. Thinking of Denise and how she died, that seems the most likely. When I test it, though, the blood type matches Bruno's. It must be spray from the head injury during his fall. On to the drop on his hip. That one is also his type. Of course, it is also possible that these two came from an unidentified third party—I'm testing only blood type, and his is a common one—but the point for now is that it isn't Penny's or Denise's.

Then comes the smeared patch at his knee. That one is tougher, because there's also dirt there. Dirt on both knees, in fact. That had been there when Lilith brought him, so it isn't from his "fake" fall. It could be from work earlier that day, though I don't know how often an engineer needs to get down and dirty on a site, especially that far into the build. All this should be irrelevant. Who cares how he got dirt on his knees?

I do. Because he also got blood on his knee. And that blood type? It matches Denise's.

April and I are rewrapping Bruno's body when the door slaps open and boot steps thump through the waiting room. The doorknob jiggles. Then it jiggles again as someone heaves on it.

"It's locked," April says. "Do you have a medical emergency?"

"It's Gunnar."

"That does not answer my question."

I shake my head and open the door. Gunnar walks in. His gaze flits to Bruno's wrapped body and then back to me.

"I've been looking for you," Gunnar says.

"Can I help you?" I say.

He grins. "The question, as always, is whether I can help you."

I sigh. "Do you have something for me, Gunnar?"

He starts to answer. Then he looks at April. Back to me. Back to April.

"Hey, are you guys, like, sisters or something? Well, half sisters."

That has April tensing, her voice brittle as she says, "We're full sisters."

"Really? Huh." Another close look before he eases back. "Cool. Anyway, I need to talk to Casey here."

"Detective Butler," April says.

I motion at the rear door. "Come on, Gunnar. Let's take this out back."

Before we leave, he turns back to April. "If you get lonely while you're here—"

I give him a push toward the door.

"I'm just saying, if your sister wants to play doctor—"

Another, harder shove as I open the door and prod him through it.

Once he's gone, I turn back to April to say goodbye, but she cuts me off with, "Did that young man just suggest I'm 'playing' at being a doctor?"

"No, no. He's just . . . I'll explain later." *Not if I can help it.* "Breakfast?"

"I eat at seven."

"I'll be here."

Storm is out on the back deck waiting for me, and I walk over to pat her head as she stands up.

"What have you got for me, Gunnar?" I say.

He leans against the railing. "Would you agree that I am a valuable member of this crew?"

"I have no idea. Yolanda is in charge of construction. Is there a problem?"

"But I have proven myself to be valuable, right? To you? I've brought you tips. I keep my eyes out. I helped with that lady's body, and I haven't told anyone there *is* a dead lady."

"Thank you . . ." I say.

"I want to stay," he says. "And I'm not on the list."

"Ah." I lower myself into a chair. "Yolanda has scheduled you to leave early."

"Your husband did. He doesn't like me." Gunnar flexes, muscles rippling. "It happens. Especially with guys who marry up."

"Marry up?"

"In looks. You're hot. He's . . ." A shrug. "Averagely decent. I don't know what the deal is there. Maybe the money."

"The money?"

"I know this is his town. I've heard things. You two built it, which means your guy must be loaded, even if he sure as hell doesn't look like it."

I open my mouth to protest. Then I just shut it and shake my head.

"Point is that I don't blame him for feeling threatened," Gunnar says.

I bite the inside of my cheek. "Eric doesn't feel threatened. Yolanda made the initial lists, and they discussed it, and Eric finalized choices. If you're not on the list, it isn't personal."

"If you say so. . . ."

"Eric is head of security. That means that he's only going to notice you if you're a threat to security. If he decides you're trouble. In that case, he wouldn't ship you off without a conversation. Have you had that conversation?"

"Conversation? The guy hasn't said two words to me."

"And I'll bet that's exactly what most people in this crew would also say. He's here to work, and he's focused on his work.

Even if you were in his bad books—which you are not—that wouldn't interfere with whether or not you're on 'the list.' Getting this town finished is his priority."

"I'm a damn fine worker." He rests his hip against the railing. "Yeah, I don't bring specific skills to the table, but I pull my weight and I do what I'm told and, hell, if you just need someone to haul shit around, play workhorse . . ." He flexes his biceps. "I'm your man."

"I will have a talk with Yolanda and Eric, but if they've already made the list public, it's hard to swap you out without an explanation. Maybe if there's someone who didn't want to stay . . . ?" I rise from the chair. "Let me see what I can do."

"You mean that? Or are you blowing me off?"

"Fifty-fifty."

He snorts a laugh. "At least you're honest."

"I try. The problem is that we have a time crunch, and I have two dead bodies, and I am not unsympathetic, Gunnar, but I really do need to get back to work."

"It's almost ten at night."

"Like I said, I have a time crunch. My day is not yet over. You have, however, been helpful to me, and so I'm not completely blowing you off." I head for the deck stairs. "I will talk to Eric and Yolanda."

"Start with Yolanda. She's in the forest."

I pause midstep. "What?"

"She snuck off. I saw it from my perch. That's what I came to tell you."

I glare at him. "You mean that's the lead you were holding hostage until you got what you wanted."

He lifts his hands. "Hey, I didn't hold out for a promise. Just a good-faith show of intent."

"You want to prove yourself? Find Eric. Tell him to meet me at the path."

"How about the other guy? Will? He seems cool. Can I tell him?"

"If he's the one you see first, yes. Otherwise, talk to Eric. He doesn't bite."

CHAPTER TWENTY-EIGHT

I'm not surprised when it's Anders who joins me at the mouth of the trail.

"Gunnar said you need backup. Eric was just over by the commissary, but he said you wanted me."

I shake my head. "He thinks Eric feels threatened by him. Sexually threatened."

When Anders stops laughing, I add, "Also, I am clearly with Eric for the money," which sends him into a fresh gale of laughter.

"I've always wondered that myself," he says. "If it's not money, what is it?"

"His outsized . . . personality."

Anders chokes on another laugh. There had been a time, before I got together with Dalton, that Anders and I had flirted with the idea of being more than friends. It'd been tempting. He's an amazing guy, and I couldn't remember ever being so damned comfortable with someone. But that comfort comes from the kinship of meeting someone and clicking because you see so much of yourself in them. We even have a matched set of emotional baggage. For friendship, it was the perfect recipe. Anything else would have been disastrous.

"Gunnar is just a little bit extra, isn't he?" Anders says.

"That is an excellent way of putting it. At least he likes *you*."

"I am very likable."

Storm stops and looks up at me. I'd had Gunnar grab Anders instead of doing it myself because I needed a moment to get a scent marker for Yolanda. I'd seen a sweater she'd left behind in the town hall, and I have that now. Storm has been following the trail but now looks up and then turns to the left, where a faint path branches off the main one.

"Good girl," I say. "Go on."

She leads us along that secondary path, and we fall silent as we head deeper into the forest. It's ten thirty and while it's light in town, the trees bring dusk early here.

I lower my voice. "How are you doing?"

"Excellent, really. Seeing my sister's family . . ." He inhales. "I dreaded that, as much as I wanted to see them. I think part of me was hiding in Rockton, and I want it to be different now. I think it can be." He glances over. "How are you doing? I know this isn't how you planned your arrival."

"It's not, but the town is . . . well, perfect. Except for the unexpectedly early arrival of dead bodies."

"Worst welcoming-committee gift ever."

"No kidding."

We go quiet, knowing our voices carry. When I catch the crackle of undergrowth, I whisper for Anders to retreat. We all do, as quickly and quietly as we can, until I find a spot to easily leave the path. We take it, and I crouch in the shadows with my arm looped over Storm.

A moment later, a figure appears on the path we just left. It's Yolanda, heading back toward town.

Anders gives me a questioning look, but I shake my head. I don't want to confront her. I want to see where she went.

We wait until she's far enough past us that she won't hear any sound of our passage. Then we return to the path and continue along it. We keep going for a least a half mile.

"Is the mining camp this way?" Anders asks.

I point behind us.

He sighs. "My sense of direction has not improved."

We are indeed heading away from Mark's camp—and away from Penny's trail and where we found Denise and where Lilith found Bruno.

Finally, when we've gone another quarter mile, Anders slows and inhales. "Is that . . . ?"

I take a deep breath. "Pot smoke?"

"Could be a skunk," he says. Then he makes a face. "Right. No skunks up here. You'd think I'd remember that after five years."

I pat his back. "You are brilliant at so many things, but there's a reason Eric doesn't like you going into the forest alone."

"Yeah, yeah. But that is pot smoke, right?"

"Yes, and if this is Yolanda's big secret, I am going to throttle her."

"Eric might beat you to it." Anders pushes aside a branch to let us pass. "We had a talk about that. He knows you're right not to push, but it's killing him to just let it drop. This can't be the answer, though, right? She's not going to interfere with an investigation to hide the fact that she's indulging in a legal narcotic."

"I'd like to say no, but the problem might be that she's doing it for stress relief, and she doesn't want anyone to know she's stressed. She's a woman in charge of a big job in a typically male environment. She needs to seem invulnerable. No emotions. No stress."

"I guess so."

"The more likely explanation, though, is that she's meeting someone, and they're the one smoking up."

"Smoking up?" He snickers. "Does anyone still say that?"

I lift my middle finger. "You know what I mean. The secret is not the smoking. It's who she's meeting, and they smell like cannabis smoke. I've caught a whiff of it in town. We were allowing it in moderation, like alcohol. Edibles were preferred—to avoid the issue of smoke—but it wasn't prohibited."

"Presuming it's regulated, though, you should be able to find out who's been requisitioning it, which will . . ."

Storm has stopped again and is politely suggesting we may want to veer to the left. We follow her and the smell gets stronger.

"Yeah, that's not lingering on clothing," Anders says. "Someone was smoking, and not that long ago."

When Storm stops a few meters in, we find ourselves in a small clearing with a log that seems to serve as a chair, given the boot prints on one side of it. I'm examining those when Anders says, "And what do we have here?"

I turn as he pulls out a backpack that had been hidden in thick undergrowth. I take it and carefully open it. Inside, I can see a shirt and jeans, reeking of pot smoke.

"That is private property," a voice says behind us.

Yolanda walks into the clearing and puts out her hands.

I lift the backpack but keep my hold on it. "So you are confirming that this is yours?"

Her eyes narrow before she forces the look away and gives a short "Yes."

"You have been coming into the forest, changing your clothing and smoking cannabis?"

"Yes."

"And this is your big secret? The one that you couldn't share with me, even in confidence, instead forcing me to consider you a primary suspect when a few words would have cleared up the misunderstanding."

She says nothing.

"Seriously?" I shake the bag. "You know this is legal in Canada, right? That no one would give a shit about it, and if you were really concerned about your image, you could have brought in edibles?"

"Edibles don't work for me." She turns to Anders. "You can leave now, Deputy. Take the dog back to town. Casey and I will return together."

He looks at her and then laughs. "Uh, no."

"I need to speak to her in private."

"Then you'll come back to town and do so there. This 'secret' of yours doesn't make any sense, so I'm sure as hell not leaving you here with Casey. If you're concerned about me sharing whatever you tell her, my record speaks for itself. I know how to keep a confidence."

"When you're sober, maybe, but I am aware you have a drinking problem."

He stares at her. "Wow. That's . . ."

"Blunt? Yes. And no, your friends didn't tell me. I need to know who I'm working with, and that is important data, which I obtained."

"All right then. I have a problem. I could say I haven't had more than an evening beer in nearly two years, but that'd be none of your business. Your concern is that I might not keep my mouth shut when I'm drunk, but if that was an issue, how long do you think I'd have lasted as town deputy?"

"That was out of line, Yolanda," I say. "But obviously Will is right. No matter how incredible he is as a deputy, Eric would have let him go long ago if he had a problem keeping confidentiality. I respect your right to privacy. I really do. But you've been throwing your weight around, blocking me on an investigation that you claim to want. If you insist on privacy for this discussion, then we're having it back in town, because I'm not staying out here alone with you."

"Fine." She takes the backpack from me and returns it to its hiding spot. "Let's go."

CHAPTER TWENTY-NINE

Once we're in town, I expect Yolanda will want to talk at the town hall or—for added privacy—our house outside town. Instead, she heads to the clinic.

"April will be in there," I say. "She'll have gone to bed by now. It's after eleven."

"Then I would like to wake her for this conversation."

I'm about to comment on that when I see a light on in the clinic. "Looks like she's up late."

I leave Storm with Anders, and the two of them set out to find Dalton.

The clinic front door is open, but when I go inside, the one between the waiting room and the clinic is locked. That's why Gunnar hadn't barged in earlier. April has been locking it with a note telling people that it is past clinic hours and if they have an emergency, they are to ring the bell on the rear door instead.

I double-check that light emanates from under the door. Inside, a cupboard door clicks shuts.

"April?" I say.

No answer. The squeak of a shoe on the floor, which she

insisted be easy-to-clean linoleum. I glance over my shoulder at Yolanda. Then I reach for my gun.

"April?" I say.

Still no answer. Gun in hand, I consider my options. If there's someone inside, the back door must be unlocked. But would April leave it that way after the other night?

I turn to Yolanda and whisper, "Do you have the key—?"

The door opens, April standing there. Her gaze drops to my gun.

"You are lucky I'm the one who opened the door, Casey," she says. "We have a killer in town. You don't want to be sneaking about carrying your gun."

"I'm carrying my gun because I thought it wasn't you behind that door. You didn't answer me."

"I was in the middle of a task." She looks at Yolanda. "It is rather late, but as long as you are here, I will require an assistant tomorrow morning."

"An assistant for what?" I ask.

"Unpacking, of course. I realize we are on a tight schedule, and I wish to complete my unpacking so that I may assist with other tasks."

"You don't need to—"

"I will," she says, lifting her chin. "Kenny is arriving in two days, and he is unfamiliar with the construction crew and will require an aide he is comfortable with."

"Ah." I look at Yolanda. "April has a point. If you can spare someone for a few hours, we should do that."

"Three hours," April says. "Up to four, if you send me someone incompetent. But I would like Nanette, and she will do it in three."

Yolanda looks ready to argue. Kenny doesn't actually need April as his carpentry aide. This is about April, and if my sister wants something—wants it enough to make up excuses—then I'm making sure she gets it.

At the last second, Yolanda bites back whatever she'd been about to say and instead mutters, "Fine. Whatever."

Yolanda prods me into the room and shuts the door behind us.

"It is very late," April says.

"I have Parkinson's."

April frowns. "You think you have—"

"No, I have it. Diagnosed last year."

April's frown grows. "This was not disclosed to me." She looks my way. "Why was this not disclosed to me? Parkinson's disease is a serious condition, and I presume it is still early, given her age, but I still needed to know this."

I throw up my hands.

"No one knows," Yolanda says. "It's a private medical matter, between me and my doctor."

"*I* am your doctor, for all intents and purposes at this moment, and thus I needed to know it." April pauses. "I believe Casey did mention mild prosopagnosia. That is a potential—though rare—symptom. Parkinson's is also rare among people from the African diaspora. Are you certain of the diagnosis?"

"Very certain. My grandfather—Émilie's husband—had it. A special little gift from that side of my family."

"I'm sorry," I say. "I really am, but presuming that's why you're smoking cannabis, I still don't see the need for that level of secrecy."

"My grandfather's disease nearly destroyed Gran. To see him like that, with all their money, all their connections, and nothing she could do. You know what happened to Petra, right? Gran swooped in and saved her when she was ready to give up. Well, after Pops died, I did that for Gran. Everyone else saw what she wanted them to see—a tough old bird who'd accepted his decision to end his life and made her peace with it. I saw the truth."

She walks to the window and looks out, her back to us. "I dropped everything to stay with her because I was terrified of losing her, too. And now I'm supposed to go to her and say I have the same thing? At my age? Hell, no. I am not telling her, and part of that is because I won't do that to her, but part of it is because I don't want to spend the rest of my life undergoing whatever radical new treatments she finds for me, and I don't want her spending her last years looking for them. You better believe I'm hoping for those treatments, and I'll take whatever my doctor suggests, but if this is the fates cutting my lifeline short, then I'm making the most of what I have left."

Yolanda turns to face us. "And that was a bit of a speech, wasn't it?"

"I'll need to know your current treatment regime," April says.

Yolanda looks at her and laughs. "I like you, Dr. Butler."

April's brows knit. "That's . . . good. But I still need to know your regimen, in detail, as well as having access to your medical files. Presuming you have not had a checkup in months, that will be the first order of business. I realize you will not want to surrender that time, given your current schedule, but I insist."

"Yes, ma'am."

"You are aware that I specialize in neuroscience, which means I am very conversant in the nature of your disease? You may discuss it with me and expect a professional level of comprehension."

"Always good."

"Casey mentioned cannabis. I presume that means you have tremors."

"Mild ones."

"And the cannabis helps?"

"It does."

"Good. We will discuss that." She looks between us. "Is there anything else?"

"I can leave if you two want to discuss it further," I say.

"No," April says. "It is late, and I am going to bed."

We say good night. Then we step out onto the porch.

As the door closes behind us, Yolanda says, "I won't apologize for disrupting your investigations."

"And I won't apologize for outing your medical condition. You could have just told me that you were going into the forest to smoke cannabis for a medical condition. I might have insisted on seeing actual evidence of cannabis, but it's an odd enough excuse that I would have accepted it."

"I couldn't trust that."

"So you made sure I couldn't trust you." I shake my head. "Whatever. I'll keep your secret. It's none of my business. I'll tell Eric what you were doing out there and that it's a medical condition, and he'll leave it at that."

She nods abruptly and walks away, chin up, gaze forward. I watch her go, and then I set off to find my husband and my dog and get home.

Dalton accepts the explanation, as I knew he would. As I would have, too. I understand why she doesn't want Émilie knowing, even if I question how long she can sustain that secret.

Parkinson's is a terrible disease. I've never known anyone who had it, but I remember a coworker whose mother did, and I recall the stories he confided in me when we worked together. Why confide in *me*? It happened sometimes. I was a woman in a job with a lot of men, and if they mistook my gender for a sign that I'd be a good listener, empathetic and understanding, well . . . well, I guess that wouldn't be entirely wrong, even if it's not how I see myself. I did listen. I did empathize. I did understand. Does that mean I'll cut Yolanda slack? Not a chance, because that's the last thing she'll want.

In all that excitement, I temporarily forgot what I found on Bruno. Dalton and I discuss that, too. Without a DNA test, I cannot absolutely say it's Denise's blood. But it could be, and if so, then that plus the dirt on his knees suggests he knelt beside her as she was dying, her blood soaking the ground.

If Bruno is the killer, then there's no justice to find here, and that comes with something like relief. Denise was collateral damage. That's horrible, and I feel for her and for her poor husband. She came to surprise him, and she stumbled on a plot to steal his claim. She may even have tried to defend that claim, threatening Bruno with her little pocketknife. He took it and—in the panic of seeing his prize disappearing—stabbed her before he knew what he was doing. Or stabbed her to defend himself. Or stabbed her with all due forethought, making a cold and vicious choice. Whatever the answer, he has paid the price.

That still leaves Bruno's partner in the wind. And our architect in the forest. Are those things connected? They must be, but I'm no closer to a definitive answer to that question than I was this morning.

CHAPTER THIRTY

Over an early breakfast on the back deck, we plan our day. Dalton wants to start a more systematic search for Penny. We know where she went, and we've been focused on that area—and, to be bluntly honest, on hoping to stumble over her while pursuing Bruno or Denise's case. We both need more before we give her up for lost. Our chances of finding her alive are slim, but as guilty as we feel about that, it's unlikely we'd have seen a different outcome if we found her on day one. If she is, somehow, just wandering around the forest, then with the warm weather and plentiful fresh water, she'll still be out there. But that is not the scenario either of us expect.

Option one is that she overheard Bruno and his partner, and they killed her. But that also seems to have been Denise's fate. How likely is it that two women both overheard a plot—in the middle of the Yukon wilderness—and were both murdered for it . . . their bodies left in different places?

No, option two is seeming increasingly likely. Penny is Bruno's partner. She went out to meet him at Mark's mining site. Denise found Bruno—or both of them—and died for it. Penny pushed Bruno off a cliff and then met with him outside town and has been hiding ever since. In that scenario, there is still one permutation where she is not a cold-blooded killer: if she saw Bruno murder Denise and that's why she pushed him off a cliff and now, not realizing he's dead, she's in hiding from *him*.

Whatever the answer, we cannot devote all our time to finding her. Nor can we abandon her. So we come up with a plan, one that will see us working on the construction project until midmorning, and then heading out for three hours to search, returning to the project and going back out to search another grid after dinner. At this time of year, we have the advantage of increasingly long days of sunlight, meaning we can hunt for Penny while still putting in an eight-hour shift for Yolanda.

Between Anders, Dalton, and myself, only Dalton is truly adept with a hammer and saw. Anders and I are suburban kids, who grew up taking coding classes instead of woodworking. We expected to follow our parents' example of calling in experts for repair work. Oh, we can manage the basics, like a clogged toilet, but here we're mostly going to get in the way. Dalton takes on general crew work, while Anders and I are on hand to fetch tools and carry wood and "hold this."

It's nearly time for Dalton and me to leave when a scream rips across town. I drop a plank and run, Storm rousing from her doze to charge along after me.

A voice rises from one of the residences. A man's voice, babbling in panic.

It's the men's residence, and there are several people working inside—the building is only partially finished, and completion has been prioritized so this can house the new arrivals. As I swing through the door, footfalls thud behind me and I glance to see Dalton.

We tell Storm to wait outside—along with a handful of

others who've raced over to see what's happening. Inside the door, we pause and listen.

"I don't know what you're talking about," the man's voice says. The French accent tells me it's Pierre.

"Don't give me that bullshit. Where is she?"

Is that Nanette? Another woman's voice comes, telling them both to calm down, but Nanette tells her to step aside.

Dalton and I proceed down the hall. Most of the doors are shut. Three at the end stand open. As I near the first, I can tell the voices are farther down, and I'm about to pass when I see someone in that first open room. It's Gunnar, holding a drill. He raises his hands and shakes his head, as if to say he has no idea what's going on.

"Stay in here," I whisper.

He gives me a thumbs-up, and Dalton and I continue on. Pierre and Nanette continue to argue, variations on what I've already heard. Nanette is accusing him of something, and he has no idea what she means.

The next open room is empty, but there's a drill on the floor, with scattered screws around it, as if someone dropped it fast and ran.

As we approach the last door, Dalton falls back in behind me. Neither of us has our gun on us—that's not the message we want to send in town. If this sounded dangerous, I'd send Dalton to grab it, but from what I hear, it's only an argument.

I angle myself where I can peek in without being spotted . . . and I see my mistake. Pierre is in the corner, holding what looks like a level, his hands raised. There's another woman—one I haven't had much contact with—backed against another wall. And Nanette stands in front of Pierre, wielding a scalpel from the clinic.

There's no time to retreat and grab a weapon, and I wouldn't anyway. That would only make things worse. I lift my own hands and step into the room.

"Nanette?" I say calmly. "Can you please tell me what's going on here?"

She doesn't look my way. Her attention is on Pierre.

"He knows what happened to Penny," she says. "He did something to her."

"I don't know what—" Pierre begins.

"Pierre?" I say. "I'll speak to you in a moment. First, I'm asking Nanette what's going on."

"She's holding a knife on me," he says. "That's what's going on. This crazy—"

"That's not helping," I say. "Nanette?"

Pierre cuts in before she can answer. "Aren't you going to tell her to put down the weapon? She's holding me at *knifepoint*."

This is not exactly true. She's three feet from him, and I recognize that stance. I'd been in her shoes fourteen years ago, holding a weapon on someone to show him I was serious. To confront him with what he'd done and scare the shit out of him and make him admit it.

I'd had no intention of hurting him. The weapon was just a prop. It was a mistake, a horrible mistake that I will never forgive myself for, but that is not what's happening here. A scalpel isn't a gun. She's not going to pull the trigger in a moment of blind rage, and I've eased forward enough to grab her if she lunges.

"Nanette?" I prompt again. "Tell me what's going on."

She lifts her free hand. A necklace dangles from it.

"I found this in a clinic drawer while I was helping your sister. It's Penny's."

When Pierre tries to protest, she waves the necklace at the other woman. "Is this Penny's?"

"It is," says the other woman. "She always wore it."

"And now she's gone, and it was stuffed at the back of a drawer. A locked drawer. One that only Pierre had the key for."

"Then how did *you* get it open?" Pierre says. "I gave the keys to the new doctor. She had access to that drawer. So did you, obviously."

"If I put it there, would I be here confronting you with it? And it sure as hell wasn't Dr. Butler, who arrived two days after Penny disappeared."

"All right," I say. "We can resolve this easily enough. I'll fingerprint the necklace. If Pierre didn't take it, his fingerprints won't be on it."

I'm bullshitting, of course. It's a chain with a pendant the size of a dime. The chance of getting a usable fingerprint is laughable, but panic crosses Pierre's face.

"Fine," he says. "Yes, I put it in there."

"And then lied?" Nanette says.

"Nanette?" I say. "Can I ask you to lower that scalpel and let me handle this, please? He's admitted to it."

"To taking the necklace. Not to hurting her."

"I *didn't* hurt her," Pierre says. "I had nothing to do with her disappearing. That's why I lied about the necklace. If you'd come to me and asked—without threatening my life—I'd have told the truth. I wasn't going to admit it while you were holding a knife on me, ranting and raving."

"*Pierre,*" I say sharply. "That's enough. I didn't hear ranting and raving."

"Nanette did ask him calmly," the other woman says. "He denied it. That's when she pulled out the scalpel."

"She caught me off guard," Pierre says. "I didn't understand what she meant at first. She was talking about me having something of Penny's, and I had no idea what she meant. I found a necklace outside the clinic, and I put it in the locked drawer, planning to turn it over to Yolanda, but then Penny and Bruno went missing and with everything that came after that, I forgot about it."

"You didn't know it was Penny's?" Nanette says.

"Of course not. If I did, I'd have turned it over after she disappeared."

"You seriously didn't recognize it?"

Nanette lifts the necklace toward me. When I reach out, she passes it over. It's a very old Roman coin in a gold bezel.

"Kind of distinctive, huh?" Nanette says. "More than one person asked her about it. In grad school, she'd worked on a project in Rome, finding ways to keep an ancient building from toppling over. Everyone said her plan wouldn't work, so she backed down, and after a few things failed, they tried her idea and it did the trick. The necklace was a reminder to have faith in her work."

"I never saw it," Pierre says. "I'm sorry."

"He's lying," Nanette says.

"I don't memorize jewelry—"

"—on women you chase even after they very sweetly—but firmly—turn you down?"

"Can confirm," says a voice behind us. It's Gunnar, still holding his drill. "I saw Penny shoo Pierre off multiple times. Guy didn't take a hint."

Dalton grunts in annoyance. He's been quiet, but now he's looking at me, knowing how I'll react.

"And no one saw fit to tell me this?" I say. "When I was going around asking whether there was any conflict between Penny and other members of the crew."

"I wouldn't call it conflict," Gunnar says. When I glare, he raises his hands in a gesture of surrender. "Fine, yeah, he pestered

Penny, but so did a few other guys and they all backed off weeks ago, including Pierre."

"I wasn't pestering," Pierre says. "I was interested and letting her know it. When she wasn't interested back, I gave up."

"Only after Kendra staged an intervention," the other woman mutters. She looks at me. "No one mentioned it because, for women on a job, it's par for the course. Kendra told him he was overstepping, and he backed off."

"Or he *seemed* to," Nanette says. "But now there's this necklace."

I turn to Dalton. "Would you escort Pierre to the station? Gunnar, can you please tell Kendra I need to speak to her."

"I didn't do anything," Pierre says.

"If we were sure you did, you'd be going in handcuffs," I say. "You're being taken in for questioning. Nanette? You'll be at the clinic?"

"I will."

"I'll check in with you if I need more."

"Isn't she being arrested or something?" Pierre says. "She threatened me with a knife."

Dalton takes his arm. "You don't admit to something when asked nicely? You'll be asked a lot less nicely the next time. Remember that when Detective Butler is questioning you."

CHAPTER THIRTY-ONE

I interrogate Pierre. He sticks to his story. Yes, he found Penny attractive. Yes, he pursued her. But once he realized she really wasn't interested, he backed off. Okay, Kendra may have talked to him about it, but that's just because he misunderstood Penny's signals and thought he was making progress. Once he discovered otherwise, he backed down in embarrassment.

Then he found the necklace and, no, he really *didn't* realize it was Penny's. He found it out behind the clinic. The clasp was broken. He brought it inside and locked it away, since it seemed valuable. That was the morning after Penny and Bruno disappeared, but at the time, he hadn't heard the news, and he'd been working in the clinic. When the news came, he never made the connection and forgot all about the necklace.

Do I believe him? I think I can buy the possibility he didn't recognize it as Penny's necklace. Others noticed it because it was interesting, but it's not as if it was a five-inch disk. The rest is harder to swallow. He finds a broken necklace, and when he hears that a woman is missing, he never thinks that might be connected? Yet the story we've heard is that Penny was seen going into the forest on her own. A broken necklace suggests abduction, and no one has suggested that.

So what does the necklace mean?

Could Penny's disappearance be unconnected to her walk in the forest? Could she have come back and then been attacked as she reentered town? Could Pierre have attacked her, found the broken necklace later, and stuffed it into a locked drawer, knowing only he had that key? Or could he have taken it as a souvenir?

I don't like the part where everyone seems to have known Pierre was pestering Penny, and yet I can't pretend I'm surprised that no one thought it was significant. Kendra apologizes and feels terrible, but he wasn't the first guy she had to speak to about "overactively pursuing" a member of the crew. She also had to warn a woman who was pursuing a guy.

In Pierre's case, it was garden-variety pestering. He was interested and wasn't taking no for an answer until someone told him to cut that shit out. Penny hadn't been fazed by it. Just uncomfortable and feeling a little guilty that a guy was so interested and she wasn't willing to "give him a chance."

I have Pierre show me where he supposedly found the necklace. It was caught on a bush right behind the clinic. I search for signs of any disturbance there. Marks on the ground? Broken twigs? When I find nothing, I call Dalton over. He also declares there's nothing. Next up is Storm. We give her a scent marker for Penny, and she finds nothing.

All this makes Pierre's story more than a little suspect, but he swears by it. He was at the clinic for two early appointments—verified by those who had the appointments—and between the two, he stepped onto the back porch for a coffee. He saw the necklace glittering in the bush, retrieved it, and figured a couple had been fooling around in the forest and it broke. His next appointment arrived, so he took the necklace inside and stuffed it into the locked drawer and then forgot about it.

I don't know what to make of this. Unfortunately, I seem to be in the minority. Nanette has already spread the story of the necklace, as has the other woman who'd been there, and Gunnar has done his part confirming it.

The only person not calling for Pierre's head seems to be me. Okay, Dalton and Anders agree that we need additional evidence before taking him into custody, and Kendra is more worried about the mob mentality, as is Yolanda—the latter being less "worried" than "pissed off."

Kenny is due to arrive tomorrow, and he's taking over the carpentry from Pierre, so Yolanda wants him on that plane out. His presence is now too distracting to the others.

We try to eat lunch in the commissary, but the continual stream of people demanding to know what we plan to do about "that man" has us retreating to our house to eat. Anders volunteers as Pierre's personal assistant, helping him with his work while keeping him safe from the others.

Dalton and I settle on the back porch with the remains of our lunch. Dalton kicks back, feet up, beer in hand.

"Nickel for your thoughts," I say.

"They aren't worth that much."

"Yolanda might be right," I say. "Ship Pierre out tomorrow. Make sure everyone knows he's under house arrest down south and hasn't escaped justice. That fixes the disruption, but if he did actually hurt Penny, then we've shipped out the only person who knows where to find her body."

"Yep."

"And if he didn't, then she's still out there, and I'm left focused on investigating Pierre rather than hunting for her."

"Yep."

"You know you're not helping, right?"

"I do believe I already evaluated the value of my opinion in this matter at less than a nickel." He takes another slug of his beer. "I can't get a read on Pierre. I don't like his attitude, but being whiny and defensive isn't a crime. I don't like the story about the necklace, either, especially when there's nothing to suggest an altercation there, but it also makes sense. Guy goes out. Spots it. Brings it in, stuffs it away, and forgets it. Could he have not noticed it on a woman he liked? Hell, when you first came to Rockton, I certainly noticed you. First because you pissed me off. Then because I wanted to figure you out. Then because I found you utterly compelling, as much as I didn't want to."

"Thanks . . ."

"But despite all that—and working side by side—it took me a while to notice you were wearing a necklace. I don't think I'm a clueless guy, but I wasn't interested in your jewelry."

"I think the only thing I can do right now is contact Émilie and have her set an investigator on Pierre's backstory. I know there was a basic background check but let's see if there's any history of predatory—"

Storm lifts her head from the deck and growls, her gaze fixed on the forest. I peer into it, but see nothing. The dog pushes to her feet, still growling, head lowered. Something is out there. Something or someone.

Dalton gets to his feet first. He peers into the forest and then grunts and plunks back into his chair. "If this is a social call, don't be lurking around the forest, making our dog nervous."

"I am not lurking," a voice says. "I am approaching at a measured pace. Also, I am not the one making your dog nervous."

Storm moves to the edge of the back deck, hair on end as she growls. The source of unease glides into view. Lilith's gray wolf, Nero. The woman herself follows. When Nero reaches the clearing behind our house, she says something to him and he stops.

"May we approach?" she asks.

I lay a hand on Storm's head as I murmur that it's all right. The wolf enters the yard, with Lilith beside him. They stop again at the edge of the porch.

"May I?" she asks.

When I nod, she asks Nero to stay, and she climbs onto the back deck. Her gaze goes to the beer bottles.

"Would you like one?" I ask.

"I would. Thank you."

I go inside and take one from the icebox, which is a deep storage space under the floorboards. Permafrost is a pain in the ass for building, but it's a wonder for refrigeration.

When I bring out the bottle, she says, "That must be expensive, flying in cases of beer."

I hand it to her. "We won't be. We brought in these for the bottles, which will be cleaned and refilled by our local brewmaster, who has her own recipe."

"Local brewmaster?" She shakes her head. "Millennials."

She opens the beer and settles into a chair. Storm sits on the edge of the deck, watching Nero, who has settled onto the ground, head resting on his paws. When Storm shifts position, his ears twitch, the only sign that, as calm as he looks, he's watching this potential threat to his human.

Lilith examines the back wall of our cabin. "That is wonderful craftsmanship."

"I could say the same about your place. I've already asked Eric to paint woodland critters on this one for me."

He snorts and chugs his beer.

"I wouldn't," she says. "On this style of home, it would look like one of those van murals. Well-intentioned and enthusiastically done but . . . ill-advised. Stick to whimsical woven creatures peeking from the grass."

"You make me whimsical woven creatures, and I'll keep that bottle refilled."

She smiles and shakes her head. "Trading already. I'd be flattered if I didn't know you're just eager to prove yourselves advantageous neighbors before I fly down on my broomstick and turn you all into hares."

"Rabbits," I say. "Or goons."

That makes her laugh, even as Dalton frowns.

"It's a children's song," I explain to him.

"But in that version, I'd be a good fairy, which I am not," Lilith says.

"I bet you could be, though, with generous offerings of handcrafted beer and other luxuries unavailable to forest dwellers, even successful nature photographers."

Her brows rise. "Look at you, Sherlocking all over the place."

"I got a hint on the photography, though it made me recall that part of your house didn't have windows. A darkroom. Nature photography is the obvious answer up here. Successful is a guess based on those boots."

"Can you tell what I had for lunch, too?"

"Cold beer, taken from an underground icebox, enjoyed on a sunny wooden deck. It may eventually be accompanied by a smoked salmon sandwich, but I'm not as good at seeing into the future."

"Well, if that sandwich is a serious offer, I'll take it, and then I will end the socializing part of my visit and get to business."

Dalton rises and heads inside to fix the sandwich. Storm also rises and seems to contemplate descending to the yard. She hops off the other end of the deck, far enough away from the wolf so she can approach slowly.

"Is that all right?" I say, gesturing at her.

"Nero has little experience with other canines, but he is not a nervous beast. This is her territory, and he will respect that."

I watch as Storm lumbers over, only to stop a few feet away.

Lilith waves at them. "You don't need to worry so much about her. She is as careful as her people. May I ask how old she is?"

"Three. And Nero?"

"About the same."

The wolf lifts his head to sniff the air and then lowers it again. Storm approaches and circles him, sniffing from a distance.

"Has she encountered wolves in the wild?" Lilith asks.

"A few. Most keep their distance, though she did have one who was very interested, and she thought that was great . . . until she realized he wasn't looking for friendship. She was in heat."

"Ah, the plight of being female. A male seems friendly. You entertain the hope of frolicking through the forest, only to discover that he just wants to jump you."

"Right? So she's being careful right now. Also she's not in heat, which helps. She does have a canine friend, though, and he's at least half wolf. A similar situation to Nero's—we found him as a puppy, his mother dead."

"Is he here? Nero might react a little more strongly to a young male."

I shake my head. "He'll be coming, but probably not until later this year."

Dalton brings out a plate with a flatbread salmon sandwich, two kinds of pickles, and homemade potato chips.

"You're hired," she says as she takes it. "I like my dinner at seven."

He shakes his head and drops back into his chair.

Lilith takes two bites of the sandwich. Then she sets the plate on her lap and reaches into a small backpack at her feet. She extracts a homemade leather bag and passes it over.

I open the bag and pull out a woman's glove.

"I found that early this morning," she says. "I thought it might belong to your missing woman."

It's a woman's knitted glove. Not expensive, but warm. We'd bought them by the boxful for the crew.

"Is it yours?" she asks.

"Our brand, yes. Presumably from one of our women workers."

"Can't be many of those on a construction site."

"Two-thirds, actually. But there's an easy way to check this one."

I head into the house and come back out with the bag containing Penny's scent marker, along with two more gloves, which I'd taken from the stockroom for my own use. I set all three gloves on the deck.

"Storm?" I say.

She circles wide around Nero and hops back onto the deck. I hold out the scent marker. Then I point at the three gloves and ask if any of them belong to the same person. Nero rises and watches with interest as she delicately sniffs one glove and then the second and then the third. She returns and touches her nose to one and then looks at me.

"That's Penny's," I say as I give Storm a thank-you pat. "Where did you find it?"

"Between the miner's camp and the mountain."

"Can you take us there, please?"

"If I can get a jar of these pickles to go."

CHAPTER THIRTY-TWO

We're in the area where Lilith found the glove. When we near it, she stops and surveys the landscape. Nero gives the slightest grunt, as if hating to interrupt her train of thought. Then he walks three paces to the left and looks into the forest.

"Yes, of course," she says. "Thank you, Nero."

We follow them in. Storm is sticking close to me, and it feels fifty percent like protection and fifty percent like a child hanging close to her mother in the face of other, unfamiliar children. When we've gone about ten paces, Storm stops and gives a low growl. Nero looks back, as if startled that this seemingly calm canine has randomly decided to threaten him. Then he sees that she's looking into the forest.

Nero takes a step in that direction. I do, too, so I can see past a thick tree trunk. When something moves, I stop. It's a fox, maybe ten feet away, tall and leggy and staring at Storm. Nero makes a noise, and the fox's attention swings that way. It looks between the two bigger canines. Then it turns and runs.

Storm gives a harrumph of satisfaction. Nero looks from her to the fleeing fox, and she does the same, gaze swinging from one to the other, as if saying "Aren't you going to chase that?" When the answer is clearly no on both sides, I swear they nod in satisfaction, as if both recognizing the other as a reasonable and civilized beast, one who will warn a fox away from their people, but does not see the smaller canine as either a threat or a plaything.

"So polite," Lilith says. "I am terribly fond of Newfoundlands. We had two growing up. You could not ask for a better temperament in a dog. Less slobber, perhaps, but not a better temperament."

"Less slobbering *and* less shedding," I say.

She smiles. "That, too. Now, the spot is just up here. I can see the marker."

When I peer ahead, I see it—a strip of bright yellow ribbon tied to a tree. She takes us over and bends to point at the undergrowth.

"I found it there," she says. "I also found signs of passage heading toward the mountain, but Nero isn't a scent dog, and I lost the trail once it hit open ground."

I take Penny's scent marker from its bag and show it to Storm. She barely sniffs it—she recognizes that this is the scent I'm interested in from the glove. But when she snuffles around, she takes longer than I expect. Then she whines and looks at me.

"Could the trail be too old?" Lilith asks.

I'm thinking when Dalton, who has been nearly silent since we left Haven's Rock, takes the scent bag from me and seals it. He puts it back into my bag while making sure Storm is watching. Then he bends beside the faint trail leading toward the mountain and gives her the command to follow *any* scent she picks up.

She looks from Lilith to Nero, and Dalton shakes his head. "No, not theirs. Anything else? Scent? Follow?"

She grunts in understanding and a little relief. He's not asking her to follow the trail of the woman with the glove, which is good because she doesn't smell it. He's also not asking her to follow the trail of the wolf and woman standing there, because that would be very odd. Her task is simply to play an old game. Find a human scent trail and follow it.

As we set out, Dalton and Storm take the lead. I fall back with Lilith.

"Your dog is telling us the woman's scent isn't on that trail," she says.

"Correct," I say.

"Which means someone else had her glove?"

"Possibly, though I think the answer is that Penny didn't lose it. It fell off."

"Fell off?"

"While someone was carrying her." I pause. "Carrying her body."

Once Storm understands that she is free to follow a trail that does not belong to the missing woman, she has no trouble tracking whoever came this way. She keeps going another couple of hundred feet, up the rock at the mountain base. Then she stops and looks up. Rock juts skyward, a slab too perpendicular for Storm to climb.

"Cave," Dalton says.

I glance back. He's retreated fifteen feet and is shielding his eyes as he looks up. I walk beside him and do the same. When I see nothing, he boosts me, over my protest and Lilith's soft laugh. It works, though, and I see the dark shape of a cave opening.

We ask Storm to stay with Lilith. Then we both scrabble up the rock to the cave opening. It's just big enough for a person to fit through. Dalton takes out his flashlight and shines it in. The tunnel floor slants downward for about ten feet. Then it drops into darkness.

"I'll go in," I say.

He hands me the flashlight. "Stay at the top."

"I know."

I leave my pack on the ground. Then I crawl in. It's big enough for that, though it soon narrows to the point where I need to hunker down into more of a slither. As the tunnel floor tilts more, I lift my hands to brace against the wall so I don't slide all the way down into the hole up ahead. I touch something tacky and pull my hand back under the light.

I shine the beam on the wall to see a smear of dried blood.

As if someone had been struggling to move a body through the tunnel, pushing or dragging it.

Pushing or dragging Penny. Her corpse.

I'm careful to avoid that blood smear. If I don't find a body, I'm going to need to come back and take a sample.

A little farther, and I reach the drop-off. It's a straight-down chute, and as I peer into it, the clock rewinds to another cave, one where a killer had stashed the bodies of women he'd been holding captive.

I need to take a moment and steel myself before I look down. When I do, I see ash-blond hair, and rage fills me. I ball my fists and resist punching the wall. Another moment to compose myself, and then I shine the flashlight down.

It's Penny. This time, there is no mistaking her. The chute opens up after the drop-off, and at the bottom, twenty feet down, it's wide enough for her body to lie on its side, fetal position, knees drawn in. There's something by her hand. A dark object that I can't make out. There are pieces of what looks like aluminum foil nearby, catching the light.

Garbage, I realize. Someone must have used this tunnel for climbing and dumped garbage down there. Which is still odd.

Something about this is *very* odd, and while my brain keeps returning to those wrappers, I push that aside and stare down at Penny's body and—

The positioning. Her killer dropped her down that chute. She should be sprawled at the bottom, not lying so neatly in that position, as if . . .

As if she hadn't been dead.

I can make out the dark object now. It's a water canteen. Penny is lying, fetal position, at the bottom of a pit with a water canteen and what looks like protein-bar wrappers.

Empty wrappers.

Heart hammering, I lean in as far as I dare and lower the flashlight. I shine it on Penny's face. It's completely still. Strands of hair hang over it. Hair that isn't moving with breath. I shine the light on her neck. No pulse that I can see. Same as her chest. She is completely still.

We're too late.

She was alive, and now she is not, and we pissed around conducting a half-assed search for her while we rescued a guy who is probably a killer and identified a dead woman who has nothing to do with us. Penny was alive, and we didn't find her in time, and this is my fault.

Deep down, I know that's not true. I may have felt as if I wasn't doing enough to find her, but we *were* searching, even when common sense said that she was either dead or hiding because she was Bruno's partner in crime.

Still, I blame myself. And still, despite seeing her lying there, unmoving, I scramble up the slanted tunnel, calling for Dalton.

I'm halfway back when the tunnel goes dark, Dalton's form filling it as he crawls as fast as he can.

"Casey!"

"Right here," I say, shining the light so he can see me. "I found Penny. I—I don't think she was dead when she was dropped in there but . . . She's not . . ."

He curses and crawls faster, motioning for me to turn around. That takes some doing, but one of my new Yukon hobbies is spelunking, with Anders as the expert and Dalton an enthusiastic amateur. I get myself turned around and head down the slope.

"It's tight here," I say.

"Got it."

I reach the end. He can't come up beside me—it's far too narrow for that—but it doesn't matter, because I'm not staying at the top.

"Hold," Dalton says when I start turning around to descend. "Assess, please?"

I resist the urge to scowl. He's right. I'm about to climb down into a pit without being completely certain I can get back out.

"I have about twenty feet of rope in my backpack," he says. "I'll go get it after you're down, but I'm not leaving you in there until nightfall while I make a round trip for more."

I turn back to the drop-off. "Fifteen-foot drop. I think I can climb down but . . ."

"But if it were an easy climb, she wouldn't still be there," he says, voicing what I just realized. He lowers his voice. "Slower, Casey. Please. I don't want to leave you in there, and I don't know this Lilith woman well enough to leave her with you."

I take a deep breath and shine the light over the sides. "Yes, I'm going to need the rope. For safety. I can rappel down with that."

"Hold on then."

As he retreats, I curse myself for not making sure he had rope before dragging him in here. I could already be rappelling down by now.

And does that small delay matter? I'm examining a dead body.

I'm still tapping anxiously when he returns. I'm already turned around and I've found a slight indent where my one foot can rest below. He shakes his head at that but says nothing. He gives me the rope, and I wrap it around my hand as he secures his end. Then I stuff the flashlight into my pocket and start down.

It's a slow climb. So damned slow. The walls are smooth, with only the slightest ridges for my feet and even those aren't enough to keep me from sliding. I really do have to rappel, boots pressed against the stone as I inch down. The short rope doesn't help. There isn't enough extra to wrap it around my waist or for Dalton to feel confident in his hold, and that means I can't just zoom down.

Finally, when I'm a few feet from the bottom, I let go and drop. Dalton's curse echoes at the top as he scrabbles to the edge and glares down at me.

"Sorry," I call up. "I'm fine."

"Didn't break your damn ankle to save sixty seconds?"

"I know, I know."

I run to drop beside Penny. I touch her cheek. It's cool to the touch. I slump back onto my heels. I knew this. I really knew it, but I couldn't help hoping.

"I'm sorry," Dalton's voice drifts down.

"I knew it."

"Still sorry."

I manage a wan smile his way as I turn on the flashlight and then angle the beam down to Penny. "Okay, so we're going to need to move her, which as you said, is a problem. It's a two-hour hike back, and it's already late afternoon."

"We can do it," he says. "I'll try bribing our local forest witch to watch her, and we'll hoof it back for more rope and supplies."

"Can you go talk to Lilith?" I say. "I'll start examining Penny. If Lilith won't stay—and I can't blame her—then I need to conduct a preliminary examination before we leave Penny, just in case whoever put her in the hole comes back."

I swing the light up just in time to catch his expression. "Yes, I know that's highly unlikely. Whoever put her down here also left food and water, which is gone. It was almost certainly Bruno. He put her in here and then his partner pushed him off the cliff, and when we rescued him, he decided not to mention Penny . . . even on his deathbed."

"Is it possible to kill a dead guy?"

"I wish," I mutter.

"Be right back."

While I shine the light up, Dalton uses the hole to get himself turned around, and my breath catches once, when he slips, just a little. Then he's in the tunnel. He pulls up the rope and goes.

I turn to Penny. She's lying on her side. There's no sign of decomposition, which tells me she hasn't been dead long.

What if we'd been a little faster? Walked faster? Run? What if Lilith didn't have a beer and sandwich before pulling out the glove?

No, that's not fair. Penny has almost certainly been dead for hours. The cool cave has warded off early decomp.

I leave her lying on her side as I check her for injuries, remembering that blood. It comes from her head. There's an ugly contusion on the back of it. That's the only obvious sign of injury.

Hit from behind. Hard enough to knock her out. Not hard

enough to kill her. Bruno can't bring himself to finish the job, so he carries her the kilometer from Mark's camp to here, where he must have seen the cave. Lowers her in and leaves food and water, in case she wakes up. She does, but the walls are too slick to climb, and she can only eat and drink and wait.

And wait . . . for help that never came.

I roll my shoulders, regaining my focus. When I see her neck, I remember the necklace. I shine the light on her throat as I look for signs of the chain cutting in, as if it had been ripped off. There's nothing. She must have lost it earlier and—

A flutter of movement at the base of her throat.

I blink. Then I press my fingers to the side of her neck and close my eyes and concentrate and there it is: the faintest pulse.

"Eric!" I shout as I hear him in the tunnel above. "She's alive!"

CHAPTER THIRTY-THREE

While Penny is alive, she's slipping away fast. Whoever put her here might have left a canteen of water, but there's a small pool of it in a divot, and I can picture her, fumbling in the near blackness of the cave, woozy from her head injury, spilling that precious water and only getting a few mouthfuls. She's badly dehydrated and suffering from God knows what injuries I didn't find.

Dalton lowers water right away. Penny's unconscious, though, and nothing I can do will wake her, so I'm stuck dribbling liquid through her lips, knowing it's not enough.

"We need to get her back," I say. "I don't know how to do that. Maybe you could run it, but then people need to come and get her, and I don't know if we can even hook her up to an IV down here—"

"Casey?" Dalton gently cuts in. "We're getting her out."

"But we only have—"

"I've got this. We have light until nearly midnight, remember? We can do this. Give me twenty minutes. If you need me, shout. I'll hear you."

He crawls out of the tunnel, and I am left alone with Penny, dribbling water between her lips, careful not to choke her, and then when she doesn't choke, worrying that she's too far gone. I feel a pulse. I know I do. But it's weak. So damn weak, and the town is two hours away, more than that if we're carrying an unconscious woman, and what if she doesn't make it because we chose the wrong option?

Dalton knows what he's doing. Trying to get her back to town—even if we fail partway and have to run for help—is better than me waiting here with her, praying Dalton gets back with help in time.

It's less than twenty minutes before Dalton returns. He's brought woven vines to extend the rope. My shaking hands fumble attaching it, and then I have to get the rope fastened around Penny.

I get it under her armpits and heave her up and then help, as much as I can, while Dalton pulls. It is not easy, and it is not graceful. It is hauling an unconscious woman out of a pit, and then, once she's up, dragging her along the tunnel. I do not want to even think of what additional damage we're doing. Nor do I want to think of how deeply unconscious she must be not to wake during the ordeal.

Once she's out, Lilith has a look but, like she's said, she's not the forest healer kind of witch. I undress Penny quickly to check for wounds I've missed, wounds that might mean we shouldn't be carrying her five kilometers back to Haven's Rock. There's nothing. Just the head injury. I get a little more water into her while Dalton and Lilith fashion a stretcher. Then Storm pulls it while Dalton runs ahead to bring back help.

We're about halfway when running footfalls thump toward us along the path. Lilith disappears into the forest with a quick goodbye. Then Anders and Dalton appear. Anders checks Penny. He's brought a makeshift IV, but declares that she's stable enough to make the rest of the journey to where April is preparing a proper fluid drip.

We get her to town and into the clinic. Then it's time for me to surrender her to April and Anders, while we take up vigil on the back deck.

Penny is stable. She's badly dehydrated, and April is concerned about that blow to the head, but not enough to start fretting that she can't handle this. She has it under control, and now it's just a matter of waiting for Penny to wake.

Waiting for Penny to wake and tell us what the hell happened to her.

I suspect Bruno did this, but Pierre remains on my list. I even consider Mark. What if that's where he was that night, instead of hunting? Penny stumbled over his camp and he hit her from behind, realized what he'd done, and dumped her into that cave? Except that dumping her with food and water but letting her die only makes sense if whoever did it was no longer around to go back for her, which works for Bruno. It doesn't work for Pierre or Mark.

I do have one clue to pursue before she wakes. Or two clues, to be precise.

I'm in the town hall with Yolanda, having just updated her on the situation. Dalton made us coffee before he slipped out with Storm, and now that I'm done with my story, Yolanda is silently processing. I've told her everything, including about the mining camp and the theorized plans to steal it. Does that mean I trust her completely? No, but I trust her enough to take this risk in hopes that, with her knowing everything, she can be more helpful.

I stare down into my coffee cup while she thinks it through.

Gunnar wondered why I chose Dalton, and one answer lies in this cup. It lies in the million things he does because he knows me, from slowing me down in that cave to not giving me too much shit for jumping to figuring out how to get Penny out while I panicked to bringing me a coffee and a cookie because I'm stressed and exhausted. Normally, I reciprocate all that, but I've been so caught up in this case that I can't, and that's okay. I don't have to feel guilty about it. I just make a mental note that I owe him.

"Penny will be okay?" Yolanda asks after at least five minutes of silence. It's not the first time she's asked, and my answer doesn't change.

"She's stable. April says it's mostly dehydration. Possibly a little hypothermia. Also a head injury, which is concerning, but April believes she'll wake up soon."

Yolanda crosses her arms and leans back in her chair. This is clearly not the answer she wants. After a moment, she sits up again. "Why aren't you questioning this photographer woman? Isn't she the obvious suspect?"

Before I can comment, she leans forward and continues, "I don't like her story. It's too weird."

"Up here, it's all weird."

"All right. So you can accept that a successful professional woman goes full-on hermit in the Yukon wilderness where she *continues* her career of nature photography while taming a wolf for a pet. If that's feasible, then why not a woman who brought a tame wolf-hybrid pet with her and pretends to be a wilderness photographer while scouting for mining sites."

"I'd accept that."

"Good." She picks up her own coffee cup and takes a deep drink before setting it down with a clack. "So we can consider Lilith for the role of partner in crime. She pushes Bruno off a cliff, returns later and realizes he's not dead, so she threatens him into silence if she brings him to town. She also hits Penny and, again, can't bring herself to kill, so she eventually leads you to her. Penny didn't see who hit her from behind, so Lilith is safe."

I could point out the many, many holes in this theory, but I settle for the main one.

"Whoever put Penny in that cave carried her at least a half mile," I say. "That's how she lost her glove, and it's why Storm didn't pick up her trail."

"This woman has a dog, right? Possibly a wolf-and-sled-dog hybrid."

"Yes, but there was no sign of Penny being dragged, and that would have left a trail Storm could follow. She was carried. Bruno was definitely big enough for that. Pierre is probably big enough. Mark—the miner—is small, so that'd be tough. And I don't care how strong Lilith might be, if I couldn't carry Penny, neither could she."

"This Mark fellow. Let's talk more about him."

"We can. First, though, I need you to look at what I found in the cave with Penny."

I open the bag I brought and take out the plastic canteen and wrappers. I lay them on the desk.

"Are these from here?" I ask.

"Looks like it." She checks the protein-bar wrappers without touching them. "That's the brand we have. We have boxes of them in the commissary, free for the taking. The canteen is definitely the brand we use. Everyone was given one on arrival. There are also extras in the commissary in case anyone misplaces theirs. Most people marked theirs. They get left lying all over the place, and no one wants to be using someone else's by accident."

I use a cloth to pick up the canteen and turn it over. We don't find any markings on it.

"Check Bruno's room for his," Yolanda says. "But either

way, those items definitely come from here. I'm not even going to speculate that whoever put them in that hole just happened to have the same brand of both."

"Meaning not Lilith and not Mark."

She hesitates, and I know she wants to find another explanation, one that doesn't mean a member of her crew left Penny in that pit to die.

"It was someone from town," she says finally.

"I think we need to put Pierre under house arrest. At the very least, for his own safety."

Anders gets Pierre into "house arrest." Once the town is done, we'll actually have a place for that—there will be a small apartment over one of the service buildings that we'll use for storage, in the hopes it never needs to be used for actually putting someone into semi-confinement. And now we require it before it's even fully constructed.

For now, Pierre is put into Mathias's apartment over the butcher shop. The problem with that is the need for a guard when we can't spare anyone. I'm at the point of wondering whether I'm overreacting when Nanette and two others show up, demanding answers about Penny and wanting Pierre arrested.

I don't see the beginnings of a mob—I have dealt with that before—but I do see the first inklings of serious trouble. So house arrest it is, with a rotating guard consisting of me, Anders, and Dalton. The plane carrying Kenny, Isabel, and Phil cannot arrive fast enough.

I'm on the first shift, which means hanging out in the future butcher shop and writing up my notes. The sun is dropping when Anders shows up.

"Penny's awake," he says, and I'm off the second he promises to take my place guarding Pierre.

I arrive at the clinic, all too aware of the déjà vu here. Two missing people. Both found seriously injured but alive. Both unconscious. Penny was stable, but so was Bruno two days ago, and we still couldn't save him.

I won't let that happen again, even if it means putting a guard on Penny's door. Someone in this damn town tried to kill her, and they will not get a second chance.

I get inside to find Penny sitting up and sipping juice from a cup.

"She insisted I crank up the bed," April says. "I said I would prefer her lying down but it was that or she'd crank it herself. She has twenty minutes in that position, and then the bed goes flat."

Penny manages a wan half smile and says, in a papery voice, "Thank you, Dr. Butler."

"I will leave you with Casey while I attempt to find some ice chips for you." April turns to me. "I know you need answers, but please don't overtax her."

"I won't."

When April is gone, I introduce myself properly and then pull over a chair.

"Can you tell me what happened?" I say.

"I'll . . . try," Penny says. "But I don't remember much after I was hit on the head."

"That may come back."

She nods. Then she says, her voice so soft I have to lean in to hear her, "Dr. Butler said Bruno is dead."

"He is."

She nods, and the nod just keeps going, as if she's so lost in her thoughts that she forgets she's doing it.

"I'd like to start at the beginning, if that's all right," I say. "Why did you go into the forest?"

Her lips twitch with a smile that doesn't reach her eyes. "Proving my mother right, apparently. Curiosity does kill the cat. They might have nine lives, but it eventually catches up." She sips her juice. "I'm going to be honest, even if it does make me look rather silly."

"I'm not here to judge. Whatever you did—whether it now feels silly or reckless—what happened to you was the result of someone else's choices. I'm here to find out who did it and make sure it's handled appropriately."

"Thank you, although I don't think that's an issue now." She takes a deep breath, and when she continues it's faltering, with long pauses as she struggles to get it all out. As much as I'm tempted to tell her to rest and talk later, I don't dare, in case she takes a turn for the worse. "I was eavesdropping on Yolanda and Bruno. There were things about this job that seemed odd, and I began to suspect it wasn't a research town."

"So you listened in on the fight."

"I did, and it was about the schedule. Yolanda wanted to get things right, and Bruno just wanted to get them done."

This matches what Bruno told me, so I only nod.

"Which was weird," she says.

That gives me pause. "Weird how? Yolanda wanting it done right or Bruno wanting it done fast?"

"Bruno wanting it done fast. I know that engineers can get frustrated with architects, just like the construction folks can get frustrated with both of us. But Bruno was arguing about the bonus . . . which he'd already earned."

I frown. "Already earned?"

"He hit his target. So did I. It's up to the crew and the trades now."

I'm confused for only a few seconds before I understand what she means. The main work of the architect and engineer is done. They're staying on-site to help with problems or issues implementing their designs, but by this point, the speed really is in the hands of Yolanda and the rest of the crew.

"So what was Bruno's point in pressing for speed?" I say.

"He claimed it was for the others, that he was just thinking of them, but that wasn't the guy I'd been working with. Others complained about being up here. He seemed happy, even talked about maybe staying on longer in case there were any engineering problems. I got the feeling he was stalling. He'd promised his wife he'd give her at least three months—she wanted more—and then suddenly I hear him singing a very different tune. I thought maybe he'd been allowed a call home, and his wife was ready to try again."

Or he found a gold mine that he couldn't exploit until he got his ass home, which he needed to do before Mark went south again and filed his claim.

I say, "So you overheard the argument and thought it was strange."

"Right. Then they come out and Yolanda goes marching off into the forest. She seemed distracted, but then she stopped and made sure no one was following her. That piqued my curiosity again, and I followed."

"Did you see where she went?"

Penny's cheeks pink. "No, because I'd foolishly gone into the forest at dusk without a flashlight. I just kept following the trail until I realized I'd lost her and the trail. I thought I was heading back in the right direction, but I obviously wasn't. I kept going, and then there was a moose that freaked me out, and I ran."

"Moose can do that."

"They're so *big*. I was already scared, realizing I was lost, so I ran. When I heard water, I thought of the streams near the town, so I went that way and I found someone camping there in this camouflaged tent with a weird setup in the stream. Of course, I got curious again. Then I heard someone coming and—"

She inhales sharply. I keep my expression calm and wait.

"It was Bruno," she blurts. "He had this look on his face, like he was even more surprised to see me than I was to see him. And then . . ."

She swallows. "And then I don't know what happened." A short laugh. "I mean, I know what happened, obviously. He hit me on the head. We must have talked. He must have said something to explain why he was there, and when I turned away, he clocked me in the back of the head."

"You don't remember what he said."

"It's a blank after I saw him. Then there's a flash, when I hit the ground, only it wasn't hitting the ground after he hit me. It was falling into that . . ." She shivers. "That pit. I fell onto rock and woke up, and Bruno was there, in the darkness. I could just make him out, leaning over me. He said he left me food and water and he'd be back. He said . . ." Another hard swallow. "He said he was sorry."

At a sound near the door, I rise and go over as April taps on it. She wordlessly passes me a cup of ice chips.

"Just a few more minutes," April says.

"Five should be enough."

She nods, and I shut the door and take the chips to Penny. She tips the cup to her lips and takes a chip, and it clicks off her teeth as she shuts her eyes.

"God, that tastes good. Water is amazing, isn't it?" Her eyes tear up as she opens them. "I spilled the canteen in the cave. I fumbled and it spilled, but I told myself not to panic because Bruno would come back. I had no idea what happened, but he'd come back. Then he didn't and . . ."

I take her hand and grip it while tears roll down her face.

"Now he's dead," she says. "Part of me wants to leap on that as an excuse. Down there, in that pit, not remembering what happened, with everything fuzzy, I don't think I actually realized that he attacked me. I'm not sure what I thought. It was such a muddled mess. Somehow, we must have come into this cave, and then I fell, and he'd gone for help. Now, knowing he died, I keep thinking oh, good, he didn't abandon me. There was a reason. Then I remember he's the one who put me there and . . ."

She starts to shake, eyes shining with rage as her fingers tighten around mine. Her voice lowers and she whispers, "I'm glad he's dead." Then her eyes widen. "No, I don't mean that."

"He did a horrible thing to you, even if he intended to go back."

She's quiet for a moment before she says, "Did he know he was dying?"

I realize what she's asking. I could lie. I don't. "Yes."

"And he still didn't tell you about me." It's a statement, not a question.

"No."

She leans back, closing her eyes and releasing my hand. "All right. I do mean it. I'm glad he's dead."

"I don't blame you."

CHAPTER THIRTY-FOUR

The case seems as if it should end here. We know who attacked Penny and who put her in that cave and left her to die. Bruno. Who is dead. Except, if I were talking to a crown attorney, they'd tell me—correctly—that I only have enough evidence for part two and three of that solution.

Based on Penny's testimony, we know Bruno left her in the cave. The crown would want proof, but I'm sure I can lift prints from the water canteen and wrappers and even the cave walls if I need to. We also know Bruno didn't save her when he had the chance—he knew he was dying and the only thing he told me was that he'd been pushed off a cliff.

That leaves an unresolved question of who hit Penny. I think it was Bruno. Penny thinks it was, too. It makes sense. He finds her at the camp. They talk, and he comes up with an excuse for why he's there. She relaxes and turns away, and he hits her.

That is logical. But without any proof, even her testimony, a defense lawyer could easily argue that a third party hit her. A random third party? That'd be a tough sell. But it wouldn't be random, would it? Because we already know that someone pushed Bruno off that cliff. Someone that he met with again the night before he died: his partner in stealing Mark's claim.

Bruno's partner is here in town. They were conspiring with Bruno to steal that claim. Then everything went to hell. First, Mark's wife showed up. Was that before Penny? Is *that* why Penny was attacked? Not because Penny saw the mining operation—she still doesn't even know what it is—but because Bruno or his partner had just killed Denise, and Penny was about to see her dead body?

Someone hits her over the head. They argue about what to do with her. Bruno puts her in a virtual prison while they figure it out. Then the partner realizes Bruno is a liability—stealing a claim is one thing; murdering one woman and confining another is a whole different level. Partner pushes Bruno off the cliff, only he survives, so they meet up outside Haven's Rock to negotiate. We appear and the partner runs back to town, where we lose them. Bruno dies, and the secret is safe . . . until Penny is rescued.

Penny needs a full-time guard, and I'm not trusting anyone other than myself, Dalton, and Anders for that.

Anders handles guard scheduling. That was part of his job in Rockton, where he was in charge of the militia, which will continue here.

We move Pierre to the prison cell in the town hall, where we can post a guard at the front door and lock Pierre inside.

Once that's done, I have two more things to tackle. A clue I've overlooked, plus a tip from something Penny said.

I zoom back to the clinic.

"Hey," Dalton says, looking up from his book.

"I need to ask Penny something," I say. "I know April wants her resting, but it'll only take a moment."

"Since I'm not April, I'm not going to stop you."

I slip past him with a squeeze on his shoulder. When I open the door, Penny is lying flat in bed with her eyes closed. I hesitate in the doorway.

Her eyes open. "I'm not sleeping. I did quite enough of that. Come on in."

"I have one last question." I hold up the necklace. "This is yours, right?"

Her hands go to her neck, patting as if expecting to find it there. "Yes, that's mine."

"When did you lose it?"

"I didn't. At least, I didn't know that I had."

"When did you last notice it?"

She pauses. "I don't think about it much. I put it on in the morning and take it off at night. I definitely had it on that day. Wait! At one point, when I was running from the moose, I ran into a branch. As I was clawing it away, my fingers snagged the necklace."

"Did it break?"

She shakes her head. I thank her and leave her to her rest.

That means someone *put* Penny's necklace in that bush. It couldn't have been Bruno. At the time Pierre found it, Bruno had been lying at the bottom of a gorge. The distance between Mark's camp and here is too far for Bruno to run back, stage the necklace, and then return to talk to his partner and get pushed off that cliff.

That means Bruno's partner staged it. Tossed it into the bush to be found in the search for Penny. Making it appear as if she'd been abducted.

That theory rests on one very dubious piece of evidence— Pierre's story about when he found the necklace. If Pierre is lying, it *could* have been Bruno who staged it, after he was brought back and snuck out that night. What if he staged it along with another clue that pointed at his partner, a clue his partner got rid of . . . because Pierre is his partner. Pierre finds the necklace after Bruno sets it out. He hides the clue, takes the necklace, and locks it into that drawer.

I track down Yolanda next. She's sitting on the front porch of the town hall, where Anders has asked her to watch over Pierre. She's drinking tea and staring into space.

"How is she?" Yolanda asks, without looking over.

I put one foot on the deck. "She seems fine, and Eric is guarding her."

"Good."

"I need to speak to you in private. Can we go inside?"

"Those walls aren't soundproof."

"That's fine."

She hesitates, and then she understands that I don't care if Pierre overhears. In fact, I might even hope he does.

We go in, and she settles into a chair, cupping her mug and sipping from it. She's quiet tonight. Muted. I don't comment on that. The cause is obvious. Bruno is dead, Pierre is in the cell, and Penny is under guard after being left for dead by Bruno, after possibly being attacked by Pierre. Or, if not Pierre, then someone else on her crew.

I tell Yolanda what Penny said about the argument Yolanda had with Bruno the night he first disappeared.

"He made it seem as if he was fighting for his bonus," I say. "But Penny says that was secured."

"It was. He came up with a bunch of bullshit about being worried for the crew, that it wasn't fair for them to risk their bonuses because of delays they couldn't control. The obvious answer would be to extend the deadline, which I said we would if the delays were truly outside the crew's control. Then he started going on about how people expected to be home at a certain time. I figured he meant him. He wanted to fix things with his wife, and he was getting antsy. Now I see the truth—he just wanted to make that . . . claim thing."

The mining claim, she means. She's being careful with her language with Pierre in the next room. If he's Bruno's partner, then he knows what we're talking about. If he isn't, then we're sure as hell not telling him there's an unclaimed gold find out there.

"Bruno was in a hurry to get home," I say. "Because he had no way of making the application while up here." I pause. "Did he ever try to get access to your sat phone? Come up with an excuse for using it?"

"No."

"Has anyone tried since his death? Suddenly needed to use the sat phone or suddenly needed to go home?"

She hesitates. Then her lips form a silent curse as she turns toward the door leading to where Pierre is being held.

She lowers her voice. "He's been demanding to leave since that uproar with Nanette earlier today."

I walk to the cell and unlock the door. A scuffle sounds within as Pierre dashes away from his eavesdropping spot. When I open the door, he's on the single cot, his arms folded.

"I'm hungry," he says.

I point at the box of food on the small dresser.

"I want something else," he says.

I hold open the door. "Go on and get it. We'll wait here."

His scowl deepens. Considering how the others feel about him, he doesn't want out. Or, at least, not unless it involves a flight south.

"I hear you want to leave," I say.

He waves around the cell. "Yes? For obvious reasons?"

"Which are . . . ?"

His look suggests I'm losing brain cells at an alarming rate. "I'm stuck in a cell for my own safety. People think I have something to do with what happened to Penny."

"What if I said you could fly out tomorrow, but you'll be taken into temporary custody while I complete my investigation?"

"Thrown into a real jail cell?"

"No. House arrest in a suite at a resort, with room service and a TV."

He looks at me. "You're serious?"

"I am. However, as this is an active investigation, you'd be escorted there, and while your room would have TV and other entertainment options, you'll have no access to the internet or a phone or any communication with the outside world until either I've completed my investigation or your work term here ends, whichever comes first."

"Fine."

"That's acceptable? No outside contact?"

He throws up his hands. "I don't have that here, do I?"

"All right. I'll make the arrangements."

I back into the main room and lock his door. His eagerness to agree doesn't mean he isn't Bruno's partner—he could think he can still find a way to submit that application once he's left Haven's Rock. But it's a definite strike against that theory, especially when Yolanda says Pierre didn't demand to leave until *after* he found himself in danger. As he rightly said, it's obvious why he'd want out.

I make sure the front door is locked, and then I take Yolanda onto the back porch. As I step out, a wave of nostalgia washes over me. Our new town hall might not be exactly like our old police station—we made improvements—but this back porch is, and Anders and I are the ones who insisted on it.

Our old station back porch was Dalton's office. Even when

it was below freezing, he'd sit in his chair and gaze into the woods and think. It was a mental trick—he relaxes in the forest, and so having that view let him fully sink into his thoughts. Anders and I replicated this deck for him, even using timbers from it that Yolanda's company had reclaimed. But part of it is for us, too. Our earliest good memories of Dalton are from that deck, when his defenses lowered and we saw the man behind the facade, and we decided this was a superior officer who deserved our trust . . . and our friendship.

Dalton's chair is there, right where it always is, with a can of rusted beer caps below it. Has he seen this yet? In all the commotion, I don't think he has, and when Yolanda goes to sit in Dalton's chair, I tense.

She notices the movement and nods to the chair. "Eric's, I presume?"

I wave toward it. "Sit. He won't care."

"But you would." Her lips twitch as I protest. "How about this one? Is that yours or Will Anders's?"

"We don't have specific spots to sit. Kind of depends on Eric's mood."

Her lip twitch turns into a smile. "Whether he's in the mood for company or not?"

"Yep."

She lowers herself into the middle chair. "I can't get a read on him. Gran warned me about that. For you, too. Now, with Will, she said it would be easier. What you see is what you get. I'm not sure that's entirely true either."

I make a noncommittal noise. "Depends on what you see. If it's the easygoing deputy who does as he's told, then that'd be about fifty percent accurate."

"And fifty percent conserving his energy for when he finds something worth being less chill about?"

"Pretty much." I pull my legs up under me. "So Pierre wanted to go home?"

"He did."

"And that only started when he went under house arrest?"

She thinks back and then says, "Yes. Now that I think about it, he was on the undecided list for early departures. You have your carpenter coming in tomorrow and your doctor is already here. We offered Pierre the option of staying through to the end or leaving early, and he was fine with either."

"Which was yesterday, after Bruno was dead but before Nanette accused him of killing Penny."

"Yes."

That swings the pendulum farther in favor of his innocence, while not entirely exonerating him. He will remain a suspect until we know the identity of Bruno's partner.

"Did anyone else ask to use the sat phone since Bruno died? Or suddenly have a reason to want to leave?"

She hesitates.

"Yolanda . . . ?"

"Kendra asked to use the phone yesterday. But it was . . ." She shrugs. "It was a Kendra kind of request. *Hey, do you think there's any way I could use your phone, and if not, that's cool, I was just checking.* It was her niece's birthday, and she hated not calling."

"So did you let her use it?"

Another pause.

"That'd be a yes. Did you overhear any of the conversation?"

Yolanda sighs. "No, and letting her use it was against the rules, but it's Kendra. Nice people are hard to say no to when they make a reasonable request."

"I'll need to check your phone and have someone run the number she called."

"Sure."

"No one else asked to use it? Or suddenly wanted to leave?"

"No."

I pause as a thought forms. My first reaction is that it doesn't work because it's backward—the opposite of what I would expect from Bruno's partner.

Unless it's not.

Unless his partner isn't eager to make that application. Not just yet.

I push that aside for a moment and ask the reverse question. "You mentioned Pierre having the option to leave or stay?"

"Right."

"Did anyone who was due to stay ask to leave instead?"

"A couple of people, yes. They saw the chance to get out earlier." She gives two names that aren't even on my list of remote possibilities. "Then, after the trouble with Pierre, Nanette asked to leave. She was uncomfortable being in a place where we might have had a murderous stalker. She suggests there's . . . history there, which made me promise we'd get her out if we could."

She means Nanette suffered at the hands of a stalker or a partner, and would understandably want to go. Or so Nanette claimed as her explanation for wanting to leave early, and it's the kind of excuse that would have most women doing exactly what Yolanda did—understanding the context and promising to help if they could.

Could Nanette have lied? Yes. But there's another possibility I want to pursue first. I'm presuming that Bruno's partner wanted to leave ASAP, just like Bruno did. Bruno might not have been angling for an early release, but he absolutely didn't want to stay longer than necessary.

How much of that was wanting to make the claim application?

And how much was wanting to tell his wife about the claim?

What if the partners weren't ready to make the application? I know it requires on-site visits and physical staking of the land.

What if Bruno had been ready to apply, but his partner wasn't? What if Bruno had all the information for that application—as someone who'd worked on mining operations—and that was the power he'd wielded over his attacker, the reason he'd felt comfortable meeting them.

So, you tried to kill me. Have you realized the problem with that yet? I have what you need to make that claim.

If that was the case, Bruno's partner wouldn't be arguing to leave.

They'd be arguing to stay.

I rise from my chair. "I need to speak to Gunnar."

"Gunnar?" Yolanda shakes her head. "He wasn't trying to go home sooner. He was fighting like hell to . . ." She curses. "He *really* didn't want to go early, when I thought he'd be weaseling his way onto that first flight back to civilization."

"Exactly."

CHAPTER THIRTY-FIVE

Gunnar's "perch" is over a half-constructed storage building. It's framed and roofed, but the sides are only partly on. He parks himself in the loft, tucked into the roof shadow, and from there, he can see the entire town.

He can watch people, like Bruno, slipping out when they aren't supposed to.

Penny said she followed Yolanda out of curiosity. That's natural. Yet Gunnar saw Bruno coming and going and never wondered why? I don't buy it.

As we head toward Gunnar's perch, Yolanda takes me looping around one of the residence buildings. Once we come around the back, the moonlight hits Gunnar's perch.

"He's there," she mutters. "See his damn boots?"

I peer up and, sure enough, in the shadows there are two soles, toes pointed up, as Gunnar surveys his domain from on high. When Yolanda tries to march out, I stop her. I map out an alternate route, and we back up into the forest and circle around that way.

The first level of the storage shed is roughed in. It has walls and a door, and that door is shut. It isn't locked, though. There's nothing inside to protect yet.

I ease open the door and poke my head through. Silence from above. That we saw just one pair of boots suggests Gunnar isn't "entertaining," but I still listen. When no sound comes, I creep inside, my flashlight shaded to a dim glow.

There's a ladder right in front of me. I brace one foot on it, testing for noise, but like everything else, it's sturdy and when I climb, it doesn't so much as creak. I continue to the top. Yolanda follows, and I don't try to stop her. I'll take the backup. I'll just make sure she stays at my back, out of danger.

At the top, I ease out my gun. I hold it low and out of sight as I make my way across the plank floor of the loft. When I see a shape to my left, I stop short, but it's only a pile of blankets. My light picks up a box of condoms on the floor.

Ahead, Gunnar sits against a post. I can only make out his lower legs and boots from this angle, and I approach with caution. When a board creaks behind me, I go still, but Gunnar doesn't seem to hear it. I continue until I'm a few feet from that post.

"Gunnar?" I say. "I'd like to talk to you."

He doesn't answer. He doesn't move. His legs stay completely still. I race forward, gun out, bracing for what I'll find.

When I see the boots and legs, my gut twists because that's all I see. Gunnar isn't leaning against that post. There's *nothing* against that post. There are jean-clad legs and boots and—

"Son of a bitch," I whisper, as I realize I'm not seeing some grotesque tableau with only part of a corpse.

I'm seeing a setup. A pair of boots propped on their heels, attached to a pair of jeans stuffed just enough so that anyone looking up from below, at the right angle, sees boots and lower legs and presumes Gunnar is in his perch.

I stride over and shine my flashlight beam on the boots and jeans.

"Can you tell if those are his?" I ask Yolanda.

She picks up a boot and checks inside. "Yep." A check on the laundry tag on the jeans. "Also his. They're labeled."

"How many pairs of boots does he get?"

"One, but everyone has sneakers, too, for off duty—whatever they brought up with them. And they have four pairs of jeans."

I look down from the perch. "I've been told that Gunnar entertains up here."

"That's one way of putting it."

"He said women come up and visit if they see him here."

"So I've heard."

I look from the open end of the loft to his boots. That's risky, isn't it? Setting up a dummy version of himself when his "guests" know that seeing those boots means he's open for company?

Yes, those are his boots and jeans, but that doesn't mean he's the one who put them here.

I check the area. There are crumbs, from snacks of some kind, and two empty beer bottles. There's also a blanket, presumably for cool nights.

I head into the main part and walk to the other blankets. There are several of them, along with a pillow and that box of condoms. There's also spermicide. Plus a sleep mask and what looks like a bathrobe belt, the purpose of which I won't speculate on.

I head to the ladder. I reach the bottom, where Yolanda left the door cracked open for light. I'm reaching for it when it opens and I nearly run into a dark-haired woman whose name escapes me. She stops short and then flushes.

"Uh, sorry," she says. "I saw the door ajar, which means Gunnar is, um, open for visits." Her cheeks redden even more as she says, "You, uh, need to close that when you go up, so no one walks in on you."

Behind me, Yolanda chokes on a laugh. The woman looks over my shoulder and sees her, and there's a moment where she *still* thinks she knows why I'm here, and her eyes widen, presuming Yolanda and I were both here for the same reason . . . together. Then she claps a hand to her mouth.

"Oh, my God," she says. "I'm so sorry. You're talking to Gunnar about the case. Obviously. I didn't mean . . ."

"It's fine," I say. "He's not here anyway."

She frowns. "But I saw his boots just a couple of minutes ago."

"It's not him," I say simply. "And we're the ones who left the door open when we came in. So that's the signal? If it's closed, he's otherwise occupied?"

She flushes and stammers, and behind me, Yolanda says, "Detective Butler doesn't care why you were here and neither do I. Consenting adults and all that. She's asking for the purposes of her investigation."

"Oh, um, right. Yes. Kind of. The closed door just means he's not accepting, um, company. Sometimes he has someone else visiting. Other times, he just wants to hang out by himself. A closed door means turn back."

And by this point in the job, Gunnar will have his established cadre of "guests," all of whom understand and respect that closed door. If he wants to be alone, he shuts it. And if he wants others to think he's up here alone, he stages it and then closes the door, and everyone who knows about his not-so-secret perch spot will see his boots and think he's up there . . . which means he's free to do whatever he wants, and go wherever he wants, and no one will be the wiser.

Yolanda and I head to Gunnar's apartment in the men's residence. His is the one closest to the door, which is why he'd been the one to answer that night when I went looking for Yolanda. Or did he answer because he was lying awake, figuring out what to do after shoving Bruno off a cliff? And did he just *happen* to be assigned the room by the door, where he could easily slip in and out?

No, that wasn't accidental.

"What Gunnar wants, Gunnar gets," Yolanda mutters as we search his quarters. "He's a manipulative bastard, and to be honest, I liked him for it." She pauses, her hand on a dresser drawer. "Not that way."

"Never suspected and wouldn't judge if you did. My past contains a string of hot guys who came one hundred percent commitment-free."

"Same. But I prefer not to be part of quite so large a cast, and I don't hook up with the crew. That crosses lines. The thing about Gunnar is that he was openly manipulative. He didn't try to hide it, and so people actually let him get away with more shit."

"They were charmed even as they knew they were being manipulated, because he didn't hide his intentions."

"Yep, good-looking guy, happy to provide eye candy and more, who also has—despite appearances—enough of a brain to carry on a decent conversation. He wanted this bedroom, and he got it, not by throwing his weight around, but by asking for it and making promises to get it."

"And then conveniently forgetting the promises," I say as I search under Gunnar's bed.

"No, *that's* why he gets away with it. He keeps his promises. He was a damn fine worker, and I was impressed enough that I told Will Anders to let him stay when he asked. Now I realize the bastard knew exactly how to manipulate *me*."

"By being a good worker."

"Yep." She closes the drawer. "You finding anything?"

"Nothing." I look around the tiny room. "And I do mean nothing. If I didn't know better, I'd think this was a spare room with some clothing in it. There's not a single personal item. What do you know about him?"

She pauses, thinking, and then shakes her head. "Nothing, really. He comes with a stellar job history, and that's all I cared about. Gran would have run a basic background check, but now that I think about it, I don't know *anything* about him."

"That's unusual, isn't it? On a job like this, everyone working together?"

"It is. Hell, even I talk a bit. Someone mentions a divorce, and I say I've been there. Stuff like that. I've talked to Gunnar many times, and I still couldn't tell you the first thing about him."

CHAPTER THIRTY-SIX

I tell Dalton what I've found, and then it's time to shuffle duties
yet again. It'll be twilight soon, and we need to find Gunnar.
That puts Anders on Penny-watch while Dalton and I head out
with Storm.

Earlier in this investigation, I'd thought about how much
easier it was tracking someone who didn't know we had a
tracking dog. The reverse is also true. Gunnar knows about
Storm, and he is being damn careful. His trail heads straight
for one of the streams outside town. He took off his shoes and
waded in, and it'd be damn cold, but it's not midwinter. The
water would only be uncomfortable.

When someone walks in water, a scent dog needs to find out
where they left it. That means walking up one side and down
the other, hoping to find that narrow patch where they stepped
out and then headed inland. We take the far side first, presuming he'd head that way, but after close to a half mile, we have to
admit there is no way he walked that far in cold water without
his feet going numb. Back to the side closer to town.

As we walk, my brain spins. Storm and Dalton don't need me to track, which means I'm free to think, and I'm working through the case with Gunnar as Bruno's partner. Does anything not fit? No. It all works, but only in the sense that there's nothing I know of to prove Gunnar couldn't have done it.

Gunnar sees Bruno leaving periodically. Gets curious, mostly—I suspect—because it could be an avenue of manipulation. Oh, Gunnar doesn't strike me as the blackmail sort. Like Yolanda says, he's too forthright for that. He'd just let Bruno know what he knows, and that would give him power.

He discovers that Bruno is going out to Mark's claim and checking it out while Mark isn't there. Bruno and Gunnar strike a bargain to share the profits.

Then Denise shows up while they're scouting the site, and they have to kill her. That same night, Penny also shows up, having tracked Yolanda and gotten turned around and gone too deep into the forest and then followed the sound of the mining equipment in the water.

This has been my theory all along. Both Penny and Denise saw too much. On the same night? Does that make sense?

I've been overly focused on Penny and Bruno, with Denise's murder being—unfortunately—just another complication. It works even better if, as I theorized, Denise was dead when Penny showed up and that's why Gunnar hit her from behind, getting her out of the way before she saw Denise.

But now that theory crystallizes with a different face in the role of "Bruno's partner."

What if . . . ?

I have a question, and it's easy enough to answer. I should have answered it sooner, but again, Denise's case fell to a distant priority compared to the rest.

"Fuck," Dalton mutters. "Gunnar must have gone the other way."

I rouse from my thoughts to realize we're back near Haven's Rock. Dalton's peering downstream, in the direction of the lake. We'd headed upstream because that's the direction of Mark's mining site. Of course, that presumes Gunnar was headed there. He could also have gone in the other direction, toward the lake.

"You have your gun, right?" I say.

Dalton lifts one brow, as if to say this is a silly question.

"Gun, flares, first-aid kit, flashlight?" I say.

"Yep." He lifts a shoulder, indicating his backpack strap.

"Then would you be okay continuing on if I swapped spots with Will? I need to check something in town."

I tell him my question, and he nods.

"Tell Will I'm heading toward the lake on this side of the stream. Make sure he has his gun and a light. He can catch up."

I'm at the clinic alone. I sent Anders to join up with Dalton. April has headed to bed, and I've only run up to say that I'm doing something for the case and not bothering Penny, who is sound asleep. That's all April cares about, and she leaves me to it.

I have taken Denise's body out of the under-cabin cold storage. That is, sadly, a necessity in a town like this, where if someone dies—hopefully of natural causes—we would prefer to return their body to their loved ones as soon as we can . . . which might take a few days. Mark has left us with Denise's body, on the understanding that we may need to investigate more.

We have her body unwrapped, and I'm combing through my notes.

Time of death is far from the precise science we see on television, where a suspect is exonerated because the victim died between midnight and one, and she has an alibi for that hour. The only way you're going to get that precise is if there's proof the victim was alive at 11:59 and found at one. It's worse up here. Denise had been found in a pit dug into the permafrost and we've been keeping her in cold storage. All that slows the rate of decomposition.

In Rockton, I often joked that I was getting a feel for Sherlock Holmes–era detection. That's not entirely true—I do have access to some more modern methods—but I'm no longer the police detective who makes a few general observations and then calls in the crime-scene techs. I am the crime-scene tech. So I've immersed myself in forensic science, especially older methods that don't require modern technology. Not having a photographic memory, I have invested in books, putting as many as possible onto my new tablet. Now I'm at that tablet, skimming a book I've read.

I know the state Denise was in when I found her, presumably about fourteen hours after her death. She had barely begun to decompose, but she was past rigor mortis. That generally sets in about four hours post-death and lasts about eight hours. Under normal conditions, then, if she had died twelve hours before, I could have expected to find her either in rigor mortis or out of it, being in that gray area.

However, there are factors that can affect that, and I use the book to confirm what I remember—that cold temperatures slow it down. I know approximately what the temperature would have been in that pit. Running calculations, I can reasonably conclude that, if Denise had been dumped in there right away, she'd would not have passed through rigor mortis by the time I found her.

What if she had been left at ground level and dumped much later? That doesn't work either. First, it would mean she'd have been in rigor when she was moved. My preliminary examination didn't support that, but again, that's inexact. The bigger issue is that I know the temperature that night. It'd been down near freezing, and when I run the same calculations at a slightly warmer temperature, the window only shifts slightly.

Bruno was spotted going into the forest after ten at night. He could not have gotten to Mark's camp before eleven. If he showed up and found Denise and killed her, she'd have still been in rigor when I found her late the next morning.

What if Bruno's partner killed her earlier?

Mark says he headed out hunting that evening. Even if Bruno's partner killed her at eight, the timeline doesn't work.

Add in the state of mild decomposition I'd noted, and I'm going to lay a solid bet that Denise had died earlier that day. Much earlier. And the more I think about that, the more it makes sense. She came to find her husband, using three sets of coordinates in the same general area. That's going to take time. She isn't going to have a pilot drop her off any later than early afternoon. The chance that Mark was gone hunting when she showed up is unlikely. Not impossible, but still highly unlikely.

In light of that, it's a little coincidental that Mark chose that night to go out hunting . . . and just happened to get lost and not return until the next morning.

Bruno or his partner didn't kill Mark's wife.

Mark did.

He knew we were looking for missing people. People who'd been wandering around the forest the night after his wife's death. We provided him with the perfect setup.

You had two people go missing? You still have a woman missing? And you found my dead wife? Clearly these three things are connected.

I hadn't said she'd been murdered, but this still gave him an explanation he can use if I admit the truth.

Hell, I'd jumped to that conclusion myself. It made sense, if his wife had come for a surprise visit on the same night Penny went missing. He said she must have arrived that night, and I bought it because, again, it made sense.

That's not what happened.

Denise's death had nothing to do with Bruno and Penny. It was just coincidental timing.

Why would Mark kill his wife? Well, he'd admitted that he hadn't told her where he was because he didn't trust her to keep it a secret. He said she didn't understand how important it was. What if she understood just fine . . . and still couldn't be trusted?

It was a second marriage. His first wife had been an active partner until her death. It's nice that Mark found someone else to share his life with. Unfortunately, she didn't share his hobby, but it happens, right? Except it's not like a couple having different favorite sports. Mark spent months each year alone in the forest, hunting for gold. Was Denise okay with that at first . . . until she realized how much it would affect their lives together? Was she okay with it because he had her convinced his jackpot was just around the corner?

Whatever the reason, Mark didn't tell Denise where he was and she wanted to know. She came up here and died. I am now certain he killed her. If she'd been shot or died from a blow to the head, it could have been a tragic accident, but that isn't what happened. She was half naked when he killed her.

They reunited. They may have had sex—there was that empty condom wrapper in her pocket. Then he killed her and hid her body in a pit he'd found while surveying the area. Hide her body. Hide her belongings elsewhere. If she is found, she won't be identified . . . unless I tell him we found a dead woman and he realizes he might not need to hide her after all.

A wilderness-hiding serial killer murdered my wife and attacked two other people. I'm shocked, distraught, horrified . . .

I wrap Denise's body again and head up to April's bedroom. She doesn't have her earplugs in, and she's only half asleep.

"I'm sorry," I say, "but I'm going to need you to stand guard over Penny."

She rises on her elbows, blinking.

"I had to send Will with Eric," I say. "They're out looking for Gunnar."

More blinking.

"I'll explain later," I say. "But I've found something I need to discuss with Eric, and if he hasn't found Gunnar's trail, I'm going to pull him off that for tonight. Can you watch Penny for a bit? It shouldn't take long."

She doesn't answer. She just rises and takes her robe and wraps it around her as I hurry back down the stairs. I stride out of the clinic, locking the door behind me. Then I stand on the porch and look up and down the street.

As much as I want to just go after Dalton on my own, I know better. This isn't urgent. I just want to tell him what I've found out and—let's be honest—maybe I'm feeling anxious about Dalton and Anders being in the forest where they could bump into Mark. Even if they did, Mark would play it cool. Still, I can't take that chance. To Dalton and Anders, Mark is a grieving widower. To Mark, they are the people who could ruin everything for him—not only unveil his secret mine but arrest him for his wife's murder.

One wrong move. One misunderstood word. That's all it will take, and while I hope to hell Mark is asleep at his camp, I can't take that chance. So I am going after Dalton and asking him to abandon the search until morning. But it's not urgent enough to warrant me running alone into the forest, where Mark might not be wandering around, but Gunnar certainly is.

I need to take five minutes to grab backup. I also need to be sure Gunnar hasn't returned on his own.

I look around, my gaze passing over a few people I've interviewed but don't know well enough to ask—or trust—to escort me. I spot Kendra talking to another woman, and I take one step toward her before remembering she'd used Yolanda's sat phone. I'm sure Gunnar is Bruno's partner, but I can't take any chances.

I jog toward the men's residence. I make it to the door before Yolanda hails me. I turn to see her striding my way and step aside to talk quickly.

"I'm checking to be sure Gunnar isn't back," I say.

"He's not. I've been keeping an eye out from his damn perch. I saw you return earlier, but then I lost you before I got down here."

"I had to check something. Will is off with Eric. I don't think Bruno or his partner killed Mark's wife. I think it was Mark."

"The miner?"

"Right. Now I just need someone to accompany me into the woods to tell Eric and Will and bring them in. We have two threats out there, and I'd rather call off any search until morning."

"Agreed. I'll go with you."

When I open my mouth to protest, she says, "Do you trust I'm not involved in this?"

"Yes."

"Is there anyone else you can say that about in town right now? I'm presuming your sister is watching Penny. If you want April and I to swap jobs, she can go with you."

"No, this shouldn't take long. I know where they were headed."

CHAPTER THIRTY-SEVEN

As we head out, I explain what I found to Yolanda. I do it under the guise of bringing her up to speed, maybe even showing that I recognize her status in town, but that's a bit disingenuous. I'm still working through this new theory, and if we have time to kill while on the move, I'll use it to bounce my ideas off her. Though, in my defense, that obviously implies that I value her opinion, so if she thinks it means that I trust her, that's not entirely false.

"There's one piece of evidence that could contradict it," I say. "I found Denise's blood type on Bruno's knee. There was ground-in dirt and some blood."

"Which matched her type—not her DNA—meaning it could be someone else's."

"Yes. I'm also thinking he may have knelt in it at the camp."

"Sees what looks like damp earth and kneels to examine it more closely."

I nod. "We know Bruno was at the camp. Penny saw him there. Mark could have actually gone hunting, as he claimed, or he could have been getting rid of Denise's stuff. He's gone, and that lets Bruno and Gunnar poke around the camp. Bruno sees the blood and kneels in it. Penny shows up and things go south."

"Works for me."

"Lots of speculation," I say. "I might be wrong about the specifics—what exactly happened and why exactly they did what they did—but the basics seem solid."

"Mark killed his wife and hid her body. Penny stumbled on Bruno and Gunnar at the mining camp. One of them knocks her out. Bruno confines her in that cave, and then Gunnar pushes him off the cliff. Probably because of Penny. Bruno couldn't bring himself to kill her, and Gunnar realizes he's a potential liability. Kill him. Let Penny die. Only Bruno is alive. Fortunately for Gunnar, that didn't last long and he didn't seem to sell out Gunnar, but now Penny's back and God knows what she's said. Gunnar runs."

"Something like that."

"Can we just let him keep running? Hope he falls over a cliff himself?"

"At this point, it's tempting," I mutter. "I have no idea what we'll do about him or Mark." I remember who I'm talking to and clear my throat. "Sorry. Tired and frustrated."

"It was easier when you could just turn them over to Rockton's council, huh?"

"We'll handle it."

"Gran will. I was serious when I said I don't think restarting Rockton was a good idea. It failed for a reason. Because it fundamentally cannot function as designed. You already have two people dead."

"Two people who have nothing to do with the purpose of the town."

I sidestep around a pile of bear scat and point it out with my flashlight.

"See?" she says. "I rest my case."

I glance back and arch my brows.

"I just blamed your town for two deaths it's not responsible for," she says. "And you didn't even retaliate by letting me step in a pile of shit. You're too nice. Too fair. These deaths may be unconnected, but that's the nature of a place like this, where a guy can murder his wife, hide her body, and get away with it."

"You have a point. Down south, he could murder her, *not* hide her body . . . and probably get away with it."

She throws up her hands. "Whatever. I am not going to win this argument, so I surrender. You'll do your best, and you might even help more people than you harm."

When I don't answer, she says, "*Fine*. You *will* help more than you harm. I just don't understand why anyone would take on that responsibility when it comes with that much risk. But we agree to disagree, and as for your earlier concerns, like I said, my grandmother will fix whatever needs fixing. That's her role. Fixer."

"Not sure I'm comfortable asking her to handle murderers and murder victims."

Yolanda snorts. "Because she's a nice old lady?"

"Oh, I don't doubt she can handle it."

"You just don't want her getting her hands dirty? Gran knows what she signed up for, and she knew it when she and Pops took over Rockton before we were born. Things may have gone downhill after they took a managerial back seat, but these will not be the first criminals—or bodies—Gran has had to deal with. Even without the peculiarities of Rockton, shit happens up here. Gran can handle it. The question is, can you?"

I glance back at her.

She ducks a branch. "You want the anti-Rockton, where putting in a jail cell is a precaution you hope to never need.

That ain't happening, Casey, and I think you realize that. You must."

I say nothing and continue down the stream, watching and listening for Dalton and Anders.

"You have to shift the goalposts," she says. "You *will* need the jail cell. You *will* need a police force. And you *will* need Gran's help. Once people start coming to Haven's Rock, no matter how careful you are, shit is going to keep happening, and the goal, I presume, is to send more people home in plane seats than you send home in body bags."

I shake my head.

"Okay," she says. "More in plane seats than body bags *or* handcuffs. Even at its worst, Rockton did that. The biggest danger you face out here is suffocating under the weight of your own expectations. That goes for all of you. I'm not sure you can handle it."

"Thanks."

"I'm not sure I could handle it, and I'm a helluva lot less nice than you. But the point—"

A boom rocks through the silent forest. I lunge and knock Yolanda down.

"Gun," I whisper.

She stares at me as we huddle against the ground, and I can see her brain processing, still confused. I want to laugh. How does someone this tough—this competent and independent—not know what a gunshot sounds like? Because she might be all that, but she's also not someone who comes from the sort of neighborhoods where you hear that sound regularly. When she hears a loud noise, her brain thinks, *Was that a firecracker, a car backfiring?*

Her confusion lasts only a second before she realizes that what she heard was indeed gunfire.

We stay down as I listen. I'm trying to figure out where the shot came from, but it happened so quickly that I only caught the *bang* of it.

Dalton's Smith & Wesson? Anders's big-ass Ruger Alaskan .45? I don't think so. It's not possible—at least for me—to distinguish between different firearms at this range. My brain says that neither Dalton nor Anders is going to fire unless absolutely necessary, and it is highly unlikely to ever be necessary. My gut says that I heard that exact same sound only a day ago . . .

When Mark fired his warning shots at us.

I keep straining to listen, and thankfully Yolanda stays quiet and lets me. Yet as still as the forest is, I don't pick up any unexpected sounds. Not voices. Not a shout. Not someone running through the forest.

One shot, and then silence.

I look around. We're nearly at the lake, and there hasn't been any sign of Dalton. The stream is narrow enough that there's no way we'd pass him heading along the other side.

Dalton found a trail, and he's following it, and I have no idea where that's taken him. I only know that someone fired a single shot, and now the forest is silent.

Was it Mark firing off a warning shot at Dalton and Anders?

The sun has started to drop. Shadows mean he's not going to see distant figures moving in the forest and know they're human.

Yolanda looks over sharply and whispers, "Did you hear that?"

I close my eyes to listen. I'm about to say I don't hear anything. Then a man's voice comes, raised, snarling something in anger. It comes from off to our right, in the direction we'd take to get to Mark's camp.

A shout. Then another shot, and this time I pinpoint it. Behind us and to our right. There's a mountain there—the one closest to Haven's Rock.

"I need to investigate that," I say.

"Um, of course? Especially considering your husband, friend, and dog are all out here."

"I mean that *I* need to go, obviously, and you should head back to town."

"Didn't you bring me as backup?"

"To help find Eric. Not to investigate gunshots."

"Consider the liability waiver signed. Now go. I've got your back."

"How about a weapon?"

Yolanda reaches into her pockets, feels around, and pulls out a stubby pencil.

I slap my pocketknife into her hand, and we set out.

I don't like this. I don't like it at all. Someone has fired multiple shots, and I strongly suspect it is a man who murdered his wife, and I'm leading a civilian toward those shots. I would much rather send Yolanda back to town. But she's not a child. She's a woman who definitely knows her own mind and makes her own choices, and the more I argue, the more determined she is to accompany me.

I don't sit there while I argue. I'm on the move, and she's behind me, and eventually, I have to accept that it would be more dangerous to send her back alone. Also, the more we argue, the more likely our target is to realize someone is coming.

We've caught the sound of shouting a couple of times. One voice, I think. Male. Could be Mark. Definitely not Anders or Dalton.

I use those shouts to zero in on our target. They are at the mountain, near the bottom. Once we draw close, the voice stops, but Yolanda picks up the sound of someone scrabbling on rock. Her hearing is better than mine, and we go another twenty feet before I hear the same thing.

Mountains come in all forms, even in the same geographic areas. Some can be scaled with good pairs of hiking boots and lungs. Just keep going up, through trees and brush and over rocky but navigable areas. Others require actual climbing gear, and they're for the pros. And then there are the ones in the middle, climbable but not meant for an easy afternoon hike. Those require a lot of navigating and a lot of scrabbling over difficult terrain.

Those noises come from a section of mountain that fits squarely in the last category. Sparse trees, mostly stunted and scraggly. Lots of rock. Someone is up there, moving around, and once I can see the mountain in the fading light, I stop and hunker down, squinting and listening.

Whoever is up there has gone silent. Did they hear us coming? Is it the shooter?

I can imagine Mark perched up there, spotting Dalton and Anders below and firing off warning shots. But we heard what sounded like someone desperately trying to get away. And we heard those angry shouts.

The shooter has pinned someone down on this mountainside. They're up there, far too exposed with the scrubby tree cover. They're moving, trying to get to safer ground. Darting from spot to spot.

Yolanda and I crouch in the shadows of a huge pine tree, both of us scanning the area above. Then, without a sound to give them away, a figure appears. They're hunched over and moving slowly. We're about a hundred feet away, and from this angle, I can only make out light hair.

"Is that Eric?" Yolanda whispers.

I want to say Dalton would never be so foolish as to scrabble along a mountain making the noise we heard earlier. But he would if he wanted to draw attention, as he did the other day when Mark fired at us. It might also not have been Dalton we heard, but Anders moving in another spot. Whoever is up there is taking it slow and moving soundlessly.

Moving soundlessly, yes, but I can see them easily, their figure dark against the light rock. Dalton would know better, wouldn't he? Unless he was desperate to distract attention from Anders.

Please tell me you know what you're doing, Eric. Please tell me you don't think you're hidden.

"Is it Eric?" Yolanda whispers again.

"I don't know." *God, I hope not.* "But I'm going to move out and warn whoever it is that I can see them. Stay here please. If you see the shooter, whistle or something."

She nods, and I creep from our hiding place. I survey the area and see a good spot. There's a line of smaller pines, little more than saplings. If I can get to it and on the other side of it, whoever is up there should be able to see me without me being seen by anyone else.

And if the person I'm looking at is Mark? Well, then, I can dodge through that line of trees and stay hidden. But I really don't think it's Mark. Even doubled over, the person seems taller and bigger overall.

I dart to the line of small trees. I'm moving along it, my gaze on that figure, waiting for them to see me. Then they turn, peering down as if they saw a movement, and their face comes clear.

Gunnar.

Shit. It's Gunnar. That's who Mark is shooting at.

Did he catch Gunnar on his claim? Chase him back from it and catch up here?

But Gunnar's trail had been heading the opposite way.

Unless that wasn't a current trail.

Damn it.

I hesitate. I think Mark is chasing Gunnar. I think Mark killed his wife. I also think Gunnar tried to kill both Bruno and Penny. So what should I do about this?

I'm tempted to back off. I don't see or hear any sign of Dalton or Anders, and I now suspect they were following an old trail, which means they're nowhere near here.

Back off, and let two killers fight it out.

Police Detective Casey Duncan would not do that. Haven's Rock Detective Casey Butler could . . . if she was absolutely, beyond any doubt, certain that these two men were both killers. If they'd confessed or been seen killing their victims. Without that, I revert to the police detective who must do things by the books. The difference is that as a detective, I had to do things that way to keep my job, and as a detective here, I do it because it's right.

I check on Yolanda. I can't see her—she's hidden and staying there. That means she's safe enough.

I ease along the row of saplings, trying to get Gunnar's attention. He's looking down, but he's not seeing me. I raise a hand. The movement catches his attention. He glances over, spots me, and visibly slumps in relief. Then he starts gesturing wildly. Telling me what's going on, I presume, but I suck at charades from across a room—I sure as hell can't do it from fifty feet away.

What I can do is a simple return message of my own. I point at trees behind him and jab my hand down. Telling him to duck and stay hidden. He shoots me a thumbs-up, swivels . . . and a shot shatters the silence.

The shot hits Gunnar and, as if in slow motion, he pivots almost gracefully. Then he falls, and he keeps falling, right over the ledge, crashing into undergrowth below.

I don't rush out. I wouldn't even if I *didn't* suspect Gunnar is a killer. The shooter is on the mountainside. Rushing out would only make me a target, and I can't help anyone if I'm pinned down by gunfire.

I wait, counting off seconds under my breath. I'm watching the spot where Gunnar fell, still fifty feet off the ground. I'm waiting to see him rise, even struggle to his knees.

Nothing.

Is he dead?

Rocks tumble over the edge, off to my left. It's the shooter, scrabbling along, making his way to his victim.

If Gunnar's not dead now, he will be soon enough.

Shit.

I check for Yolanda. I can't see her, which is still good. I point up, telling her I'm going to get to Gunnar. She doesn't pop up, frantically telling me not to do something so foolish. She trusts that I know what I'm doing.

Or she doesn't give a damn. If I want to get myself shot, she's going to let me.

I laugh under my breath and shake my head. No, she trusts my judgment, and I appreciate that.

Time to do some climbing.

CHAPTER THIRTY-EIGHT

I'm making my way to Gunnar, trying to hurry while also trying to stay silent. And it isn't only the shooter I need to worry about. Gunnar saw me. He could be playing possum, ready to leap up and knife me when I try to help. The fact that I consider this might suggest I've watched too many movies, but it actually just means I spent too much time in Rockton. Which, granted, might mean Yolanda is right to say I take too many risks, especially when it comes to saving someone I'm worried might murder me for trying.

The moonlight provides enough illumination, and I'm dressed in dark clothing. I pull up my hood and cinch it, minimizing the amount of skin exposed. I might not be as pale as Gunnar—who fairly glows—but I can still be seen in the twilight.

I dart from tree to tree, and while every squeak of my boots and crunch of dirt sounds as loud as gunfire to me, the shooter doesn't seem to hear it. I'm going to need to climb soon. Gunnar is on the ledge about thirty feet off the ground, and the best spot I can see will require a combination of free climbing, scrabbling, and clambering. Yes, those are all different things, and if you spend enough time around mountains, you come to know the difference.

I pause to assess my path. The problem is that once I hit the climbing area, I'll be exposed on the mountainside for two sections. I need to know where the shooter is. Or, more importantly, what their line of sight is.

I squint up. Rocks crunch far overhead, and when I blink to adjust my vision, I spot a figure. Not just a figure, but a figure holding a rifle. It's almost certainly Mark, because it looks exactly like the figure I saw on a ridge two days ago.

He's peering over the edge, as if trying to find Gunnar. When he paces along that edge, I realize he's not trying to *find* him. He's trying to figure out how to *get* to him. It's almost a straight drop from where he stands. He points the rifle down, as if seeing whether he can line up a shot. Then he pulls it back. He doesn't actually see Gunnar. He just has a very good idea where he is and can't find an easy way down.

After another moment of pacing, Mark slings the rifle over his back and strides to his right, away from me, heading for an easier path. I wait until I'm certain he's fixed on that path. Then I ease out and begin my ascent.

For the first part, I can scrabble, staying upright as I pay more attention to noise than speed. This is where I'm most likely to send down a mini-avalanche of dirt and rocks. I get through that, and if I make any sound, Mark presumes it's just Gunnar moving around. His steps continue in the same direction, his booted footfalls loud in the stillness.

Next comes a bit of clambering, where I'm hunched down and grabbing what I can to help me up. Finally, I reach the first actual climb. I edge to the left, where I can get behind a protruding rock that will, with any luck, hide my ascent.

While this part makes me more easily spotted, it's silent, as

I place one foot on a solid spot, grab another, and haul myself up. It's also slower, and it seems to take forever to scale ten feet. I'm finally lifting my head over the edge when I hear a snort.

I go still. Something is on that ledge. I can hear it, snorting as I disturb its sleep. Then a thick musky scent washes over me. I stay frozen, barely daring to breathe.

As careful as we are about bears on the ground, we're more likely to encounter them here in their mountain homes. I peer into the shadow of an overhang, ready to scramble back down—

A shape lunges from the darkness. Something big and pale and charging straight at me. My brain screams a warning and an order: *Let go.*

My fingers release the rock, and I fall back, and my feet slide off. It seems to happen in slow motion, and in that moment, I see what is charging me.

A sheep. A Dall sheep.

Goddamn it.

I flail to grab the ledge again, but it's long gone and I'm falling backward. I hit the rock below. Pain slams through me, stealing my breath and then my brain in fresh panic when I can't breathe. I roll over . . . and start sliding down the slope.

I jam my arms out, stopping my slide. I'm on my stomach, staring at the last ten feet of the way down, and I can't get my breath. I can't breathe. I can't move. I fell on my back and broke something and—

And I rolled over, didn't I? I stopped myself from sliding down this slope, and my hands and feet are both dug in to keep me here.

I'm okay.

Relatively okay, at least. Everything hurts, and when I try to rise onto my hands and feet, I gasp and find air and fall to my stomach again.

I'm winded. That's all.

Okay, I don't know whether that's all, but that's the story I'm telling myself. Just winded.

When a shadow moves past me, I convulse and twist to look up, only to see the sheep, yellow eyes with elongated pupils watching me.

I resist the urge to shake my fist at the sheep. There was a running joke in Rockton that the only things that hadn't killed anyone were the Arctic hares . . . and even that was only a matter of time. The mountain-dwelling sheep might not be particularly dangerous, but out here, everything can be deadly under the right circumstances.

I'd startled this ram from sleep. It panicked and charged . . . and I panicked and fell. No one's fault, and I settle for a quick grumble in its direction as it shakes its curved horns at me. Then I push up—

A gun fires, the shot hitting the dirt less than a foot from my outstretched hand. I yank away and half wriggle, half jump back into the shadows, and if my body screams in protest, I don't even notice.

Another shot hit six inches from the last one. Six inches in my direction.

That is not a warning. Not at all.

Mark saw me fall, and he's shooting at me.

I twist and scramble up, gritting my teeth as my body begs me to let it be, let it rest. I get up to the section I'd climbed, back pressed to the rock, and then, carefully, I ease to the right. That's the same direction as Mark, but going the other way will expose me more. I tuck between an overhang and a bush.

I rest there, catching my breath. After a moment, I roll my shoulders and stretch my limbs as I assess damage. They hurt like hell, but they all work. I take a deep breath. While that also hurts, there's no searing pain of a broken rib. I can breathe. I can move.

When I taste blood, I wet my lips and realize I bit the lower one in my fall. An abrasion on my cheek pulls as I move my face.

I'm fine.

Fine enough anyway.

Or I would be, if I weren't stuck under this damn overhang, pinned down by a guy with a rifle who knows where the hell I am.

"Casey?" a voice croaks from above.

Gunnar. Shit. I'd forgotten Gunnar. That's why I'd been climbing this damn mountain, right?

"Shhh!" I say.

A shot fires. It hits somewhere to my left and bounces off the rock. Gunnar goes silent.

I pick up a chunk of rock near my hand and pitch it down below.

"You really think I'm going to fall for that again?" a voice shouts. A voice that is undeniably Mark's. He's far off to my left. Heading this way? Heading the other way to get down the mountainside and circle back? Or just poised in place, waiting for me to stick my head out.

Damn it.

I pat my utility belt. Dalton has the backpack, and I didn't bother grabbing a second one. After all, I was just popping into the forest and bringing Dalton back. I gave Yolanda my knife, so I have my gun, a flashlight, matches . . .

And something else.

I take it out and smile. It's a firecracker. We carry flares, in case of an emergency, but they're not exactly pocket-sized. I'd bought these as a backup, though Dalton grumbled that I just wanted the excuse to set off firecrackers, which is not entirely wrong.

I have two of them. I take one out, light it, and then pitch it as far as I can.

The firecracker lands in a tree, sparking and popping.

"Is that supposed to scare me?" Mark calls. "Oh no, she has a machine gun!" His laugh ripples down through the forest.

When something moves in the trees below, I go still, my heart hammering. *Tell me that's Dalton or Anders. Please, tell me . . .*

Movement flashes in the forest just below me. I focus and see it's Yolanda.

Before I can react, she throws a rock. It lands below where I'm perched on the mountainside.

"Really?" Mark says. "You're just going to keep trying, aren't you? I know where—"

Yolanda runs. She dashes from her hiding spot and races to another one. Mark fires, but he can't see more than I can, which is just a dark blur of movement. She does it again, running into another stand of trees farther away.

It takes a moment before I understand. Then I realize what's happened. I threw the firecracker to alert Dalton, but Mark thought it was to divert his attention . . . which it did, momentarily. Yolanda's rock landed below where I am, and he thinks I used the two to cover me while I climbed down, and now I'm making a break for it. He's fixed on "me" down below.

Did Yolanda do that on purpose? If so, it's a dangerous ploy, and I hope to God she stays where she is and doesn't decide he needs another clue.

In the meantime . . .

I creep back to where I'd been, in that hidden climbing spot. I grit my teeth and start the ascent. This time, when I reach that ledge, the ram is waiting, back in his spot, watching me.

I pretend not to see him, get onto the ledge, and keep going, and he thankfully lets me pass. This next part is a scrabble. I put one foot up, and it's clear that I am not going to do this without making noise. Shit.

I could go back down. Forget Gunnar. After all, he's still my prime suspect for Bruno's partner. Just get down and find Yolanda and then go after Mark once she's safe.

"Gunnar?" I whisper, as loudly as I dare. "How are you?"

"Shot."

"I'm going to stop him and come back for you."

There's a pause. One so long that I know he's about to say no, don't leave, he needs help. Instead, there's a nearly inaudible "Okay."

"Are you all right?"

Another pause. Then, "Sure. Go on. Get him."

Damn it, that's not what I want. Gunnar isn't all right, and he's lying, telling me to go after Mark because it's the right thing to do, which makes it a hell of a lot harder to dismiss Gunnar, telling myself he was Bruno's partner, the guy who shoved Bruno off a cliff and left Penny to die.

Is he being helpful because he's innocent? Or because he's guilty and building his alibi?

I really was the victim here. I even pretended I wasn't badly hurt so you could catch the real killer.

I place one careful foot up and then grab what looks like a well-rooted vine. I lean into my foot and brace. I make it two steps up before dirt tumbles, and I freeze.

Nothing.

Where the hell is Mark?

Not here. Not paying attention to me. That's all I can care about right now.

I make it the next few feet, and then I'm at the second climbing spot. This time, I can't hide. I can just move fast. Thankfully, it's only about five feet, and then I'm throwing myself onto the ledge where Gunnar is.

At the last second, I remember that I'm supposed to be cautious. I remember that he could be faking his injury and spring at me.

I hit the ledge and awkwardly roll, as if that's going to protect me. Also, I just vaulted onto the ledge after falling ten feet onto rock and every muscle screams at once. I execute a weird scrabble-and-twist as I grab for my gun and get my back against the rock.

"Hey," Gunnar says.

I look over to see him propped on one elbow as I'm pressed against the rock, holding a gun on him.

"You came," he says, more croak than words.

I only nod.

"Can I lie back down now? Before I pass out?"

There's blood pooling under him, and I motion for him to lie down. Then I reholster my gun and crawl over to him.

"So," he rasps. "I got shot. How's your night going?"

I shake my head and check his wound. He's been hit in the hip. It's bleeding freely, but the bullet didn't seem to hit anything that'll make him bleed out. He can't move, though, not without risk of doing more damage.

"At least I didn't get shot in the ass," he says. "Close, though."

I take off my jacket and fold it under his hip and up over the wound. "Press there," I say.

"It's a lot of blood."

"You'll be fine."

"Getting the impression you're not happy with me right now, Detective, and I think I know why."

"Um-hmm."

I peer down as I think of how I'm going to handle this.

"I shouldn't have gone after him."

I glance over. "Gone after who?"

"The miner guy. I know the rules. No going into the forest, but I was up in my perch, and I saw him skulking around, and I didn't like it. Yeah, his dead wife's body is in town, and maybe he decided he doesn't trust us, but I just . . ." A one-shouldered shrug. "I didn't like it."

"Okay. So you took off and just happened to have clothing to stage up there?"

"Yeah, well, sometimes I make it look like I'm there while I take a walk in the forest. The stuff was already in the loft."

"So you just took off after a potential killer."

"I should have gotten you or your husband or Will. But no one was around, and so I figured I'd check it out myself. Only apparently, I make a shitty detective, because he caught me."

"Caught you . . . ?"

"Sneaking up on him. He tricked me. Damn—" Gunnar pauses, and I notice sweat trickling down his face, as if talking is costing more energy than he's letting on. "I fell for a really obvious trick, and he caught me. He said he knew another woman had been brought to town and wanted to know if it was the missing one."

"He noticed us bringing in Penny."

"Seems so. He wanted to know if she was alive. I said yes, and he freaked out, demanding to know what she said. So I said Penny saw him the night she was hurt."

"What?"

"Yeah, I'm a shitty detective. Or a pretty good one who

makes shitty choices. He was already freaking out, so I threw that in."

"You lied and said Penny recognized him to see what he'd say . . . while he had you at gunpoint."

"When you say it like that . . ." He tries to pull a face but only winces in pain. "I hit a bull's-eye, though. And he didn't shoot because he wanted more information—what had Penny said, who knew about it. I played along, buying time, and then I ran."

"And he shot you."

"Eventually."

I shake my head.

Gunnar continues, "But he's obviously the one who tried to kill Penny, right? That's good to know."

How sure am I that Gunnar is telling the truth? Not enough that I'd turn my back on him, but what he's saying clicks a few more pieces into place.

Penny says she saw Bruno at Mark's camp . . . and then everything went black and she woke to Bruno leaving her in the cave. Which means Bruno was definitely there, so if Mark panicked when Gunnar said Penny saw him . . .

Gunnar isn't Bruno's partner.

Mark is.

CHAPTER THIRTY-NINE

I leave Gunnar with a promise that he'll be fine, and I'll get back as quickly as I can. Then I go after Mark. Getting to him is as dangerous as getting to Gunnar. More dangerous, because by this point, he's given up on climbing down to me. Yolanda has gone silent, and he's realized he's better off focusing on the bird in the hand. He's heading back to his original path to Gunnar. That means I need to head left and then up. It also means there's almost no way to do that without being seen, and being seen means being shot.

I do love a challenge.

I have the advantage of Mark thinking I'm down below, cowering in the bushes, far enough away that I can't shoot him with my handgun. He's moving resolutely, confident that I'm out of the game and Gunnar is flat on his back, possibly bleeding out, but definitely not hopping up to attack him anytime soon.

I consider my options and decide to get fancy. I'm going where Mark will least expect trouble: over his head.

There's a scrabble spot to my right. That's where Gunnar

must have been heading when he'd been shot. He'd seen the gentler slope and been hurrying toward it with the intention of sliding down the mountainside as fast as he could. I want to go up—not down—but the theory holds. The only problem is that Mark is heading this way, meaning he could see me. I move fast and get past the easiest stretch to make it to one with more scrubby trees and bushes. From there, it's a relatively easy run up the mountainside. If I make noise, I don't care. I just need to move.

I get twenty feet above the route Mark's taking. There's an actual path here, presumably from the sheep, and I follow it. It's not straight—it twists and turns—but it stays relatively level, and it's easy to follow, and best of all, it's outside Mark's line of vision.

Now I *do* care how quiet I am, because I'm getting close. If Mark has heard anything before, he's dismissed it as mountain-dwelling critters. Gunnar has been disabled and is not going to be scampering around anytime soon. He's especially not going to head up the mountain.

I can hear Mark's footfalls plainly . . . right up until something stops him in his tracks. I'm getting close, and I rock on my toes, eager to cover the last few feet. Rock scrapes under his boots. I ease down a few feet and crouch to peer through a bush down at him.

He's there, closer than I thought, and he's on the edge doing exactly what I am—peering down. He'd come along a path above Gunnar to get to him faster, and now he needs to descend. He thinks he's found a good spot to do that, but it requires an actual climb, because he's on a ledge. He's thinking it through.

I creep past him and then slide down to land behind him. He wheels, swinging the rifle, which would work so much better if

I weren't right there. I grab the barrel. Perhaps not my best idea ever—and it would give Dalton heart failure—but I'm less than a foot from Mark. When I grab the barrel, he pulls the trigger, and there's a moment of sudden heat as the shot flies down the long barrel . . . and harmlessly past me.

I yank, and that catches him off guard. He lets go of the rifle, and so do I, and it goes goes tumbling down the mountainside.

"Hello, Mark," I say as I lift my own gun. "Seems you're having a really shitty night."

He starts to back up.

"Careful," I say. "There's a reason you stopped here. This is where the ledge ends. The only way out is down. Straight down. Or past me but . . ." I waggle my gun. "I wouldn't advise it."

He still eyes my gun. He notices that my finger isn't on the trigger, and so he's considering whether he could get past me before I fire.

"The answer is no," I say. "One sudden step my way, and you'll see how fast I can pull this trigger."

He still looks around, searching for another option.

"It's almost as high as the cliff you pushed Bruno off, huh?" I say.

He only glances my way, and then returns to looking up and down and even behind him. I try not to take offense at that. I really do.

"You should have checked to be sure he was dead," I say. "Should have also checked on Penny. Or didn't Bruno tell you where he put her?"

"If this is where I'm supposed to confess all and beg forgiveness, you're going to be sadly disappointed, Casey."

"Detective Butler."

He snorts. "You're private security. Rent-a-cop."

"That was my cover. I'm an RCMP investigator for the Yukon division, specializing in mining fraud. Bruno screwed you over. He didn't trust you, and he realized he was in over his head, and he cut a deal, one that included a payout. Not as much as he'd have gotten from the mine, but this one was guaranteed."

Mark blanches. Then his face hardens. "I don't know what Bruno told you, but I'm not mining up here. I'm investigating a possible claim site. That's what you government assholes insist on, isn't it? We have to come up here, find a site, stake it out, and *then* file a claim and hope we can get to it before someone sneaks in and cleans it out."

"I'm beyond caring about the mining fraud," I say. "I'm far more concerned with the two people you tried to murder. Your partner and an innocent woman who heard too much."

"I didn't do anything to that woman. Bruno hit her, and then he took her away and said she'd be fine. We argued—I couldn't believe he'd hit the poor lady. Next thing I know, he's swinging at me, like he's going to knock me out, too. I pushed him away, and over he went."

"Must have been pretty hard," I say. "There's a handprint on his chest." Now, that's that biggest whopper I've told yet, but Mark flinches.

"I don't know how I pushed him," he says. "He was trying to push me off the cliff, and I panicked and did whatever it took. Self-defense."

I nod slowly. I know he pushed Bruno off that cliff, and I'm sure he's the one who knocked Penny out. Not being an actual RCMP investigator, I can't do much about either. Both victims survived their ordeals at his hands, and I'm more concerned with the one who didn't. But it's not time for that. Not yet.

"You met Bruno in town the night he died."

"I don't know what you're talking about."

"You then skirted through town to divert us, make us think whoever he met was from there."

"I don't know what you're talking about."

"You had nothing to do with what happened to Bruno or Penny?" I say.

"I never said that. I said I didn't kill them. Self-defense for Bruno, and yes, I witnessed what happened to that woman, but I sure as hell wasn't about to tell you. I presumed she'd gotten back to town—I thought that's what Bruno was doing. You said she was still missing, and I had no idea where she might be, so I kept my mouth shut."

I nod slowly, as if assimilating and accepting this. "You and Bruno were partners, as you've admitted."

"I was his damn *victim*. He found me staking out my mining claim, and he saw that I'd found gold, and he was a fucking mining engineer. He knew what I had, and he wanted in or he'd steal it out from under me. That's what your damn laws do. Screw over hardworking miners who are trying to follow the rules."

"Bruno sees you've found a site with gold—which you are *not* currently collecting—and he demands a share."

"Yes."

"He also promises, I'm sure, to help, since he has the connections and experience."

"I didn't need his damn help."

Mark can make up any story he wants now that Bruno is dead, but I suspect there's an underpinning of truth to this one. Bruno found the mine while poking around in the forest on his off time. He recognized the area as a potential location for gold in the creeks and rivers flowing from the mountains. He hoped to find a few flakes, a souvenir and a way to pass the time. Instead, he found Mark's site.

He would have told Mark that he could help. Connections, resources, expertise, whatever he needed. He'd have pitched himself as a partner, but there'd have been a threat underlying that, too, because Mark hadn't yet filed his claim.

It wasn't quite the hostage situation Mark asserts. It wasn't a fully voluntary partnership either. That made it uneasy and volatile, ripe for trouble, which came when Penny innocently found herself in Mark's camp just when Bruno had stopped by to talk to him.

Bruno talks to Penny, makes up some story that she would have accepted. She wouldn't know a placer mining operation when she saw it, especially at night. But Mark panicked and hit her, and then Bruno panicked and put her in that cave until he could talk to her and buy her silence. Only he died before he could return.

"All right," I say, again willing to accept this half-truth. "Explain why you shot one of the construction crew tonight."

"I have no idea who I shot," Mark says. "Some crazy man came charging out of the woods, shouting at me for getting too close to that secret construction site."

"What?" Gunnar's voice comes from below us. "That's not what happened at all."

"Yes," I say. "He's still alive. And his hearing is apparently fine. You caught him following you, and he said the missing woman had identified you as her attacker."

"Which is a lie."

"So you shot him for lying? Seems extreme."

"I fired warning shots. One hit him."

I nod. "Okay, that's possible."

"What?" Gunnar says again. "Those were not—"

"Enough from you," I call down to Gunnar. "You can give a full statement later, along with the statement from Penny, identifying Mark here as her attacker. But you're alive, and she's alive, and I don't think the department is going to pursue that nearly as much as the other charge."

Mark says, "I did not work an illegal claim. I told you—"

"I don't care about the claim. I care about your wife."

A pause, as if he'd forgotten all about Denise. Then he says, "My wife is dead. One of those construction bastards killed her. Probably Bruno. I don't know why I didn't see that before—"

"Denise died earlier that day. While Bruno was in town with an alibi."

"And I was out hunting."

"You claimed to have gone hunting that night. The night you also pushed Bruno off a cliff."

"I lied, okay? I went earlier that day."

"We found your fingerprints in the pit where your wife was buried. They're on file, and I matched them."

"Because I came back from hunting and found her dead," he says, matching me lie for lie.

"You killed her," I say. "You finally struck it rich, and she showed up, and there'd be no way to hide that from her. No way to be sure, either, that she wouldn't go home and shoot her mouth off, telling people what you found."

"*Telling* them? Selling my claim, you mean." He stops and pulls back. "I mean, maybe she'd have sold it. I have no idea. That's why I didn't tell her where I was. I didn't trust her. But I didn't kill her either."

"You suspected she'd sell you out. That makes more sense. She'd see the mine and go home and find someone to buy it. That's why she came out. Not for a reunion, but to spy on you, see what you were up to. Something you did or said made her suspect you'd finally hit it big, and she hacked your computer and found those three sets of coordinates. She came out and pretended to just be here to surprise you, but you knew better. You started the reunion—had sex or were getting ready for sex—and you stabbed her while she was half dressed. In your panic to search her pockets, you missed the napkin with the coordinates, which came out when you were burying her."

"Never happened."

"No?"

He crosses his arms. "Nope."

"You are under arrest for the murder of your wife. You have the right to retain and instruct counsel."

Mark lunges at me. I'm ready for it, and I kick him, sending him toppling back. He rights himself and springs again, and I hit him with the gun barrel.

"Do you want me to shoot you?" I say. "Because I'm not. You are going to stand trial—"

He kicks, and I don't quite get out of the way in time. His boot connects with my shin. That stings, but I'd be fine if I didn't stagger back; something about the move makes pain rip through my side, reminding me that I'd fallen off the mountainside twenty minutes ago.

When my side stitches, Mark takes advantage and tries to shove me. Not a shove backward, where I'd just fall onto my ass—no, he shoves from my left side to push me over the edge. That's where he screws up. In trying to kill me, he misses the obvious opportunity to knock me out of the way. It's an awkward push that I easily brace against and use to duck out of his reach.

I raise my gun, the barrel less than a foot from his face. "Get back."

"Or what? You'll shoot me?" He sneers. "We both know you

aren't doing that, *Detective*. You think I'm fooled for a second? That I actually think you're a cop?"

I lock down my expression. "You want my ID? Put your hands on your head, and I'll get it out."

"You know what I mean. You're not a real cop. You're a quota-filler. A woman and a minority. That's two boxes checked off. Please don't tell me you actually think you got the job because you deserve it."

I laugh. That's not fake—I can't help it—and his face darkens.

"Do you honestly expect that to work?" I say. "You think I haven't heard that five dozen times, from five dozen guys who all thought it was going to make me break down in tears? Oh my God, you're right. I'm a fraud!" I look him in the eye. "Or is it supposed to make me mad. Piss me off enough to shoot you. If that's what you want, Mark, you're going to have to do a whole lot better."

"You think I'm taunting you? Death by cop?" He snorts. "Do I seem distraught, Detective? You won't shoot me. You won't even take me in." He waves down toward Gunnar. "If that's your partner, he's out of commission. If your partner is the guy you pretended was your husband, I don't see him." He makes a show of shading his eyes and scanning the forest. "Nope, no sign of backup. That means you're alone, and there's no way a little thing like you is taking me in without shooting me. So let's make this easy. You're going to let me go, and I'm going to forget all about this."

I only shake my head.

"That's not an offer," he says. "I'm telling you what I'm go-ing to do. I'm going to walk away, and I'm not going to hurt you. Not going to shove you off this cliff like I did to Bruno. Not going to crack you over the head like I did to that chick. Not going to stab you and let you bleed out, like I did to my double-crossing bitch wife. You should have seen the way she looked at me, the *shock* on her face. Why, Mark. *Why?* Well, no, she didn't say 'Mark' because that's obviously not my real name, but she did cry and beg—"

"Still not shooting you. Also, it's getting late, so if we can wrap this up, please?"

He lunges at me. I back out of his reach.

"Nope, not shooting you for that either." I whistle. "Hey! I could use a bit of help here! He's unarmed. Biggest problem is that he won't stop talking."

Mark swings at me. I duck it and backpedal again. Then a sound comes from below. Not Yolanda's shout but a familiar birdcall.

My laugh drifts down the mountainside. "'Bout time you showed up."

"Heard the firecrackers," Dalton's voice drawls from trees below. Then he appears. "Thought you were having fun without me."

"She is," Anders says as he steps out. "Can't you tell?"

"Let's try this again," I say to Mark as he stares down at the two men. "You are under arrest for the murder of your wife. You have the right—"

Mark runs at me. I back up, but at the last second he veers. He jumps. It's not a plunge-to-the-death. It's a leap, him aiming to jump down past the rock and land on the softer slope below.

"Eric!" I shout.

Mark is in midair, and Dalton and Anders are already running. They're off to the left, about fifty feet from where Mark is jumping. If he manages his jump and runs on an angle, he might actually get away.

He does manage the jump. He lands on the softer slope . . . and one foot slides. He tries to correct fast, and his other foot flies out and he slams to the side, head cracking against the rock face he just cleared. He crumples and starts sliding down the slope.

I spin, lower myself fast, grab the edge, and hang off it for a second before dropping. I hit that softer ground, but my feet also slide, and I'm scrambling, fingers grabbing at the slope in panic . . . before I realize I'm basically surfing down on my stomach.

I let myself slide, and then I'm on my feet, and I would be running, if my entire body weren't screaming in protest. Fortunately, Anders has already reached Mark.

Dalton races beside me, grabs my elbow, and steadies me.

"Fell earlier," I say, wincing. "Hurts."

"Do I want to know how far you fell?"

"No."

He shakes his head and helps me to Mark, who lies on the ground. I'm about to ask if he's all right. Then I see the angle of his neck, and I slow down.

Anders looks over, meets my gaze, and shakes his head.

Mark is dead. Broke his neck with that crack to the head. It hadn't seemed hard enough to kill, but he'd hit at just the right angle. A freak accident . . . not unlike the one that killed Bruno, so I guess there's some justice in that.

Mark got what he wanted . . . even if, in the end, I think he decided he didn't actually want that at all.

CHAPTER FORTY

We get Mark's body back to Haven's Rock. Or close enough to it that we can sneak it in and hide it with Denise's under the clinic. Again, there's justice in that, his body ending up in the same place as the wife he murdered.

I let Dalton and Yolanda look after Mark while Anders and I take care of Gunnar. He'll be fine, though he's going to be laid up for a few days. It's nearly dawn before we have him in the clinic bed, April taking over.

I'm preparing the instrument tray while April talks to Anders on the back porch.

"So I guess I get to stay now, huh?" Gunnar says.

"At least until you're back on your feet," I say.

"Oh, I think I can still help out after that. I'm a helpful guy, right?"

"You almost got killed following a murderer into the forest."

"Which helped you catch him. If not for me, who knows what he'd have done next. I took a bullet for you guys."

"Fine. If April clears you to work, you can stay until the end."

"How about after that?"

I stop with a stack of gauze in hand.

Before I can speak, he says, "We can talk about it later, and don't worry, I won't resort to blackmail by reminding you that I know a whole lotta things you'd like kept secret."

"You just reminded me."

"But I said I won't use it as blackmail."

"By bringing it up, paired with a demand, you're—" I shake it off. "We'll talk later."

He smiles. "I know we will."

Later that morning, a plane lands. April and I are out there to meet it. It touches down, and the doors open. A woman appears. She's in her mid-forties and glamorous even in hiking boots, jeans, and a jersey. She has light brown skin, silver-streaked hair, and a pinup's figure. Isabel, first off the plane, naturally.

"Oh, look," she says as she taps her boot toe against the box beside me. "A coffin. We must be in Rockton."

"Haven's Rock," I say. "Which means that's a poor crew member who suffered a fatal accident."

"Fell off a cliff and impaled himself on a branch?"

"Something like that."

We don't hug. Neither of us is the type. She only shakes her head and calls back over her shoulder, "Hurry up. The bar opens at four, and I have a feeling everyone here will be ready for it."

The others are stalled in the plane. Phil is giving orders to the pilot. Then he appears. Fifteen years younger than Isabel and looking like the catalogue-model version of a corporate guy, with his pressed shirt, glasses, and perfect jawline. Phil gets out, sees the wooden box, and sighs.

"Accident," I say.

"Should I open the bar at three?" Isabel says.

"Perhaps." Phil looks around. "Where is Yolanda?"

"Hiding, probably," Isabel murmurs. "I know I would be." She looks at me. "He has a fifty-point list of things to discuss with her."

"Forty-six points." He looks at the box. "Starting with the lack of security to keep people from wandering into the forest and blackmailing the local miners."

I wave him toward town. Isabel lets him go and draws my attention to the plane, where Kenny has just gotten out. He's in his late thirties, white, with brown hair, a boxer's build, a cane, and braces on his legs. April is right there waiting for him, and as he smiles at her, my heart melts a little. He directs her off to the side to make way for someone else. A woman moves into the open doorway. She's in her eighties, tiny and fit with perfect white hair, and wearing outdoor apparel as stylish as Isabel's.

"Émilie," I say as I walk over.

She climbs down and clasps my hands. "Off to an interesting start, I hear."

"That's one way of putting it. I'm sorry you had to come out so soon."

"Oh, I'm just using that as an excuse. Let's get this poor fellow loaded into the plane, and then we'll head inside and talk."

Bruno's body goes home, along with his bonus and extra money for his wife. Hush money? I hate to call it that. He really did die of an accident, but yes, Émilie is going to be generous with her condolence compensation.

As for Mark and Denise, they will disappear into shallow graves. Mark deserves that. As for Denise . . . I don't know enough to say whether she does or doesn't, and so I will allow myself to feel a bit of guilt chased away by the reminder that there was nothing else to be done. They will vanish, and Émilie will handle their disappearance in ways that I'm better off not knowing.

I spend the rest of the day dealing with the investigative cleanup while the others transition into their new roles. By the next morning, Émilie is gone, and I only have one task remaining: clear away Mark's mining operation.

Dalton and I will do that together, and I'm looking forward to a bit of couple time after all the chaos. We didn't sleep a wink two nights ago, and last night, I was asleep before he came to bed. This morning I wake to coffee and a muffin with a note that we'll meet up at eight to head to Mark's.

By 7:50, I'm on the front porch with Storm when footsteps crunch and I hurry down the steps like a teenager waiting for her date. Instead, Yolanda walks from the strip of forest between our house and the town.

She lifts her hands. "Don't worry. Your husband is coming. He's been temporarily delayed, and I offered to run a message over along with this." She hands me a thermos.

"More coffee?" I say. "He definitely wants me caffeinated."

"That's from Isabel, and I have a feeling it contains more than coffee." Yolanda shakes her head. "That woman is a force of nature. And her guy is a royal pain in the ass. Pretty to look at but . . ." She shakes her head. "Far too many alphas in this town. Kenny seems nice. I think we need more Kennys."

"We do need more Kennys."

"Notice how I slid that 'we' in there?" She leans against the railing. "I'm not going to beat around the bush, Casey. I already told Gran that I'm staying."

"Staying . . . ?"

"Yeah, I hear you're already stuck with Gunnar, at least until he gets bored and flits off, which I suspect will be soon enough. I'm also staying. I have things to work through, and I've decided I want to work them through here, and the polite thing to do would be to ask you, but I've never gotten anything I wanted by being polite. If you want, I'll give a PowerPoint presentation on how having me here is worthwhile."

"Mmm, I'll pass, but you might want to do one up for Phil."

"No kidding." She tucks a curl behind her ear. "I didn't ask Gran either. I told her. She's fine with it. Petra was her eyes and ears in Rockton, and I'm taking on that role here, even if you'd rather have Petra. I'll pull my weight, and I won't demand a damn thing."

"I know, and I understand."

"And you're absolutely thrilled to have me on board?"

I smile. "I am not completely devastated to have you on board."

"Fair enough." She lowers herself to the deck stairs. "Grab a couple of mugs and share that special coffee with me, and we'll wait for your man to show up."

We arrive at Mark's camp and . . .

I stand where his tent had been, looking around at the empty site. "This is the place, right?"

Dalton's on one knee, rubbing his hand over the packed ground.

"This is where his tent was," I say. "Am I imagining that there's no trace of it? Not even a peg hole?"

He straightens. "You're not." He circles around the site, studying the ground, even pausing now and then to touch it.

"Someone didn't steal his stuff or break camp for him," I say. "They erased all signs—"

A bush crackles to our left. We both wheel, hands going to our guns.

"Hello!" a man's voice calls. "We are coming to greet you, with our weapons holstered and hoping for the same consideration from you."

We stay where we are, hands still on our holstered guns. I put my other hand on Storm's head as she growls.

A man appears. He's about fifty, white, with silvering hair and a smile that shows off perfect teeth. He's dressed head to toe in expensive outdoor gear. Flanking his rear are two younger men, one wearing sunglasses despite being deep in the shadowy forest. One glance at them, and I know they're his security detail. They have the bearing of ex-military. Both have their hands on their weapons, but at a wave from the man, they withdraw their hands, and we do the same.

The man in charge continues to smile. "I thought we might see our neighbors sooner or later."

I bite back the urge to say, "Neighbors?" That's what he wants, and I can tell it's better not to give him that satisfaction.

"We're looking for someone who was camping here," I say.

"As are we. We were supposed to meet him yesterday to complete our transaction, but there's been no sign of him, so we removed his camp, as a courtesy. Before any of the local wildlife got into it."

Dalton's expression darkens. "We were coming to check on him, not steal from him."

"Did I suggest that? I apologize. I do think we might have something of yours, though." He waves to one of his guards, who takes a backpack from his shoulder.

My backpack. The man doesn't ask if it's ours, just sets it between my feet and Dalton's.

"I didn't tamper with the cell phone," he says. "That's far too difficult, I'm afraid, merely for the hope of finding the rightful owner and returning it. I fear, however, that our mutual friend did use your satellite phone."

We say nothing.

He continues, "One would think he'd have one of his own, but these miners are so paranoid that they shoot themselves in the foot, trapped out here when they most need to contact the outside world. It seems he ran into a bit of trouble and was most desperate to have someone else take over his claim. We negotiated a price, and I was supposed to meet him here to complete the transaction. But now he's gone. That's most troubling."

"So you came out here to buy his claim," I say, arching my brows. "And now he's missing? You're right, that *is* troubling."

The man only laughs. "Believe me, we'd have nothing to gain by harming him. I prefer a properly completed transaction, but since he is temporarily missing, and time is of the essence, we will move forward while awaiting his return."

"Move forward with his claim?" Dalton says.

"With the management of his claim and the construction of a somewhat larger camp." He nods in the other direction. "We'll be breaking ground about a mile that way, which is why I said we seem about to be neighbors. You are, I believe, responsible for the settlement our mutual friend mentioned."

I try not to stiffen, but Dalton does, and the man laughs. "No need to worry. We know *you* are not a mining operation, and so we are perfectly fine having distant neighbors. As for what you are doing?" An elegant shrug. "This is not a place where people worry about the business of others. We have no interest in yours, and you have no interest in ours. Correct?"

Dalton answers, "We're not miners, like you said."

"Good. Then I believe we will get along fine. In fact, there will almost certainly be an advantage to having others so close.

Shared resources and all that." He flashes that smile again. "We'll need to meet for drinks sometime. At a mutually agreed-upon location, maintaining the privacy of both our operations."

Don't come here again. That's what he's saying, and I can bristle, but I sure as hell don't want him near Haven's Rock. My brain is still reeling with the implications of this development and trying not to panic.

Dalton only nods, his expression calm. "We'll leave you to it. We'll skip the drinks. I don't mean to be unneighborly, but we have a lot to do, and I'm sure you do, too."

"We do. I like your thinking, young man. No need to overdo the neighborly parts. Good fences and all that."

Dalton scoops up my backpack. "I figure this is about where you'd like that fence to be?"

The man purses his lips and squints into the forest. "Maybe a half mile that way?"

"Works for me. Just as long as you know it goes both ways."

"And *that* works for *me*." The man nods. "I'll be seeing you." Another flashed smile. "Or not seeing you, as the case may be."

Dalton nods back, and we turn and make our way back to our side of that dividing line. We say nothing until we've passed that half mile. Then Dalton mutters "Fuck."

"Yes," I say.

Fuck indeed.